FLEABAG

– BOOK 2 –

FLEABAG

– BOOK 2 –

SOMEONETOFORGET

Podium

Copyright © 2025 by Theodoros Zapris

Cover design by J Caleb Design

ISBN: 978-1-0394-5408-8

Published in 2025 by Podium Publishing
www.podiumentertainment.com

Podium

FLEABAG

- BOOK 2 -

CHAPTER 1

Fixing itself was not a matter of difficulty, not this time.

It was relatively stable. Extremely injured, but not dying.

It was simply an issue of time. It was so thoroughly injured that just fixing itself would take a couple days.

Unfortunately, there wasn't much time for rest. Not with all the scavengers eating its prey all around it, and trying in vain to chew into the wolf itself.

The rat gnawing at its tail was particularly annoying, because it just *wouldn't give up*, despite having made no progress in chewing through the burnt remnants of its fur to get to the meat underneath.

Not to mention that it was lying right next to an extremely abundant source of meat, according to the two or three antennae that hadn't been snapped or torched off yet, and it wanted to steal its prey's biology before it deteriorated too much.

All these thoughts led to the simple realization that it had to eat, and get moving. It had to find some little hole or somewhere quiet and just sleep everything off.

It was finally outside the innards of the human nest, back to a familiar place, so it wasted no time whatsoever in changing its "hands" back to paws and getting rid of the cartilage blocking its ears from the open air, the process of reinstating an older version of itself very easy on both mind and resources.

Fixing its injuries was a lot more costly.

Its skills were so *frustrating*. It had full memory of what it had been up to during [Maddened Frenzy], and it was confident it could have avoided most of the burnt fur and the jagged trails of flesh in its abdomen if it had the presence of mind to *care* about dodging beyond the most basic of instinctive reflexes.

And its poison.

Its damned poison.

It had *completely* forgotten it even had poison available when the fight started. Completely and utterly. It could have injected the thing with more than enough of that neurotoxin to render it a flopping bag of meat within a minute, but it was so panicked and surprised that its mind just forgot in the sheer heat of the moment.

It could have come out of all this relatively unscathed if it hadn't been stupid.

With teeth tightly shut in frustration and pain, it breathed in the unpleasant scents of its prey's insides, mixing with the chemical rivers' scents, quickly moving around in [Devourer] and fixing things, big and small, one by one.

It could process whatever this thing was and what it had gained from it, *after* eating it and finding a safe spot to recuperate.

As soon as it had confirmed everything it wished to fix, it pushed away the [Devourer] skill and turned to the symbols' updates.

You have progressed on your Path.
[Hound of the Keeper] Level 18 → Level 21

Attribute Points Available: 3
-Attributes:
Strength (+1)
Speed (+1)
Dexterity (+0)
Endurance (+8)
Perception (+1)
Resolve (+1)
Intelligence (+5)
Soul (+1)

Three "points" felt . . .

Not nearly enough for the amount of pain it had gone through to acquire them.

Its foul mood was already getting fouler—

And would this stupid rat *give up already*?!

It snapped back into [Devourer] for just a moment, switching to manual change, and twisted its tail around, forcefully jabbing the rodent with the poisonous fang at the tip of its tail, right between the ribs, squeezing the tiny gland in its tail absolutely dry in the moment it took for the rodent to process the attack.

Then it flicked the damned thing away, despite the eye-watering pain of its faulty vertebrae grinding together.

As it felt its twitching assailant spasm on the stone, it disregarded its annoying screeches and turned back to the system, exiting its skill to "stare" at its attribute points.

Its main issues so far were still Endurance, as it seemed like the world was utterly determined to do its best to kill it, and Intelligence, because Intelligence made the [Devourer] skill understand more about what it was eating, giving it access to more tidbits it could use. Like the mana cells. If it didn't have the Intelligence to understand those, it wasn't sure if its skill could so smoothly incorporate them into its body like it had.

It also allowed its brain to process more information, and faster, which was seemingly the best way to prevent information overload. It also considered that maybe the skill was getting faster and easier to use because of Intelligence. It *felt like* that was the reason, but it didn't really know.

That attribute also helped the wolf with using the "mana" things indirectly, because of visualization, more capacity for imagination, and things like that.

On top of all those reasons, it kept having the realization that it was, in fact, not nearly as intelligent as it had assumed. The constant slipups confirmed it.

It still couldn't get over the fact it *completely forgot about its poison.*

So in truth, nothing about its point distribution had changed. Endurance and Intelligence were its main tools to stay alive and thrive.

Endurance (+10)
Intelligence (+6)

The attribute screen faded, and a small wall of symbols replaced it.

-Acquired Skills:
You have gained the Skill [Danger Sense - Level 1]
-[Pain Resistance] has Leveled Up. Level 21 → Level 23
-[Infection Resistance] has Leveled Up. Level 8 → Level 9
-[Poison Resistance] has Leveled Up. Level 15 → Level 16
-[Corrosion Resistance] has Leveled Up. Level 5 → Level 8

-[Restful Awareness] has Leveled Up. Level 19 → Level 20
-[Tough Skin] has Leveled Up. Level 7 → Level 12
-[Bloodrush] has Leveled Up. Level 5 → Level 6
-[Sonic Blast] has Leveled Up. Level 3 → Level 5
-[Tremor Sense] has Leveled Up. Level 4 → Level 5
-[Maddened Frenzy] has Leveled Up. Level 1 → Level 4

The only skill it really cared about was [Danger Sense]. Even just the vague idea of a seventh sense dedicated to notifying the wolf of surrounding danger sounded incredibly valuable. It assumed that it would feel like that prickle on the back of its neck that it had felt a moment before the thing's tail slammed into the bridge.

As for the rest?

It was, once again, not terribly impressed. It would never complain about tangible, visible progress, but the effects of most of those skills leveling up would be rather minute changes, so it brushed them aside and went back to resting, just enough for its bones to knit themselves back together.

It could deal with the pain of most of its injuries, but trying to walk with bones made of frayed tissue would feel like trying to force a bag of unsupported meat to walk properly. So it prioritized its bones and relaxed.

Unfortunately, a downside of [Restful Awareness] skyrocketing in levels was that if it had any subconscious issues or worries, they would constantly tug its mind out of rest. So while its body rested, its mind continued to race with errant thoughts.

Its most prominent worry was actually about its human. It had no idea where she was, because the moment it activated [Maddened Frenzy], [Pack Hunter] completely stopped regarding her as an ally.

It was likely that she died, because to put it bluntly, she hadn't exactly been strong. It couldn't come up with a way she could have survived being flushed down a flaming river, never mind how susceptible humans were to the toxic air down at the abandoned floor if that's where she also ended up.

It was a rather bitter thought, one that made its chest tight and burn with a strange phantom sensation of sadness, but there wasn't anything it could do about it. Death was a regular, ever-present part of life. It had been fully aware she could die at any moment.

It was just . . . sad and disappointing.

After all the trouble it went through, all the fun they had together, she died. It was just . . . it didn't feel nice. And it was likely that she died because of the wolf. If it had reacted faster and kept them on that bridge . . .

Ah. This was the first time it had ever felt "guilt."

It was very unpleasant.

It really wanted something to kill or fight just to take its mind off of it, preferably something weak enough to not cripple or severely harm itself.

That thought made it pause, a light reprieve from its depressed mood.

The dogs.

Those were just free food at this point, weren't they? They'd be nice to let out some of its self-directed frustrations on.

There were a *lot* of them around the human nest, and they were even weaker than humans. It had seen some of them gang up on a human and eat them, but for the most part, they scurried around humans and tried to avoid them, clear signs of a weaker pack.

Sure they had fur, and it would be annoying to eat them, and many of them were little more than skin and bone and diseases, but they were an extremely easy source of food it could prey on.

Then it remembered that it had assigned the bottom half of its body to be covered in glowing moss, so it put that idea in a corner of its mind for later.

That was something it had to work on. It hadn't even considered life on the outside world when it added the moss.

It just wasn't used to planning things in advance for later. It had lived its entire life up to this point going day by day, the concept of "the future" wasn't even something it could ever focus on or be certain would ever arrive.

Now that it *was* relatively sure it had a future, it had to start actually planning. Or at least attempt to.

A slight problem to its plans of hunting the dogs for free food was that they were all on the upper part of the human nest, above this abandoned part. Among humans, it had no idea how they would react upon seeing its rather . . . healthy and sizable frame, and the glowing moss on its bottom half. Judging by how they reacted to the wolf having glowing eyes, they would either stare incessantly or react like that human that tried to capture it with some kind of mana skill.

So, if and when it ran out of things to hunt for in the abandoned floor, it would just get rid of the moss in favor of its old fur and go skulk about on the upper parts of the human nest, hunt and wipe out the dogs.

Mostly because they were free food, but it could not deny a slight hint of spite and anger remained in its mind about how the dogs had treated it when it was small and weak.

Now, *they* were small and weak, and it would have a lot of fun ridding the human nest of all of them.

Oh, and the rats. It *hated* those damn things. They'd been some of the most consistently terrifying and infuriating parts of living in the human nest. It had gone so many times into an exhausted nap, only to wake up to a screech from some rodent that skulked out of some tiny crevice, and it had to be constantly ready to jump to its feet and run to the humans so they'd kill the thing, or try to lead the rat into some dangerous crevice or canal predator to kill it for the wolf.

Come to think of it, that was probably how it learned to pay attention and use its environment, so it had been a learning experience.

It was still terrifying to its tiny, old self, however, and it really wanted to let out some of its aggression on the vermin. [Devourer]'s incessant, soul-deep hunger seemed to agree.

Judging by how the rat behind it had stopped twitching already, and how it had spent half an hour trying to chew through its fur and skin, they weren't strong at all, at least not anymore. Free food, *again*. And entertainment.

It had lost its human, and it couldn't deny that it was a little . . . no, it was *very* depressed about it, especially considering that it was mostly its own fault, or so it felt. But the future looked bright for itself. It had grown a *lot*. The thirty-foot behemoth it was almost lying *inside of* proved that beyond a shadow of a doubt. The human nest was full of food, fights, and entertainment to be had. It had lost its human, but it had gained insurmountable strength compared to what it had before.

So while it wanted to curl up into a ball and mentally mourn how it lost the only pack member it ever had, it knew that doing that would be useless.

It would . . . give her a howl. That felt appropriate. It would give her a howl as an apology, and a show of mourning, like it had seen countless dogs do before for their fallen kin, and move on to greater things.

Its mind ruminated on memories for a while, but eventually, with a heavy sigh, it moved on, because that was all it knew how to do.

Plans. It had to learn how to plan.

One of its main problems was that it wasn't sure how humans would react to its changed form. So it could just . . . walk into the nest and *see* how they reacted. If it was negative, it could just run away into the shadows.

The floor above was quite densely populated by humans, but there was an absolute heap of machinery to navigate through, higher, unlit walkways around and under them, and plenty of alleyways it could prowl through without drawing much, if any, attention from the humans. It could easily stalk around the human nest without getting noticed, especially considering [Echoes of Oblivion].

That activity might become a bit harder on the floor *above* that floor, but it had only been there once or twice by sheer accident, and had no reason to revisit it.

It still remembered when that random human threw some kind of spark missile at it for seemingly no reason.

Actually . . .

Its memory was rather hazy, and its nose was not *nearly* as great as it was now, but it was pretty sure it could find that human again by his scent.

Something to entertain for later, once more.

Mostly because thinking of human scents brought it back to its human and made it feel bad.

It thickened its vocal cords significantly in preparation within [Devourer], and rested.

Eventually, its bones were healed, just enough for the wolf to stand and walk around its prey, so it woke up, shaking off the vast amounts of burnt fur it had detached, most of it peeling off in half-melted chunks, and it opened its single fully healed eye to observe a few wriggling maggots, gently glowing green, chewing through its prey's meat.

It wasn't particularly bothered. More food on its food.

It would also answer the question of what would happen should it try to eat something alive.

The pain was . . . not mild, but not enough to deter the wolf from forcing itself upright on shaking limbs, [Pain Resistance] giving it the ability to hobble around at the very least.

Most of its bodily injuries were healed only to the extent that they wouldn't deteriorate while the wolf ate its prey.

It really needed to find a way to make eating things a faster process.

A rather absurd but efficient idea came up as its eye roved over the charred, leathery mass sprawled out before it, and it let out a long, tired breath.

This was . . . going to take a *long time*. And it probably wouldn't even taste good. It really had to eat a human again. If nothing else, just for the better taste and texture.

But first . . .

A howl for its own.

It remembered the first time it used [Sonic Blast], the way it poured emotion and memories into mana and let it out in a short, violent burst. This was the opposite of that burst, but the principle was the same.

It gingerly sat on its haunches, staring *through* its prey's mutilated neck.

It had to draw that emotion out, and pour it into its howl. At least to make this feel *proper*, in a sense, even if it wasn't sure of how humans mourned their dead pack members.

The best way to draw that emotion out that was to simply go back to the beginning, go through everything.

And slowly, it drew the memories forth, categorized them, from the start to the end. The human playing with her mana in the stairs. The fight in the trash pit, them against a few hundred rodents, the endless road down the pipe. Her fingers in its fur. The fight against the insect. Halfheartedly playing on the support rods. Sleeping next to each other.

The emotion built, and built, and its body wished for a way to express it, to relieve it.

It poured a slow, steady stream of mana into its lungs and took in a breath, one so deep it felt its lungs start burning from exertion. [Mana Conversion] and the mana cells in its lungs got to work sucking the mana out of the air, providing the wolf with a steady stream.

And so it let it all out, slowly, feeling its vocal cords be used to the verge of snapping, but holding, as the slowly building howl vibrated the metal and stone all around it, slammed into its ears incessantly, enough for a serious bout of ringing to fill its ears.

Across the fourth floor, workers, trackers, predators, cultists, they all slowed their steps, their thoughts fleeting as a strange keen echoed and filled the wasteland like a wave.

It was like the sound of someone pressing too hard on a violin's strings, mixing with a wordless wail full of loss, an eerie sound that bounced and echoed and rattled against the metal, swirled through the smog and fog, pierced through their ears to clutch their hearts, and twisted their spine in eerie unease.

By the time it faded, not a single soul on the fourth floor was moving. The communication lines stayed eerily silent.

Motion resumed, haltingly. Most ran, protocols and basic self-preservation driving them forth to retreat, away from whatever made such a sound.

Not all, however.

"I'm not complaining too much. I just wish—" he replied through the mask's speaker and immediately cut himself off as a sound built up in the air, like the beginning hums of a song.

Except it was no tune, nor melody, but a single drawn-out keen that slowly built itself up into a howl.

Niet stiffened, hand already clutching his short sword, glancing around them with clear nervousness.

Him? He just focused entirely on the sound, tilting his head up. Part of him was captivated by the mere sound, the emotions it forcibly wrung out of his withered heart. Another part of him was curious and terrified at the same time.

Despite both sides of him warring for dominance, a single memory ran through his mind.

A meeting, held almost eight months ago at the Prospectors Guild, telling them to report any doglike creatures they might have run into or seen during their work, for a hefty monetary reward should the creature be caught because of said tip. Something offered and paid for by a dungeon baron.

His first instinct was to go back to the guild right this moment and try to report it before anyone else did, then realized how pointless that would be.

That howl was *loud.* There were likely at least a dozen other people across the floor right now that had the exact same thought he did, maybe younger, maybe closer to the guild, maybe faster than him.

What they didn't have was experience with trapping and hunting. Even after all these years, his Path remained the same, not only in the system but in his heart. He'd still trap rodents and slugs and all manner of curiosities to increase his level, but also because it was fun.

And as the howl faded, its distorted echoes still flooding through the mask's speaker, he considered the reason that baron wished to find this creature.

Considering how, for something like a dog, the only way to survive down here would be if it was exceptionally mutated or Awakened, the answer was obvious.

Awakened dogs were very rare. Awakened dogs that were strong enough to withstand life on the fourth floor were . . .

Unheard of, actually.

And if it was mutated to high hell, it would still be much stronger than a regular dog. It would still fetch a *lot* in an auction.

Greed warred with caution for a brief moment, and as even the remnants of the echoes faded, he made up his mind.

"Niet. How would you like to make a few hundred gold crowns?" he whispered, breathed out into the mask's microphone, and he saw his friend's mask snap to him so fast he swore he heard something in his spine pop through the grimy bodysuit.

He seemed to consider it for a moment, his head and gaze drifting in thought.

He understood why. This would be dangerous. And neither of them were exactly in their prime anymore.

Then Niet gave a sharp resolute nod, sheathing his sword.

He smiled, an unusual formation for his wrinkled skin and fading musculature.

"It carried a lot, and echoed even more. And the only large open areas in the fourth floor—"

"The canals." Niet cut him off.

He nodded, turning around and briskly walking toward the nearest guild lift, glancing at the magic compass in his hand and hearing loose metal plates grind and creak beneath his steel boots.

Something in his gut told him this was a bad idea, but temptation overpowered his caution.

"Let's go grab my old gear, friend. We've got a dog to catch."

Life was an unfair, psychopathic bitch.

And she was absolutely certain that said bitch had a grudge with her.

It was a long series of unfortunate coincidences she couldn't even bother to count or recite at the moment.

Long story short, she was fucked over by being unlucky several times, in the worst timing and manner possible.

So she'd gotten assigned to *this* bullshit.

She'd gone from being a half-respected gangster under a respected crime lord's boot—or dungeon baron or whatever the fuck they called themselves— to this. Lugging around almost eighty pounds of gear, looking for some fucking *dog* in the fourth floor. Day in, day out.

For *a goddamn month*.

It wasn't just the time sentence for her fuckups, it was the fact that her task was fucking *pointless*. There was no fucking dog, and even if some dirty mutt could somehow survive down here for longer than ten minutes, there would be no fucking way of fucking finding the fucking thing, for fuck's sake.

Fuck.

And because some plucky rumor about some adventurer and a dog reached her boss's ears, her sentence was doubled, along with how many people were sent down in this shithole.

This place wasn't nearly as big as the third floor, but it was still fucking *massive*. There were hundreds of others being forced to scour around this shithole 'cuz of Mister Crimelord Dungeon Baron Manny or whatever the fuck his name and title was, when they would need several *thousands* to even catch a whiff of a goddamn dragon if it decided to live down here.

It was just wasted manpower. Wouldn't they need her and everyone else they could use up above? The situation was tenser than a stretched, fraying piece of string. One or two guards, or gangsters, being killed, could ignite the shitstorm. Everyone was looking for a reason to lash out.

But did Manny fucking Ironskin or whatever the fuck give a shit? *Noooo*, he wanted to find his lost pet or something.

Unfortunately she couldn't complain to anyone, nor voice these thoughts without getting her limbs cut off and thrown into a sump, so she complained to *herself*. Like a sane individual.

Probably.

She just continued to stomp through gravel, plates of steel, and cracked stone, trundled through oceans of bolts and scrap metal forming hills that blocked half the thin metal alleyways she wished to go through, with just a shitty fucking compass to guide her back once her *ten hour* shift was done.

This endless bullshit was driving her insane.

Fucking stupid fucking—

Then she heard it.

She tensed, her spine going stiff, her gloved hand braced against a twisting pipe, as if made from rope and turned to metal, her right knee to her chest as she was about to squeeze through a mess of pipes to continue her meaningless wandering.

There was something about the sound that so openly declared mourning and loss, that she couldn't help but let her mind wander to those she herself had lost, people she hadn't thought of in months.

It was also exceptionally eerie. It felt like she'd just sat and listened to a requiem, the parting eulogy of someone far more significant than her, and she couldn't shake off the goose bumps that rose on her skin because of it.

It was like a siren, declaring, *Here you will find death.*

It took almost a full minute of sitting frozen for her to realize what she'd heard, breathless, from how fucking *loud* that was. She could swear her eardrums *hurt*.

Her first action was to check the speakers on her gas mask, gingerly tapping along the plastic circles clamped around her ears.

No, they worked just fine.

And she was . . . *probably* not hallucinating. She hadn't taken any cloud-sugar with her.

It took a few seconds for her mind to start processing what to do and what to make of that sound.

First of all, that was so *fucking loud*, holy shit.

Which meant that it was probably close to her.

And it also meant she'd been completely and utterly wrong in almost all of her assumptions. And that she could get out of this chore of a job if she could capture it.

Her hand jerked down to the comms tablet that had been bouncing at her hip for two weeks without use, and she hesitated.

If she could capture it without any help, how much rep would she get on the streets? That thing had some *lungs* on it.

Actually, how dangerous was it?

She brought up the system screen, her lips pressing into a thin line.

Level twenty-eight. There was no *way* she'd lose to a fucking mutt.

As she turned around and began to sprint toward the direction that haunting howl came from, she could have sworn something was staring at her through the smoggy alleys and pipes, yet despite checking around her continuously and seeing nothing, the feeling never faded.

She disregarded the feeling after a couple minutes as she vaulted over a buzzing engine, chalking it up to nerves and anticipation.

Hanging across wires and prowling beneath bits of debris, she never noticed the small entourage of spiders that seemed to follow her with their beady red eyes.

Gears creaked.

The hiss of a hundred chassis drawing breaths, a hundred fans whirring to life behind metallic chest plates, the buzz of electrics, they filled the air, the empty space behind him warming with presence.

Incense and oil fumes filled the air, and Archbishop Varmond rose, hands unclasping.

A question whispered.

An answer eluded it.

A question demanded answers of form. Of self. Of creation, of futility. Of negative value, and the transaction of flesh and metal. The maddening crown that could not be worn, the incompatible conjoining in nirvana.

A question of perfection, lost.

Through the temple's vents, a wordless, distorted wail longing echoes and loss flutters into his ears.

A question of perfection, found.

A series of clicks, and he unfurled. Hydraulics hissed like angry hydras, metallic joints clicked and cracked into place as his true body formed, pressed, compressed, decompressed, reformed, a silent demonstration of near perfection, of flawless machinery.

He gazed at the symbol, scrawled onto a tattered red cloth with black paint. The eye gazed down, down.

A veneer. A lie.

Soon, brother. He whispered in his mind with a voice that wasn't his, and he turned.

A sea of yellow eyes extended before him as he towered above them. Contempt and hope raced through him.

"Soon. The hands of the clock wear away and fade. The answer nears. The eyes shall find it." Three voices rumbled through the gramophone in his chest, and a fuzzy, distorted melody long lost to the tides of time began to play, a fathomless importance reverberating through flesh and steel, through wires and crystals.

The melody tingled at a phantom heart within his frame, an ancient memory.

A memory of loss.

Of ascension, broken.

Of perfection, lost.

Of perfection, never found, but perhaps echoed in another.

CHAPTER 2

Her confidence in beating this dog without severely injuring or killing it had very, very sharply declined the moment she laid eyes on it, after almost a fucking *hour* of sprinting around trying to find the damn thing without getting lost.

Not because it was particularly gigantic or intimidating, despite its strange form, but because it was eating something several times bigger than itself. Like, fucking eight times bigger. Without stopping at all, biting whole ass chunks out of it.

Without being disturbed by *anything*.

She didn't for an instance think that this thing was what killed the . . . what looked like the mutilated remains of a spearhead shark. It was something that it probably just stumbled upon and decided to eat, because she couldn't fathom how something that small could kill something that large. It just didn't make sense.

She was still confident she could beat this thing into the fucking dirt before hog-tying it and slinging it over her back, whistling merrily all the while over her free trip back into the Beakers' good graces. She just wasn't sure she could do it while holding back. Accidentally killing this thing was a genuine concern. Baron whateverhisnamewas was *very* insistent about catching the thing alive.

It was just the attitude of everything *around* the thing that made her hair stand on end.

Whether it was the carnivorous vines around the canal that seemed to actively lean away from the massive free meal right next to them, the acid flies that only seemed interested in melting the carcass's tail as far away from the dog as possible, or the sump frogs and acid slugs, everything that came close to the massive carcass to scavenge some easy pickings, they all very quickly turned around and left.

And she knew that *nothing* in nature, or as close to nature as one could get inside this shithole, would ever give up a mountain of free food without a valid reason and concern.

She idly noted the withered signs posted occasionally up and down the miles-long expanse that stretched to her right as she observed from a lightly vibrating venting pipe a few hundred feet above her catch, her left leg swinging as she hugged her right.

Something about this all felt off, and she wasn't sure what. Just to be safe, she mentally noted the canal number and sign, in case she needed to call in assistance from the comms tablet.

After a brief moment of self-reflection, she sighed and rolled her eyes at her own attitude.

She was being *such* a fucking *pussy* about this.

It was just a fucking dog, and even if she couldn't beat its ass with her bare hands, she had a thirty-pound harpoon gun she'd been forced to lug around for two weeks. And a healing potion she could feed the thing once she'd sufficiently tied it up, to prevent it from bleeding out.

"All right, come on, it's showtime, you jittery fucking bitch." She murmured to herself, a familiar phrase she'd muttered to herself before every cage fight, and hopped off the pipe onto rusty metal with a worryingly loud bang. She stayed crouched for a moment, nailing her eyes on the dog's form below.

Besides a twitch of its ear, no reaction. It just kept biting giant chunks out of the carcass.

Holy *fuck*, how much could this thing eat?

Beginning to unstrap all unnecessary weight from the filter canisters to the backup respirator, she only kept a single flare, a healing potion, and the comms tablet on her belt.

Just as a precaution.

She picked up the harpoon gun, checked the crank and arrow, and began stalking closer with a deep, steadying breath, ducking beneath a crisscrossing box made of wires and squeezing through tight crevices for the best shot possible.

It turned its eyes to the tail currently getting melted by glowing flies, and after throwing its head back and swallowing a giant chunk of oddly textured organ that almost got stuck in its throat, it clacked its teeth shut and began limping over to shoo them away.

It wasn't very interested in chewing up the thing's digestive tract.

It was *very* interested in how this thing got its tail to be such a devastating weapon.

Thankfully, its tail was about half as wide as its main body, never mind its gigantic, arrow-shaped head, so it took little more than forty-something minutes to eat through it all, up to the base of the thing's spine, which, oddly enough, had hip bones connected. Without any legs.

Weird. And redundant.

With only a vaguely cylindrical piece of meat left, around six feet long and half as tall, almost two hours after it began eating, it was quite honestly more than sated. Even [Devourer] seemed more than content enough. Its diminishing reserves had been restocked to more than it had *before* it went down into the enclosed spaces of the human nest, [Devourer] wasn't hungry for once, and the wolf's jaws were beginning to hurt from constantly biting and chewing and tearing out chunks.

For . . . probably the second time in its life, it considered actually leaving free food behind. It didn't want to waste another hour with this. It had to get going and find some crevice to sneak into—

A distant click and a faint whistling sound made its ears shoot up, and it detached from its prey, planning to crane its head around to investigate the odd sound, one that didn't quite fit with the normal ambiance of the canal's surroundings.

The ghostly prickle of a needle at the side of its mind from [Danger Sense] made its head snap to the left before it could do so, just quick enough to see an arching blur fly out of the foggy reaches of the walkways above, just a dozen inches past its head.

It slammed straight through its left hind leg, the skin and muscles not enough to stop the projectile without its fur to assist, the impact jerking its hips to the side from the force. It yowled in pain and surprise, forcing its protesting body to jerk back and turn away from its assailant.

It didn't need four limbs to run, despite its awkward half-changed paws.

Right as its claws dug through the stone to propel it forward, with its left leg curled up to its stomach, the metal *pulled*, three jagged points digging into the inside of its thigh and using its own flesh to pull it back.

Its chest and jaw slammed into the stone as [Bloodrush] activated and it began getting dragged back with unreasonable speed. Any attempt to resist the pull only shredded its flesh further, so it didn't hook its claws into the stone at all, instead squeezing as much adrenaline out of its sac as it dared to, throwing its left paw back to hook into the stone next to its hip.

It twisted its waist with as much force as it could muster as it pulled with its paw, launching its body backward, granting it some relief from the pain. Its left eye saw the tense steel cable that led to the metal in its leg, and without hesitation, it backhanded its claws through it, sending it reeling back to whoever held it.

Its antennae, the few that had regenerated, writhed against the floor, feeling the vague vibrations of someone or something dropping from one pipe to the next.

Its eye focused on the piece of metal, and in the few seconds of respite it had gained, it pressed its palm on the blunt back of the arrow-shaped thing, forcing the metal through its flesh with a pained whine-snarl.

Then it moved its left hand under its abdomen between its legs, and with a flick of its finger, cut off the sharp, spiky bits that had been hooked into its flesh, then moved to the outside of its thigh to yank it out.

Then it realized that it would only bleed even more should it do that, and instead cut off most of the metal with a flick of its finger to make it less awkward to run, and quickly turned around once more, sending one last glance to the human that had attacked it for no reason before it began running.

As its assailant sprinted out of the fog, however, it paused, its lips curling into a sneer, its eye narrowing.

Its body was still wrecked. How long could it run for before it would have to activate [Maddened Frenzy] and get itself even more injured than before? Five minutes? Ten? It was *fast*, normally, but could it run with two hands instead of paws, heavily injured, and without using one of its legs? While bleeding the entire time?

Realistically, it *couldn't* run away.

But as it used its single functioning hind leg to hop its bottom half around, turning to face the human, it came to a simple conclusion, one that might be born of overconfidence for all it knew, but felt *right*.

Why *should* it run away?

It was so *tired* of running.

And this was just one human.

As hundreds of feet rapidly turned to dozens, the human slowed down, its knees bent and its fists held loosely in front of its body, slowly closing in.

In the dim light, it couldn't see any sort of weapon on the human, at least none that it could recognize as such, so it idly wondered if he was holding on to some other hidden trick—like whatever he had used to shoot it.

Because there was just . . . no way he was actually planning to fight the wolf with his fists.

This wouldn't even be an actual fight if he tried that.

Yet even as the distance closed, and the wolf silently glared at the human, it took nothing out to wield.

Maybe its wishes for an easy fight were less unrealistic than it had thought.

In fact . . . it could probably kill him without even fighting.

It just had to crack the mask.

And then it could just let it die without interfering, before inevitably biting its head off.

Despite its desire to coil its tail for a strike, it allowed its appendage to wag a little, restricting the snarl in its chest into a low rumble.

This fucking thing was making her skin crawl.

Not only was it almost completely hairless, giving her a very good understanding of just how fucking *muscular* the damn thing was the closer she got, the way it had dealt with the harpoon made no fucking sense.

She'd fucking *blinked* and the steel cable had detached from the harpoon somehow.

The more attention she paid as she slowly circled the dog, the more hesitant she became about fighting this thing.

The harpoon that should be in its leg was nothing but a thin hollow pipe now, without the head or the tail attached, two clean cuts. The canine's body was covered in cuts and deep, jagged wounds all across its back and shoulders, which were disturbingly humanoid, and the way its single glowing eye followed her with an intelligent, laser-steady focus made her hair stand on end.

Twenty feet of distance slowly turned to seven. One lunge from either of them would start a fight.

But neither of them moved, even as her eyes followed the steady stream of blood that dripped onto the stone from its injured leg.

Then its tail began to wag and its lips began to curl into a snarl, a low rumble building in the air, and the feeling of something not adding up only increased.

She felt like she was in the cage again, having to fight some blood-crazed psycho with a giant grin on their face at the prospect of beating someone up. Those were the fights one wanted to *avoid*.

Its body language, from the low stance and the reluctance to move, screamed defensive, while the way its almost humanoid hands gripped the stone below, the low, rumbling growl that sounded more like an engine's purr, and the wagging tail, they all screamed "I want to fight."

It was so contradictory she couldn't tell what this thing was going to do.

Despite her wounded pride, her instincts and the bizarre way this thing looked and acted sealed the deal.

Her left hand went for the comms tablet, and the dog's—no, the beast's eye, followed the movement, hopping once to realign its bottom half with her, still crouched but significantly more tense all of a sudden, its tail curling strangely.

So the mutt understood the concept of "weapons" and the danger they posed. It had to have been around humans for a while—

In an instant, it blurred forward and to the side, whipping its lower body toward her by using both of its legs to kick the stone as it used its hands to stabilize its upper body in place, adding to its momentum and torque, its back facing her as its thick, muscled tail blurred straight toward her face.

She jerked back, a practiced movement.

Not quite far enough. She hadn't realized how goddamn *long* its tail was.

She activated [Challenger's Focus] just in time to watch in near slow motion as the strange black thing at the tip of the beast's tail slammed through the glass of her gas mask.

Boxers learned how to not close their eyes when facing an incoming hit, as it would only hinder them in a close fight.

And that was the thing that doomed her, as in that moment of panic, her natural reflex to close her eyes simply did not occur, beaten out of her from repeated bouts in the ring.

Shards of glass, big and small, slammed into her open eyes, and she let out a cry of surprise and anguish as she backpedaled in a panic, almost tripping over herself and spinning in confusion. Her legs buckled and she almost careened forward before managing to catch the ground with her fist and spin, pushing off and away from where she thought the beast was.

Where she *thought*, because no matter how hard she tried to focus and stop herself from blinking, her vision was nothing but a blurry sea of grimy green and gray and red, with a single undulating dot of gold glaring at her through the muck.

"F-fuck! FUCK!" She snarled, backpedaling further while keeping some unstable form of a stance as her left hand fumbled with the comms tablet, struggling to remember where each button was. She slowed just a bit and straightened, despite the panic clawing at her heart, in the hope the damned dog would keep away long enough for her to call reinforcements if she just *pretended* to have her shit together.

That blurry golden dot disappeared, and something slammed into her ankle as she took a step back, just hard enough for her lead boots to scrape at the floor and make her lose her balance. In the middle of falling onto her back, she curled her left leg in and stomped where its tail was, all her points in Speed allowing her to do so before it pulled back.

She was rewarded by a slight yelp before her hips and back rolled onto the floor, and she carried the momentum by curling her legs and rolling back, ass over head, and staggering upright, unbalanced, feeling fear and agony claw at her mind and body.

Every breath felt like a million fish hooks were being dragged through her nostrils and into her lungs, a deep-seated feeling of wrongness permeating her body.

The scrape of nails on stone sounded out from in front of her, and in a move both desperate and fearful, she jerked her upper body low and threw out her fastest right hook.

Her fist moved through something solid as if it wasn't even there, the flesh and bone splitting effortlessly, the tendons snapping, before her knuckles slammed into the top of wet, hot, rough flesh, a sandpaper tongue scraping at her pinkie.

A split second before the agony registered, innumerable sharp points clamped around her wrist, and with a twist, she felt the flesh, the bone, the tendons, everything, be sheared off, like paper meeting scissors.

An ear-grating, shrill scream left the human's lips—a female, it noted from the scent—as her mutilated hand lay comfortably nestled into its jaws, covered by some kind of skin-fitting covering. It quickly spat it out, watching with concern as the human backpedaled, tumbling over her own legs, hyperventilating and clutching at the clean-cut stump on her right wrist, agonized, choking groans leaving her lips as blood dripped down her face from her punctured eyes.

She was being *loud*, and the wolf was fairly certain she was just going to attract more of her kin to it if she kept it up. It was concerned about having to fight *more* humans. Besides, it didn't really hate humans, so despite wanting to fight and kill this female, it had no reason to draw it out or toy with her.

It had to kill her quickly and leave, leaving her corpse to be food for the various vermin of the canals. It was kind of a sad situation for the wolf to be in. All that meat, *wasted*.

Her free hand let go of the stump, fumbling for some kind of vial at her waist as the wolf patiently hopped and prowled around her. She downed it in what seemed like a single gulp, before tossing it with force toward the wolf, a couple feet off the mark.

It quickly wreathed its claws in darkness and stopped its instinctual growling to deny her its rough location, watching in both fascination and annoyance as skin quickly formed over the bleeding stump.

The human fumbled for the strange metal device as she backpedaled even farther, posturing as if she was fine, despite the way her legs quivered and the way her fear was so thick in the air it could almost note its undertaste from beneath the acrid chemicals.

A series of strange beeps and clicks came out of the device as her fingers pressed as many buttons as they could reach, and it tilted its head, the device's design reminding the wolf of those strange grated boxes that would make a bunch of noise, whether it was some human speaking or some cacophony of sound that humans seemed to enjoy listening to.

It paused, its eye widening as it realized what she was trying to do. As she opened her mouth, bringing the device to her mouth, the wolf put down its injured leg and rushed forward.

"HELP! JACQUELINE HERE, I NEED HELP, CANAL F TH—" The human was cut off with a wheeze as the wolf's shoulder slammed into her midriff, its left hand curling down and behind her knee before raking through, severing the tendon in her legs without issue, as its right hooked into her lower back, the farthest it could reach, and sheared through her back, severing the end of her spine.

It knew all the weak points of a human. It knew how to disable her without effort, and so it did, its eye nailed to her elbow.

As her torso reeled back, her hand extended, and the wolf saw its opportunity, unwinding its neck and opening its jaws to clamp onto her elbow, its canines scraping against one another as its front teeth cut through her forearm.

A violent jerk and twist as they fell, and the device flew through the air above their heads along with the human's arm.

Some buzzing voice responded through the device as it clattered to the floor, but the wolf didn't care enough to listen to what the human on the other end was saying, focused on shutting up the human below it as fast as possible.

It knew what humans sounded like when they were calling for their kin.

A breathless cry of terror and pain left the human as she threw her arms above her head and neck, and the wolf, left without a choice, started clawing through, its jaws closing around the single forearm the human possessed as she jerked and writhed around, its claws hooking into her shoulder muscles and raking through, jerking its jaws back and to the side, a clumsy maneuver that didn't manage to sever her defense, only partly cutting through her forearm due to her stump smacking into the side of its face from the motion and not allowing it to twist further.

Without her shoulder muscles to help her arms move, and her legs completely paralyzed, it didn't matter. Its right hand's "fingers" clamped around her elbow and pushed it up, away from her head without much effort, allowing the wolf's teeth to cut through flesh and thick, threaded cloth.

Its tail felt along the human's limp lower body before jamming into her suit in vain, the fang not sharp or strong enough to pierce through the thick suit.

As the human's upper body continued writhing, her chin tucking into her neck, it twisted, throwing her severed forearm to the side and opening its jaws as wide as they would go.

Then it snapped forward.

Its canines cut through her eye sockets and cheekbones effortlessly, and without anything to block it but the human's annoying screaming and bucking, it began trying to dig its fingers into her neck, trying to either cut through her spine or neck, to make her *stop making noise already*.

Its hind leg, the functional one, kicked its lower body up in the air, then kicked down at her stomach right as its weight came crashing down, the impact making her abdomen curl and her mouth open in a breathless wheezing cough.

It saw an opportunity and immediately blunted its teeth, yanking her head up and sideways by pulling at her skull, the tips of its fangs scraping at the edges of her brain.

It lifted its right paw, phasing its claws through her open mouth, down her right cheek and jawbone, before turning and *finally* managing to cut into her throat, her gurgling screams as frustrating as they were worrying.

It snarled, a rising, sharp sound, and engaged its pained, torn muscles as much as it could, trying to force its fingers deeper into her neck, being blocked by her blood-soaked chin as she desperately tucked her shoulders up.

In frustration, it gave up and grabbed on to the detached jawbone it had cut through, then yanked back with all its strength, the guttural crack of snapping bone and tearing flesh predating the animalistic, gurgling screech of agony that the human let out as the wolf's arm trembled with the effort of trying to tear her jaw off.

It just wanted to jam its claws into her spine and be done with this, but she would just *not* give up.

It flattened its ears to save its hearing from the sound, and with urgency and genuine anger, let go of her head by cutting through with its teeth and yanking back. It quickly grabbed her half-connected jaw with its left paw, its stubby half-transformed fingers barely getting a decent grip, then wrenched to the left, exposing her flopping tongue and neck.

It formed a rough fist with its right arm and punched the side of her head, just strong enough to expose her neck further, and it jammed its snout into the exposed flesh, opening its jaw progressively and allowing its teeth to cut through tendons, arteries, and flesh.

Unfortunately, no amount of twisting would reach her spine, so it adjusted its grip, blunted its teeth, and yanked her half-limp, spasming body off the ground.

Its hands rose to the back of her neck, and with a forceful rake of its claws and a twist of its own trembling neck, the human died with a final jerk, her spine severed completely.

It adjusted its grip on her neck, then pushed down with its hands on her torso and pulled up with its back and neck. With a sound of wet, tearing paper and a spray of delicious blood, her head finally detached, making the wolf jerk back from the sudden lack of resistance, leaving it hanging from the left side of its jaws by a few scant ribbons of flesh.

It had *really* missed the taste of blood.

Even as [Bloodrush] faded, it didn't feel particularly tired, its breaths only mildly heavier than normal as it breathed through its catch.

It was just injured and frustrated at its current circumstance. It wanted to relax for *one day* without something trying to kill it. It was almost tempted to crawl back into the tunnels for some peace and quiet.

At least it could take the only part of the human it cared about, her brain, and run away to eat it somewhere safe.

Because there was *no way* not a single human had heard her cries for help, especially judging from the urgent voices coming from the little metal box thing she'd been holding on to.

As if the world sought to validate that exact thought, another prickle from [Danger Sense] made the wolf instinctively duck and throw itself to the side in an awkward hopping manner, dropping the human's head and letting it roll away as it turned its gaze skyward.

It snarled at the shady outlines of two humans crouched atop a precariously positioned walkway that connected two leaning towers of steel, more than a hundred feet up and away, but both clearly focusing on it.

It had to run away, so it turned and . . .

Stumbled over its own feet, its shoulder and the side of its snout smacking into the small pool of blood cradling the human's corpse. Confused and alarmed, it pushed off the ground, planning to resume its attempt to flee, and saw the world begin to rock side to side, as if the wolf were in a barrel floating down a stream.

Something tugged and prickled at its back, and it twisted, almost falling over, staring uncomprehendingly at the half dozen tiny metal spikes that dotted its backside, swaying and lightly bouncing with each movement.

It understood why it hadn't felt them, considering how much pain it was still in, but *when* had those gotten there? Had the humans above thrown the spikes down?

A word for them formed in its mind as its vision blurred and the world tilted, sending the wolf drunkenly stumbling onto its side, watching the glowing canal twist like a worm across its vision.

Needles.

A wide, heavy net covered the wolf and squeezed its adrenaline sack dry, the conflicting chemicals in its bloodstream battling for dominance, and it snarled in effort as it ground its knuckles into the stone, getting up and taking six stumbling steps before the adrenaline was overpowered, its limbs and fingers getting tangled in the net.

It didn't even have the energy to swipe its claws through it.

It fell unconscious, and immediately its mind flitted away into [Devourer], frantically trying to disable and target the poison in its veins.

It wasn't paralyzing poison, so the wolf didn't have experience with how and what it was doing. It seemed to move through its bloodstream and into the brain, and then act like a hyperefficient version of melatonin, forcing its mind to rest.

By the time it forced its quickly flagging mind into properly programming its mana cells into attacking the poison, however, its chemical bonds seemed to have altered and changed, and eventually, it couldn't even understand what it was doing or looking at, its mind succumbing to a deep sleep.

"HELP! JACQUELINE HERE, I NEED HELP, CANAL F TH—" The voice cut off with a thud and a wheeze on the public channel, and across the fourth floor, gangsters, mercenaries, and hopeful nobodies alike all paused, some replying with requests for location and details.

But *all* heard the ensuing bloodcurdling screams, the gut-wrenching gurgles of agony, the spine-chilling snarls, the sounds of tearing flesh and snapping bones, distorted through the speakers, until all that remained was the low static of a damaged comms tablet.

And in a metal tower, nestled into the walls of the third floor, a pale, gray face curled its lips into a sneer as it listened to the replay, an hour late.

Newly regrown limbs crushed the crutches they held in trembling fists, while steely eyes glared at a complex machine of mana crystals and countless buttons and wires sprawled across a dark, carpet-less room.

"I *knew* you were alive, you fucking *mutt*," he snarled under his breath and swept his glare off the hub machine, and onto Kolak, his brown eyes staring back at him, unflinchingly.

Good.

"Get Mason in here. And the comms crystal that's labeled 'Trackers.' *Now*," he growled, and didn't wait to see Kolak nod before he grabbed a hold of the boxlike microphone, pushing the WLF-SCT button with enough force to hear something crack.

He brought the microphone to his mouth and cleared his throat.

"To everyone currently assigned to the fourth floor on dog-catching duty, this is Baron Manos Ironheart. And I will make myself *very, very* clear," he rumbled, planning on doing his best to make it as clear as possible how serious this was and how fucking *furious* he was.

But then he remembered that many of them were tracking groups, mercenaries, and people he had little hold over, as well as how he couldn't make it obvious how *important* this was. Thus, he forced out a hissing breath between clenched teeth to calm himself down.

"If you do not catch that fucking dog soon, you will all either be out of a job or a floating corpse in a gutter, depending on your incompetence and efforts. My patience has *limits*. So I'll add further incentive: Whoever brings me that dog, *alive*, will be paid their weight in gold, and will have one favor granted by me, within reason. I'll relay new instructions through your superiors."

He was met with silence as he tossed the microphone aside, letting its curled cord swing it along the edge of the machine.

He was going to burn this fucking floor to the ground if he had to, to find that wolf.

CHAPTER 3

"Miss? Are you Lady Anna's escort?"

Katherine tore her eyes away from the dark mansion looming above and beyond the towering spiked fence, and calmly turned her gaze to the guard that had approached her, briefly roving over his weapons, his demeanor, his stance.

He looked more like a tin bucket, but she supposed that it was effective in keeping away trouble, something that was sorely needed with how the third floor was being right now.

She nodded.

"Yes, I am. Is she coming outside soon?"

His expression twisted into a light, sympathetic grimace.

"I'm afraid Lady Anna has been forbidden from doing her usual, erm . . . stroll. Security concerns, and with the situation outside being as it is, I'm sure you understand. Lady Anna said she will send a letter to your apartment when your services are required again. I'm afraid I'll have to ask you to leave now."

She stood for a moment with a blank space in her mind, an empty void where a directive and a purpose used to be.

Her hands hid within her coat pockets as she turned and walked away without a second word.

Two empty, soulless eyes slid across terrain and flesh and cloth alike, unseeing, wandering without a clear goal.

She would never *not* be thankful for what Emhreeil had done for her. Years and years spent ruminating and fantasizing about freedom, what it would be like. But she couldn't claim that it was a wholly positive thing for her, to suddenly be free.

She wasn't used to stagnation before attaining freedom. This feeling of not having anything to do. There was always something. Some chore to do, some preparation, some command, schedule, or person to help. She also wasn't used to being so directionless. When she'd been granted freedom one afternoon, without any warning but a vague sentence spoken days ago, she realized how lost she was within the limitless paths laid before her.

How the world could feel so very empty when it suddenly became so vast, and the only one who occupied it was her, alone.

It felt like breathing manually, like she was overthinking her every step until all she could do was stumble and wonder why the more she thought about it, the more unstable her path became.

Red light eventually filtered into her vision, and her steps slowed, struggling to bring focus to her gaze as it moved over tinted glass.

Her eyes rose, inspecting the establishment, the corny quotes of eroticism plastered all over it.

She'd been to this brothel many times. Never as a client or worker, of course. She'd follow Lady Anna and do her job, standing guard as she healed whoever she could, however she could, nothing more and nothing less.

But for a brief moment, she considered it, just this once. Maybe laying with someone would clear her head. Fill that numb, cold void.

Then she remembered what she'd seen inside such establishments, in the back rooms where no clients went. Teenage girls beaten bloody, goblin girls, little better than children, curled in unresponsive balls, eyes somehow emptier than her own.

Her eyes lost focus as she turned and kept walking.

She needed something.

Anything.

As a child, twenty-something years ago and an entire sea away, she'd watched from underneath the stands in the fighting pits between people's boots, day after day, whenever she had free time. The way people fought, the way they moved. The way they died, blood and broken teeth mixing into the orange sand.

It hadn't taught her how to fight *well*—that was a work of labor between herself and Lady Anna's instructor—but it had taught her better than most.

She could try that. Find some bar a little too large to be reasonable, wander down to the fighting ring usually held below. Maybe waltz into the third floor's lower reaches, amongst wooden boxes and firelight within metal barrels, pay for two gaunt unfortunates to fight for her amusement in their improvised fighting rings, wrestling in the gray mud.

Would that fill the void with nausea or nostalgia? Maybe guilt as she'd wonder what Emhreeil would think of her for contributing to that?

She kept walking, dispassionate, lost in her thoughts.

The noise around her rose and fell, from growled whispers in the tight confines of alleyways to buzzing little market streets, selling trinkets and dungeon curiosities, supposed maps and miracle potions, a hazy, empty mass of senses that molded together in her memory before quickly slipping away altogether.

Maybe she should have been more careful, paid more attention, but she just couldn't find it in herself to care. Coupled with the fact the third floor was rapidly turning into a war zone, something like getting mugged was the least of her concerns while roaming the streets.

She did have to dodge out of the way of a pickpocket a few times, though. Children, always.

Eventually, her eyes moved over a vaguely familiar alley, a quaint little tailor's shop at the corner, and just beyond it, a familiar square.

There was an orphanage there that did some minor medical care for cheap to fund itself, tucked away behind a blocky apartment building, just behind the square's main street. She could honestly only remember it because she'd seen her first-ever Awakened stray somewhere around here. And because it was the first time she'd seen a skill cast spend so much of Lady Anna's mana, just for an ear infection.

Her mind transitioned from that thought, wandered to all the times she'd helped with things big and small as Lady Anna did her work, positioning her patients, giving her tools and the like, like an assistant.

She wanted to do something along those lines. Try to be like those people she admired and appreciated.

There weren't a whole lot of those. At least not by comparison. Emhreeil was always what first came to mind, then Sir Carmian Kervile, Lady Anna's father, and Lady Anna herself. Part of it was their kindness, but she was not self-aware enough to know the deeper reasons as to why she admired them, and she did not care to be introspective about it either. It was what it was.

She slowly wandered forward for a few seconds, the bottom half of her face obscured by her coat's high collar, staring down the cramped alley, before eventually deciding on what she'd occupy her time with.

A bright red uniform, with metal pauldrons engraved with a gear, torch, and a chevron underneath, hurriedly jogged past the alley and out of sight.

Like being suddenly doused in cold water, her senses sharpened and flitted back into her mind, the fugue she'd been entrenched in snapped in an instant. She stopped in her tracks, turning around without a second thought.

The faint, chaotic background sounds in her mind processed, turning from empty noise into yelling voices and the scuffle of clothes and shoes grating against stone, into the sound of impacts and grunts, a concert of struggle.

Her steps slowed once more, until she'd ground to a halt, indecision gnawing at the back of her neck. Wisps of smog passed through the entrance of the alleyway, dancing around the metal bars of its open gate, obscuring the outside world. The alley suddenly felt so much more private than it was. A little piece of the world, cut away for her convenience, to give her a moment to think.

She tightened the collar around the bottom half of her face, the acrid stench of wandering chemicals lessening, her eyes observing the uneven grimy cobbles underneath her boots, the barred window sinking into the floor just beside them as she listened.

It didn't sound nearly as bad as some other scenes she'd had to turn away from since a week ago. There were no screams of agony, no explosions. There was no sound of shattering glass and quickly roaring fire. There was no group of guardsmen beating submission onto random passersby just to send a message.

No sound of blades whistling through the air.

It sounded like a minor scuffle at best. Someone got too uppity, maybe their spine was a little too rigid to bend down for a chest-puffed guard. She wanted to intervene, truth be told. She wanted to fight, even if just to feel her blood pump with adrenaline, in a fight where the stakes were not death but a single beatdown.

But there was no . . . weight in that thought. No drive, no fuel.

It was like saying she wanted to be eating fresh bread tonight. It felt empty, muted, and passionless.

Her steps resumed, a faint direction in her mind.

A church, a house of healing, a clinic, the aftermath of a battle. Anywhere where she could help with her meager medical knowledge, attained through observation alone, she'd go there. In fact, why stop there? She was terrible with children, but she was great with chores. An orphanage, maybe, or one of the Crow's Church's soup kitchens, she could help there as well.

Because she had to do *something*.

And the only way left to go was down, all the way to the bottom of the third floor.

Cobbles slowly turned to textured metal, alleys opened to vast squares and overhangs. Her eyes peered through the railings at the countless lights below and above, some obscured by wandering clouds of smog, some drowned out by wires and cables.

In a seemingly meaningless alley, a group of tense, quiet strangers formed, waiting for the lifting platform within to get back up, and she moved in to stand amongst them.

At first, she'd been baffled at how and why everything was so chaotic in the dungeon. A tiny alleyway could hide within a massive, busy store, while in the most hard-to-notice places one could conceive of, laid countless lifts to take people up and down through the gargantuan metallic plates that formed what one could easily be described as a beehive of a country.

The lifting platform's upper mechanisms whirred to life, and she kept all senses but her sight on her surroundings as she politely pushed through the crowd, curiosity tugging at her.

With one hand firmly grasping a pipe beside the latticework door of folding metal, and her ears open for anyone rushing to push her, she extended her neck and leaned forward a little.

Four cables as thick as her arms, of magisteel alloy, extended down a dark metal shaft, several hundred feet deep, and in the small open area she could see at the bottom, no bigger than her thumbnail, was another sprawl of homes and factories and streets and towers of various purposes.

She had little appreciation for the arts, having spent more than a decade in Emhreeil's home. She'd grown used to them.

But there was still something infinitely humbling in the nigh-infinite scale of the dungeon. In the fact she was but one worthless soul, letting time flit by among a dozen million more, trapped on a colossal island people called a country.

A tiny dot of black quickly ascended, a metallic contraption just twelve feet wide and long, more of an open-top box than a platform.

She leaned back into the safety of flat ground, without her back exposed to anyone, and pressed against the wall like everyone else, a silent aura of distrust in each of their searching eyes, hers included.

The platform rose to their level soon enough, with a loud, off-key ring and a flash of red light.

The folding metal doors creaked and groaned for a moment, attempting to move on their broken rails, before giving up, and through them squeezed in a small crowd of people, some wearing colors, some not.

Two of them, guards.

There was a sudden spike of tension in the air, in the way even the hushed whispers of conversation and the shuffles of clothes suddenly turned dead silent, the way two dozen eyes nailed themselves to the two of them within the cramped alley, hers included.

The senior guardsman's steps paused as he looked at them with a subtle weight in his gaze, as if weighing a decision, while those from below simply wandered onward to continue their day.

She idly remembered hearing something about a curfew, declared by the Guard to those who would listen.

But then again, crime lords, average people, religions, and businessmen ruled the third floor. Few listened to the Guard.

A decision was made in the tense silence, and he tilted his head down a little and said something in a polite manner as he pushed through, something she didn't quite catch. It somehow sounded snide, like an attempt at a joke, despite most likely being an attempt to defuse the tension.

Her eyes flicked to a young man's shifting hands, the pointy end of a shank moving about his pocket, his grimy scarf wrapped around his nose, highlighting the scaled ridges of his cheekbones, slowly drawing her attention to the hatred in his eyes.

She knew what was about to happen, and wished no part in it. She maneuvered between a dozen different people that were trying to leave the tight alleyway, and brushed shoulders with another dozen, flitting into the slowly refilling platform.

Some hesitated between looking at the tense scene and getting on the lift, delaying further. Seven people joined her on the platform, most mimicking her behavior if they were able. Back to the bars, eyes shifting and observant, and gazes heavy.

As the lift's mechanisms groaned to life and her organs began pulling upward from the suddenly rapid descent, the sounds of a struggle flared high, just out of sight.

The descent continued, uncaring. Her eyes flitted up, the pitch-black confines of the shaft lit by only the dim yellow light crystals just outside the alley. The chorus of yelling voices and meaty thuds quickly elevated to elated yells and cathartic spews of profanity, the cracking of bones.

Her eyes flicked back down.

Two versus two dozen. They never had a chance. They'd probably die.

She couldn't find it in herself to care. Much like with everyone else down here, it was difficult for her to look past the uniform and look at the person wearing it. Many were even worse than said uniform.

Faint light burst from around the rim of the platform and washed over her boots as the shaft rose quickly above them, like a curtain peeling back to show the wider world.

Cautious or not, she couldn't stop her eyes from wandering to the side, admiring the scant few moments of beauty one could find down here, in the countless glittering light crystals and light bulbs, spotlights and occasional enchanted signs gently glowing purple. Much of the dizzying complexity of the dungeon was being obscured and distorted, blurred by wandering pockets of smog that looked like innocent mist from afar, rather than gray-brown clouds of poison.

Her gaze drifted to the left, observing the nearby tower, a massive cylinder-like structure, customized progressively to add balconies and banners and cables and a myriad other details. Towers that were created just as much for structural support as they were meant for decadence, to those who could afford such.

Maybe if she had high enough Perception, she would peer into one of its countless windows, beyond the mirror enchantments, and see those within staring back at her, eye to eye, for just once.

Her head turned, looking through the bars and trying to figure out if she could recognize any of her usual routes from above.

Despite their quick descent and the vast distances, she could. The gigantic piles of gravel and the dark spot of slave lodgings were nestled near the walls in the far distance, barely visible due to distance and smog, one of their most frequent visits. Half-forgotten explanations were brought to the forefront.

Lung burns from chemical gasses, paired with inhalation of mana crystal dust, leading to lung rot, people coughing out shimmering blood, then bits of their own lungs, until they would inevitably die. Interaction with unprocessed, raw mana crystals without any alchemical lead protections, leading to severe mana poisoning. People who had used mana before, or had developed their mana circuits to any degree, would likely die screaming within a few months.

Slave mines rarely had anyone within them that lasted for more than five or six years. Especially considering the vast majority of slaves were goblins, which were notoriously fragile.

It was where Lady Anna had gained the vast majority of her levels.

And current beliefs.

Treatments there were . . . out of her range. She was no mage, she had no in-depth knowledge of how anything worked inside someone's body, and she had no skills to cleanse people's bodies like Lady Anna.

Brown eyes shifted, moving from one spot to the next. She faintly recognized the blue-painted banners of two clinics extending high above their surroundings, miles apart, of blue syringes and a scalpel, intertwined, topped off with light crystals hidden within blue-tinted glass, lighting the dimly lit streets they were nestled in with soothing blue, easily spottable from anywhere.

Which was the entire point, from what she knew. The sheer contrast of blue against dark gray, browns, greens, and striking yellows and oranges, made it difficult not to notice them.

They were more . . . *official* clinics, however. House Tillenhall's clinics. They had standards, and would not accept some random nobody's help, even a minor one, not without hurting their reputation and prestige, which was already waning as far as she knew.

Her eyes continued as the world below grew closer.

Some flickers of red and green, purples and enchanted signs that looked like they were moving, just barely. Brothels and casinos, bars and general hot spots of recreation. She dismissed them.

A *lot* of flickers of fire, of writhing masses nestled within alleys and squares.

Even from up here, she could hear the faint roar of their chants, a faint glimpse of undulating masses, turned toward some unknown speaker.

It was rather bizarre that the faces of the brewing civil war were a union of religious figures, crime lords, and *adventurers* of all people.

Yet Lady Anna's irate ranting when questioned on the absurdity of this made more sense the more she observed.

She could understand why the religions got involved. The Six-Eyed Crow's Church had many beliefs and genuine grievances that spoke to the people. They were aligned on the same tracks, for the Six-Winged Dove was always one step away from using the nobility above to prosecute them out of existence, which was a sentiment the common people shared heavily, if one simply removed the religious aspects and replaced it with a common hatred of those above, that had been brewing for four hundred years.

The cultists of the Struggler's Mantle wished to capitalize on the situation to legitimize themselves, throwing their lot in with the Crow, citing that struggle and war with those considered as "stronger," were . . . the . . . meaning of life . . . ?

She couldn't quite remember.

The Gatekeeper's Church was, as usual, painfully neutral and quiet in her eyes, though Lady Anna had said something about a missive that spoke of the tragedy of lives shortened or some such. But they had no real stakes in any of this, so she could understand. It was the same case for the other minor religions.

The crime lords that called themselves "barons," as if in mockery of those above, were the only real authority that existed in the lower ends of the second floor, and all around the third? It was painfully simple. They'd carved themselves a place in the dungeon, and thus wished to keep the influence of the kingdom as far away as possible. There were rumors of an alliance, at least temporarily.

Which she also understood. They saw a bigger threat to their survival than each other, and banded together.

It was all a bit complicated, but much of it made sense.

But *adventurers?* Much like Lady Anna had eloquently said, there was no reason for the Adventurers Guild in the third floor to put its foot into the meat grinder that was to come. In fact, it was in their absolute best interest to shut up and be quiet until this all blew over, so they could continue doing what they usually did, without any real consequence or change.

There were ideas as to why, maybe due to the guildmaster's origins, or due to the fact many adventurers had come to consider the dungeon their home and saw the heavy hand that the upper capital used in trying to assert control over it.

But those reasons all felt . . . weak. It felt like the guild had decided to put itself in the ring, and half the adventurers just followed because they wished to complain about the portals being shut down to better control the flow of resources that trickled down to the third floor. She doubted any of them would put their blades where their mouths were.

Then there was the fact that all the common people were split between wanting this war to happen or prevent it, to keep the dungeon as it was or to allow the kingdom to bring order, exchanging one group of uncaring exploiters for another, but with the vague hope of stability and peace that the dungeon barons could not and *would* not offer.

Above was . . . very tense. Below was slowly and steadily turning into a war zone the more people resisted and the more things escalated from both sides. The Guard kept pushing harder in an attempt to assuage the worries of the highborn about the "dungeon terrorists," or simply to not lose face by appearing incompetent. Perhaps even for petty revenge. She had little doubt that the standing army would soon be called forward, however small it was in comparison to Carmera's population.

Civil war was a fast reaction in her mind. Something that just sparked like a candle and burned until either side won.

This had proven her wrong. It was a painful grind of butting heads and trying to see who would back down first, until heads turned to swords over the course of many, many days filled with chaos and conflict.

It was annoying and too dangerous for her to reasonably entertain involving herself with.

She also didn't doubt that those above simply wanted to institute order in order to begin collecting taxes properly, something which the gangs have made an impossibility for decades, collecting said tax themselves.

It was so tiresome.

In fact, why was she wasting energy thinking about all this? It was all such a headache to sort in her mind. So . . . complicated. And it was all for something that, in truth, she could not care less about beyond a surface level curiosity to know who would next hold the leash around the dungeon's neck.

A white flash of light extended up to the sky before being devoured by the smog from within an alley with the faint crackle of lightning, fading away in an instant.

With a defeated sigh, her eyes moved down to stare at her own boots.

She'd have to go even lower. Much, much farther down, close to the entrances of the fourth floor. She doubted any of the Guard would have gone down there yet. They were stretched unimaginably thin among the second and third floor.

So she would head deeper and deeper, until she found someone or somewhere to help, like Emhreeil or Lady Anna likely would.

It was almost ironic, that the deepest reaches of the third floor had suddenly turned into the most peaceful and safe.

They descended past roads and bridges, past metallic platforms hundreds of feet wide yet still cramped with shops and people, and her eyes drank it all in.

The lifts were commandeered by the gangsters a while ago, so she'd only taken their services once or twice, unwilling to part with a few coppers for their use. But with how things were right now, neither side cared enough to station people at the lifts. And she could not deny that she had been missing out.

The buildings and factories below eventually rose around the platform, drowning out the lights and intertwining levels, embracing her back into tense mundanity.

The hiss of enchantments and a slight rocking of the platform was the preamble to the platform once more being embraced by a metallic shaft, correcting the platform into fitting properly, and she lifted her head, staring up at the numerous buildings and facilities glued onto the top of the level above, nestled just underneath where she'd started her descent, at all the numerous complex yet muted sights she'd gone past.

Or their undersides, rather.

Their momentum suddenly slowed before halting altogether, and she was jerked out of her idle thoughts with the muted thud of the platform sinking into place. Her eyes fell to observe the doors, and as they creaked aside, their intertwining bars folding to let them out, her eyes flicked to the group of five guards huddled around a close circle just to the left.

The way everyone on the platform had a shared moment of hesitance was mildly amusing, but the red light started flickering, and thus, they were forced outside, squeezing past each other.

Fortunately, besides a wary look by a couple of them, nothing happened, and she filtered out of the alley with everyone else, continuing to walk through the streets.

It felt so different, yet the same.

There was a sense of . . . energy, energy that always seemed to be lacking in the third floor, outside a select few places. It was the best way she could put it.

That sense of life and activity.

It was in the char marks of liquor bombs occasionally painting the metal and stone beneath her feet black, in the way she would turn out into a big street and see the remains of makeshift barricades made of sheet metal and fabrics and wooden pallets, shoved against the walls for people to drag into place whenever necessary.

In the way people's eyes had lost some of that . . . that fog of apathy. That cold sheen of distrust. Not much, but some.

The distant, rhythmic chanting of words she could not quite make out certainly added a hint of unity and community this place didn't seem to have before.

She wished to slip back into her usual fugue and wander through the streets, down to her destination, but with such a stark difference, such developments happening all around her, it was difficult to do so.

It was curiosity that made her steps slow, before eventually changing direction, vigor renewed.

She wanted to see what the chanting was about.

It took more than a few minutes of maneuvering through alleys and some of the more open, wide streets, but by simply following the chanting and the cheering, she eventually found her way. She walked through an alley, turned her eyes to the right, and was met with a loose wall of people dressed in browns and grays and blacks, rough worker's pants, and a myriad more, pumping their fists up with passion.

It felt so strange to see something like this, on the third floor of all places. And she was . . .

A little too short to see what was happening. Curse her genetics. Though she was sure being malnourished as a child did not help with that.

For once, as she approached someone to ask them a question, it didn't feel like she was about to have a mental spar, or impromptu interrogation. If anything, the sheer . . . energy of the crowd, it felt like it was seeping into her somehow. She kind of . . . liked it?

Even if the chanting of "off with their heads" was a rather grim one. And very loud.

"Excuse me, sir?" she asked and lightly tapped a middle-aged man's shoulder, jerking back when he whirled around, eyes wide and wild, before settling on her and relaxing, his shoulders drooping.

"Succubi's tits, you scared the shit outta me." He groaned, almost yelling to be heard over the chanting, before taking a deep breath through his nose and resetting his shoulders. "Whaddya want?" he asked, not quite cagey, but not exactly friendly either.

"I was just wondering what exactly this is all about. I haven't been paying much attention," she asked—well, more like yelled—and the man's brows rose.

"What do you *think* it is? Buncha spooks got caught by the Beakers. They're executing the bastards. Wanna stick around? Ye might catch one o' their heads!" he exclaimed with almost childish excitement, gesturing vaguely behind him, and as if on cue, a round whirling object rose above the crowd and fell in an arch, spewing blood all the while. The chants broke into roars of elation and savage glee, and the man turned around, leaning and jumping to catch a glimpse, roaring along with them, fists raised high.

Her nose wrinkled as she fought to keep the disgust off her face.

Any positive feelings she might have had about this odd congregation vanished in an instant.

These people were acting like animals. And to some extent, they had been treated like animals, so she could . . . *kind of* understand them.

That didn't mean she had to like it.

As she turned and walked away, she idly wondered if "spooks" was the new slang for the guards or if the people getting executed were just some rival gangsters.

She sighed through her nose as she began making her way to one of the numerous lift stations, preparing herself to part with a few coppers.

By the time she got there, even her prodigious stamina had been getting somewhat wrung dry. Between dodging conflicts, trying not to get lost, and the sheer distance, her Endurance meant that she'd negated an exhaustion-induced coma in exchange for her feet being in constant pain.

And the gondola trip was not nearly as entertaining as the platform. It was essentially a repurposed train segment stripped bare and turned sideways before being connected to a wire lift system. She was not well versed in the history of the dungeon, but judging by the flaking paint and the numbers on the segment, this was likely ripped from an actual train and dragged down here for this purpose.

Not very confidence inspiring.

It also had much less visibility to start with.

Additionally, it was slow, the descent was diagonal rather than straight down, and she couldn't relax at all, as the "gondola" was not very stabilized. Gentle rocking was fine, if a bit annoying, but coupled with the stomach-cramping heights stretching out below her just beyond the windows, it made her feel like a stretched wire on the brink of snapping, tense to the core.

By the time the lift slowed and the disembarking horn sounded, she felt almost twice as tired as when the ride began, basically stumbling out of the moving death trap along with the other two dozen passengers.

Many headed for the factories, twisted titans of glass and steel and pipeworks in the distance.

She stood for a moment, watching the crowd disperse and allowing the knot in her stomach to unwind itself before turning and walking toward the railing, eyes meticulously flitting through the eye-hurting mess of complexity that was the dungeon's deepest habitable reaches.

No blue lights. No banners she could see. No clinic signs.

Then she saw it, the sign of a Crow's Church, six feathers arranged in a star, each cradling a beady eye in the middle, each glowing a soft red, towering hundreds of feet into the air with the help of a thick metal tower at its base. Nearby said church, she thought she idly recognized a soup kitchen, near the glass factories. And as she turned her head and leaned forward a little to squint, in the distance, she could vaguely remember the red-painted roof of an orphanage.

None of those destinations were *close*, but it was close enough for her poor feet to handle.

And they were the only places she could see from this position that fit her goals.

So she began the long trek down once more.

"Just hold him down?" she asked, just to confirm, and the nun, clad in a feathered cloak of what she assumed were black-dyed chicken feathers, turned to smile and nod at her.

She breathed out slowly, a hiss of a sigh, and set her left forearm across the man's knees and her right hand across his chest.

She wasn't sighing because she didn't want to do this, she was sighing because she was, frankly, completely exhausted. After working in the soup kitchen of this specific church for almost four hours, and walking what she estimated to be twenty-something miles total today, she could barely walk straight anymore.

Which was a good thing, honestly. She didn't mind. She was planning to go to that orphanage after she was done here, if she didn't collapse first.

But trying to hold someone down while feeling like a sack of rocks was not her idea of fun.

He was a little too out of it to react or understand what was happening, and by the time he felt the nun's bone saw rake through his lower leg, a twisted, inflamed mess, it was too late for his screams to change anything.

It was over in ten seconds, and she kept holding the man down as another nun came and used a single burst from a sprinkler full of healing potion on his stump, a diluted mix, just barely enough to hasten the healing process to where the blood would clot and stop the bleeding.

Then she was practically shoved out of the way in the cramped confines of the back rooms, which she provided no protest to as she waited for the nameless nun to finish her work.

It took a while.

And so did every other patient after him. It was a slow, slow grind, where minutes felt like hours.

The vast majority of it was actually far more mundane than the first person she helped with. Bringing warm water, throwing out dirty bandages, helping with minor things as the nun did the brunt of the work.

She still felt like a walking puppet, but at least the strings guiding her had some semblance of purpose.

In the dead time as the nun finished up with setting back the blankets of a sickly old man, she turned to observe the room with a tired gaze, and her eyes immediately jerked to the underside of a single, strangely well-taken-care-of bed in the corner, drawn there by subtle movement where there shouldn't be any.

Big brown eyes within a scruffy little green head topped with brown hair stared back at her, and she dumbly blinked at the goblin that had seemed to claim the underside of a patient's bed as its lurking place, clad in a severely oversized red shirt and hugging a rucksack seemingly made of said shirt.

"Is that supposed to be there?" she questioned, not bothering to turn her head around, continuing the odd staring competition she'd started with the goblin.

"What?" the nun asked, before a soft "oh!" of realization left her. "Yes, it is. It's the patient's. Normally we'd turn away those who practice slavery, but judging by how attached and loyal it is, we assumed it's been treated well. As well as . . . some other factors," the nun cryptically said, and she turned around to stare at her blankly.

Oh, she should probably do the eyebrow thing.

She tried to raise a questioning brow, but the movement was awkward and twitchy, so she instantly gave up and returned to her deadpan expression. She was just not used to emoting.

"You can't say something like that, in that tone, and expect me not to ask what those 'factors' are," she said, and a smile spread across the woman's motherly face.

"I know, I'm just hesitant to speak of them. Things have gotten much more tense since, uh, more tense," the nun fumbled, the smile disappearing, before her head turned, regarding her with a single critical eye. After a few seconds of stillness, she tucked the sheet fully under the mattress and sighed, getting up to look her in the eye.

"It's not exactly a secret, but try not to spread this around. We don't need more trouble than we already have here."

She nodded wordlessly. The nun gestured to the bed with her chin.

"Long story short, that girl killed a guard and a guard captain in one of the processing facilities nearby, walked out covered in blood and gore, wearing the captain's clothes and jacket, all the insignia scratched off, and collapsed in the middle of the street just outside. It wasn't anything amazing in the greater scope of things, but it certainly gave some people the realization that the guards are just meat and bone beneath their fancy uniforms. Some factory workers stumbled onto her and brought her to us about two days ago."

She couldn't quite contain the mild widening of her eyes as she turned to look at said patient.

They looked more like a breathing skeleton from afar. She could see the lines of their bones through the blanket. And they'd killed two guards that she herself would have trouble dealing with individually, never mind together.

"That's . . . impressive," she simply said, too tired to convey *how* impressive that was though her tone, then tilted her head just a smidge. "What's her problem? Besides severe malnourishment?" she asked, much like with all the other patients she wished to satisfy her curiosity about.

"Well, she's likely not going to make it, so I doubt there's any reason to focus on her," the nun said in a rather subdued tone, and Katherine let her brows furrow into a light frown.

"Why wouldn't she make it? She just looks skinny. And . . . absurdly pale," she added, a little awkwardly.

Because being pale in the dungeon was normal. Being almost as white as the sheet that covered you wasn't. Everyone, unless a traveler or of someone desert descent, was pale as a corpse down here. The woman's skin, if removed of scars and bruises, was a couple shades away from porcelain white.

"She breathed in a lot of toxic fumes. Some occasional, thankfully mild, seizures because of it." The nun sighed as she began, and started walking toward the patient's bed. Katherine dutifully followed behind her.

"There's signs of some substantial chemical poisoning, but we don't know the specifics," the nun whispered, her voice heavy. "She's also a little out of it in general. Keeps muttering about blood, rats, and vampires. Keeps vomiting out anything we put into her besides simple water, so we've been trying to give her some simple broths, but the moment it gets any more complicated than a bit of salt or chicken broth, she starts vomiting again. And while the Crow cares for the forgotten and the broken, and thus, so do we, I'm afraid we cannot afford to inject her with healing and nutrition potions until she improves, nor afford the services of a healer Pather. I expect her to pass soon. Best I can do is make it painless for her and pray to the Gatekeeper to bring her soul to rest."

A shared silence passed, before the nun sighed once more, then turned toward her.

"Go to the kitchen and ask for some water with chicken broth. The girls will know what you mean. Bring it here, will you?" the nun asked, and she simply nodded, turning away to fulfill her task.

Two minutes later, she was expertly balancing a slightly-too-full teacup in her hands as she walked back into the large "sick room," then lethargically made her way to the nun, who seemed to be considering how many blankets would be too many to put on the woman in the bed. Her eyes moved to the woman's face, or what remained of it, and she had to suppress a sympathetic grimace, one that became increasingly difficult to conceal as more of the woman's body was revealed as the nun removed the blankets to replace them.

She'd seen comparable injuries before, but still. That had to have *hurt*.

Half her nose and right nostril seemed to have either melted or been torn off. Her ears were much the same, just two tiny nubs of healed flesh remaining where the outer ears should be. A good fourth of her bottom lip looked to be missing, as did a good fifth of her upper one, as well as a decent chunk of both her brows. She was completely bald, and it did not look like the result of a haircut as much as it did the result of poison and chemical burns. Tiny pockets of flesh were missing all along her face, cheekbones, and jaw. Not to mention the state of her fingers and the numerous pockets of discoloration on her skin.

Likely another result of chemical burns.

Judging by the way the blindfold around her eyes sank into her sockets a bit, she wasn't sure she even had eyes.

Her right arm had been cut off and seemingly cauterized in the most crude way she'd ever seen, and she could easily count the woman's ribs with a glance. Her legs were both swamped within two thick casts, her right all the way up to the thigh and the left just under the knee.

Her eyes roved up to return to her face, but she paused as her eyes moved to her neck.

A really, really long neck. Just long enough to be strange on a human, just short enough to not be creepily uncanny.

"Is she an elf?" she blurted out, blinking rapidly in surprise, and the nun turned to her, her brows furrowed in confusion.

"Why would she be an elf?" the nun asked with a genuine sense of curiosity.

She tried to gesture toward her neck with a jut of her chin as she moved a little closer, careful not to spill the hot drink in her hands.

"Really long neck. Besides their beauty and the ears, that's the third way to tell an elf apart from a human. Oh, and they don't have hair on their bodies, at all. That, uhm, fuzz," she fumbled quietly, remembering how confused and fascinated Emhreeil was when she realized that normal, average people have hair on their arms, even if just a little bit.

That had been almost a decade ago, and she still found the memory funny.

The nun made a sound of realization, tilting her head as she nailed her gaze on the woman's long neck, then moved her hand to feel along the woman's knee, which was something that would have been a lot more inappropriate if it wasn't being done by a nun.

"I guess she is. Or was, soon." The nun sighed and turned to her, gesturing toward the woman. "You've a steadier hand than I, from what I've seen. Try to *very slowly* make her drink that. If she says something, just vaguely agree; she seems to like that. I will go deal with some more pressing tasks. I'll be back soon to give you something else to do."

She nodded and crouched down beside the bed, scooping her right hand beneath the woman's nape and gently lifting as the nun walked out of sight.

A murmured jumble of nonsense left the woman's mouth as she said something that . . . *vaguely* sounded like "blood" mixed in with other gibberish.

"I see. That's very interesting. I'm sure you're right. Could you drink this for me?" she said in the best impersonation of comfort she could muster for a complete and utter stranger, her voice almost as tired as the woman's.

It somehow came off incredibly sarcastic, which was not her intention at all, but she was too numb to feel embarrassed about it.

The woman seemed to actually pause, her head turning toward her just a little, her left hand twitching up, the phantom sensation of *something* brushing against her face making her tense in surprise.

"Kaaht?"

She wasn't numb enough to not freeze in place once her mind processed that croak, clearer, more energized than anything else she'd heard from the woman so far.

A voice that was scratchy, soft and lyrical, tired and grumpy and likely still half stuck in sleep. A voice she'd heard a thousand times, spoken in almost that exact tone, heavy with sickness or exhaustion from nights spent without sleep.

Her eyes frantically jerked from spot to spot, progressively widening. The slight slant of her brows, their rough shape. The curve of her lips, a familiar bow shape. The oval-shaped face, the tiny crescent scar on her left cheek, from a slap that involved a nail and a lot of blood.

Her hands shook, one caressing skin she'd never thought she'd feel again, the other struggling to stop the cup from clattering to the floor, her breath frozen in the middle of a gasp.

"Ihm . . . misst . . . eew," the woman, the person that couldn't be, slurred out, and Katherine felt her chest tighten, her lungs, eyes, and heart all burning in tandem for different reasons, each heartbeat feeling like a fist slamming into her ribs, her pulse pounding along the sides of her head.

"Gods above, what happened to you?" she breathed out, her voice warbly as hot salt raced down her cheeks, her eyes examining every scar, every injury, big and small, with renewed horror.

The cup shattered in her palm, but she felt neither the scalding burn nor the shards of porcelain digging into her palm, water and soup mixing with her blood. She took a deep, stuttering breath, trying to calm down, crush her emotions and find how she could even begin to process all this and find a way to fix it all, loosening her fist to let the chunks of porcelain tinkle against the floorboards, the scent of antiseptic and sickness flooding her brain.

Her eyes opened to the sight of a skeletal arm jerking away from the bed to grasp her hand with speed that genuinely startled her, yet even that paled in comparison to the sheer numb shock she felt when she saw Emhreeil. Emhreeil, the girl who ate like a sparrow, poking and nibbling at her food like it was about to attack her, all for the appearance of etiquette. The girl who would jam her open mouth against her bleeding palm and suck like a starving leech—her dry, sand-paper tongue licking at her wound as if it were the only source of liquid for miles.

She couldn't even process what was happening, blinking rapidly to try and clear her sight of tears, staring mutely at the disturbing sight before her, tense as stone, her jaw hanging open, her emotions an utterly dizzying whirlwind of ecstatic joy, horror, pity, confusion, disbelief, and complete bafflement.

None of those emotions faded for an instant.

Not when Emreeil detached and gasped for breath almost a full, incredibly long minute later before passing out again, muttering about how much she missed her, not when she broke into a dead sprint toward the nearest relay station and almost got into a fistfight to force herself within, not when she called in her favor in a frantic panic, not when she marched into the church three hours later with an entire squad of House Kervile's best and walked out with a mumbling skeleton cradled in her arms, a terrified little goblin trying to hide in her shadow.

Shaile groaned. "Can you stop doing your interpretive dance and just tell us what you're thinking? It's been a goddamn *hour*."

"Yeah," Dyce agreed, "I . . . don't mean to pressure you, but just because we're the first to find the scene doesn't mean we have all the time in the world to do our job."

He ignored them, setting another careful step, [Wild Recreation] working in tandem with his senses and expertise to forge pieces of the puzzle from minor clues, sticking and gluing them together to form a greater picture.

That picture was one that bode ill for them if they wished to get the full reward. Tracking paid well, but if they could catch this thing . . .

He was getting distracted, so he abandoned that line of greedy thinking to focus on his job.

He continued prowling around the decomposed remains of the gangster, tilting his head left to right, horizontally, and almost upside down, his slitted eyes buzzing from one tiny indentation in stone to one specific splash of blood against the floor, tracking its pattern, mentally retracing it, forming the wound, the angle, before flicking to the next.

Another twenty minutes of grim silence passed, filled with his coworker's idle chatter, background noise he easily filtered out to focus.

Then he let out a long, long breath and straightened, patting his coat down and smoothing the fabric.

If only he could also forgo the mask as well, but alas, not even *his* [Poison Resistance] could blindly tank all that flew in the breeze down here.

"I've got quite a lot," he began, and didn't bother waiting for questions or requests from his annoying audience before continuing. "Pessimistic estimate: This thing is extremely, extremely dangerous. We shouldn't even consider taking this job. Optimistic estimate: This thing is really dangerous and really lucky. The risk is a bit more than usual, but more than worth it. Pick whichever you want, for I have no clear verdict."

Their silence was enough.

He pointed to the claw marks in the stone.

"Claw marks. No broken stone fragments, just dust. Clean cuts. No brute force. About an inch deep. Extremely dangerous claws, could likely cut through basic metal armor without much effort. Could be some skill, but if it's not a temporary effect, forget melee unless no other options are available. Too dangerous."

He turned and pointed to the decomposing corpse. Or its pieces, rather.

"Decomposed for the most part, with the exception of the acid flies eating some bits here and there. The dog's scent likely triggers basic scavenger instincts, which explains why we even have any remains to work with. Meaning that it's fairly dangerous, even by this floor's standards. Additionally, the way this person was killed is extremely alarming."

He moved closer, grabbing the right pants leg and hauling it up, pointing at the clean cut behind the knee with his other hand.

"Cut straight through the leg tendons, the joint, and an important artery. Clean, single cut."

He grabbed the corpse's shoulder and flipped it onto its chest, then pointed at the blood-caked gash across its lower back, something he noticed while almost touching the floor with his head. The so-called interpretive dance.

"Single cut across the bottom of the spine, likely with the purpose of partial paralysis. Lack of scrapes against the stone by the heavy lead boots of the gangster supports this theory. She fell and was paralyzed. Then torn apart. Either a very lucky string of cuts . . . or our dog has fought and killed so many people it knows all their weak spots. Could also be some skill that shows weak points, though that's unlikely."

He walked to the rotting, mangled sphere that once was a head and picked it up, grabbing the loose jaws and spreading them open sideways to show his coworkers, swatting away an errant fly that buzzed out from beneath its hanging tongue.

"Area around the jaw, including cheeks, neck, and jawbone joint, was cleanly severed. The inside of the mouth has puncture wounds as well, from its claws. But under the neck and between the two ends of the bottom jawbone, the entire area was not severed, but ripped apart through brute force. The broken jawbone supports this. Coupled with the puncture wounds inside the mouth and the single puncture wound on the underside of the jaw, this dog has human hands. Thumbs included. It grabbed onto the jawbone and tried to rip it off manually. Which requires . . . well, more strength than the average person in the level-ten range."

And this was where Shaile opened his obnoxious mouth again, waving his hands in the air like a clown.

"Whoa, whoa, whoa, hold on. I don't care *how mutated* that bastard says it might be, what fuckin' dog has human hands?"

"A mutated one. Useless rhetorical question. Moving on." He let go of the skull and kicked it away to tumble off into the canal, before pointing at the charred remains of *something*.

"Giant slab of meat back there. Mostly eaten by various things, but it was obviously part of something fairly massive. This thing is either an opportunistic scavenger that came here to feed on a carcass, or it can bring down opponents roughly five to nine times its size, assuming it's normal sized."

He turned to point at the two pieces of metal innocently sitting about thirty feet away.

"Harpoon shot. Went through our prey, then got cut off. Assuming the person who got mauled wasn't a complete troglodyte, they shot the harpoon first before coming close. Which means this dog did everything I mentioned just before, after being impaled by an iron bar as thick as my finger. That means it isn't easily disabled, nor easily frightened."

He turned to point at scuff marks and needle points that his coworkers likely couldn't see.

"Circle-like indentations in the stone. Tiny puncture wounds in the stone, done by needle. Following the trail of blood and the splatter patterns, the dog likely killed the woman, tore her head off, and just a couple feet away, was attacked once more before it could eat anything. Needles were probably some kind of hunter gear, poison could be anything, the circles were likely netting weights. It was taken down, then netted, then dragged away to about . . . there." He pointed about sixty feet away, to a pile of person-shaped charcoal.

"Scratch patterns are simple. Some kind of small container, cage, or box. Judging by the faint footsteps of dried blood being on the left side of where the cage was, there was likely a second person on the other side. They put the dog in the cage, then person number one betrayed person number two. Poured alchemic oil on them and burned the corpse to be rid of any evidence or insignia. Sloppy job, but it did the trick, mostly. Judging by the less burn-able parts of the outfit, though, like the lead boots, they're likely from the Prospectors Guild, or one of the cleanup crews they have around here for wading through the canals. Workers, in short."

Silence reigned for a few moments.

"Can you follow the trail of this guy?" Dyce tried, and he scoffed in reply.

"Of course not. Do I look like a clairvoyant to you? This place is massive, and the footsteps would fade out after a couple minutes at most. I don't even need to check to know they went straight to the nearest lift. After that, I have no clue. Just follow simple logic. Why would two people grab a dog that Ironheart's been clamoring after and *not* bring it to him?"

Dyce tilted his head, rubbing at the chin of his mask.

"They're either working for a rival, want it for themselves, or wish to sell it for an even bigger profit. Judging by your words, they're not wrong about possibly getting a far better deal if they went with either of the latter options."

"Good, so there are some neurons still firing in that tumor you call a brain." He snorted.

"Go fuck yourself, Tracer." Dyce sighed tiredly, getting off the wall he was leaning on, and began fiddling with the comms tablet to report their findings to the boss.

Tracer just sat in place, his eyes roving over every inch of his surround-ings, to no avail.

It felt like he was being watched, yet he couldn't find the eyes that fol-lowed him.

And he felt many of them. He could be wrong, of course, and he was certainly no stranger to the odd bout of paranoia, but this felt too . . . solid. Too real.

"We'll do our report back on the third floor. Let's go."

Dyce sent him an annoyed look, likely seeing this as another challenge to his authority or something juvenile like that, but he only had to glare at him and gesture with his eyes at their surroundings for him to get that something was up and nod along, his features relaxing into understanding through the muck of his gas mask.

"Yeah, good call."

CHAPTER 4

By the time the poison that forced its mind to stillness had faded and it had gotten its bearings, it had become distinctly aware of three very strange things.

One, it was *not* dead. Which was a pleasant surprise that made it very confused, because why were the humans trying to *catch it?* Food for later?

Two, it was actually tied up in a way that made it nigh impossible to do anything. Both its front paws were dragged behind its back, then put into two very tight cuffs, with two metal spheres sitting tight around its newly formed paws, while the same went for its bottom feet, each individually shoved into a tight, locked sphere of iron.

Then there was some weird cage of metal *very tightly* affixed to its snout and clamped onto its head for stability with leather strips, so it couldn't bite anything if it tried. Its tail was the only thing that had any semblance of mobility right now.

It wasn't *helpless*, but it was fairly close.

It was a very anxiety-inducing realization.

Three, whoever caught it had somehow fixed a lot of its injuries overnight. The superficial ones, at least, like some of the muscle tears and burnt skin. Its bones still felt frayed and fragile, and its body was still in pain, but it felt much better.

It assumed that the human had given it one of their weird healing vials while it was out, which it wouldn't complain about, but *why?* It didn't make any sense to heal your food. It also didn't make sense to go through all this trouble just for food, considering how much easier it would be for a human to feed itself *without* going through the task of restraining it like the human had.

It had left an entire six-foot-long pile of meat right next to itself. What was the point of grabbing the wolf? Humans made *no sense*. It was *so* annoying.

Maybe they had some actual reason. Maybe they just got curious about how different it looked to the average canine and wanted to poke at it, which was what the wolf would do in their position, or maybe they knew it was a wolf and . . .

That thought led it down a dark trail of increasingly worrying ideas, because it was then that it questioned: If they knew it was a wolf, and went to such trouble to capture it, what was the reason? Why was it the only wolf it had ever seen in the human nest? Did humans collect them? Or kill them? Why?

Would it meet other wolves if it just waited in its cage to see what would happen? Should it do that?

It was both confused and hesitant, but with the amount of questions that were mounting up, and the lack of answers only continuing, it discarded that trail of thought.

Mostly because its own survival was much more important than getting to meet another of its kin, and it had no reason to believe humans knew what it was. They most likely just wanted to poke and prod it precisely because of their lack of knowledge. Which was a much more optimistic line of thinking than "they might just want their food fresh."

Twisting, it tried to get comfortable and grumbled at the needlelike pinpricks racing up and down its forearms.

So annoying.

Another thing that had severely annoyed it was the fact that it hadn't been able to dissect the poison at all. By the time its mind began functioning again, it had only managed to decode the way it seemed to change its own composition all the time by using various chemical reactions and unique gland cells, not all the variations that poison had.

It was immune to about three of them. It had no idea how many more variations there were.

The pattern of mild but constant change was something it lightly modified and added to its own poison, with about three different, equally potent variations, which then transitioned into the tedious process of preparing its immune system and mana cells into attacking any of its own stray poison that might end up in its bloodstream. But that was the only current good that had come of the whole ordeal, besides it *not* being slow-cooked over a fire right now.

It grumbled in frustration, still trying to get comfortable, twisting around the tight confines of its cage, which would be little more than paper if it could *move*. The lack of a thumb bone should have made it easy to slip the cuffs off, but they were tight enough to cut off circulation, and moving around only made them tighter, somehow.

And without any momentum, it was fairly sure it couldn't just snap the device apart with brute force.

The front door to its cage seemed fairly loose, thankfully, so it did the only thing it could.

Which was to very, very awkwardly curl up against the back of its cage, position its shoulder to the door, and start trying to bust through with sheer force of boredom and frustration, using its tail like a weak piston to add momentum.

That "padlock" thing looked brand-new and solid, but it had nothing better to do than test the structural stability of its cage before its captor returned in the vague hope the latches the padlock was going through would snap.

Or rather, that was its internal explanation for the illogical action of wanting to pound out its frustrations on something before resting and healing itself.

Despite its back paws being encased in metal spheres and sliding all over the floor, it was able to squeeze itself into the corner by shuffling around with its shoulders before exploding forward, its left shoulder slamming into the door as its head and snout ground against the floor, lacking room to twist.

The metal banging of its cage door filled the small metal room. A single window filtered yellow light through its bars from the other side of the room. Covered in discarded fabrics and the cloying scent of an aged human male, its vibrations picked up on something.

Something both infuriating and hopeful. That made it pause in the middle of dragging its shoulder across the metal for another crash.

It was a little metal lock that held its cuffs closed. Or at least it *felt* like a lock.

Its cuffs were essentially just a rectangular piece of metal with two holes in it that led to the spheres around its hands, with two chains on the inside that would tighten whenever the wolf moved, locking its hands in place and forcing them to curl into fists. The mechanism was . . . mind-bogglingly complex.

However, there was a tight seam running through the rectangle between its wrists, of interlocking pieces and fine machinery within. It was a circular arrangement, of multiple dozen little pieces, and it was all wrapped around a locking mechanism that was, by comparison, quite simple.

Which was not simple at all, the more it parsed through the vibration's information.

How did it know what a locking mechanism was?

It didn't. It just had a vague image in its head of what one was supposed to look like, much like all the other information in its head about machinery that had proven utterly worthless.

Until now.

It knew that humans would somehow fiddle with these lock things, and they would pop open. Though this lock seemed different. It had seen humans messing about with a padlock many times. And it had a perfectly mobile tail that it could use to fiddle with said locks, much like a human, minus the fingers.

It took a long, deep breath and let it out in a growl.

It hated how helpless it felt, and was thus more than willing to keep slamming into its cage's door. But all that would likely accomplish was making the wolf exhaust itself.

So it started flaring its antennae instead, twisting as much as it could, the side of its face squished against the bars as its bulky upper body prevented it from turning around. It began kicking at the floor, the iron spheres around its back paws making the process extremely strange and awkward.

It didn't take long for it to pick up everything there was to learn about the lock, its antennae easily feeling all the minute details of its innards.

But *seeing* and *feeling* a mechanism was not even close to enough for the wolf to puzzle out how it actually functioned. It was full of little springs and cylinders and a lot of tiny, twisting parts, but, to put it bluntly, it was all useless information, because the wolf had no idea how any of it would or *should* move.

Something was obviously meant to be put into the hole, and that was the only concrete, useful information it had garnered about it.

It wanted to sleep and maybe put everything it had learned about that spearhead shark to use, which was a *lot* of things, but at the same time, it was a bit hesitant.

When it had no room for error, it could not really experiment with its body. It *could* add that braided muscle, but its bones were *made* to bend. The sheer power of those muscles contracting would turn its body into a squiggly, bendy mess whenever it went all out due to all muscles being connected to bone and using it as a base for their power.

It was fairly sure that feeling its bones twist and bend mid-fight would only be disorienting and confusing.

And it *could* densify its bones to compensate, severely limiting the bendy nature of them in favor of stability and power.

But it was just too hesitant to try and escape the human nest while not being fully sure of what its body was doing and was capable of. Experimentation was for when it had room and time to commit to it, and a relative guarantee that it wouldn't trip over its own feet.

As it squeezed its sleep sack dry to go back into [Devourer], it sighed and watched its moss-covered bottom half, admiring the pretty light, until its eyes grew heavy and "sleep" embraced it once more.

It only increased its inner plant-based armor to wherever it could without limiting its mobility, adding a few wide strips of braided wood-like fibers across its abdomen and some small patches along its arms, then added the braided muscles it had gained from the spearhead shark to its tail to increase its strength and mobility. The plant-fiber armor changes would likely be completed far too late and were still ridiculously costly, but it had enough essence to not worry about its resources for the moment.

Another thing it changed was something it very much regretted.

The moss fur.

It had taken way too long, and it felt a little too heavy, too inflexible to be comfortable. Likely wouldn't be as good of an armor as its normal fur was. Coupled with the plentiful sources of food around the human nest and its impending escape, it didn't have any real reason to have it. It was an interesting experiment and it looked nice, but that was it. It got rid of it all, replacing it with its normal, coarse, thick fur.

After directing additional essence to healing its injuries, it added a few antennae to its tail. It had enough Intelligence to not get overwhelmed, so it was no problem.

Afterward . . .

Well, all it could do was try to puzzle how to unlock its cuffs, and wait to learn its fate. But first, to jam the chains around its wrists.

Writhing red veins of fat tissue and nerves crawled out of the little pockets on its forearm, some thick, some thin as strings, and slime quickly followed, squirming between, and within all the mechanisms that moved the chains.

It retracted them, content with knowing they would soon dry and jam everything inside, and rested.

There were two locks on the door of the room. One seemed to be . . . logically impossible. But based on how it would pop open when the human would prick his hand with a needle and push it onto the lock, it assumed it had something to do with mystical human stuff it couldn't understand.

Thus, it ignored it, flexing its wrists to try and get some blood into them. Jamming the tightening mechanisms hadn't worked, unfortunately, unlike what it had expected, and the cuffs were thus as tight as ever.

The second lock was much more useful, because it very closely resembled the mechanisms between its wrists.

Unfortunately, the human wouldn't use the damn thing. He'd always come into the room, try to prod the wolf with a needle, which it fiercely objected to, managing to break three of them before the human stopped trying to use its oddly specialized stick to poke it through the bars, then sit around for a bit, fiddling with the human-communication device for an hour at a time before talking to someone for three minutes.

Then he would just go outside, lock the door using the blood lock, and walk away, farther than its perception could reach.

It was infuriating, and it could do nothing but inwardly fantasize about ripping him apart for being so frustrating without likely even realizing it.

And capturing it. That too.

Another thing that was a simultaneous problem and a boon: time.

It had spent about two days under this covered cage, judging by nothing but instinct, and while that granted the wolf plenty of time to rest and the possibility of its inner plant-fiber armor to be done by the time its escape started, it was both bored and anxious the entire time, and that combination was *really* wearing its patience and nerves thin.

At least it had plenty of time to practice human speech and nitpick its body for tiny improvements to make, like making its blood clot faster when exposed to open air, making its tendons even thicker, and adding some reinforcement to the shoulder joints.

Because flexibility sacrificed stability, and it was tired of its shoulders popping out of their sockets during fights. It happened with the golem and the shark, and it was a huge annoyance beyond the pain.

With a long, long exhale of boredom, it got back to practicing the words its human had taught it.

Head, neck, chest, stomach. Oh, and haste.

* * *

Its ears straightened as its head tried to snap up. Its antennae started writhing as, for once, the human did not stop at merely using the blood lock as he left, but started pulling some bits of metal out of his pocket.

A change of routine.

The human brought his hand to the door's handle, and to the lock beneath it. [Bloodrush] activated, its Perception getting boosted by the skill just well enough for it to feel everything within. The little metal thing, which the ether informed it was a *key*, its grooves, the way the key entered and the pins were pushed up one after another.

Then a twist while the little free-moving cylinders of the lock moved, and the mechanism locked the door as the human walked away once more.

The wolf was far too busy thinking about the contraption to pay attention to the human's retreat.

It was . . .

Actually rather simple, after seeing it in action. All the pins and springs were of a different length; all it had to do was align the pins with a groove on the inside of the lock, and then the whole cylinder could twist.

Of course, the key to the door had about five large pins while the one inside its cuffs had about twelve tiny ones, but it knew exactly what to do now to escape, assuming that *locking* was the same action as *unlocking*, but in reverse. Which, by simple observation, seemed to be the case.

It knew that actually making a key on its tail made of bone, while judging the proportions on nothing but *feel*, would be an exercise in delicate attention and a lot of frustration, but it was all it had to work with.

Its antennae writhed with the spheres and on the fringes of its cage, its tail twitching ever so slightly as it moved along the edges, and it hurriedly put itself to sleep to get to working on the key.

The human got back a lot faster than it had expected. Just an hour later, he'd unlocked the door, then started erratically picking things up and tossing them aside, then pacing, before eventually going to the corner, reaching over an oddly shaped metal bowl thing embedded in the wall, and turned a handle on top of the metal pipe that was aimed into the bowl.

It was very strange to feel water rushing straight up within a pipe, and the wolf idly wondered how long it had been since it last actually drank something that wasn't blood. It kind of missed the taste of water, that refreshing feeling. The specks of dirt in it just added texture, in its opinion.

After this was all done with, it was going to find a nice spot to drink water at, even if it had no need for it due to [Devourer].

After a couple minutes of the human drinking water and pacing, the wolf grew bored. And it still had a key to design, so it prepared itself to sleep once more.

Then the human picked up a familiar blanket and walked over to the wolf's cage, and it felt with puzzlement as the blanket was thrown over the top of its cage. Again.

It sat unmoving, blinking at the brown covering on its cage.

That was . . . just annoying. Watching the new colors was at least entertainment. The dull brown was boring.

Then it felt the human take out a knife, and it tensed, minute complaints forgotten, poison fang ready to try and reach through the bars and neutralize the man. The bars were *tight*, and its tail was thick, so it couldn't quite reach, but it could at least try.

The man grabbed the blanket and cut four lines into it, above the metal holds at the four corners, then got to work putting the holds through the blanket, and the wolf relaxed as it realized what he was doing.

Then the human sheathed his knife again and put his hands on the circular holds, bending his knees and tightening his core.

Oh.

This was going to be *horrible*.

Its cage rocked, and with a heave, the human slid the cage over his knees, dangling and holding it over his pelvis as he straightened.

"Fucking . . . hundred-pound mutt." The human grunted.

It was, indeed, horrible. It *hated* every second of it as the human stiffly walked back to the door, every motion rocking its body back and forth and to the sides.

The door swung open and was quickly kicked shut. The human readjusted his grip a little and walked out into the outside world. Its eyes curiously flicked to the edge of its cage, under the blanket, its discomfort momentarily forgotten.

It was instead replaced by a primal, instinctive fear, its body locking up as its eyes widened.

The fear of heights. Which it didn't have, it thought, but the sheer *amount* of empty space between itself and the ground was so vast that it couldn't help it.

That would explain why it couldn't feel the ground anywhere, just a vast expanse of metal above the room and a complex of metal beneath its feet before its senses faded.

The thin grated walkway they were on was more of a series of thin galvanized metal platforms stapled onto the side of a small complex of metal rooms, all seemingly designed for humans to live in. And said metal rooms were hanging off the bottom of a gargantuan plate of metal, like a . . . blocky beehive.

It felt its stomach churning uncomfortably with every step as the human turned to the right and began walking in the opposite direction of where he'd come from, the mixture of primal fear and intense discomfort actually making it nauseated.

It had the comfort of knowing there were another dozen walkways spaced in the exact same manner just beneath it, but that was a thin comfort considering it could see the lights of the human nest so impossibly far away that they were blurry despite its humanoid eyes.

Never once had it thought something so all-encompassing and endless as the human nest could be reduced into nothing but tiny little boxes and moving dots the size of ants, light crystals the size of a pinprick in the distance.

And there were so many layers to the whole thing, platforms and bridges and wire lifts connecting it all together.

It even saw *purple* somewhere, before it winked out of existence. It was the most bizarre color it had ever seen.

The sight, in total, was both mesmerizing and terrifying.

The human walked past a couple rooms much like his own, through a strange little room filled with cables and mechanisms oddly reminiscent of the human speaking device, before the walkway curved right, leading to a roughly rectangular staircase, extending all the way to the bottom of the complex building, and all the way up above, through the giant metal plate above.

If the human *walking* made it nauseated, it would have dry-heaved when their upward journey began, had the overlaying grates of the staircase not hidden the endless drop below, each step swinging the cage left and right in the human's arms.

The vibrations, already faint and muddled due to being filtered through the human's flesh before reaching the wolf's cage and tail antennae, didn't provide much insight into where exactly it was. The tight, cramped staircase just went on and on, up and up, seemingly nailed into place within an empty metal shaft, judging by the redundant wires and random open pipes, sealed shut with some kind of solidified . . . rocklike paste?

The word "concrete" came to mind, as if it was its own thought, as if it was just remembering something it had briefly forgotten, and it resisted the urge to growl at the word.

It *knew* that it did *not* know what "concrete" was, and the fact that there was something just randomly planting knowledge into its head without asking was mildly discomforting. Even if it was useful information just before, considering the "lock" mechanisms, and never a negative thing so far, *right now* it was a rather irritating reality.

Or maybe it was just more irritated about its situation being outside of its control and it was more easily frustrated than usual because the human was swinging it around like he was *trying* to make the wolf retch.

It had absolutely no trouble with motion sickness. It could run in a circle for an hour and only come out of it mildly disoriented.

But that was because it could *control* or at least *feel* how its body was going to move, allowing it to mentally and physically brace itself for it.

This had no rhythm, and the human's gait was so sloppy it was a wonder how *this* thing was what caught it. It didn't have much in the way of pride, but this was just . . . insulting. A single flick of its claw and this human would drop dead. Or would stumble over his own uneven feet and drop into the void below.

A particularly uneven step made the human overstep to balance, smacking his shoulder into the metal wall, and coincidentally, the wolf's cage.

It snarled, jamming its legs into the corner to ram its shoulder into the left-side bars of its cage, the impact further unbalancing the human and almost making him fall on his ass as his breath was driven out of his stomach.

Then he suddenly just seemed to lose all signs of weakness and tiredness, stiffening his body and clumsily straightening himself, fixing his grip on the handles of the cage and readjusting the cage to be supported by his stomach.

It stiffened in surprise, then its eyes widened.

That was almost *exactly* what the wolf itself had done many times. Make a mistake, stumble, get tired. And then it would activate [Bloodrush], one of the skills it had been given by the symbols, and move on, energy renewed and with more than enough power to compensate for crappy balance and position.

And that made it question whether or not the humans had the symbols too. Because the way the human had so stiffly and quickly recovered, it screamed of him activating a skill.

It . . . frankly was not sure why it had assumed that nothing else had access to the symbols. It had chalked up any strange things, biological impossibilities and strange developments it had seen to the humans' mystical ways of using the mana energy, such as that terrifying metal-head human that was dead yet moved around as if living.

"To think I had to kill Niet just to have to do this shit by myself . . ." the human's withered voice grumbled, and their journey continued.

It kept relatively quiet, feeling oddly shaken and unsure by what it had just noticed. Humans' biology cemented them as weak and absolutely worthless without their tools. But in an actual fight, it was confident it could just as easily kill any human, because their biology was just . . . pitiful. They had really good stamina and reach, and that was about it.

But if they had access to the symbols, every encounter it would have could be completely different. One human could have put everything in Endurance, thus rendering it a useless scratching post for the wolf, while another could have poured everything it had into Speed, and simply run around the wolf in circles, or just run away entirely without the wolf being able to do something about it.

If humans had access to the symbols as *well* as all their crazy mechanisms and mana constructs, it would actually have to rethink how it distributed its attribute points.

Endurance and Intelligence was already a rather thin strategy for its physical well-being, considering the various tricks and tools the humans had at their disposal, but if they had access to the symbols as well, then almost every attribute gained value. Nothing incredible, but something to think about. Speed would have to be the next attribute it could invest in, considering it had just acquired braided muscles, which were easily twice as strong as its regular ones, and . . .

Once it had some room to breathe, it would sit down and think about all this in a bit more depth.

At least the human seemed to be paying more attention to the rocking of its cage now, so it forced itself to calm down and curl into a ball, narrowed eyes glaring at the glimpses of the outside world it could see through the fluttering of the blanket covering it.

It was just about ready to activate all its skills and hope for the best, because it genuinely could not deal with this anymore.

The more tired the human became, the worse his stability got, and all it could do was slide a couple inches forward, then back.

Then forward and back again. And again. Thump. Slide. Thump. Slide.

It had been something like an hour, and it was starting to feel delirious.

It was in this state of mind that it decided to try something it thought was futile just ten minutes ago, which was to try and jam its venom fang through the man's uniform.

Which had proven to be exactly as useless as it had expected, the man immediately noticing the sharp bit trying to dig through his uniform and into his stomach, and dropping the wolf's cage on the steps as he jumped back.

After falling down the steps in a rolling cage, and with the human having decided to hold its cage longwise right after, keeping its tail far from his body, it could confidently say its efforts were rewarded with more misery than they were worth.

After that, the wolf began paying as much attention to its surroundings as possible, mostly to try and distract itself from the nausea and mounting irritation. They'd moved up a long shaft, exited out of a tiny door hidden in a little nook beside a broken water pipe and a cracked-open gutter grate, and then the human went to some kind of open square to meet up with some other humans, who started escorting him.

And the more time went by, the more it began focusing on nothing *but* its surroundings, any idle musings on trying to sleep and craft a key forgotten.

It wasn't sure why, exactly, but the air was just . . . a lot cleaner than it could ever remember it being, besides in that one moss-covered room, way down into the human nest. Which made it think that it was really, really far away from all the places it knew.

That was a rather uncomfortable thought.

Its assumption was very quickly confirmed when the alleyways they started moving through seemed wide enough to have ten humans walking side by side, and the roads they were flitting through became wide enough to have *thirty* humans walking side by side.

It had *never* seen places this . . . open, besides that one time it had accidentally stumbled into an open space, across from a gargantuan tower, and almost got hit by a bolt made of sparks from some angry human.

Of course, that was not the only difference. The streets were more even, the floor was universally more flat and just more . . . traversable, and from the couple dozen feet it could feel through the human's vibrations, there was a lot less . . . chaos, in general. It was all in the details.

No pipes sticking out of random places, no barred alleyways barely thick enough for a human to squeeze through, and all the walkways extending over the small human nests had actual metal supports that people had to weave through as they walked under them.

There were, of course, a dozen other tiny details, but it eventually let them slide away from its mind and solidify into the vague thought that wherever it was, it would be much easier to navigate than what it was used to.

There were also fewer people walking around than it was used to.

Significantly fewer. It could feel dozens and dozens of humans sitting in their metal boxes all around, above, and sometimes even *below* itself, but the number of them wandering the alleys and streets were so *few*.

It idly wondered if something had happened in the nest, because there was nothing it could notice that would justify all the humans hiding inside their miniature nests like this. No poisonous gasses, no telltale rumbling of a collapsing factory, a sight it had caught a glimpse of once, near the start of its life, many months ago, and no fighting.

Well, any more than the usual amounts of fighting that the humans did.

It had been a *long* time since they'd started moving, and the human and his followers didn't seem inclined to stop anytime soon. It let out a long sigh, its frustration having been already spent, and its mind and body now well accustomed to the uneven rocking of the human's gait.

It squeezed its melatonin sack dry as soon as it had produced a bit more, for the third time, and tried to empty its mind, fall into sleep. And despite how incredibly *uncomfortable* it felt to do so, it even sheathed all its antennae into its fur and flattened its ears, for the sole purpose of trying to sleep.

It took a few minutes. Its mind continued brushing along the edges of a lucid awareness, and eventually, what felt like seconds later but was likely several minutes, it felt its mind slip under, embraced in restfulness.

Now to craft a key as fast as it could before the sounds of its surroundings and the annoying rocking would wake it back up again.

The process was not fast whatsoever. It had to focus on vibrations to properly calculate sizes and distances for the key's grooves, and the more it focused on them, the less solid its grasp of sleep became. External stimuli and sleep just didn't work together. The deafening sound of grinding pulleys and humming electrics, the rocking of its cage, none of them helped the wolf whatsoever.

Mercifully, there were extended periods of time where its cage would be put on the floor, free of interference.

It had to stop every couple glimpses to allow its mind to sink back into rest, before the next bout of fast-paced mental measurements took place, and it would add another groove into the key.

It was in the middle of confirming the height of the third groove when its vibrations picked up on the fast-paced steps of a human marching toward its cage, and before it could react, light flooded its cage, a stark, sickly white.

Forcefully pulled out of its sleep, its eyes snapped open in a squint, and its lips curled into a snarl.

Now it was going to have to start all over again on the groove.

It wanted to bite the man's head off *so bad*.

Or at least it wanted the irritating light beam *out of its face*.

"Are we sure that thing's alive?" The nameless escort asked, leaning back and blowing out his cigarette smoke out beyond the bars, idly watching the Great Tower's countless lifts and platforms moving beyond, above, and below them, their own lift a single speck within a complex web of metal and glass. "It hasn't moved or made a single sound, and we've been escorting you for like three hours."

"Check if you want, just don't antagonize the damn thing. It's really pissy," he warned, too tired to give a shit about maintaining the mystery, and he watched dispassionately as the young man took his flashlight off his belt, pressing the button on the shaft as he marched to the beast's cage and lifted the blanket.

It was pointless, really. The mutt had thrashed and refused any kind of nutrition and water he could give it, whether it was by needle or tube, and it somehow still seemed just about ready to turn rabid at the slightest provocation.

Not to mention how it woke up six hours later from poison that was supposed to put it to sleep for at least four days.

In short, it was fine and *very* healthy. Somehow.

He couldn't help but tense as the man pointed the flashlight straight into the cage.

He was still somewhat paranoid about the damn thing somehow getting free, very vividly remembering the horrific screams that had guided him and Niet to the thing's precise location.

He was very glad he wasn't going to be the one carrying it from now on.

A sharp snarl like a bark boomed out of the cage with enough volume to make them all jump, and in an instant, a deafening metal bang filled their lift as the cage screeched forward a few inches with a sudden jerk. The man jumped back as if burned with a rather undignified exclamation of surprise, stumbling back before falling on his ass, and he stared with slightly widened eyes at the two rings of golden malice glaring at the man from within a pitch-black cage.

Then they slid over to him, and its pupils might as well have turned into needle points, a low rumbling like the menacing purr of an engine making the metal beneath his boots and at his back vibrate.

It made his hair raise in goose bumps, his shoulders instinctively raising to hide his neck at the memory of the way the thing had *ripped off* that woman's head.

He couldn't wait to be rid of this mutated biomancy experiment or whatever accursed freak it was. Holding it next to his soft, squishy stomach wasn't helping. Getting out of the apartment had given him such anxiety he was sure he was going to be having stomach cramps for the next week.

The brown-feathered corfid woman Pietre had personally sent was the one to grab the blanket and cover the cage back up a mere moment after the growling started, and after another moment of rumbling, the beast seemed to calm down, silence returning to their group once more as the lift continued rattling its way up the Great Tower's spine.

"Well, it's definitely alive," the man awkwardly quipped as he picked himself up off the ground, trying to scrape together some sense of dignity, and returned to his spot along the bars.

He tuned out of their idle ribbing and banter as he closed his eyes, leaned back against the bars, and returned to doing his favorite thing.

Absolutely nothing.

Much as it wanted to stay awake and feel for its surroundings, it was much more interested in escaping, and had thus managed to keep itself asleep for long enough to get to the seventh groove of the key.

Unfortunately, the room they'd put it in was just too *infuriatingly* loud to concentrate. And too tantalizing. Progress had slowed to a crawl.

There were so many damn animals in one large room, their cages stacked on top of one another. And it was torture for the wolf, because it wanted to eat every single one of them.

It had never seen *any* of these things before. There were four-winged birds, there were lizards with wings, small, six-legged furry animals, a quadrupedal furry thing that meowed incessantly, there were human-sized lizards that had the rough anatomy of a canine, there was even some strange, round creature covered in what felt like . . . rocks, leather, and crystals?

There was even some absurdly large moth as big as the wolf's head that had some kind of artificial environment in its glass tank.

It couldn't see any of them due to the blanket still on its cage, but it could damn well feel just how different and varied the life in this room was. Never mind how many new smells were assaulting its sensitive nose with every inhale. It was *so hard* to tune it all out and focus on the key.

The moment it got out, if it was fast enough, it could have a small feast on its hands before cutting a hole through the bricks and getting out of here. Unfortunately, it did not have any faith in its luck, so it decided to plan for the worst-case scenario, which would be that it might only have time to eat one, maybe two things in this room before it had to run.

So it would have to pick carefully.

It turned off its hearing by dissolving the microscopic hairs in its cochlea in seconds, and squeezed out some adrenaline as it woke up, just to take a quick look. Its right hind paw slammed into the floor in a steady rhythm.

The canine-shaped lizard was . . . boring and uninteresting in its design, besides the tail.

It was *long* and covered in bony spikes, none of which seemed decorative whatsoever. And judging by the vibrations, it was a fairly complicated setup of little muscles made to flare or flatten the spikes, and a strange configuration of tendons underneath that it couldn't quite understand the purpose of.

That thing's tail would be number one.

It turned its attention to the rest of the chaos filling the room. The ball-like thing covered in crystals was by far the most interesting thing, but its cage was more of a thick box of closed metal, and the wolf couldn't find something all that useful for its continued survival on the thing.

It kept looking, but finding something useful based on nothing but vibrations was a tall order.

Sure, it *could* eat that screeching beaked bird thing, but it didn't really feel like it needed feathers, and while flying sounded *great*, it had no idea how it would go about doing such a thing when it was so heavy. How huge would its wings have to be? Would it fit anywhere if it added wings that could actually carry it? And if it messed up, how likely was it to die?

Questions like that made it steer away from the flying creatures, instead turning to other quadrupedal creatures.

There was a six-legged thing that had a strange neck and head biology, with two giant curling horns coming out of its head near the eyes. It looked both strong and intimidating. Unfortunately, it was also within a box of metal, and thus cutting into that, and killing it, before eating the head and neck, would take far too long.

Then, some strange, small, furry thing, tucked into a large cage and . . .

It was *very* interesting.

It almost looked like a tiny dog, but its tail hair was flat, and its body felt almost like liquid, impossibly flexible. Its nails were somehow embedded into its paws, and as it stretched, the wolf felt them flex outside of its paws, something that would definitely be useful to have for itself.

It was the thing that kept making the grating meowing noise. And it was small enough that the wolf could easily chow it down in two or three bites.

Its targets decided, it got back to making the key.

It was halfway through the twelfth groove when it felt a small entourage of humans barge into the massive room, among them the human who had originally captured it. He was hurriedly walking beside a strange fat man who waddled with speed, while the other men and women followed behind.

It decided to be optimistic and go back to its key, hoping they were there for another animal.

As always, being optimistic meant that it was *wrong*, because they were heading straight to it.

The fat man said something it couldn't quite pick out, and it saved its progress on the key, fixed its hearing, then filled its veins with a bit of adrenaline, flashing itself awake with a light shiver, its eyes squinting at the yellow light glinting off the wooden floorboards below the blanket and straight into its eyes.

The musty smell of a hundred different animals within one enclosed room was quite suffocating, now that it had the mental capacity to notice.

Two humans marched forward among the small jungle of cages and enclosures and put their fingers through the bars, each holding one of the handles and pulling with speed, dragging the wolf toward the middle of the room, a squareish area clear of cages.

It eyed their fingers with disdain as its chest tightened with anxiety, and it briefly considered poisoning them to death, watching their lungs stop breathing due to complete and utter paralysis.

Its poison didn't just disable nerves after all. It was a neurotoxin. It *destroyed* them unless washed out or regenerated. However, with seven humans in the room, that would likely only make its position worse.

It decided that the best thing it could do was precisely nothing. Just wait to see what would happen, wait for an opportunity.

Such an opportunity did not seem like it would come, as two more humans approached its cage, and the first two stopped dragging it, throwing off the blanket.

The fat man wordlessly extended a hand to its original captor, and after the key exchanged hands, he made a noise for one of the humans, who turned around and deftly caught it in midair.

Its eyes and attention both briefly stuck with the strange man, both curious and confused. The man was . . . eye-catching? His coverings were ridiculous to the point of being actively restrictive to movement, covered in strange frills and pointless machinery, like the clocks ticking away on top of both his shoulders.

And his metal arm was somehow moving with the grace of a normal one. It had seen metal arms and legs plenty of times before, and had just accepted that humans could somehow make it move, but watching a fake limb move with such fluidity felt downright *unnatural*.

In the moment it took to observe the strange man, the key was shoved into the padlock and twisted. Before it could puzzle out what was going on, the door flew open.

"Wave this around the mutt, will you, gentlemen?"

Between varying human coverings, it saw a needle prod exchange hands, and a human hand darted into its cage, grasping at the leather straps pushing into its face and head, pulling with strength that felt like a ton of bricks, like it was trying to rip off both its head and the muzzle.

Another two hands fisted into its shoulder fur and pulled, dragging it out of the cage as it remained stiff and silent, its eyes tracking the prod with laser focus.

It *refused* to get poisoned again, this close to escape. That stuff was *potent*, and it did not wish to wake up in another unknown place again, without having any say in it, nor knowing where it even was.

And just considering its luck, they'd probably change its cuffs and render its progress null.

One of the four people surrounding it took it from a tall, lanky man, and started holding it as if he was about to jab.

It didn't want to raise their guard, but it had to draw a line, and this was it.

Its lips raised into a deep, rumbling growl, its thick vocal cords and [Logotexnia] putting an extra dose of intimidation into it. Its fur spiked across its back, and its tail curled with the intent of jabbing the human in the leg the moment he twitched.

Despite the hands holding it down, one on the back of its neck, one on its right shoulder, and two pairs holding on to its legs and pulling them back, it was just about ready to activate every skill and hope for the best.

The man turned to the fat one and did some sort of head jerk, to which the fat man responded by doing an up-and-down head jerk.

The needle approached, and it thrashed side to side, twisting and yanking the humans' arms around as it struggled, pouring more mana into its growl, feeling the floor vibrate beneath its chest.

"All right, enough," the fat man said, and the needle prod retreated, the black-haired man who wielded it passing it back to the tall, lanky man.

"Seems you're right, my good sir. Likely some kind of experiment. Doesn't like needles, very . . . strange changes to what looks like a purebred, or something close to it. A damn good-lookin' specimen, I must admit. Very dark fur, very canine face. Snout's nice and long. We can only speculate, but point is, this little fella looks strong, healthy, and besides the slightly-too-wide shoulders, the closest thing to a purebred I've ever seen. What you've brought me . . . could be worth its weight in gold." The fat man made some kind of laugh-bark, then put a hand on its captor's shoulder.

"While I'm not convinced its eyes glow because it's Awakened, and thus I cannot claim this to the auction members, I can assure you this merchandise will sell for a *lot* of gold crowns. Likely quadruple digits. If it was tamed it would sell easier, and had we some guarantee it's Awakened, that price would likely go up eight or so times." The fat man's voice was like the deep croaking of a canal frog.

Its original captor's heart sped up to an almost dangerous degree, and the wolf simply continued sitting inert on the floor, pinned and just barely holding back the growl in its throat, its lips curling and uncurling in fear and rage both.

It hated this. *It hated this.*

It felt like it was a skin-wreathed skeleton again, a little helpless pup that could die at the whim of something stronger at every single moment. Were they talking about which one would get which cut of its body to eat?

"Besides the regeneration . . . its claws. Saw the thing cut straight through a reinforced uniform when it was drowning in that maintenance fill and clawing its way up."

Something at the edge of its soul but just barely beyond, just barely untouchable, flared to life, whispering *half lie* into its mind without using words or pictures, and the wolf only stiffened for a moment before it remembered that it had that useless title. Something about breaking illusions because it saw a higher being. Witness of Divinity, whatever "divinity" meant.

It hadn't paid attention to it since it hadn't activated before, ever, until now. It was a *little* curious, because it didn't get the sense the human was lying from its mere sounds, but from all its sensory options. It felt the half lie in the vibrations, in the aftershocks of his feet shuffling against the floorboards, in the way he *looked* as its eyes flicked to him.

But it still didn't pay attention to it, because it simply did not care about the humans lying to each other, even if it was a good distraction from the turmoil in its chest. It instead paid attention to another exchange of keys, which were given to the man holding its right leg in place.

The man unlocked the metal sphere that had been crushing its right hind paw, and it clicked open, clattering to the floor. It stiffened, struck with the desire to kick at the human's throat just to kill him.

"Check with this," the fat man said, and tossed some kind of little tin bottle. The human at its leg caught it.

Then he adjusted the wolf's paw, his grip still made of iron, almost tighter than the sphere it replaced, and quickly phased the tin bottle through its nails.

"That's either enchanted nails or it has some kind of skill," the man said, blinking at the four perfect lines cut into the tin bottle, turning it slightly to observe what it assumed was the cut its claws made. Then it turned the bottle and put it up in the air, almost showing it off.

Maybe it should have blunted its nails if they were getting this much attention.

And there was also a human sneaking about on the rafters above, which it just noticed.

What was going *on?*

The human sounds continued, and it stayed relatively silent, even when the humans rolled it over onto its stomach. Its teeth gritted together with enough force to hurt its gums, and it kept both [Bloodrush] and [Maddened Frenzy] at the edge of its mind, just in case, its eyes flicking momentarily to the dark silhouette nearly gliding across the rafter beams with movements that were nigh perfect.

For a moment, their eyes met, and the man stiffened before redoubling his pace.

Was this some scavenger or something?

"Don't see a dick, so it's a female. And it seems more than healthy enough for today's auction. Though we might be cutting it a bit close. Do we clean it up?"

"Yes, usual process. Try not to irritate our canine friend too much. She's got to look good and calm for the showcase. Let's see if I can convince people into thinking she might be Awakened . . ." The fat man hummed, and the human at its right paw quickly put the sphere back on.

It was turned over onto its chest again, and grabbed once more by the strong human before being shoved face first back into its cage.

Which . . . was actually good; now its tail would reach the lock much easier. The door rattled shut behind it, and it stood still as they locked it back up.

The human on the rafters began to slip away, prowling through and under crisscrossing iron rods, vents, and shoddy supports, and it carefully felt his path, wondering where he was going. Maybe he knew a way out, if he knew a way *in*.

And he did. He unlatched a metal plate the wolf hadn't noticed could open, lowered himself through it, put his feet against the two walls separating the insulation of the building, and slid down a tight space just between, just wide enough for the human to shuffle through, chest and back rubbing against the metal walls, and it felt his fleeting steps as he climbed up some iron support rods, then aligned himself with a rather shoddy-feeling plate of metal and foam.

One that seemed to be connected by nothing except a single loose rusty nail, hanging on via nothing but friction. That was probably how he'd gotten in here.

It stopped paying attention as the human began slamming his shoulder into the panel, knowing the fastest path to the outside now, and focused on the humans surrounding its cage.

Unfortunately, after they all broke off and walked away, it didn't get to sleep one more wink, as just a minute later, four of them returned, three carrying some kind of machine full of water connected to a hose and the fourth holding some strange metal device with a pinched mouth.

What followed was . . .

Rather cleansing, actually, besides the deafening sound both devices made as they blew clean water and hot air all over the wolf's form.

It quite enjoyed itself, contrary to what it had expected. It was such a rare feeling, to be *clean*.

Until one of the humans got closer to the cage and started spraying nose-burning chemicals all over it. Not burning because they were genuinely toxic, but because their scent was so intense it felt like it was burning the insides of its nostrils with each breath.

If it wasn't for the overwhelmingly powerful scent, it would have smelled wonderful. As it was, it was utterly infuriating. Curse humans and their stupid useless noses.

Sneezing for the twentieth time in a row, it wondered what the point of all this was, trying to ignore the mounting dread in its stomach and enjoy the sensation of hot air washing over its body and drying its fur.

It took a long time, but eventually the humans seemed satisfied with how clean the wolf had gotten, and after tilting its cage around to get rid of some water pooling at the bottom, and blowing hot air at it for another ten minutes, they slid its cage back among the racks, and the wolf huffed as it settled down to rest and finish its key.

It would be out of here soon. It already felt over half of the key having grown on the bottom of its tail tip, next to the venom fang, hidden under bushy fur. Just one more groove and an hour or two to grow the bone key, and it was *out of here*.

It noted that it actually kind of liked how puffy its fur felt as it slipped back into [Devourer].

"Dyce."

Tracer's careless voice growled through the comms tablet without warning, and he held up a hand to the fox-masked man, who gave him an understanding nod, the table between them littered with reports, stray blackthorn cigarettes, and a barely comprehensible map of the dungeon from the side, crumpled and faded from where their fingers had rubbed the ink off from use.

The smell of cigarette smoke, aged leather, and paper had made the atmosphere quite relaxing to him despite the stress, until now.

He brought the tablet close to his head, pressed his thumb into the mana sink, and a transparent bubble of undulating, pale gray force sprang into existence around the tablet and his head as he leaned back into the soft couch.

Then he used the tablet to hide his mouth, because all these bastards knew how to lip read, and sighed right back into the oversized microphone.

"What is it?"

"I found it," Tracer breathed out, sounding like he was one step away from falling over and sleeping, and he blinked at empty air for a moment before blowing stray bangs of black hair out of his face, confused at both the unusual tone and his words.

"You—what?"

"I *said* I found the *fucking* thing," Tracer growled, his breaths deep and lethargic for a few pregnant moments, before Dyce's eyes widened in understanding.

Looked like he wouldn't be needing all these scout teams he'd been planning for.

He didn't say anything as he bolted to his feet and almost stormed out of the room, stomping straight toward the only genuinely private room the Fox Den had.

She wasn't a caretaker.

Still, she did her best.

All the black-scorched chitin along her arms and fingers was a testament to that.

Mirena sighed, dropping her face into her palms, all four of them, caressing the harsh plate that made up her forehead, the mask just below.

She barely felt it, but it was a far more pleasant sensation to the feeling of the liquids that formed and filled her insides boiling under her exoskeleton every time she'd have to help Holo move.

The soft sizzle of water slowly turned to boiling, to hissing and foaming, and warm, hot steam was siphoned out through a shoddily welded pipe in the ceiling, the beaten-up bathtub just beside her steadily starting to glow orange along the bottom, the soft shades of firelight dancing through the steam acting as the only illumination in the dim room.

Besides the two little suns that took the place of Holo's eyes, half lidded and far away, projecting her wandering gaze like spotlights with every sway of her head.

Watching the crescent lights that swayed along the brick wall was, at least, mildly entertaining.

Without looking, her bottom-right arm extended behind her stool to reach into the small bin by her side and pulled the pin on her latest emergency device, feeling hundreds of tiny runes within invert and activate. The way the energy was swiftly entrapped within the runes, the mana crystal at its core was spewing out all of its power and slowly began powering them.

It was a satisfying feeling. The feeling of something clicking together and working, just as she'd envisioned.

With a casual toss, the device was thrown into the spasming, boiling waters of the bathtub, just barely missing Holo's sternum.

It didn't take long for the boiling water to calm down to a shimmering simmer, then mere warmth and the faint wisps of steam, the orange bottom of the metal bathtub quickly cooling down.

The faint whisper of a word was slurred out from between Holo's lips, and her eyes flicked to her face from between three hands' worth of fingers.

It wasn't a pretty sight.

But then again, it never was to begin with.

It just wasn't so glaringly obvious before. The fact she was so closely tied to her element that she was a mere misstep away, a mere overexertion away from becoming an elemental spirit. A mindless mechanism of the world, consumed by her nature.

The scariest part of it all was that Holocaust would probably love nothing more than to surrender herself to just that, were she a little more lucid.

Like cracked obsidian, her skin was black and peppered through with glowing veins of angry orange, pulled taut over whipcord muscle and veins of magma, all pulsing with each heartbeat. Every inhale made the temperature in the room rise by several degrees, her veins flare and flicker as if her insides were nothing but flame, and every exhale made it drop just as much, her veins dimming like fire losing its oxygen.

She didn't understand how any of this worked. In fact, it simply did not make sense to her, based on what she knew about the average Pyrokinetic. She also didn't know how Ghoul knew everything about it to the point he could deduce what was happening by staring at her for a few minutes, but she trusted in his word.

And his word was that it would take a long time for her to be safe using her powers as liberally as usual. She was sure it would take much longer for Holo to learn how to control herself, stop her from frothing at the mouth at the mere *sight* of something flammable. Ten steps forward, a hundred back.

As long as they could keep her from turning into a spirit on purpose the moment she felt like that was a genuine possibility, for some reason she didn't understand, she'd recover.

Holocaust attempted another barely legible imitation of the word *thanks*, slurred and half of it too low for her vocal cords to even voice out, still barely conscious despite the ice bombs slowly trying to cool her down.

Her mandibles clicked into a V-like shape beneath her mask, which twitched into the ghost of a smile, if only for a moment.

She had hope, at least. Things were getting better.

All she had to do was keep this up for another hour until the runes of the cooling pod had finished imprinting, and she could put Holo in there to rest again, free of her consciousness, which was no doubt squirming for something to burn.

This was like . . . a glorified fever, truth be told. A very dangerous one, but still a fever. She just had to keep her cool.

It would be much less stressful to go through all this if Ghoul were around as much as he used to be, but without Holo dogging his heels, and cut off from their allies, he was always doing *something*. Always looking, plotting, learning.

She kind of missed having someone conscious around . . .

The water soon began boiling once more, and her bottom-right arm extended back, grabbing another grenade.

As the pin was pulled with a small click, she could have sworn Holo's eyes briefly sharpened, the black holes that served as her pupils narrowing, before they hazed over once more.

Her mandibles clicked into a V-shaped smile for another brief instance, but the light feeling in her chest remained.

Yeah.

Holo would be fine.

Just had to have a little hope and optimism. Even if some dark corner of her mind whispered to her that she was just trying to delude herself, it was easy to ignore it, because it didn't feel like she was.

A black spider writhed and bucked within his right fist, its fangs feebly trying to poke holes into his gray-toned finger, its legs flailing and struggling to find purchase and escape, to push his vice-like grip away.

Ghoul stared into its eight eyes with a hundred of his own, a faint echo of contempt within his covered gaze, and it writhed ever more, its legs breaking and snapping on his skin from its efforts.

The consciousness within fought the little predator for control, its natural instincts battling against its mistress's control.

His left hand tightened around the pipe he was holding on to, and his eyes languidly rolled within their metal confines, watching every inch of the walkways, buildings, and streets below, the depths of the gutters peering at him from within the murk of the alleyways, hundreds of feet away.

One pair saw the temperature, with senses he could not describe if he tried. Another idly rolled within its case, and he watched the faint echoes of radio signals struggle to move through the metal jungle. Another watched the faint discoloration of electricity flowing through the wires next to his bare feet, all else around him an empty void besides the most minute sources of static.

Another pair glanced around, noting the various elemental energies, their meek remnants in the air.

A man, with his head ducked and his hands shoved deep into his pockets, walked with haste through the alley below, and one pair of eyes watched the determined resolve and paranoia flood the air around the man like a human radiator.

Another peered into his skull, into his brain, looking for lucidity, consciousness. Faint whispers of caution, the background image of a guard's uniform floating around within his subconscious. The tiny inklings he could see, nothing less and nothing more than surface thoughts or presently subconscious ones.

And he peered even further, deeper, past the brain and into the metaphysical concept of the "mind."

Through it, like a chaotic tunnel with a trillion different paths, the eyes traveled, searched within moments, and peered at mere glimpses of the collective racial consciousness the man was a part of, a loose, undefined bubble unto space-time, where its edges melded with another. All confined into the black dot that the human's head had been turned into from the vast distances. Like staring into a swirling, endless void.

Yet all he was, was a simple, normal human. With some distant hint of beastkin in his blood, only a tiny bit of overlap to another bodiless concept too vague to be determined with his limited vocabulary.

The eyes writhed and dissected all in sight, peering through all as well as each other.

The spider twitched violently within his grasp one final time, and with a hundred eyes, he turned to stare at it, his head just barely turning.

The mind within spoke of blood, witchcraft, and more besides, a collective consciousness as chaotic as the people it was a creation of. It felt . . . artificial, born of artificial differences put upon countless different people throughout the ages.

Patchwork, almost.

He brought the spider a little closer, his left hip settling against the metal to his left as his right leg curled and settled flat against the wall, relaxing against the steel that stopped him from falling off the second floor's ceiling and into the quiet streets below.

Not that such a drop would hurt him.

"Did you think I wouldn't notice?" he asked plainly.

He wouldn't receive a reply, of course. Spiders couldn't speak.

"You are not as subtle as you think you are. Not when in sunlight, watching the burning wreckage, and not when in shadow, trying to extend your web beyond what you can handle."

A muted hint of alarm roiled within the mind he saw nestled deep within the spider, but it was . . . filtered. Through distance, magic, and the spider's tiny speck of an existence. Even the faint sense of alarm faded in an instant.

Still, it meant she understood.

He brought the limp predator ever so slightly closer, his head tilting.

"I will drink your blood for that. Whether it happens tomorrow or in a thousand years, it will happen. I don't believe in forgiveness. Until then, however, I think I'll have a taste of Miaro," he murmured, and allowed his cold, dead, stretchy flesh to twist into a wide shark-toothed grin full of iridescent black steel and gray gums, the tendons of his neck peeking through the corner of his "lips."

The spider began convulsing feebly once more, Arach's control slipping.

"After all, you coven bloodsuckers all taste the same, don't you?"

With a satisfying crunchy squelch, fluid and chitin burst from within his clenched fist, chitinous legs popping and plummeting below. The smile faded in an instant, all expression disappearing from his face.

His eyes calmly observed the cloaked figure that confidently walked into the auction house, just in time to cut off all long-range communication, and his long, dry tongue idly licked along his open palm, licking off bits of cracked chitin and softer bits of the arachnid's insides.

Spider tasted like little more than salty slime.

He blended into the metal behind him like an illusion, his concept of self and environment melting together, to the point where should someone even look straight at him, all they'd see would be a black silhouette, their mind would instantly dismiss it as nothing more than a meaningless shadow, not worth a single thought, much less a second glance.

Their eyes would hold a thousand times more interest for the window beneath him or the wires above him.

And so, he waited for his opportunity, silent.

CHAPTER 5

As Miaro settled in amongst the crowd and took his seat, his sister's instructions clear within his mind, he prepared himself for a very long, very boring evening.

He could have been feasting on some cute girl's blood right now, or smoking a nice pipe of Maniac on top of some vent along the walls, watching the humans fight for his amusement below.

But no, he had to sit here and run another meaningless errand. Because Ironheart was hunting for a dog and dear old Mother wanted to grab it out from underneath his hands.

He couldn't give less of a shit as to why, truth be told, beyond a passing curiosity. He'd only agreed to doing it unconditionally because he wanted to see the veins in Ironheart's forehead bulge when someone told him they'd lost his newfound dog obsession for the twentieth time.

Not that he was likely to actually witness that, as the bastard would probably assign him to scout duty for the umpteenth time, but the thought that it would happen comforted him.

"Just act like yourself and they'll never suspect you," my ass.

He sighed, sinking lower in his seat out of boredom, his eyes and thoughts wandering across glittering chandeliers and the faded painting on the ceiling of this little theater imitation.

He couldn't get close to anything important. Even in the dungeon trip he'd been dragged to, he'd been stationed near the entrance. He didn't even fucking know how Ironheart managed to lose all his men and his limbs. It was just a giant waste of time.

But if he complained about it to his brothers and sisters or, god forbid, Mother, he'd just be inundated with a bunch of condescending bullshit about how he was a fledgling or how he needed to gather experience with something lower risk.

Like experience mattered when he could become invulnerable with a single thought. He wanted to fucking *fight*. Not split himself into a hundred pieces and just *watch* everything like some kind of low-maintenance mirror system.

Being a glorified errand boy for *both* sides he was working for *sucked*.

He'd probably get another "review" from Mother's handler telling him off for being so shit at blending in or something like that, but he would rather peel his skin off than wear the mess of cloth and machinery that was the fashion standard for everyone else in the room.

In the background of his meaningless internal complaining, the bids kept climbing higher as animal after animal was dragged onto the massive theater-like stage and then dragged back behind the scenes, until the numbers got so high he couldn't quite contain his curiosity. The magic-blocking bracelets around his wrists tingled as he straightened up a bit from his slouched posture to peek at the "merchandise."

Considering the heights that the bids were reaching, he'd been expecting a goddamned dragon to be preening on the stage.

Instead it was a *cat*.

These people were paying the yearly combined income of a thousand average people to buy a useless pile of fur that had been driven near extinction because it couldn't even kill rodents to save its species.

He slunk low into his seat once more as he idly tuned out all the bullshit, only keeping an ear out for any variation of the word *dog*.

It took two and a half hours, but eventually, he did hear it, and he'd damn near pulled several muscles as his head snapped straight up, eyes flicking to the moderately sized cage sitting right beside the . . . owner? He looked like the owner, because who the fuck else would have two giant golden clocks embedded into his suit and be *this* goddamn fat?

Unfortunately he was at the beginning of a long and annoying-as-hell spiel about how dogs were both a man's best friend but could also be forged into something more, blah blah blah, some bullshit about potential, and then finally, *finally*, he dramatically grabbed the blanket covering the cage, and with a practiced flourish, tore it off.

It looked much nicer than any other dog he'd seen before, and its fur was a black so dark it looked almost artificial, as if a biomancer had done it. The yellow glowing eyes looked pretty badass as well, he would admit.

But beyond that, it was pretty underwhelming.

It just looked like a *relatively* purebred dog on what he assumed were lethal amounts of enhancement drugs, mostly due to the muscles visibly bulging out from underneath its fur and its slightly larger than normal frame.

The crowd's gasps didn't seem to agree with his assessment.

And when the starting bid was announced at *two hundred* gold crowns, he knew that it would likely cost Mother a *lot* of money to win this auction.

Unfortunately for Arach, she couldn't interfere with him in this place, warded so heavily against magic. Unfortunately for *Mother*, she gave him a "tab" letter to their house, so he could burn as much money as he liked, at least in this one auction.

Making his family lose a considerably larger amount of money than they had to out of pure spite was rather childish, yes . . .

But it was also funny.

A smile played on his lips.

It knew what was waiting for it just beyond the curtains, even if most of the context it had garnered was done while it was finishing up the key.

Still, it was such an immensely weird feeling to be placed at the absolute center of attention, and have what felt like at least a hundred and fifty or so humans all just . . . staring at it.

Its eyes briefly flicked to the fat man, drawn to his gesticulating hands, and the strong man from before crouched in front of its cage, unlocking it and swiftly dragging it out once more by the straps of leather around its neck and head.

It stayed resolutely stiff, ignoring the way its heart seemed to be trying to crack its ribs with every beat. Even as the human moved it around like a sack of meat, showcasing it to the humans, the most resistance it provided was trying to hide the more unique aspects of its body, like deflating the slime veins as much as possible to not draw attention to the odd squishy pockets along its legs and back, and making the antennae, fang, and key within the tip of its tail all hide in its thick fur.

It couldn't believe how terrible its luck was.

The key was literally *minutes* away from hardening enough to not break when the wolf would twist it into the lock, being the thin, fragile piece of bone that it was. Had it worked a little faster, it would have been out of here by now.

Thankfully, from what it had felt, the cages of all the other animals that were dragged onto this strange wooden stage were quickly returned to the room they came from, so it was sure the same would happen to it.

The problem was the fact that said room was now utterly *flooded* with people. Whether they were part of the fat man's people or the people in the crowd with their strange coverings and gaits, it didn't particularly matter.

Its prospects of a *peaceful* escape were quite gone by now. It would have to do something more drastic, and soon.

Its best chance was to get back into that room, cause as much chaos as possible, and use the distraction to grab whatever it wanted and run.

The strange tempo of the humans on stage speaking into a boxy device, followed by various humans in the crowd raising their hands, continued.

On . . . and on . . .

By what felt like the passing of half an hour, both its heart and mind had calmed down, even if the ever-present anxiety remained.

Because while having so many eyes on itself made some instinctive part of itself squirm and whisper *danger*, all the while [Witness of Divinity] kept whispering in its head about lies, there wasn't anything particularly exciting in sitting chest down on a stage within a cage and doing absolutely nothing but waiting to pass the time so it could go back into the room.

Eventually, the humans raising their hands reduced themselves to two, then only one, a strange-feeling human clad in pure black coverings.

His flesh felt more like . . . solid air. Like a structure made of tightly packed dust, in a way. But the weight still felt right. It was just bizarre. It wondered what it could gain by eating him.

Then it was dragged back through the curtains on the side, the strong human delivering it backstage before he let two other humans pick up its cage as he turned and went to pick up the last cage, a small lizard with wings curled up within.

They passed other humans, walked through the back of the closed area behind the stage, and went through another set of doors. It watched with boredom as they turned to the cage room and walked inside, unable to use its tail's vibration sense but already knowing the building's layout inside and out by now.

Besides, [Tremor Sense] worked without the antennae. It could still feel about fifty feet in all directions if it could touch the floor and not have everything filtered through the two squishy humans carrying its cage.

After talking to some other of their kin next to the room's entrance and slapping a piece of paper on its cage door, the two humans carrying its cage continued, weaving through the dozen or so people in the cramped, absurdly loud room, and sliding it back onto the same spot it had occupied for the past couple hours, before hurriedly speeding away to continue their tasks.

Finally.

Its key was ready, and had been for a while, having finished hardening halfway through its odd stage session.

It just had to figure out the way to cause the maximum amount of chaos to cover its quick snatch and escape . . .

Which wasn't all that difficult. It was in a room *full* of irate, varying, and relatively dangerous-feeling animals.

Its tail uncurled from around its hind legs, and the wolf brought it before its eyes, the tip unwinding to reveal a protruding bone next to the black chitinous venom fang. Shaped like a perfect key.

Its tail squished between the top of the cage and its back before it began trying to align the key with the tiny groove between its wrists. It had gotten completely used to the prickling of bad blood circulation by now, but as it shifted a little to allow its tail to twist more, it realized that its cage felt remarkably smaller compared to when it had first woken up inside it. And so did its cuffs.

It might have to cut back on the growth hormone boost. Now that it had noticed how much it had grown and how quickly, it was worried about under or *over*estimating its reach and stride. Thankfully, it didn't *feel* much heavier.

It had *so many* things to work through in [Devourer] that it was honestly kind of dreading the notion of going through them even after it got to a safe place where it could relax. Auxiliary micro-brains, bone-pocket skin armor, braided muscles, specialized impact-absorbing scar tissue, its bones, and if it could nab the strange furry thing and the reptile's tail, those things as well.

Its trail of idle thought about how much stuff it would have to go through once it got out of here was interrupted by the key's tip finally sliding into place, and it stiffened, very, very carefully pressing it in.

To its immense relief, the key slid forward without issue before tilting with a little click as the venom fang lightly hit the steel just beside it.

Then, it awkwardly twisted its tail, the tendons and braided muscles all straining with the odd cork-like movement.

And without any dramatics and a simple click and the grind of its curled-in fang's joint scraping at steel, the cuffs abruptly snapped open and off its hands.

Getting its arms out from being trapped along its sides and the cage was *very* annoying, and it was fairly sure it had pulled a muscle or two by the time it managed to squeeze its right forearm past its pectoral muscles and the floor, before raking through the muzzle's straps with just the tip of its claws. A bit of thrashing and twisting, and the muzzle was shoved into the corner of its cage.

Another couple minutes of squeezing and shuffling, and it managed to finally bring both its arms in front of itself.

For a moment, as it stared through the back of its cage, it stopped, mentally planning a route, trying to pick the most troublesome and irate "allies" it could have in its quest to make everything devolve into chaos.

The six-legged horn thing was its best bet. Its body language was perpetually pissed, and judging by how thick its metal box was, and how it had hooves instead of paws, it was likely dangerous but not fast enough to be a threat to the wolf. It had also been considerably more angry after it got dragged on stage and the humans did some strange mana things to its box.

Thankfully the lock holding the door closed wasn't buried all that deep within the metal.

With a deep breath of preparation, it tilted its wrists and hooked its nails along the top and bottom of the bars, left and right.

Smoky, inky nothingness wreathed its paws.

As it mentally sharpened its nails, it jerked its arms through the metal, the rods collapsing into a mess of bite-sized cylinders, and without wasting a single second, it hooked its nails into the wooden floor outside and kicked its cage's door with its hind legs, launching itself out of its cage and sending it crashing into the next row of cages beyond.

With a mental command for its nails to not cut through its own flesh, it brought its right hind foot forward and effortlessly cut through the metal sphere entrapping it, then hurriedly did the second, its tail caressing along the floor with its antennae, keeping an eye out.

Somehow, the sound of a bunch of metal bits hitting the floorboards wasn't nearly enough to alert anyone, drowned out by the cacophony of complaining animals dumped into one room.

Human hearing. For once, it was helpful.

It was currently squeezed between two walls of cages with just enough room for a human to walk through, in one of the many rows of cages that occupied this massive yet somehow cramped room. Chains went through the handles of each cage, connected to some spinning gear machine on the top of the room, amidst the crisscrossing bars of metal, which it assumed was for stability.

Which meant that without those chains, there would be *less* stability?

The cages themselves were all filled with strange and sometimes utterly illogical creatures, furry things of all types, some bland beyond belief and some so strange it couldn't puzzle out how they were even alive. It was one thing to *feel* them and *smell* them, but to see how they looked just added another level of bizarreness.

Most of the creatures nearby, however, it gave only a cursory glance. These actively cowered back into their cages, squeezing themselves into the corners and keeping oddly quiet. Away from the wolf.

That was . . . odd. The wolf didn't look *that* intimidating, in its own opinion. The human-sized lizard canine looked a lot more terrifying.

It kicked its legs at the air for a moment to get the blood flowing back into the numb appendages, before punching the floor a few times for the same purpose, alternating hands as it kept an eye on any humans who might be passing by this particular alley made of cages with its antennae.

Its head swiveled to stare at the cowering masses of animals to either side. One had even pissed itself.

It was beset by both intense curiosity and urgency. Why were they so scared of it?

For once, however, urgency won.

Besides, something that was fearful was much less likely to attack unless attacked or approached. So it wasn't particularly hesitant about freeing all of them.

It quickly moved all the way back to the metal wall, then hooked its claws at lock height, onto the far left chain holding the stack stable.

How convenient that humans made all their things uniform.

It quickly ran forward with three legs—or two paws and one arm, rather—its claws soundlessly phasing through metal links, then lock after lock, the only evidence of its actions being the faint creak of cage doors swinging open and the dull thuds of padlocks impacting the floorboards. The rattling chains slamming into the floor, however, were much too loud and alarming, judging by how it felt at least three humans pause and turn in its direction.

The first human to dash into a sprint and come into the mouth of the haphazardly made alleyway froze on sight, right as the wolf got to the last cage.

Its left arm, which was busy clawing through padlocks, hurriedly jerked forward to cut through the rightmost support chain and down into the floorboards, hooking into the planks, and without an ounce of hesitation, it kicked forward and to the right, allowing its lower body to swing as its hands remained buried in the floor.

Its lengthened tail, two times the length of its body, crashed into the cages' bars before just *barely* having the length to whip into the human's neck, fang and key both.

The human's startled shout was unfortunately something it couldn't do anything about, and neither could it do anything about how the human jerked back, collapsing on the floor with choked gurgles and backpedaling for the short few moments where his limbs still worked.

As its eyes adjusted back into a world that was more than a blur of metal and wood, it saw the makeshift alley of cages, still bereft of any escaping animals.

It *needed* them to run out and cause chaos.

With a snarl of frustration and urgency, it quickly fixed its footing and dashed forward, back to the cages.

It didn't have time to *wait*, considering how the dozen-plus humans in the room were all staring in confusion and concern or rushing to the fumbling human's side, straight in line of sight of the wolf.

It slid across the floorboards after the short second it took to run through thirty feet of cages, its shoulder slamming into the metal wall, and without caution or fear, it reached into the back-most cage, blunting its claws just enough to hook into the flesh of the furry creature cowering in the corner.

Its striped form began frantically writhing, but the wolf didn't care, dragging it out of the cage before twisting its wrist to cup the thing's form and launch it toward the humans.

The creature didn't wait to gain its bearings after hitting the floor, rolling to its feet in a frantic jerk that was blindingly fast, then running straight out of the alley, dodging the human hands grasping for it in a panic.

A couple animals on the far end of the cages followed it, all peeking outside before dashing, waddling, or slinking away to freedom, and the wolf dashed to the next cage, grabbing the odd, big-eared creature within and throwing it straight at the humans, much like it had done before.

It was sure that the motivation of having shallow injuries was enough to keep the animals it was pulling out frazzled enough to do their work.

That big-eared one was *fast*.

The room had devolved into chaos already, but things were happening fast. Another dozen humans were rushing to the room, drawn by the sudden yells for assistance. It needed more chaos.

If these things were all so scared of it, then it knew exactly how to make them run for it.

It took a deep breath, poured just a bit of mana into the air traveling out of its lungs, and snarled with its thickened vocal cords and some help from [Logotexnia], the resulting sound sharp and violent like a chainsaw.

The cages immediately emptied, an entire procession of panicking creatures bursting out of their cages and rushing out, furry, scaled, and armored, and the entire stacks to either side from top to bottom started cowering, some frantically trying to escape their locked cages. Something from above started spewing flaming liquid everywhere, trying to melt through its cage bars, and the sight of flame further increased the chaos, the stacks wavering from the sudden burst of movement and struggle.

The liquid fire hit the floorboards, and something along the ceiling flashed with light before a blaring alarm drowned out all other sounds.

Fine bits of water suddenly began spraying the whole room, further agitating the animals and adding to the confusion. The entire room was in complete panic, humans trying to help the man on the floor, running around and throwing nets to catch the fleeing animals. Water sprayed in aggressive torrents from pipes in the ceiling, while some cornered animals began fighting back with more than just tooth and claw.

Through the scent of wet animals and the feeling of its fur being weighed down by liquid, drops of water clinging to its brows, it felt oddly accomplished, taking a short second to observe and appreciate the results of its brilliant plan.

It was fairly sure it saw a three-headed bird manage to claw out someone's eye before it was tackled to the ground.

The wolf saw no reason not to make everything worse.

It took a running start before turning as much as it could in the tight confines of the alley and slamming its left shoulder into one the bottom cages to its left. The stack wavered, and the wolf dug its claws in and briefly leaned back, before slamming forward. Again, and again, and on the third time, the twelve-foot stack of cages tipped and slammed into the stack to its right. Unfortunately, instead of crumbling from the top down, it was the middle of the stack that first seemed to slide out of position.

Upon realizing how much it had underestimated the falling speed of a stack of metal boxes, it activated [Bloodrush] and squeezed a bit of adrenaline into its bloodstream, its claws raking at the wooden floorboards as its legs furiously pumped forward.

It barely slid out of the cage-made alleyway just as everything collapsed behind it with a burst of rattling metal and screaming trills, ignoring the faint tingle of caution that came from [Danger Sense], and without hesitating, it used its claws to sharply turn right and dash past the tilted wall of cages barely being held in place by chains, to another cluster of cages in the corner, only just managing to dodge some of the rolling enclosures that crashed into the floor just next to it with an awkward side jump.

The constant . . . *pinging* in its head about dangers it already knew about and was in the process of dodging was genuinely grating on its nerves.

Its annoyance at the skill faded when it felt through its antennae the motion of a human lunging forward, extending some kind of crescent-tipped rod in its path.

It simply flattened its shoulders to the floor as it suddenly halted with a tiny slide, turning its neck toward the human, its nails grinding through wet wood, and felt the air currents above its head move with the rod as it overshot and missed by mere inches, another delayed warning from [Danger Sense] brushing against its mind.

It snapped its head to the right, clamping down on the rod, and before the human could fix his balance from his overextended position, it jerked its head even further back and pushed away with its legs for added force.

The lightweight human, regardless of his strength, practically flew a foot forward, chest and arms down on the floor, and before he could raise his arms and be a nuisance like that female, it wrenched its head to the left, letting go of the rod, and dashed forward to clamp onto the back of his neck from an awkward tilted position.

It was neither clean nor quick, but in the chaos, nobody could distinguish his screams before they suddenly cut off with the sound of ripping flesh and a frustrated growl. His clawing hands, now limp, slid off the wolf's head, and its eyes opened once more.

It quickly spat out the meat and bone in its mouth, then clamped down on the gaping depression of flesh missing from the back of the human's neck, and using one paw to cut through the front of the neck, and the other to brace against his back and shove him away, began pulling and pushing, working its teeth through then blunting them, jerking its head side to side, as its eyes frantically searched the surroundings for anyone looking at it.

Besides one frozen, horrified female gaping at it, nobody seemed to notice. It was relatively out of the way to the rest of the chaos.

And finally, the head detached with a sudden jerk.

It didn't have time to eat it, so it simply extended a single thick slime vein out of the slit in its back, opening the pocket of mucus and membranes that ran from its nape down to its lower back, and jerked its head back to toss it at the appendage, which grew a few dozen smaller veins to entrap the head as it turned back to the corner of the room, where two dozen cages were haphazardly discarded.

The head was quickly drawn back and secured within the sack-like space on its back, seeming and feeling like a strange bump that was an intrusion on its body, but it simply dug the head in deeper, wishing to keep its brain safe enough to eat. The rest didn't matter.

As sorely tempting as it was to run around and glance at what that deafening crackling sound behind it was, and the no doubt worrying sight of almost two and a half dozen humans scrambling after escaped animals and tripping over each other, it had three objectives: lizard tail, small furry thing, escape.

A giant black version of the little furry thing it had chosen to take was the first to have its cage clawed open, and much to the wolf's satisfaction, the moment it passed the cage to go grab its furry snack, it felt the odd creature dash out of its cage.

The biology between it and what it wanted to eat seemed to be near identical, but it was too big. The wolf didn't have time.

It saw out of the corner of its eye as some of the humans took out some strange rods like the human who had tried to stop it, and tried to use it on the speedy black thing, only managing to stumble over each other, their allies, and a furry rodent-like thing it had freed.

It was curious that not a single human was using anything lethal, but it didn't have time to question anything. Its chance was here and it was taking it. Where else would it ever find a chance to add these two animals to its own biology?

It found its prey's small cage sitting isolated upon a wooden table, and without hesitation, it wrapped its tail around the base and threw the table away toward the chaos behind, hearing a strange yowl come from within as the metal enclosure tumbled to the floor.

It lightly jumped off the ground with its arms, then made its knuckles touch each other, wrists turning outward, then slammed its nails onto the thin metal sheet of the enclosure, denting it inward, its nails piercing cleanly through.

With a hurried growl of excitement, the metal peeled and bent to the side, and it saw the arched, orange-furred thing in the corner, hissing quite pitifully, covered in water and stray hay and little bits of oddly nice-smelling food.

Its left arm remained on the mangled metal sheet as its right flashed forward and slammed into the little creature, and before it could do much more than wildly buck and let out a choked yowl, it turned its claws and swiped through its internal organs, before hooking under its jaw and blunting its nails, carrying it out of its cage by the inside of its skull.

This thing was so small it would only need three bites, and so it didn't waste any time, tossing its twitching body on the floor before hurriedly biting off half of its torso, its tail swiping along the floor through the water to feel for any incoming danger.

There was a lot of *potential danger*, yet none of it extended too far in the wolf's direction.

But the humans were slowly bringing the situation under control, much to its worry. There were three of them wrestling the black-furred thing into the ground, two were dragging out the human it had killed through its paralyzing toxin, while two others were frantically barking at the gaping human from before, gesturing at the corpse of the one it had beheaded just out of sight.

There were at least a dozen of them either gathering the smaller animals or still trying to chase them down throughout the maze of cages, and even more humans were coming into the overcrowded room with every passing second, jogging or sprinting through the distant hallways.

Thirty-five or so people utterly flooded the clear space by now.

It didn't even chew anything, almost choking on its food as it scarfed it down with three gluttonous chomps, barely tasting the wonderful copper coating its mouth.

As its prey's tail slid down its throat, feeling like a sack of furry rocks struggling to go down, it idly remembered that it had to expand its throat a bit for situations like this, then turned around, nailing its eyes on the iron box within which the horned thing was held.

Unfortunately, a human chose that very moment to glance away from the net he was securing around the black fur, their eyes locking for a brief instance of a second before he yelled something.

It felt at least three or four heads snap toward its general direction, pausing in whatever they were doing.

It dashed forward with as much speed as it could muster.

The giant horned thing was bashing into its cage door like a rabid titan with deep, reverberating thuds, and the wolf was certain that freeing that thing would give it enough time to grab the lizard's tail and get out, with some to spare.

However, it was at the top-right end of the room, close to the corner, almost a hundred and fifty feet away, and close to the giant cluster of humans.

With how most of them were still focused on other things and pro-foundly confused by the alarm and general chaos, it believed it had a chance.

The faint whistle of rent air to its left, getting closer in the blink of an eye, made its eyes briefly twitch in said direction.

A shapeless blur exploded into a spiderweb of ropes, too close and too big to dodge, so the wolf did the only thing it knew would work.

It stopped its charge immediately, claws grinding through wood at its sides, then whipped its lower body to the right, tail dragging through water and upward with as much force as its appendage could muster. It slammed into the weighted mass from below, gathering up the ropes into a rough bunch but without the strength to stop nor redirect them.

Air gathered in its lungs as its claws hooked, the mass of ropes a mere foot or two away, and it turned its anger at [Danger Sense]'s incessant, delayed needling into mana, pouring it into its next skill just enough to be strong but safe, then released, jerking its head away as air and sound decompressed into a short, explosive screech, its body rocking backward and held in place by its claws.

From its right eye, it watched as all the water on the ground and in the air was violently shoved away, almost forming a dome, obscuring the black forms behind it, before the dome was shattered by the mass of tangled rope that slammed through it and straight into a human, sending him tumbling to the floor.

Then [Bloodrush] ended, and a bitter realization was accepted in the blink of an eye as it turned back around, abandoned its plan, and ran straight back to where it had eaten the furred four-legger, at the closest metal wall, water resuming the endless pelting of its hide.

It had drawn too much attention, and had too little time.

And it knew that it should always value caution over greed.

Even through the ringing in its ears, it could hear the humans shouting behind it, could feel their forms scrambling toward it, and it didn't hesitate when it reached the wall, jumping up and kicking at the metal with its legs and hands, claws at just enough cutting capacity to give it leverage.

It had tons of experience with climbing at this point, and thus, climbing up the mere thirty-foot wall was nothing.

Within seconds, leaving a trail of claw marks into the metal below, it had reached the top, where the wall turned into a crisscrossing network of thick metal beams supporting the curved roof above.

Its hands weren't quite as great at climbing as its more humanoid ones were, but with the tail being able to help, it wasn't all that difficult for the wolf to lunge upward and grasp onto an H-shaped metal beam with its hands, its tail wrapping around the other end.

The lack of thumbs made this very difficult to hold on to, so with a quick practiced motion, slime veins crept over its "fingers" and grabbed onto the metal, providing it with a stable grip.

It swung its body to the right, using its hanging legs, then as it swung to the left, pulled with both tail and arms, managing to swing one leg up on the beam.

Slime and veins once more crept down its paw and clung to metal, and with another awkward half swing and a throaty growl of exertion, it was on top, chest to iron and snout pointed at a vertical column that connected to the ceiling.

Just in time, as out of the corner of its eye, another ball of rope whistled through the air at it.

Within the grid of metal it was now in, it simply jumped back a little, careful with its footing, and allowed the tangle of ropes to slam into the cross section of iron, briefly tangling, before sliding off.

Then it bounded forward, jumping from beam to beam with as much caution as it could manage.

Nothing felt quite right, now that its movements were so crucial and it had room to focus on them. Its weight felt off, and its arms and legs were longer than it remembered, making it difficult to judge whether it could fit into the next gap between the beams, columns, and the ceiling. With every other leap, it messed up a little, having to use its tail and slime veins to grasp on to something lest it overshoot and slip off back into captivity.

Twice it had slipped off and ended up on the underside of the beams, and had to hurriedly swing back up before the humans threw another net at it.

Thankfully, the distance was short, so on the ninth leap, it was on the double wall the human peeker had come through, and it wasted no time in grasping the top of the wall, claws into steel, and swinging its lower body down, before realizing a problem.

The head in its back. Combined with how much it had grown, its body barely fit in the tight gap between the inner and outer wall, and that was without the bulbous bump on its back.

It shifted the human's head to its left shoulder, an awkward motion that required a lot of focus, then threw its right hand at the outer wall, its left remaining on the inner, twisting its waist a little.

With its body in a strange diagonal, it was a bit of a tight fit, but it was a fit regardless.

Hanging between the two walls, it allowed its claws to cut through, starting a fast but comfortable descent as friction slowed the fall.

Then its paws hit the ground and it lowered its right hand to the ground as its left remained extended far above it, awkwardly shuffling across the tight gap until it reached another H-shaped support rod, this time vertical and filled with smaller metal sticks within the free space.

Convenient handles, really.

Climbing while half its body hung off at a strange angle was frustrating and slow, but judging by the vibrations it could feel, the humans were grabbing ladders to go after it, which was a nice motivation to ignore its own comfort and just speed up the walls as best it could.

Then it was finally at head height for the loose panel, and it leaned back a little, sneezing out the dust that had gotten into its nose before giving the panel an appraising look.

There was absolutely no way it was going to fit through with the head in its back, and it needed some space for proper leverage, so it removed the head from within the sack on its back, simply floating it to the side with a single thick vein.

Then it grasped the metal, awkwardly turned its body around, shoulders braced against metal, and punched forward with its right hand.

The rusty nails holding the panel in place simply snapped, the panel flipping through the air before crashing to the ground fifteen feet below. Without wasting a second, it quickly guided the slime vein and its dripping cargo through the hole first, then put its right arm and head through, using its tail and legs to push its body through the small gap.

The outer wall was a mere four inches thick, so once more than half of its body was outside, hanging there with its left forearm stuck next to its waist, it simply had to wriggle, claw at the metal under itself, and push with its legs and tail to fit through the small gap, until finally, both its hands were free.

With its hips being the only thing keeping it from falling head first, it took a short moment to observe its surroundings, tail brushing against metal as its head swiveled and the slime vein crept back into its sheath, human head included.

It was just another dark empty alley, wide and smooth, and . . . strangely clean. That was unusual.

Though it could tell from the smell that blood had been spilled here a couple days ago. Blood was one of those smells that simply didn't wash off things the way humans probably thought it did.

Realizing it was distracting itself, it focused back on the alley and potential routes it could take to go back down the human nest, which it had grown used to.

The alley was cut in half by a very thin gap between two buildings, too tight to be called an alley and too high to be called a corridor, just across from the wolf.

The gap curved to the right and went under the buildings it separated, then based on vibrations, it opened to a metallic overhang that seemed to loop under the streets around itself before rising back up to another street about two hundred feet away. Some kind of shortcut.

A perfect escape, as far as it was concerned.

It also noticed a lot of people, however.

Way too many people. The room below was under control, and beyond the people within the building itself, it could feel more than a dozen people prowling *around* the building, including two of them on the roof just above it, four on the roof across, and a few suspiciously still humans stood around in places that seemed oddly purposeful.

It felt paranoid all of a sudden.

There were *so many* people around outside, in the buildings themselves, around this building's flanks, on the roof and patrolling the alleys, and it had no idea who would be trying to grab it and take it back into the cage, and who was an unknown, unrelated passerby.

[Danger Sense] sent a stab of an urgent warning into its mind from somewhere behind it, and without thinking, it kicked at the inner metal wall with its legs and tail with a deep, deafening thud, launching its lower body through the gap and tumbling through the air.

It was both luck and skill that made it come out of the fifteen-foot drop relatively unharmed, managing to bend its torso inward at just the right time to land with its right shoulder and transition it into a clumsy roll rather than face-planting and breaking its collarbones and jaw.

Unfortunately, [Danger Sense] only got more insistent by the time it had rolled to its feet, and unwilling to waste even a moment as it felt the humans on the roof dash to the edge, alerted by the sound, it ignored the pulsing pain covering half its backside and the feeling of the shattered skull embedded in said backside, in favor of clawing at the stone, dashing forth into the claustrophobic gap across the alley.

As its shoulders crested the entrance, it heard the humans on the roof angrily shout something, and turned its head to the side, just enough to peek at what its skill was so insistent about, and saw the humans jump off the roof.

Then its eyes flicked down to look into a cloud of . . .

Violently twirling black smoke, speeding through the panel it had punched out and rushing straight at it with speed it *knew* it couldn't outrun, not for more than a minute or two.

But it would try, because its instincts and [Danger Sense] both screamed that whatever the smoke was, it was something unnatural and dangerous.

It turned around in order to make sure it wouldn't trip, deftly dodging something that was in the middle of the thin corridor, barely squeezing past it, and pumped its legs as hard as it could, fifty feet passing by in a blur of exertion, its tongue hanging out of its mouth as it carefully injected more adrenaline into its bloodstream.

Then with the distant sound of a pop and a hiss of decompressing gas, the sensation of danger utterly vanished in the blink of an eye, [Danger Sense] turning off entirely just before it arrived at the curving, down-leaning stairs, and it quickly turned its head to see what happened, slowing its pace to a hurried jog as it let its body cool down.

Instead of smoke, it was a single pitch-black humanoid figure that occupied the corridor, hanging in the air, back against the stone, grasping at something close to its neck and kicking at the air, while the two humans from before were lying limp on the ground according to its vibrational senses, obscured from sight by something.

It had no idea what was happening, and it didn't care. It could feel humans bursting into motion all around it.

It turned around, and hurriedly dashed down the steps.

Clawing at his skin did less than nothing. He felt like a human toddler futilely trying to shave off bits of steel from a statue with his nails.

He hated the feeling. He was Miaro fucking Batheril, and he was not lesser than a mere fucking *ghoul*.

He curled his fist back and snapped it forward at a speed that would have rendered any mortal's head into an explosion of gore.

Instead, a sharp series of simultaneous cracks preceded the searing agony of his now-mutilated fist slamming into the bastard's faceplate with nary a twitch on his end, and his stomach heaved as he fought to keep down the groan of pain.

Ghoul's fingers tightened, crushing his windpipe, and he choked on air as he tried to speak, ask him what the fuck was going on and what his problem was, fear quickly replacing anger and pride as the reality of the situation settled in.

"You should ask Elizabeth why I'm doing this. I'm sure she'll answer truthfully to her favorite beaten puppy," Ghoul said, voice inflectionless and with only the slightest hint of mockery within his words.

Then his free left hand snapped forward, digging into his flesh, his fingers burrowing into his shoulder joint and pushing through as he thrashed in agony, trying to scream but unable to, kicking and pushing and punching at an immovable enemy that completely ignored him.

The sensation of clammy, ice-cold fingers pushing and cutting through his flesh was branded into his mind, until finally, with the sound of wet paper being ripped in twain, his right arm was torn off, and his wide, shock-white eyes filled with horror as Ghoul's mouth opened, and opened, and *opened*, almost like his very neck was splitting open.

Then it closed, his head tilting.

"Interesting biology," he commented, staring at the deathly pale arm in his grasp, bleeding dark red, then opened his mouth once more, shoving the mangled fist deep into his throat before biting off everything up to the forearm, swallowing it like a snake.

Then a mere two seconds later, he did the same to his upper arm, pushing it down his gullet with two fingers and a snakelike tongue that his wide eyes involuntarily followed.

"Three more, a little blood sample, and then we're done. Don't squirm too much," Ghoul dryly ordered after gulping.

He couldn't cry. He didn't have the capability to.

But were his windpipe not a single inch away from being crushed into pulp, he would have wailed, screamed, begged.

CHAPTER 6

The shortcut was mercifully empty of humans and was far, far more wide and open than it had any need to be.

Thankfully, that just meant the wolf could dash forward without worrying about tripping and tumbling off to its own death.

A hundred feet passed in a blur of near-pitch-black cobbles and metal support rods speeding past, out of its line of sight, and it bound up the stairs with enough speed and precision to surprise even itself, barely cutting its momentum enough to not slam into the curving wall.

As its focus turned to the vibrations, it mentally hesitated for a moment. There were too many humans. *Everywhere.*

It could easily tell which human was after it and which one wasn't, thankfully. Their frantic movements, their positions; it wasn't difficult at all to distinguish between the two groups, to figure out where they were and what they were doing.

Escaping their notice was the hard part. The moment its shoulders cleared the topmost step on the stairs, it heard one of the humans above bounding across walkways and metal-sheet rooftops, shout something out, pointing in its direction.

The way it felt almost two dozen humans all simultaneously halt and spin around to begin dashing toward it was mildly terrifying.

No, not mildly. It was genuinely scared, angry, and above all, confused, because something about the whole situation refused to click. Why were there humans sitting outside to hunt it? Did they know it would escape? Why didn't they stop it before it *could*?

It pushed those questions aside and focused on trying to find some kind of path it could take to escape.

The problem was simply that its mind couldn't map out the paths and choose one in the chaotic sprint as it rushed forward without any real direction but *away*. It couldn't puzzle out which of those paths led to a human, which didn't, which were dead ends and which led to safety. Not enough time to process the three-dimensional, mazelike surroundings.

It *did* have enough time to process that it had to change its path immediately. Humans weren't *supposed* to be so freakishly fast, but one of them was.

It bent its body to the right as its claws briefly raked through cobblestones, and before it could bleed off more momentum than it could afford, charged straight toward an empty floor nest at an angle that was far from ideal.

The fit was also tight, but it didn't have much choice, so it leapt up the moment it was close enough, tilted its shoulders as much as it could in midair, and braced itself for impact, moving one arm in front of its head to take the blow.

The sound of shattering glass was deafening, yet nothing but a whisper in comparison to the bang that echoed through the streets, ruffling its fur with a rush of air as something slammed into the door, just a few inches below where its feet were. Its downward-tilting head watched one of the hinges snap and fly off in a moment of adrenaline-induced clarity, the metal door denting inward.

It did its best to keep its momentum the same, but the landing was awkward, the angle was terrible, and the space was far too tight. It landed on its left paw and was underbalanced with its other, unable to get it under its chest in time, sending it forward and to the side, involuntarily ramming into a pile of furniture pushed up against the wall.

Its shoulders and hips met a dozen different protruding chairs, tables, and stools, which quickly tilted and fell all around it with a cacophony of metal and broken glass, its fur utterly packed to the brim with sharp bits of the stuff, which it ignored as it fixed its footing and pushed through with all haste, shrugging off the pile of iron rods clinging to its back.

The exit was far more graceful, a single clean jump through another thick pane of glass that couldn't withstand its weight, sending glittering bits of glass flying everywhere and filling the alleyway.

Behind, it felt the human's feather-light steps reach the first door and jump through, before the human promptly landed on the mess it left behind, sprawling over the furniture with an audible bark of frustration, his feet tangling in the mess of furniture and tripping him up.

It wouldn't buy it any more than a couple seconds, and it didn't have time to think.

It turned to its right, at a tiny staircase wedged between two blocky human nests, and clawed through the stone as it built up its momentum.

Taking the short, short moment of mindlessly bounding up the metal staircase to process where it had to go, it realized that it had no real idea. It just couldn't process the dense mess of sensations that it felt through its antennae.

It just had to go for whatever it felt was right. Pure instinct and hope.

Two humans were jumping across rooftops above and to its right, very fast. Three splitting up and rushing into every little alley below and behind it, too far and slow to be a real issue.

In the distance, however, it felt one of the human-filled boxes dock into a metal platform, at the very edge of its perception, almost five hundred feet away, and had a short moment of realization, like a mental "click" of something sliding into place.

If it could jump on top of one of those, they wouldn't have any way of following it.

It just wasn't sure how it was going to get there.

It reached the end of the staircase, coming out into a tiny, thin corridor lined with rumbling, clicking pipes, and it mindlessly charged forward, trying to split its attention between its movements and mapping out some way of getting to the platforms.

The fast human was quickly approaching, so it took a quick swipe at the pipes to its left as it bound through the S-shaped alley, a frustrating mess of construction that kept making it bleed off momentum lest it slam into a mess of flaking pipes.

It snarled at the sensation of the flesh around its claws burning in agony as foul pressurized liquids burnt through its flesh, but it endured for a couple more swipes before changing hands and repeating, covering its tracks with the sound and sight of pipes screaming in protest as they spewed pressurized off-color chemicals against the grimy pipes on the opposite wall.

Just as it left the alley behind, it felt the human charge into the alley, only to lose his balance by the torrents of gas and liquid beating down on his sides, slamming into a curved wall with his right shoulder before sprawling on the floor, struggling to get up and reorient himself.

Its focus pivoted to weaving through the confused bystanders filling the open street it charged into, an arduous task that slowed it down far more than it had the patience for, each shove cutting its momentum, despite the yelping humans trying to make a path for it.

Then, an idea struck.

Its tail whipped at one of the human's sharp iron rods, hanging off his back and wound around the handle, binding fur and steel together with sticky slime, guided by nothing but vibrations. As it rushed through the sparse crowd, at just the right time, right as its tail stretched to its full length, it *yanked*.

The human behind it was thrown to the floor with a startled shout as the leather straps yanked him back for a short moment before snapping, a clear rod of sharp iron clutched in the tip of its tail, trailing behind it.

It wasted no time in trying to use it, curling its tail into a spiral shape up to its tailbone, before finding a target in the form of an old human standing right in the middle of its path, looking at the crowd of humans it left behind, his eyes too high to see the wolf.

From the base of its tail, it focused the tendons and the tension into a current, trailing down each joint and bone, amplifying, multiplying, unwinding. The iron rod whistled through the air, right to left, and in the blink of an eye slammed cleanly through the old man's neck.

It leapt up his momentarily rigid body mid-fall, and in one clean movement, raked its claws through his coverings to use him as a springboard, leaping over his falling body, while the longest of the veins in its back broke through the hardened mucus sealing the sheath shut to swipe at the head, barely managing to secure it by the forehead, struggling for a couple seconds to control it but eventually managing to store the second head in the sheath next to the first.

The blood pooling in its back was rather uncomfortable, and as it mixed with the slime, made it far more difficult to rouse than it should be, but it was a sacrifice the wolf was willing to make at the moment.

The humans around it turned from yelping and a general murmur of noise to loud screams of panic. Panic which made clearing its path a *lot* easier.

And a lot more noticeable to its pursuers, but it wasn't going to be able to conceal itself for long. It was quite surrounded.

It swerved its head to the walkways above, using vibrations to make sure it didn't crash into anything. Above a ventilation pipe, far above, fifty feet to its left, it caught the flutter of a cloak fearlessly vaulting over the side of a walkway, crashing onto equal ground, out of sight.

Vibrations confirmed what it already assumed, and it turned its attention to the right.

Seven figures, split between the only two streets that led to the moving platforms. A clear road ahead, but it would be flanked on either side.

Its thinking was too . . . *flat*. There was nothing stopping it from using the three-dimensional nature of the human nests.

It lowered its eyes, following along the blurry stretch of decorated walls it was speeding past, and paused when it saw a boxlike structure of fine machinery nailed to the side of a building, wedged in a tiny Π-shaped groove within two buildings.

But it was tight enough for the wolf's purposes.

It swung its bottom legs to the left, grinding claws through stone to halt its momentum, then dashed into the little alcove, jumping just before it hit the wall and redirecting its momentum upward, scrambling up the wall two, then four feet, before it set its hind legs on top of the machine and kicked up, further speeding up its frantic scramble.

It had neither the time nor the slime left to climb safely. It was just pure, frantic clawing, instinctual shifts of its weight, occasionally blunting its claws completely to catapult itself up.

Exhaustion was its only real obstacle. Adrenaline was slowly but surely squeezed out of its internal sac, trying to offset the lactic acid that was quickly weakening its limbs as it scrambled up a hundred feet of flat iron.

The humans below, its pursuers, quickly approached, and it could only hope they wouldn't notice.

Unfortunately, the crowd of human passersby all staring at it and *pointing* dashed that hope in less than a second, and it briefly swung its head around in the middle of another rake of its claws, staring at the group of four humans and the things they were pointing at it for a brief fragment of a second before a tiny blur sped toward it with a resounding wooden *thunk*.

Instinct helped it far more than the next useless ping it got from its [Danger Sense] skill, and it raised its left leg to kick at the wall as its swung its upper body outward and to the right, arm extended into the open air.

The metal-tipped wooden stick flew past its fingers close enough to feel the wind ruffle its fur, then hit the iron wall a few inches from its chest, where its left shoulder used to be.

Before it had time to question what that *explosion* of mana that it felt for a brief moment was, the answer came in the form of golden light bursting out of the back of the stick, winding into distinct forms, then snapping down at the iron wall like the jaws of a vine-eater from the burning rivers.

One of the glowing ropes headed for the side of its chest, and in the tiny, almost instantaneous instance it had to prepare for agony, it was even more surprised to feel the rope swerve *around* its flesh to hit the wall.

Without the metal bit sticking into the iron wall, however, and with the odd mana net having caught nothing but air and sparks, the light feebly pushed against the iron for a moment before the stick bounced off, and it simply stared in mute shock for a blink of an eye as the light-net disappeared into thin air.

Then right behind the falling, spinning stick, it saw two others take aim with their wooden devices, while the fourth man began screaming into a human-communication plate thing.

It kicked at the wall behind itself, and with the crimped, quivering fingers that upheld its entire body, it pulled itself up while throwing its left arm up, covering a couple feet of distance, before resuming its tempo of frantic clawing.

It engaged its legs far more, its arms and fingers starting to feel numb, weak, and shaky, its tail curling and uncurling in agitation.

A light but firm squeeze of adrenaline flooded its body with a little more energy, and then it heard another snappy *thunk*.

It was a decision born from a sense of panic more than rationality, a sense that it *had* to rush up to the top of this building as soon as possible or it would only be delayed more and more, become slower until it would fall to its death or captivity.

It did not turn around to see the stick, nor try to intercept it. Its ears twitched in the direction of that faint whistling sound, of something sharp ripping the air apart, heard it get closer in less than a heartbeat, and with nothing but a faint understanding of its trajectory, it dodged to the right once more, flattening its chest to the wall on the side.

The muted shock that traveled through its limbs as an iron tip burrowed into its arm bone alerted it to the simple fact that it had dodged *into* the metal-tipped stick, and in the next instance, a living spiderweb of golden ropes burst out of the back end, weaving around and slithering through every nook and cranny of its torso, head and arms like a living thing.

Then they snapped shut and tightened.

Its right arm, already positioned close to its torso, snapped to the side of its waist, claws effortlessly ripping through steel, and it felt something in its neck *strain* as its head was violently jerked down, jaw pressed into its sternum and ears crushed flat. Its ribs creaked in protest as the ropes *tightened*.

Its legs kicked on instinct, startled, and it only realized its mistake when it felt all of its remaining weight move onto its left hand, awkwardly half extended, battling both gravity and a single rope trying to pull its elbow into the side of its head.

It was going to fall.

With its line of sight being a slightly dizzying height and a crowd of humans below, it wasn't hard for its eyes to snap to the fourth human in the group, who extended both arms toward the wolf and launched two metal rods connected to wires, both landing to either side of the little nook the wolf was hanging within, burrowing into the metal with surprising ease.

Then the bulky mechanisms strapped to the human's arms whirred to life as the wolf tried to figure out how to escape, and it saw the human be launched up, the wires reeling him up straight toward the wolf like a launched projectile, the harness around the human's hips sending him feet first toward the wolf, in an almost upside-down diagonal position.

There was no moment between realization, action, and reaction. It was a seamless moment where it saw an opportunity and moved without the middle ground of *thought* entering the process.

Its left hand uncurled, and it allowed the rope to wrench its arm to its head, twisting its elbow to place its claws at its right shoulder, bicep pressed against the side of its head as it abruptly began falling. Then with a quick rake of its claws, it cut through a golden rope, which somehow made all the others snap out of existence. Now free, its arms awkwardly snapped to the sides, the Π-shaped nook more than tight enough for the wolf to quickly scramble for a clawed grip on the iron and halt its fall before it truly began.

The flying human jerked strangely, throwing his arms in a frantic whirl-like motion, the wires going slack as he tried to stop his momentum, to no avail.

It pushed its hind legs off the walls to its sides, set them to the flat iron behind it, and with the assistance of its wound tail, launched itself straight at the human's form, a screech of rent metal accompanying the fireball of sparks it left behind.

The human detached the wire on the right as the left snapped into rigidity, and the wolf watched as the contraption on his arm *tugged*, beginning to swing him out of the wolf's path.

It could not reach his torso, not like it had intended, but it didn't panic, as the human was too slow, and far too late.

Its left hand reached to the left as far as it could go, aiming for the human's chest.

Gleaming white claws burrowed into the human's stomach as he tried to fly past, the wolf's jaws snapping shut around his left knee, teeth effortlessly cutting through bone and joint, and the rest of its body, momentum, and weight soon tugged the wolf into a rough swing that had the wolf inadvertently end up with a detached leg in its mouth, panicking for a grip as the human's scream filled its ears.

The human's soft abdomen didn't provide one, its claws cutting the coverings and flesh into ribbons, peppering its forearm and face with a wild spray of blood.

It swung its right arm with their momentum, spitting the leg out of its maw, the world a blur around them, and stabbed its "fingers" between the human's ribs from the back, grabbing a rib and feeling it snap as its weight settled on it.

It ducked its head under the human's wild swing, seeing a flash of gleaming silver at the edge of its sight, coming out of the human's glove, and swung its tail with its lower body, discarding the sharp rod in the general direction of the humans wildly shooting mana-filled sticks at them, and completely missing, before snapping the tail up as far as it could reach, managing to grab a hold of the human's neck.

It tried to blunt its left-hand claws, but rather than giving it a grip, that attempt simply made its claws slip out of the human, slick with blood, so it quickly jabbed forward once more, miraculously digging its hand into the human's hip at the perfect angle to grab a hold of his hipbone with the tip of its claws.

It curled its claws, blunting them before burrowing a bit deeper, and simultaneously tightened its tail, the human's panicked scream turning into a gurgle, leaving the wolf awkwardly hanging off him as they struggled for leverage.

Its eyes flicked to the building they were heading straight into from a sharp sideways angle, a mess of sharp protrusions and pipes, and another warning from [Danger Sense] notified it about something it had been too distracted to see, its eyes snapping back up to the struggling human in its grip.

Its left eye saw nothing but a thin sliver of immaculate iron spearing straight toward the wolf. Its right eye saw a complex mess of gears snap and whirl to life, pushing the rod out of the human's arm with speed it had no hope of matching.

Its attempt to dodge was not a mere lean. It pulled at the human's rib, snapped its whole upper body as far away as it could, the muscles of its waist straining, and used a tiny burst of [Sonic Blast] to propel its head away from the point of the rod.

Its efforts rewarded it with the feeling of cold steel slamming into the side of its neck, and pushing through fur and skin before impacting the thin sheets of armor it had wrapped around its neck, and . . .

Spearing through them for an inch, before completely stopping, the thick part of the rod unable to move through the tough stringlike fibers of its underskin armor, the impact of the human's strike dissipating throughout its neck and choking its next breath, a snarl of pain mixing with a rough cough as it swung its head to the left, the ends of its snout snapping shut over the human's wrist.

Top and bottom canines ground together, their tips touching as flesh and crushed gearwork machinery worked together to stop its jaws from fully closing.

It twisted, digging its claws deeper, ignoring the human's desperate struggle to pull his hand and rod away, merely clamping down harder.

It really wanted to rip the human's hand off and get the rod's tip out of its neck, but it was far too useful as a grip.

A tail around the human's neck, a flimsy, broken rib in its right-hand fingers, its claws nestled into the human's lung, and the bare tips of its left-hand claws burrowed into the human's hip bones. It was only *just* enough grip for it to feel a hint of assurance that it wasn't going to fall a solid fifty feet and get caught when they crashed.

It twisted its head as best as it could, hoping to prepare itself for impact, and felt its confidence plummet. A sharp diagonal angle, speeding toward a mess of railings—iron rods protecting the windows behind them—and the occasional pipe.

It used what little leverage and time it had to distance its body from the human's, before lurching to the right, trying to swing the human around so he would take all the impact.

Unfortunately, when hanging off a single wire, it hadn't accounted for how *easy* it was to make them spin. The world began to blur as it vastly overestimated how much force it needed, and less than a second later, it slammed shoulder first into the wall, before the diagonal angle forced its already-dizzying spin to turn even faster, and it felt the human's rib break off and stay in its fingers as they were ripped out of his chest cavity, its right arm smashing into something, its left losing its grip from the sudden jostling, and then for a single moment, it felt itself begin to fall, disoriented and unaware of where its limbs even were.

Except its tail.

It clenched with all the strength the limb had, and felt its spine jolt and crack oddly as it suddenly straightened, supporting its swinging body for a brief instance as it tried to reorientate.

Swinging. So it was upside down . . . ? Oh, right. It was staring at the ground below, of course it was.

It heard four *thunks*, almost simultaneously, and let go of the human, swung down, bringing both "hands" in front of its chest and to the left, pressing its claws into the iron, blunting them and allowing its lower body to swing from its own weight.

Its fingers buckled for a short instance, too abused and exhausted to support its sudden transition of weight, but the way they were wedged into the iron only made them ache from the weight rather than slide out, allowing it to see with relative clarity as four metal-tipped sticks slammed into the iron and bounced off, ribbons of golden light fading as they caught nothing once more.

One of the humans angrily roared something, rushing straight at the wolf, his heels spewing fire with every step, and for a brief moment, it remembered its previous realization: that humans might have access to the symbols as well. And instead of dismissing the human as illogical, it used his confident sprint as a warning that fueled its burning limbs and numbing fingers, kicking at the iron wall.

It wrenched its hands down simultaneously, effectively launching itself up three straight feet, before resuming its frantic clawing.

[Bloodrush] finally returned, a light mental ping in the back of its mind, and it activated it instantly, energy and power filling every fiber of its body, the panicked mess in its head slightly easier to parse through.

It didn't have to go *up* the entire building. It could just go through.

It clawed up to the underside of a window sill, grabbing the edge with its left hand, then with a quick back-and-forth swipe of its right-hand claws, sent the rods protecting the window rattling around and over it in a shower of metal pieces.

It punched through the glass, grabbing onto the inner wall, and with a final kick of its hind legs, it curled them to its stomach, over the sill, and used them to kick the wall, rocketing its body forwards into the grimy hallway and continue running.

It heard the roar of flame approach from the window it had broken through and felt a human's foot coverings hit the floor, immediately breaking into a sprint right behind it, and so it stomped that hint of hesitation it felt into dust, speeding up even more as it focused on vibrations, mapping out the world outside, confirming distance.

A mental preparation, to help its muscles do the motion its mind envisioned, and it felt a little more confident.

It could make it. Easily. It closed the distance, reaching the opposite end of the hallway.

It leapt up once more, breaking through the glass window for the umpteenth time with its elbows, and barely managed to awkwardly swipe its claws through the iron bars in the middle of its jump, clipping its right foot on one of the sharp remnants clinging to the window, then proceeded to tumble through the air in a wild spray of glass, iron chunks, and blood.

A short erected barrier of thin sheet metal passed by from under it, and it snapped its neck around to see its landing spot, swerving its head and neck around as its body spun, trying to keep its gaze steady.

It quickly realized it had slightly overshot.

Right as its flailing body was about to crash into the triangular top of the gravel pile and bounce off to take a hit that would likely fray its ribs, a solid thirty feet that led straight to iron, it threw its right arm out, the back of it slamming through the top of the pile and cutting its momentum just enough for the wolf to roll down the pile in a chaotic tide of dust and gravel, the pile losing cohesion as the entire thing shifted and flattened, swallowing the wolf's body.

It backhanded through the thin layer of gravel covering it with a snarl, bucking once to loosen the pebbles and frantically shaking its head to get the dust out of its eyes, then used its claws' grip on the floor to dash out of the remaining debris and toward the gate of the . . . work site?

It didn't care what it was.

The humans here seemed much more aware of its presence and all but leapt out of its path as it sped toward their flimsy gate, catching a glimpse of stark green light in the distance through the thin metal wiring of the gate.

The color washing over the people made the whole area pop out from its surroundings, and the faint motion of a gigantic box moving on wires, just barely visible through the smog in the background, made it realize exactly *what* it was looking at.

The moving lifts humans used to move around. And its sole viable plan of escape.

A seemingly endless railing crept into sight just past the grated gate, coming from the left in a straight line then gently curving left into some kind of open area flooded with humans on benches or conversing with each other, and the wolf pumped its limbs even faster as it ran past all the rumbling machinery and to the gate, swiping through the mechanism holding it shut and shouldering through in a burst of cut-up chain links, sending a small crowd of curious passersby quickly hopping back with sounds of surprise, staring at it warily, tensely.

It didn't waste time nor attention on them, turning to the right and resuming its frantic sprint, being swallowed up by the parting crowd as it ran.

Its breaths came in pants, and its limbs were burning, growing heavier with every pump of its muscles. The crutch of [Bloodrush] would end eventually. It had to be quick.

The distant roar of flame suddenly getting louder made its head turn, a stray breeze bringing forth a vaguely familiar scent.

It only caught a glimpse of a human vaulting through the window, fire spewing out of his feet to slow his fall, coverings billowing around him from the sudden fall, but the acrid breeze of the human nest carried forth his scent, straight into the wolf's nostrils, and almost made it stumble.

It was like a sudden *spark* of recognition.

It knew this human. A vague memory of dodging a ball of sparks, back when it had just gotten access to the symbols, was brought forth, a surprised face staring at it as it frantically ran away.

The realization made it almost stumble and turn around just to shred him to pieces, but the familiar, light tapping steps of the fast human from before, winding around the building to its left, and the pounding of heavy foot coverings rushing toward its path with the aim of cutting it off, were just enough for it to contain its fury.

It had to *run*. Not fight.

As its head swung forward to focus on its path, it saw a vaguely brown-green-tinted blur streak through the air to its left, flying over the railing and the mess below, struggling to keep up with the wolf.

And it was the wolf that it was following, because even from a single glance, it could see the way its beady eyes were completely glued to its form.

That was a problem. Did the humans control that thing somehow?

It *hated* flying things. It couldn't *feel* them.

Shoving aside its frustrations, it focused on taking the straightest path possible, gigantic heat radiators towering over human and wolf alike, softly glowing orange along the grid-like buildings to its right, flashing by as it rushed around and *through* the groups of people that hung around them.

Having actual shoulders made it so much easier to take impact from the sides, or push aside human legs, but they still slowed the wolf down, uncomfortably so.

The crowds thinned for a short few feet, and its eyes flicked up to the right, as far up as they could go without it moving its entire head, feeling a human dash through a small crowd somewhere around there.

A thin but incredibly tall alley, full of half-lit windows from within. Faint smog rolled in from above, just barely turning the walkways going above and *through* the buildings into blurry shapes.

Then the smog seemed to whirl into a vortex and *split* the second the human came into sight.

It saw the blur a second too late to react to the seemingly wild shot, only managing to have a mental flash of realization before something slammed into its right forearm.

Its stride broke, a pained yelp escaping its snout as its arm jerked, and by pure instinct, curled into its chest mid-bound, sending it tumbling, right shoulder first, into the floor, half a dozen humans jumping away or backing off, yelling things.

It rolled to its feet as gracefully as it could manage, using its tail to compensate for its flailing legs, and came face-to-face with a long line of liquid fire, spewing out of the flying lizard thing's mouth as its scaled form hovered above the crowd, going from left to right, carving a line into the metal.

The fire itself was little more than an annoyance, mere eight or nine inches of fire, but surprise, proximity, and instinct made it jerk back briefly, only it flopped awkwardly onto its right side, its right arm nowhere to be found, not following its commands. It stumbled upright to swing its head to where its arm should be.

To its relief, it was still there. But a familiar numbness had crawled up from its forearm and was racing up its bicep, a glass vial bobbing out of where its thick metal head had punched into its forearm.

It couldn't so much as twitch a finger.

Alarm was not what it felt, instead something more akin to panic. It *knew* how poisons worked. It was too late to get it out of its bloodstream.

Its claws dug into the stone, a single slime vein jerking out of its backside to grab onto the elbow and pull it back to sit along its chest, and it squeezed its adrenaline sac absolutely *dry*, its tail clamping around the top of its right shoulder and squeezing around its elbow with all its might, trying to slow the poison.

The chill of power was *intoxicating*. Aches vanished, limbs turned from lead to feathers, panic turned to a jittery, scared sort of *excitement*.

With a sharp bark that scared the ogling crowd into scrambling away, it dashed forward through the flames, three limbs barely slowing it down as it shouldered through legs, purposefully ramming into people's legs to make them fall and hopefully be an obstacle to its pursuers.

Still, it was just *not* enough.

The fast human seemed to vanish for a moment from its senses, before it felt him *running on top* of the railing, screaming something. Behind and to its right, it felt the shooter speed forward and vault from walkway to walkway, twenty-foot drop after twenty-foot drop, getting closer by the second. The fire human was somehow keeping up as well, its vibration senses unsure of what or *how* he was doing it.

And the *flying thing*.

It was flying right above it, just too far to be in reach but just close enough to make the wolf wary.

A burst of orange light from above made it tense, and for the second time, [Danger Sense] saved it from a nasty wound or worse, a light needle prod that seemed to follow the path of the liquid fire.

Unfortunately, that path was in front of it, so it could do nothing but momentarily dig its claws out of the metal and allow itself to half slide, slowing just long enough for the flame to hit the metal.

It tried to keep its momentum the same, charging through the liquid fire the moment it was sure that the flying lizard was done firing, but it just *couldn't* get enough speed to outrun its pursuers.

A crystal light pole quickly neared, the distance between it and the wolf closing as quickly as the distance between itself and its pursuers was, and a hasty plan of attack formed in its mind as it firmed its resolve, steeling its nerves as best as it could.

A deafening *thunk* came from behind, from the human that had fired the poison into its arm, and through sheer speculation, from the position of his arms and his device, it guessed where the projectile was going and kicked off the ground with its hind legs, curling them up to its stomach.

It felt the air whip around its stomach and ruffle its underside fur as the strange projectile rushed through where its legs were, and it caught a glimpse of a rope and three metal balls from the corner of its eyes, impacting the metal beneath.

Then, bouncing up with equal velocity to slam into its left arm, the force of it ripped its limb off the ground completely.

It tried to jerk it back down, but it was too late to fix its stride. So it leaned into it.

It curled its right side as much as it could, its left shoulder slamming into the metal, and it rolled with its momentum, then unwound its tail from its right arm to wrap around the base of the metal pole, and *pulled*, its bottom half in the air as its chest scraped at rusty metal, pulling itself away.

Faced with its pursuers, it realized in just how dire a situation it was, let it sink in, in that single second.

If it fought, it would likely die. It had been about to launch itself straight into its own death—or captivity.

It punched the metal floor with its left arm, down and at an angle, using the motion to clumsily throw the metal balls at its pursuers in the same movement by flicking its forearm up, and curled its back muscles to assist, managing to launch its upper body off the floor and use its tail and momentum to swing its upper body back around, away from its pursuers, letting go of the pole and restarting its sprint with an awkward midair twist and a desperate kick of its legs that sent sparks flying everywhere.

"Holy fuck!" a human yelled, louder than anything said before, and it braced for a projectile that didn't come.

Still, the distance kept closing. Between itself and its pursuers, between itself and its escape.

Wrapping its tail back around its arm, now at the bicep, it turned its head around to stare at the humans pursuing it, using its vibration senses to navigate, glaring back at them, eyeing the heaps of rope and wooden sticks they had strapped to themselves.

Within mere seconds, the fast human running on the railing lifted his arm, another pair of metallic balls balanced atop the triangular device on his arm.

Just sixty feet behind it, the human spewing fire out of his feet with every step gestured something, a strange whistling sound coming out of his mouth, and the flying lizard locked eyes with the wolf.

Then a small spurt of liquid fire was launched into its path, and it had to swerve awkwardly to the side, a harsh, sluggish movement, considering its single arm, almost doubling over, its pace interrupted.

Then, above where it was dodging, another spurt of liquid fire.

It couldn't move out of the way. The only way to dodge was to stop.

It clenched its jaws and pushed forward, moving its head back around to stare at the humans. It felt the liquid land on its back, feeling it slowly begin to burn through its fur, smelling it with every harsh pant.

That was fine. It had enough fur to not feel anything yet.

The vibrations fed it information, feeling the clicks and twists of the machinery on the humans' forms.

It couldn't dodge well with one arm.

Air gathered in its lungs, and it felt its world *shrink*, struggling to charge up a [Sonic Blast] and provide its body with oxygen. Its lungs felt like they were being crushed beneath a thousand tons of steel. It slowed, seeing black dots starting to pepper its vision.

It hurt so much worse than feeling fire lick at its skin.

The humans standing around had caught on to the chaos. There were none in range it could grab and use as a shield, all clearing the path for them. If it continued dodging, they'd just catch up sooner.

It had no other option.

"Now!" the fast human barked from atop the railing, and three thunks sounded, so simultaneously they combined into a single sharp *crack*.

It turned its wrist, hooking its claws in the opposite direction of where it was trying to run to, and curled its waist as it swung its lower body around.

Something in its wrist popped painfully as its full weight was halted, and it jerked its head low, almost against its chest.

Blurs of whirling metal and rope filled its vision.

It pushed the air, the sound out, more forcefully than it ever had before, charged with enough mana to tear its throat apart.

A translucent blood-speckled ball of air came out of its throat, a visible distortion in the space around it, traveling for just a mere foot.

Then the ball hit the metal and exploded, and the world turned into a spinning blur of colors and the shrieking of its protesting eardrums.

Its sight and body jerked violently as a dull impact cut its momentum, then the world spun even faster in another direction.

Then it hit the ground, a hundred little impacts peppering its bruised ribs, its flailing elbow, its shoulder and hind legs as it rolled across cold steel.

Momentum bled off quick, and it landed snout first into the ground, sliding on its numb arm for a foot or two.

It lay there for a length of time that felt negligible but still far too long, trying to remember where it was and what it was doing, why its entire body felt like it had been shoved between moving gears, the world swaying under its snout ever so slightly. Pain didn't register, adrenaline too thick in its blood to even feel a pinprick, nothing more than mild discomfort where some things had an impact when they shouldn't have.

A furious cry cut through the shrieking in its ears, and its vision sharpened, its head snapping to the left as the thrums of adrenaline picked up again.

It didn't see anything but a wall of rapidly approaching fire.

Its left hand gripped the floor, and with a buck of its right shoulder and a frantic kick of its legs, it threw itself aside, quickly glancing at the open area it had found itself in, at the dozens of humans staring at it or running away.

The searing heat that rushed past its body almost made it feel like it was being boiled alive by mere proximity, then it just suddenly vanished with a weak puff, the blinding light coming out from somewhere behind it dying out like a momentary spark.

Seven blurry, wispy forms dropped down from above, surrounding it in a thirty-foot-wide loose formation, while three similar ones seemed to slink through the distant and retreating crowd.

It awkwardly hopped with its working arm, blinking dust and tears out of its eyes as it reoriented itself, staring at the floor the way the world kept swaying back and forth, making it feel like it was about to puke.

The lifts were . . . directly behind it, their pulleys and spinning gears groaning in effort. One of them was stationary, full of humans curiously peeking through the windows at the chaos outside.

Before, it was running along a railing, on the edge of one of the human platforms . . .

Its vibrations crawled through steel, feeling a familiar section, utterly destroyed. A wall heater lay crumpled inward as if punched by a giant's fist, the railing torn clean off the iron deck and hanging over the smoggy abyss below in a twisted, bent mess. Two unmoving humans lay on the ground, one missing half his head and the other cradled within a bent metal bench, his spine snapped in two.

Wasn't it there just a moment ago?

Had it launched itself almost *eighty feet*?

It closed its mouth to swallow a giant glob of blood leaking out of its throat, finding it futile as more came to replace it, and thus focused on its body.

Its ribs were frayed beyond belief, and it could feel its wrist joint being completely loose and disconnected. Which made it quickly realize why its movements were so awkward, why its wrist refused to listen.

It focused back on itself, the humans at the edge of its vision still not moving.

Then it noticed that none of them had any vibrations. Nothing. No weight, no mass, no *body*.

Except for one person . . .

It lifted its eyes from the floor, moving them up along the shady figures at the edge of its eyesight, and glared at one of them in confusion.

The moment its eyes focused, it felt its title activate, Witness of Divinity like a switch being flipped inside its head.

It was looking at an illusion. It wasn't sure *how* it knew, but it could just tell. It was in the way it moved, stood, the air it didn't breathe, the very space it occupied, the way its form was just *not right* but not in a way it could possibly explain or understand.

The human crumpled like a statue made of dust, vanishing into nothing in the blink of an eye, and the other illusions paused in their circular prowls.

It hopped around, toward the only human with vibrations, then let its chest hit the floor and shoved its hand in its own mouth, clamping down on it with blunted teeth.

With a forceful jerk, push, and a meaty pop that reverberated through its bones, it shoved its wrist back into position, the abused joint holding. For now.

The human locked eyes with it, the furry ears atop his head peeled back in aggression, the slits of his pupils locked onto its form. The hazy blur that covered him puffed out of existence, turning his form . . . sharper, more defined, more detailed, a mess of belts and machines and latches covered by a flapping covering. His left arm was nothing but metal and wires from the shoulder down.

It was unnerving. It just felt wrong.

His green eyes glared into the wolf's from behind a black scarf that hid everything up to his nose, and he raised his right hand to the left side of his waist, his left hand grasping his fluttering back covering from his right shoulder.

The illusions all disappeared, and then in a motion almost too fast for its eyes to follow, the human's form burst into action, throwing his covering at the wolf, then lunged forward, drawing his weapon, a ridiculously thin and sharp piece of steel. He swung upward in a diagonal arc, the sharp tip almost touching his left foot, then moving in a diagonal upward angle to his right.

Exactly where the inside of its elbow would be, it imagined.

Despite *feeling* the attack, it simply did not have the speed or the limbs to properly dodge and keep its balance. Its arm jerked back as it tilted its torso sideways, drawing the arm behind its waist.

The human's covering split in two, the green-gleaming edge of his weapon flashing through it and through where its arm was a millisecond ago, his body angled to dash through the tight gap between the wolf's chest and the floor.

Its right eye only caught the blur of his left fist, crackling with lightning and gleaming with steel, before it slammed into its face.

Pain punched through its dulled nerves as electricity made its body spasm, a hazy flash of an open space and an endless expanse of walkways passing by in its vision before turning to black as its back and shoulder hit the metal floor, followed by its skull.

It curled its hind legs and abdomen as its momentum continued, managing to roll backward to its feet, ass over head. Its left arm settled against iron again, tense, curled, its right shoulder sagging to the ground as it swayed in place, momentarily blind.

It couldn't *dodge*. It just didn't have the limbs for it. The venom was almost past its bicep, worming through its veins no matter how hard it squeezed. Instead of five limbs it had three.

It felt the human stabilize and lean low to the ground, winding both his arms behind him. Another charge.

Vision returned to its left eye, the darkness filling with colors. Its sight was blurry and wavering, distorted. It saw a haze of black speed toward it, the glint of his weapon in the sickening green light helping the wolf distinguish it from the mess of blurry shapes filling up its field of view.

It couldn't figure out the trajectory, nor the distance. The world rocked below its feet, and its mind felt like it was a giant ball of cotton.

The weapon rushed toward its head, and the wolf feinted a dodge, throwing itself backward and tossing its head to the left. The mucus veins burst out of its back with practiced ease and the force of encroaching panic, dripping with blood.

The rod adjusted, and the human's foot smashed into the floor. The wolf felt the human's wrist twist, his weapon rushing straight toward the right side of its exposed neck in a straight jab.

Its tail unwound from its arm, and the wolf yanked the limp limb up, its shoulder managing to bring its right arm up, covering its neck and head.

The sharp tip barely managed to pierce through its flesh with enough force to strike its arm bone, embedding itself within the malleable fibers.

Slime veins slapped onto the sharp rod, coiling awkwardly around it, what little remnants of slime it had left quickly firming up, and the wolf twisted its waist and torso to the right, slashing its claws at the human's right-hand wrist in a wild, awkward, upward swing.

Its tail simultaneously whipped to the human's left arm as he punched forward and wrenched it to the side, just enough to make it narrowly miss its ribs instead of smashing into them, the electricity making its hairs stand on end.

The human tried to pull his right arm back, only to be caught off guard when the blade refused to budge, not quick enough to let go.

Its claws cut through the outside of his wrist in the upward swing, going halfway through it, cutting apart the joint and tendons.

Slime veins burst out of its tail's sheath and clamped onto metallic fingers, its tail tightening, and the human's middle and lower body twisted and bucked in a downright *impossible* way, managing to halt his momentum, set his feet below the wolf's falling torso, and kick himself backward, violently jerking to a halt when his arm refused to budge from the wolf's tail.

Its chest hit the ground, and it pulled with its tail, intending to reel the human in and bite his head off. Instead of the human being thrown toward it, however, the metal arm clicked and spun with a burst of steam where it connected to the human's shoulder, plates shifting, then it simply popped off.

The human wasted no time in dashing back and away, having stalled long enough for a small, scattered group of his packmates to come.

It all felt so purposeful. It felt like it was playing into their hands. Run, fight, run, until it couldn't even move, and they'd grab it. Was that their plan?

It was a good one.

It turned, feeling [Bloodrush] fade, its body feeling like a mangled pile of rocks, yet it pushed itself up, hopping on one arm to reorient its body, panting, spit and blood crusting into its fur, dripping out of its mouth, running down its snout and neck and splattering to the iron below. The human's metal arm dropped to the ground with a metallic clang as its eye struggled to focus on the humans.

The scent of burnt *everything* filled its nostrils as it judged distance with its antennae, a mere *fifty feet* between itself and freedom. It was so close but felt so far.

The humans barked something at each other, spreading out in a loose circle to better surround it, and it tried to move its right shoulder, only to realize that it had already stopped responding, the blood carrying the venom through its veins with every frantic heartbeat.

It needed its tail to fight, to run properly. And it needed to buy time it simply did not have.

It felt wrong to do, but it had no other option. It only had a few seconds before it would be too late, the poison in its arm moving into its chest.

It wrenched its head to the right, as far as it could stretch, and clamped its jaws around its upper arm, as close to its armpit as it could get, pressing down until its jaw muscles began *burning* in exertion. It tensed its neck, its one eye examining the sprinting humans rushing into the open area from every which direction. All its slime veins retreated into their sheaths.

It hesitated, its resolve cracking, doubts creeping through the gaps.

Would it really be so bad to just let the humans capture it?

They hadn't done anything to it beyond prodding it about when it was in the cage. They'd even tried to feed it. That was . . . for the most part, what it had been after, until now. Simple self-preservation. It would be safe, it would be fed. In a cage. For how long, it didn't know. Maybe the humans would keep it in a cage until it died, or maybe they'd force it to walk beside them like it had seen its distant kin do many times, a leash and collar around its neck so they could pull it around.

What felt like ages ago but was most likely a mere month or two, it would have fought to the death just to get those things. To satisfy its base needs. What more could it have wanted back then?

It wanted a lot more now.

It wanted "Emhree-eel" back. It wanted to be strong enough to not ever have to run away again, it wanted to hang off the tallest towers of the human nest and watch everything below be reduced to insignificance. It wanted to fight things strong enough to be a challenge, to get its ears roaring with adrenaline, to make that soul-deep savagery that nestled within its chains, deep in its soul, break free and *indulge*.

It wanted to have a place where it could feel safe, some nest of its own within this hostile place that seemed to exist just to kill it, capture it. Carve its own place out of the humans' nest by force if it had to.

It wanted to be too strong for any of the humans to challenge it.

The idea of walking beside a human with a collar around its neck turned from a begrudging option to an infuriating image that made its fur spike even straighter across its back. Something in its very *being* protested against the idea, even without its own opinions interjecting. Like an instinct, but deeper.

It refused to *obey* prey.

The cracks sealed, a chill of determination racing down its spine.

The machinery to its left began groaning, the metal boxes resuming their endless back and forth journeys, inching away from the platform, sailing away with all its hopes of escape on their backs.

Another needle was launched at its side, and it twisted its head, the limp arm catching the needle at the elbow.

Its teeth sharpened, its tail curled.

* * *

Tracer watched with narrowed eyes as the beast bit down on its own arm, using its head to move the limb and block the hunter's needle.

It was too precise, too accurate, too calculating.

The control it had over its own movements, the combat instinct he had witnessed as Dyce tried and somehow *failed* to subdue it, dodges that shouldn't have been possible for a seasoned adventurer, never mind a mindless beast . . .

They were *sublime*.

A shudder of excitement threatened to contort his spine, but he kept it ramrod straight, arm raised, ready to call the shot.

Then the beast jerked its head, teeth cutting through its own flesh, and he went rigid with surprise.

It snapped its jaws back onto its bleeding arm, biting out an entire chunk of its own bicep before closing them *again* where stray gore kept its arm hanging off its side, a frenzied blur of teeth and blood.

And with a final yank, its arm detached with a spray of blood and was immediately tossed aside, its prehensile tail curling around its upper arm and squeezing with enough force that he saw the muscles be visibly compressed, the steady stream of blood slowing to a trickle.

The remaining length of its tail clumsily pressed against the ground like a tentacled replacement of the limb it had just *bitten* off, and the beast crouched low to the ground, white teeth glinting in the green light as a yellow eye glared at him, at his raised arm, his confident posture.

It knew how poison traveled through veins. It knew it had to staunch its own bleeding.

It was a show of intelligence that made a grin try to tear through his stoic expression, his teeth chattering in that nervous, giddy feeling of discovery. Of *weakness*.

Its golden eye bored into his skull like a drill.

That *hateful glare*.

Did it have his scent? Would it know him? Would it remember?

Would it *hunt* him?

He had left the jungles years ago, but they had never left him. He heard the buzzing insects burrowing into his ears every night he fell asleep. He heard the sound of snapping traps in an endless beat, until all that was left was himself in a jungle that fell silent wherever he treaded.

And now here he was, despite his warnings to Dyce.

Scared.

Staring at something he'd never seen before.

Grateful that such monsters still existed in the world, to make him feel like prey again.

His arm snapped down, his veins thrumming with barely restrained ecstasy.

His voice came out as smoothly as it ever did.

"Fire."

It didn't know if its throat could handle it.

It knew that it *had* to.

[Sonic Blast] thundered through, a flash of white-hot agony that almost paralyzed it for a moment as it hurriedly threw itself between the dozen nets covering every inch of available space it could dodge into, and the lifts behind itself.

This time, it was prepared for the power its own skill could exert. It didn't try to brace against it.

It simply leaned away, allowing it to throw its body back like a pebble, slamming through a human's legs with a sickening crack as his knees snapped back and bounced off the ground, its guts clenching in discomfort from the impact.

Its right shoulder slammed into the booth that sat beside the machines moving the lifts, now vacated, denting the metal inward, and its left hand reached above, claws hooking into the open counter. It twisted its body, kicking off the ground, and threw itself through the glass into the booth right as another volley of nets, weighted rocks, and ropes slammed into the structure, the cheap metal shed crumpling like a tin can all around it, sending a flurry of drawn paper and ink flying over its head as it struggled to catch itself.

It cut through the door's lock with a swipe of its claws, shouldering through, and dashed forward, straight to the elongated box that had just detached from the platform, packed to the brim with humans, seeing them squirm through the windows.

It just had to jump on it and it would be free.

It could make it.

It could *make it.*

Then a line of liquid fire dashed a swift trail across the gap, a short feeble thing—the damned lizard flapping above as it tried to cut off its path. It charged forward, intending to go through it, when it felt a roar of mana surge into the flame, another spike of caution from [Danger Sense] making it hastily grind to a halt, sparks flying from where its claws cut through metal.

The little line of flame roared to life, turning into a blazing wall, six feet tall, the sheer heat making it snap its eye shut instinctively, flinching.

"Fire!"

It jumped to the right, leaping over one of the benches humans used to sit, and dove shoulder first into the thin gap between it and another, two amongst a long row, using the wide backs and seats as cover.

A deafening clatter of snapping metal rods and breaking screws filled its ears while it ducked as low as it could, feeling at least a dozen projectiles miss or break against metal, the flimsy benches folding like paper under the barrage, before a tide of nets was tossed on top of its hiding spot, the weights on the ends clinking against steel.

It swiped through the double layer of rope above it, cutting through, and then lifted its arm and tail to grab onto the backside of the crumpled benches to either side, kicking its feet against the ground to launch itself forward.

Straight through the flames.

It was over in a split second of suffocating heat, and its eye snapped open to the sight of a sheer open drop, split apart by a million cables forming hazy lines through the smog.

The box it was chasing after was idly cruising away, its chances of freedom going with it, riding on a lightly swaying pair of steel wires.

It turned its head to look to the right, where two other boxes were slowly inching toward the wolf's platform, and then swiftly turned left when its ears picked up on a struggling growl.

The fire human from before, one of his arms swaying limply by his side now, wrenched his fist toward himself, the fire wall collapsing behind the wolf.

And exposing it to its pursuers.

Stuck between its captors and certain death, it did the only thing that came to mind.

It turned around, ducking behind a few trash cans and a crystal pole to buy a second more, spun on its single clawed hand, and charged.

The edge rushed forward to meet it, the world spreading wide with every stride, a million lights and lines and outlines filling its eye.

One mistake and it was *dead*.

But it was getting used to that mental pressure by now.

The final stride came much too soon, but hesitation didn't rear its head. In a moment too fast to be registered, it felt something in its mind click into place, a tiny fragment of a moment where its thoughts were absolute, its body and mind a perfect union. Thought and action turned into a single concept.

Its tail curled over the lip of the platform from around its shoulder, its left-hand claws doing the same. It pulled, curled its legs to its stomach, and slammed them down on the very edge, the moment its chest crested the floor, then extended both arm and tail into the air in an instinctual pouncing motion.

For a moment, it was flying. Its mind sharpened, concussions or dizziness or adrenaline or fear all forgotten, adrenaline and wonder squeezing the world in a death grip.

Unbound by neither humans nor its own weakness, nor gravity itself, it felt, for a single, long second, what true freedom was like.

Its eye flicked down to the winding abyss of wires and towers, of distant mega-factories turned to little dots of sparking lightning, of a canvas with a million different lights peppered through its depths, and the image seared itself into its mind.

Then the moment was broken as the box full of humans it was aiming for rushed forward, the haze lifting, panic and mind-choking adrenaline carving through before it could even blink.

The sideways rectangle did not provide much space for landing, but it didn't have a choice. Its decision was made already.

The wolf's tail let go of its arm, managing to slam its middle point around the anchor that supported the entire metal box from the two taut metal cables that carried it, and its left arm desperately extended to the side.

Its ribs, already frayed, did not handle the impact well. A short, violent wheeze left its lungs as it hit the box, like a punctured balloon getting punched, and its tail and fingers instinctively went rigid.

Its tail strained and cracked oddly as its momentum tried to carry its lower body forward, only stopped by its desperate grip, and its upper body fared no better, bouncing off the box's roof for a brief moment before sliding. Its claws carved jagged lines into the smooth roof of the box, until it noticed and blunted them, just in time for its body to be half hanging off the side, elbow wrapped around the box's roof and legs scraping for a grip right above one of the box's windows.

Panting and wheezing through a bleeding throat, it could feel its pulse scream and pound through every tiny vein of its body, from its fingers to its tail, and with an effort that felt a thousand times more intense than any other activity it had been up to today, it *pulled*, an empty wheeze coming through its throat, bereft of vocal cords to form the growl it wanted to make.

It bit onto the box, hooking a single canine into the metal and blunting the rest of its teeth, and used its severely over-strengthened neck to assist, managing to drag its chest to the flat top, then kick at the metal as it pulled with its tail, scrambling sideways onto the flat roof.

Then it slumped, its blood-soaked tongue hanging out of its mouth and meeting delightfully cool metal as it fought for breath, seeing spots dancing in its vision. Its tail lethargically let go of the box's anchor to press back down on its arm, the crimson not yet having scabbed enough to staunch the bleeding.

Catching a flicker of fire out of the corner of its vision, it tilted its head just a bit, watching a steady flame licking away at its fur, sporadic and sputtering as the oils, blood, and water in its fur fought the heat and slowly won.

How long had that been there?

It didn't care enough to smother the fire. It would go away on its own.

Rather, it was more concerned with its body. Its lungs felt *destroyed*. Like they'd been thrown between two moving gears, crushed to a pulp, then strung back together and shoved into its chest.

And with the momentary hope of freedom and calmness, the pain of everything slowly began to register.

Its glare moved from its fire-licked shoulder to settle on the platform, a solid sixty feet away and half that distance above, seeing humanoid shapes flutter about the edge and snap at each other.

Then a human climbed onto the hook-shaped mechanism that loomed above the green lights, wrapped a bunch of fabric around the wire of the wolf's lift, wrapped his forearms around said fabric, and jumped off the spinning machinery.

It wasn't sure what it was expecting, but the human's idea seemed to work flawlessly, the fabric steadily speeding him toward it. Another few seemed to consider the idea, glancing back and forth, but none followed their singular brave kin.

To its right, another blur of battering wings descended, and it resisted the urge to screech in frustration as it tried to rouse some energy out of its abused body, knuckles grinding into the slightly swaying box beneath its chest and pushing down, lifting itself up on limbs burning with exertion.

It did *not* think about the unfathomable drop below. It didn't even dare look down. It didn't *need* to look down to feel the entire box and the worried humans squirming about inside.

It raised itself up, still using the end of its tail as a curled, tentacled replacement for its arm, a motion that had gotten a lot more comfortable to use since the first moments it did so, and watched.

The human's cloth started smoking halfway to its ride, and the wolf had no idea what his plan was. Had he *not* seen it use [Sonic Blast] less than a minute ago? How was he going to *stay* on the box once he arrived?

The flying reptile then screeched, wrenching itself to the side and diving straight toward the wolf, and it braced itself for a free snack, lowering itself and half turning.

Only for the blasted thing to immediately halt and flap its body backward the moment the wolf glared at it, then started flying in a wide circle to the right, forcing the wolf to turn with its movement to keep the thing in its sight.

It *hated* this thing. *So much.*

Another spew of fire was launched out of its mouth, cutting the thirty-foot-long metal box in two, and the wolf idly wondered how *much* the infuriating ball of scales could hold in its little body as it glared at it.

Then it realized what the reptile was trying to do.

Cut the area it could dodge to into a smaller piece.

And distract it.

It probably thought the wolf couldn't feel the human rapidly approaching behind it.

Just to prove the thing wrong, it ignored its screeching, keeping it in the corner of its vision while it turned to face the human, and in a bout of unexpected frustration, the lizard dashed forward to draw its attention.

A lot closer than before, a lot closer than it should have been.

Its tail unwound from its arm as its legs curled close to its stomach, tail pushing onto the box's roof like a spring as it kicked its lower body upward, sticky veins flaring out of the tip of the tail as it snapped through the air, only the wolf's claws burrowed into metal, preventing it from detaching completely from the container.

The thing tried to flap backward and halt its momentum, but that only made its wings extend far more forward than before, even if they succeeded in halting its body.

Slime-covered veins slapped onto the tip of a flimsy wing, and a single hurried surge of nerves turned the slime to an unbreakable bond that jerked the flying lizard aside with a shrill squawk. Its tail continued the swing, slamming the reptile onto the roof with a dull, light thud.

It swung its tail to the right, slamming the lizard into the rooftop with well-deserved vitriol, and just for good measure, it leapt a short distance forward, jumped up a little, and slammed its knuckles into the thing's chest with all its weight behind it, feeling tiny bones and organs crunch and squish beneath its fur.

Just like that, the infuriating nuisance was dead.

Its tail curled the veins back into their place, and the majority of its length settled around its stump again.

The human was coming close startlingly fast, his speed continuing to ramp despite the now-flaming piece of cloth keeping him away from a deadly drop.

It still had time to quickly bite off the twitching reptile's head, then its middle and wings, then its lower portion, finishing its meal in three hurried, choking gulps, barely using its teeth to tenderize anything, wincing and grimacing through the burning agony of its torn throat to hurry its prey along.

The fiery human's roar of rage and mourning was the most satisfying sound it had ever heard. Was the lizard his companion?

Good.

He deserved to feel what the wolf had felt, a thousand times over, purely out of frustrated *spite*.

The moment that weight settled into its stomach and swiftly disappeared, it focused back on the human sliding down the cables.

He had slowed down *significantly*.

And then he seemed to bring himself to a stop, gaze nailed to the platform, legs wrapped around one of the cables, ignoring the wolf completely.

Its eye flicked to a sudden flare of fire from where his gaze was directed, its attention stolen much like the human's.

The fiery human was . . . attacking his kin for some reason, then he spun clumsily, a blinding mote of light clutched in his broken arm's hand, like a crushed, compressed mass of light crystals roiling with fire.

Their gazes locked, hateful and bloodied both, and the human's shaking arm jerked up, aimed straight at the wolf.

It felt its instincts squirm and squeal in alarm.

And then the little mass of light flashed forward soundlessly, like the release of a spring.

Another moment of clarity, of urgency. The certainty of incoming death snapped around its body and mind like a thousand miles of chain, crushing them into a singular entity, bereft of worldly concerns, a mass of decision and action and reaction, emotionless and perfect.

[Devourer]'s roaring hunger and rage felt like the snapping of a chain link, the scream and grind of bending, tearing metal as it fought against the wolf's very being to rush out and consume without end, to tear and bite and gnash until the end of time.

This was the opposite. It was controlled, and it was perfectly . . .

Biological.

It felt like the flip of a switch in its mind, the crackle of a spark, but there was no disconnection it could feel. No *presence* or externality to it.

For all but a *tiny fragment of a second*, it felt like a machine geared toward survival. The basest of instincts.

The [Sonic Blast] that left its throat was pitifully weak. There was no buildup, no time to sluggishly command mana to flood its bruised, abused lungs. It was little more than a pop of a bark, but within every flaying string of wind and sound, etched into the absolute forefront of its mind, was an iron command.

Hold.

And it did.

A barely visible ball of roiling air left its snout, flashing forward in the blink of an eye, and met the ball of flame.

Before it could process the shock of seeing [Sonic Blast] *not* explode in its face, its vision flashed orange, the ball of light unveiling into a flood of pure *flame* and *pressure*.

The box underneath it *bucked*, a split moment before the invisible after-shock of the explosion rammed into its body like a wall of iron, and an empty sharp wheeze left its throat in place of the yelp it tried to let out.

Its body tried to fly backward, only saved from certain death by its nails being awkwardly embedded in the metal.

Its forearm spiked with pain as its muscles clenched with the strength that could only be born from deadly desperation, and the devastating shock of its weight being halted by nothing but its claws traveled down its arm, fraying bones *stretching* and muscle fibers snapping like strings.

The groan of creaking metal was followed by the snap of a steel bolt, and the pop of its shoulder dislocating for the umpteenth time came a moment before its body fell slack and began to slide across the harshly swaying roof, the stump of its right arm uselessly flailing for a grip from sheer habit.

Out of the corner of its eye, right between its legs, it saw the screaming form of the human that was clinging to the cable, falling, flailing as the blurry smog swallowed him.

The box tilted forty-five degrees, slowing its momentum for a moment, allowing its legs to scrape at metal, nails giving it some much-needed sense of safety.

Then the container violently swayed to the opposite side, the screaming of panicked humans below just barely penetrating the low whine in its ears as it twisted, two canines digging into metal, only barely managing to stop its body from flipping legs over head by the harsh motion.

A steady but choking flare of mana came from within the box, and suddenly, the swaying lessened, slowed.

Bubbling, bloody froth fell from its mouth and slid down the roof's box as it panted, eyes wide and all limbs taut with tension, its tail firmly wrapped around the creaking anchor of the box, now only attached to a single cable.

It heard more than saw the fire rapidly approaching, and for a moment, it just wanted to give up.

The box was moving at a snail's pace. It was hanging over an endless chasm. Its limbs were mangled or broken, only two exhausted legs working right. It was bleeding from so many places it couldn't even start to pay attention to each cut and stab. Its lungs didn't contract as much as they desperately jerked and convulsed for breath, something just not clicking right. Its nose and mouth were flooded with the scent of gamey iron.

Everything hurt.

Its left eye flicked to the strafing form of the fiery human, *flying* on two heels, spewing fire with a deafening, constant thrum, tinged more blue than orange.

A half-crescent turn at the box's height.

Then the human used his unbroken arm to correct his course, leaning forward, charging at the wolf's limp form.

Dark spots danced in its vision.

Still, it took a moment of exhausted trepidation to note that fire was still so, so beautiful, when it could see more than two and a half shades of it.

The human's upper body leaned back, a furious snarl on his face as his fist wound back, wreathed in orange-blue flame, a mere dozen feet from the wolf. His heels sputtered, momentum carrying him forward.

[Maddened Frenzy] grabbed a hold of every notion of defeat, exhaustion, passivity, acceptance of its fate, and tore them to shreds the instant it activated.

Savage glee filled him, the beast so close, so defeated. Every last ounce of mana he had fed into [Combustion Punch], a skill that Atrius had rarely used before.

He'd never had to.

His team was there. His thrakling, Mellow, was there.

Now they were nothing but corpses.

Fuck the job.

Fuck his own life.

He wanted *blood*.

Despair roiled with frenzied fury, shredding his mind like a tornado made of glass shards, scraping his thoughts away, leaving nothing but raw emotion and impulse behind.

He turned off his flight, poured what scraps of his mana were left into his fist, and prepared himself for impact, preparing to carry his momentum forward and turn the beast into smoking chunks of meat, himself likely with it.

A single yellow eye tiredly glared at him, the beast still panting as it lay on its chest, and his feet slammed into the lift's roof, his knees buckling and launching him forward as his quads protested.

The eye flashed a searing, blinding *red*, pupil and sclera melding into an orb of light.

A black blur of motion and sparks filled his sight, his fist slamming forward and down—

The limb tumbled, flew away from him, spewing blood from a mangled stump. His chest smashed into something, his ribs snapping like dry twigs as his momentum was brought to a sudden halt, and his head jerked down from the sudden motion, a slave to momentum, catching a glimpse of a mass of fur and blood burrowed into his chest.

An impact made him spin, something in his neck straining and breaking, the world a blur for a single long moment.

Then his vision was filled with the sharp, chilling sight of a snout that led to a baleful red star, glaring at him with pure madness, the sharp gleam of perfect teeth curling like sabers in his sight, spreading open, open, *open*, too wide to be physically possible, like the gleaming rib bones of a corpse spreading open to snap down on his soul, like a flycatcher.

They snapped shut, a moment of darkness.

He felt his jawbone be crushed flat, his eyes squeezed and pulped out of their sockets, his skull cracked like an egg—

"What the fuck is happening?!" someone screeched, right into his ear, and he growled wordlessly, feeling various pairs of hands struggling to keep him upright, the tight confines of the repurposed train segment making them all tumble into and onto each other.

Blood ran down his nose, his mana drained dry to absolution, and he felt something crack inside him, a metaphysical thing more than a biological one.

He choked on air, yet a smile of relief spread on his face.

He had slowed the swaying down. And hopefully, stopped their lift from turning into paste a few thousand feet below. Their lift hadn't dropped into the abyss, but due to malfunction or luck, its speed had slowed to a crawl. They might live yet.

"Open the hatch! Call for help or something!" a woman yelled, and he grimaced in frustration that he had no energy to act upon, stumbling into the

arms of some random stranger who mumbled random shit at him as he tried
to remember how to use his legs.

"Help?! They're shooting fucking fireballs at us!"

He'd never used his entire mana pool and beyond in the span of mere
seconds before. The skill's low level likely didn't help. He should have trained
harder.

"So tell them to stop!"

"I don't wanna die . . ."

He tried to raise his voice, tell them to *shut the fuck up for a moment*, certain he'd felt *something* on the roof that was likely what the bastards above
were mindlessly shooting at.

He was a fucking silver-ranked adventurer. If his hands would fucking
move, he just had to flash the symbol and everyone would likely listen, if only
for a moment.

But his hands didn't move, twitching and swaying, barely listening to his
commands and seemingly doing whatever they wished, and his voice—

All that came out was a wet cough, blood dribbling down his chin, something phantom-like in his chest squeezing.

"Something's on the roof! They're trying to kill us with it! Give me a
fucking sword!"

His vision slowly stabilized, and the muted thuds from before turned into
deafening bangs, the roof denting inward. The muted scrape of something
scratching at the roof from before turned into the sporadic screech of metal.
Something in the roof's wiring sparked, and the lights began flickering.

The scared crowd panicked even harder than before, and the constant
swaying of the half-broken lift didn't help.

Some old woman screamed and leapt away from her spot, pointing a
shaking hand at the window she left behind, the flickering lights only making it harder for him to focus on what he was looking at.

It was blood.

A steady stream of crimson, dripping down the window.

Screams turned to roars, someone pushed someone, it all melded together.
He could only struggle to breathe and focus on his eyes as some dude used
him as a hug toy, panicking, likely not even realizing what he was doing.

In between the flickers of light washing his thoughts away, a gleaming
sword was pulled.

Someone grabbed it, barking orders.

In the corner, a man was helped up by someone to open a hatch.

His body rose, his arms went through.

He wanted to tell him to sit the fuck down and wait for help. He couldn't.
The light flicked off.

It hadn't even been a second before the man's body violently jerked, his
scream cut short as his legs spasmed. The person holding his legs shouted "let
go," stumbling back and over someone curled on the floor.

The lights flicked on.

The man didn't fall, only being pulled up a foot higher by something out
of sight, a choked wet gurgle predating the tide of blood that rushed down
the visible half of his stomach, splattering on the floor, his shoes, the window.

Everyone jumped back, squeezing themselves into corners, screams of
terror making his ears ring.

This . . . wasn't how he wanted to die. To some fucking *thing* he didn't
even get to see. But his limbs barely listened to him. He had no mana left.
And not a single other person in this lift knew how to do anything. They
were all workers, civilians, factory bookkeepers.

He supposed there were worse ways to die. Probably.

The kicking, the noises, they abruptly cut off, the man going limp, and
with a wet squelch, his headless corpse limply dropped into the lift, crumpling to the floor.

A black blur shot through the open latch like a bullet, like a hole torn
in reality, pitch black beyond comprehension, and the faint impression of a
canine shape was the last thing he saw before the lights flicked off, the horrified screams of the dying and the splatter of blood being the last he ever heard
as he swallowed down the heart-stopping terror clutching at his heart, and . . .

Closed his eyes.

A second passed like a year, two, ten, thirty.

A sharp agony cut into his collarbone without warning, up his neck, and
then he felt something in his spine snap before darkness claimed him.

[Maddened Frenzy] didn't last long enough.

Not nearly long enough.

When the mindless desire for pure violence suddenly faded along with its
strength and energy, it was all it could do to not collapse on the floor right
then and there, the sudden retreat of the heart-searing anger almost giving
it mental whiplash.

Its jaw slackened, some unidentifiable mass of flesh hitting the wet floor.

It tried to take a step, just to dislodge its fist from where it was buried in
a human's chest, but the moment it tried to *move*, all its limbs crumpled like
paper.

So it simply sat there, panting, wheezing, rasping breaths through its abused throat, its entire body weak beyond comprehension and numb to the bone.

With every gentle sway of the lift, a tide of blood washed around the mounds of corpses filling its sight, bits of gore being swept by the tide.

The scent was *glorious.*

If not for the scent of death, loose bowels and slight ammonia, it would be . . . pure perfection.

If only it could enjoy it by taking deep breaths, which was nigh impossible with its destroyed ribs and lungs. It just hurt too much.

But it still wasn't out of trouble. It knew that. It had to focus.

It could still feel three skulls in its back, crushed but still coherent enough to be forming bumps on its backside.

It would probably be a good idea to *get up* and just collect more, or just scarf them down as fast as possible. There were at least thirty corpses in the silent lift. There was no chance it couldn't unlock the secrets of the human and even inhuman brain anatomy from eating all of them.

But it just didn't have the energy to do so.

It still had to . . . get out of the mess that would no doubt expect it when it got to the lift's destination. And when it tried to move its limbs, it felt like it was made of lead, nailed to the floor and suffering ten times the gravity it usually did.

Not so much as a twitch.

The lift was . . . dreadfully slow.

But so peaceful.

Silent.

The screams had been so unfathomably *loud* and *constant* it could almost still hear them if its attention began to wane further than it already had, and after everything that had happened in the past half hour, this was relaxing.

The gentle swaying, the splashing sounds of the blood moving from side to side.

It blinked once, staring at the silent metal box, the blood splatters covering the walls.

Thirty humans.

It killed thirty humans. It just . . . it couldn't understand it. It couldn't even believe that it had happened. Were these ones just so weak? Was the strength difference this vast between random groups of humans? They barely fought back. The most they'd done was an old man who had a *mean* punch, which had given it a very painful bruise on its arm, but that was it.

It didn't have the energy to think about it. It just accepted it.

A languid blink. Another.

Then it was in [Devourer], half passed out.

It considered squeezing its adrenaline sack just to get up again, but there was nothing to squeeze. It was drained dry.

It focused on manual changes, superficial but fast fixes. It healed whatever it could. It drained the blood pooling in its lungs and repaired as many of the burst blood vessels as it could, it replaced torn muscles with new strands and closed whatever wounds it had remaining with quick but thin films of skin.

Then it forced as much essence as it could into [Devourer] making blood and putting it in its body, just to replace the frankly terrifying amounts it had lost, and rested, focusing on vibrations as much as it could.

It might have been half an hour, or ten minutes, but the faint whisperings of solid ground came through the groaning roof.

And more, and more.

It forced itself to awaken, getting up on trembling, barely functioning limbs.

The platform clicked into place with an unsteady jerk that made the wolf drop to the floor again. It gritted its teeth and forced itself up again, antennae brushing the metal ground through the quickly thickening crimson slime covering it.

Its exhausted mind considered its chances of success against thirty armed humans, all waiting for it, bolts and sticks and needles trained at the metal box. And likely far tougher than the ones it had "fought" inside the lift.

There was a sewer entrance right in front of the platform. Just twenty feet.

But it couldn't even *run*.

It wracked its brain, and the only thing that came to mind was . . . mana. It had plenty of mana left. And its course of action . . .

Intimidation. And deception.

It had *nothing else* left.

The doors groaned, creaked, then finally slid open, halfway, lopsided. A small tide of blood came rushing out, the lights flicking off.

Darkness was scary, wasn't it? To humans, at least.

[Echoes of Oblivion] activated. Its slime veins, trembling and squirming and barely responding, gripped the crushed, deformed skulls in its backside and brought them out into the open air, three floating messes of flesh with the vague shape of a human face.

Its tail curled around its arm.

And with a desperately steady gait and confidence it didn't have, it started walking.

The creaking lift slowly approached, and the sound of groaning screws was all there was to grace the tense silence they held.

Closer and closer.

The lights within flickered, and as it got closer, the dark-red blood coating every window in wild splashes and dragging handprints became all too easy to notice.

He felt like he was in some kind of fairy tale, doomed to watch the reaper's boat cross the river of death as it neared.

Marleen began shaking next to him, little twitches of her shoulder. He wanted to grab her, turn and run, job be damned.

They were fucking *gangsters*. They weren't monster catchers.

Still, they had a job to do, even if it had only been barked to them through a comms tablet thirty goddamn minutes ago without any notice or warning.

The lift creaked and croaked, slowly getting closer.

There was no movement in the windows he could see. Just red. Dripping down the windows, from inside and *outside*. Shredded bits of organs and flesh were strewn about the whole roof, intestines loosely connected to a mangled chunk of bleeding flesh and exposed bone that might have once been a torso.

The metal itself was gouged out like it had been turned into the scratching post of a dragon, and he could see the rough, jagged lines of metal crisscrossing all over it even from fifty feet away, the way they'd filled with blood that dripped with every sway.

It felt like years before with a bang of metal meeting metal, it docked into the silent station, and the doors creaked open.

Blood poured out of the doors, like someone had poured *buckets* of it inside, a rush of crimson slime, revealing a formless mass of shredded clothes and flesh and gore strewn about on a dark iron floor when enough was drained out of the lift.

Nothing moved for a shocked, horrified second.

The miasma of death and blood that washed over them was so thick he could *taste it*.

"What the *fuck*?" Marleen gagged out, her breath coming out in harsh pants, a hint of hysteria in her voice. "What the *fuck*?" she repeated, her voice growing garbled, her hands shaking on her crossbow.

He wanted to tell her to calm down. He *had to*. He was the leader of this rushed hack job.

But he felt the same.

The icy chill of terror brushed against his spine, and his hands shook as he ground the butt of the crossbow into his shoulder with bruising force.

A limb, an arm or leg, he couldn't tell, suddenly, languidly stretched over what used to be a man crumpled at the doors.

His breath caught in his throat.

It wasn't *black*.

It was pure nothingness, an absolute *void*.

Slowly, as if taking its time, as if taking a stroll, a canine shape made of pure black prowled out of the lift.

On its back, three swaying tentacles holding mangled, decapitated heads. Mockingly swaying back and forth like bells, like soundless chimes, barely recognizable as more than clumps of flesh. Its left arm moved low to the ground, its right a formless tentacle that curled and uncurled with each easy step.

"Demon . . ." someone whispered, and he realized his hands were shaking so bad that he couldn't even find where the trigger was to *shoot*, to lead by example as he always did. He couldn't even *shoot*. He couldn't breathe.

Marleen let out some strange choked sob, and he heard the clatter of her crossbow hitting the ground before her footsteps broke out into a sprint, fading away.

Followed by another, and another.

"S-s-shoot," he choked out, a croak of terror, eyes wide as the beast, the demon, the monster, got closer.

Nobody did. He wasn't even sure if anyone was next to him anymore. He couldn't see anything but the horrific abomination, the bloodied lift looming behind it, and three skulls, mockingly swaying back and forth, taunting him over his fate should he do as he, himself, commanded.

The beast lazily hooked its claws around a sewer cap, just thirty feet away, and the void receded, just a little bit, to reveal a gleaming golden eye glaring at him.

He was going to die, he was going to die—

The crossbow fell from his hands, and he turned around, stumbling over his own feet, scrambling away, and ran with all his might without looking back, fearing that if he did, all that he would see would be an empty void that would consume him.

CHAPTER 7

Katherine sighed, blinking sleepiness out of her eyes as she gulped down the tea cradled in her palms with far more speed than strictly necessary. The heat did nothing for her bandages nor the injury they were wrapped around, but she couldn't really care for such a little problem right now.

Lady Anna let out an undignified groan as she shifted on the couch, her dirty-blonde hair haphazardly strewn about the pillows as if spread by an errant wind.

"This wasn't the favor I was expecting you to ask when we gave you one," Lady Anna grumbled, eyes closed, body going limp, even her voice laden with exhaustion.

"I see. Was your expectation more or less troublesome?" she asked, despite feeling like calling Emhreeil "troublesome" was a rather grave insult.

"More. Just not for me," Lady Anna replied before peeling her eyes open halfway and tilting her head to give her a scrutinizing look.

She calmly met it.

"I believe it would not be excessive to inquire as to what your relationship with that woman is. Father's been . . . *fussing*, I guess is the right word. We don't have the greatest information network, but wheedling out some concerning facts about our guest was alarmingly easy. And fast." Lady Anna's her tone hardened in tune with her gaze with every passing sentence.

She sighed again, forcing her eyes open. When had she closed them?

"She is my old master," she murmured, and took another sip, her eyes on the floor. She wasn't sure if she should have admitted that, but she trusted Lady Anna. To some extent.

"So why on *Ergos* did I spend *six hours* saving her life?" Lady Anna asked, tone light with something she couldn't quite place. It sounded quite close to the sarcastic sweetness of someone who was, in fact, quite annoyed.

She mentally blanked for a moment, wondering what Lady Anna even meant, before realizing and letting a long, tired sigh leave her lips.

"She's not . . . she's part of the family that used to own me. She's not the person who bought me. Or scarred me. She's the one who gave me my freedom," she explained, lifting her eyes, and noted with quiet relief how Lady Anna's glare softened to a curious, albeit cautious, look.

"Oh. I apologize for my assumptions."

"No need."

Silence stretched for a few seconds.

"What was her family name?" Lady Anna asked, and with backbone that was long absent in her life until now, she gave her a thin-eyed look of warning, her black eyes meeting green.

Neither caved.

Lady Anna huffed.

"This isn't curiosity. I *need* to know, in case they send someone to take her, or somehow implicate us with her. Most highborn families aren't content to just *let* their children walk off into the dungeon. *Especially* elves who have children once every half century at *best*."

She worked her jaw for a moment, gaze straying to the rich mahogany wood that lined the walls in the waiting room.

"I cannot tell you. I do not know if I can trust you with that information. Should you know, how would you guarantee nobody else comes to find out? How would you guarantee that you won't be *forced* to tell them? I refuse to let loose information that might implicate her back into politics, into people seeking to use her as leverage, or a pawn, or a trading chip. I cannot risk the chance of her family finding out where and who she is now, and taking her back."

"Why not?" Lady Anna asked, brows furrowed. "Surely going back home after all . . . *that*"—she waved her hand at the medical bay's closed door to emphasize—"would be a pleasant change in comparison."

"It wouldn't," she replied, a lot more snappily than she intended, and watched Lady Anna's brows rise in response.

"Apologies. And my reply was rather hasty. I mean more that, while maybe it would be *preferable* to living as a cripple in the dungeon, that is not our decision to make for her. And I will not elaborate further. It is not my place."

Lady Anna's eyes slid shut, and she sighed.

"All right. If you can't tell me, I'm afraid you'll have to take her and leave tomorrow, as soon as possible. She should be all right on all fronts except her eyesight and arm, as those are not things I can do anything about, nor can any healers in our employ. Should any complications arise, send a radio message from the relay station. You know our frequency. It might take a bit to reach us, but we'll get it, and I'll tell you what to do. I'm sorry for this, but . . . we're all in a precarious situation. We cannot afford to have complications like this lying around, figuratively and literally."

Katherine took a deep breath, already planning things out in her head as her eyes flicked to the scruffy green head poking out from behind Lady Anna's couch, staring at her.

Route back to her apartment, trip supplies. How to keep her safe. How to budget what was left of Emhreeil's money in a way that would get her back on her feet, to some extent. Did she have time? Room? What would she do with the goblin? Now that Lady Anna had temporarily fired her, she might have to find a different job. Maybe two, or even three, if Emhreeil couldn't work. At least until this civil war business settled down. If it ever did.

Would she have to flee Carmera with her? She didn't know how civil wars ended. Some type of massacre or genocide wasn't . . . out of the range of possibilities, at least. Considering Emhreeil's actions, if the kingdom won . . . She might have to grab her and go to Synttha.

The cost of that was . . . *enormous*. Getting a ship to and from Carmera to any of the three continents that surrounded it needed an entire armada of battleships, armed to the teeth with enough warding and magecraft to fund a small kingdom for an entire month. For each individual trip.

The entry fee to boarding such an entourage was equally over the top. Maybe if she was a close friend of the sole trade company that could afford such shipments, she could get a discount, but that wasn't even a far-fetched option.

So . . . new jobs. Multiple. As long as it didn't involve prostitution, she'd do it. She didn't mind. She'd work herself to the bone for her, as long as it helped her. She was used to it.

"All right."

They sat in silence from there, each too tired to continue a discussion that had brought itself to a close. Minutes passed, her eyes growing heavier with each second. She'd done a lot today. Six hours of pacing behind Lady Anna as she healed Emhreeil had likely not helped.

Then an idea popped into her head. Her eyes, with a small and fast struggle against exhaustion, peeled open.

"Lady Anna."

A questioning hum was her reply, and so she answered.

"Would it be possible to give us a golem's eye? Not an implant, or a flesh-graft, just . . . something she could wear around her wrist or neck, and use to see. Mana activatable, at least."

Lady Anna's eyes flitted open, half lidded and hard, staring into the ceiling for a moment before nodding slowly.

"We can do that. They're not *terribly* expensive. Should have one in a few hours of me sending the request. Now let me take a nap, please," Lady Anna mumbled, closing her eyes, and Katherine nodded.

It had been a very tiring day for both of them.

The hazy, soft embrace of sleep slowly enveloped her mind, her body slackening on the couch as the minutes ticked by.

A desperate scream pierced through the night and her heart both, drilling into her ears, barely muffled by the wall separating the two rooms.

"Katherine, calm down. She's probably—" Lady Anna started, forcing the words through a yawn, but she blocked her words out, heart clenched with worry and ears strained to hear any other sounds from within the room.

She launched herself forward, stumbling over the coffee table and sending at least four things to break on the floor, and she crashed into the door, wrenching it open with more strength than she'd intended.

She only caught a glimpse of Emhreeil's torso violently jerking up from the bed and only had the time to let out a gasp of surprise before a flash of orange rushed to fill her vision.

She took a deep breath, hearing the wolf's footsteps draw farther and farther away, struggling to keep herself calm.

Its steps grew fainter.

It will come back. It will come back. It will come back.

The soft thuds of its paws turned to less than a whisper, a mere hint of existence like the puff of a drawn-out breath, before that, too, disappeared.

It was going to come back. Emhreeil knew it would.

She gulped as seconds turned to minutes, each breath infinitesimally faster, deeper than the last. There wasn't enough air. Rational thought cracked under the weight that crushed her lungs, and as she panted, harder and harder, she clung onto that single thought.

It would come back. It had to. It wouldn't leave her.

The pipe tightened, and what was once a curved but relatively flat surface turned into a tight curve under her back.

She realized that she couldn't even hear her breaths anymore. Not a peep of sound. Nor a single ray of light. Bile rose up her throat, her stomach clenching painfully, and she opened her mouth to yell, to call it back, to scream for help. Nothing came out but a soundless huff of air. There was no scratch at the back of her throat. No vocal cords.

She struggled onto her stomach, soundlessly gasping for air, feeling the unending chill of complete and utter isolation, despair, and hopelessness pierce her very soul like a billion freezing needles. Her nails scraped at rusty iron as she wriggled, trying to scream for it to come back, for help, for anyone or anything to come to her, hearing little more than the brush of a feather against her own eardrums.

The pipe tightened, pressing into her sides, and she tried to bring her arm back, to push her body into a more comfortable position, only for her elbow to hit metal, straight metal, metal that reeked of shit and blood and clogged her nostrils with the familiar stench of death. She couldn't bring her arm back.

The first sound to greet her ears was a squeak from behind her, distant, and she froze, her convulsing lungs halting all motion, her spine being twisted like a rope between the gauntlets of terror as she clenched her jaw, feeling tears run down her face, choking on nothing, screaming for no one to hear, not even herself.

Another squeak, a chitter. She scraped at the pipe, feeling her nails break, her clothes tear, her skin be scraped off by rusty walls as she wriggled like a worm through the tight confines, soundlessly sobbing, screaming, begging. The pipe tightened, pressing tight against her shoulders, crushing her hips, and no matter how much she bucked and struggled, no air entered the black holes inside her chest, no distance was covered.

She took the deepest breath she could, feeling her ribs creak as they tried to expand, as the pipe tightened. She tried to scream with everything she had, feeling her empty stomach heave from the effort. Not even a whisper of sound came out. Empty air.

The pipe tightened, and for every inch of space she crossed, another inch tighter. Her shoulders were crushed into her spine, her hips forced to conform to the width of her waist, her bones bending from the force.

Squeaks, the soft patter of a thousand little feet.

She tried to buck, to squirm like a worm, to wriggle forward like a maggot, like the insect she was.

The pipe pressed harder, digging into her chin, the back of her head, pressing her into its shape, her bones snapping like twigs. She tried to kick with her feet, to press forward, but couldn't move an inch, the pipe ensnaring her in an iron grip, crushing, holding.

The squeaks turned to screeches.

She screamed into the void as she felt the familiar sensation of teeth digging into her feet—

A sharp, deafening *bang* to her right was the impact that made the glass mirage shatter and snapped her back into reality. She bolted upright, her abdomen cramping from the sudden movement, and a loud, sharp gasp of surprise came from somewhere to her right.

Her left arm wrenched itself forward, a hasty [Sparkburst] blowing out of her hands just to buy time, create some distance, her body curling to the right and bucking forward to slide off whatever she was lying on.

The sparks hadn't even finished rushing out of the invisible framework over her palm before she sent a wave of mana out into her surroundings, feeling rough outlines. A woman in a coat, a smooth concrete floor, shelves covered in jars, a couch.

Her legs hit the floor—

And completely buckled, without a hint of resistance.

She activated [Haste] right as her knees slammed into the hard floor, and she put as much mana as she could into a flash of [Illumina], being rewarded with a startled shout by her assailant.

Were she more experienced, less disoriented, she might have come up with a better plan, a better maneuver that could throw her to her feet in an instant.

As she was, she tried to lean back and away toward her right, put her right leg against the ground, yet only managed to step on her own left ankle, tumbling back, barely managing to stay in a semi-upright position by clutching at the sheets out of sheer reflex.

She wrenched her arm forward, intending to throw the sheets forward, a movement born from panic rather than a plan, her lips pulling into a snarl—

"Em, *stop!*"

And she froze, her body turning to stone.

She let go of the sheets, uncaring of the fact her body slid to the ground without the support, and sent another rush of mana into the room, focusing on the person hissing and rubbing at their eyes, holding a hand out in front of their head as if it would shield them from a spell, gingerly trying to step toward her.

Her jaw slackened, her mind fuzzy and muddled as harsh pants rushed in and out of her throat.

This—

She was still dreaming, wasn't she? She did that a lot lately. She could remember most of them. Was she dying?

"Calm down, please," Katherine said, her voice so familiar, so steady, so *real*, and she gritted her teeth, grabbing the edge of the bed and feebly pushing herself to her feet, legs quivering, swaying in place, gulping in greedy lungfuls of air, making sure to keep her hand turned toward—what she hoped was—Katherine, sending a steady stream of mana to fill the room, to *feel* every inch.

Memories slowly rushed back to her, of burning chemicals that melted her skin, of a spray of blood meeting her face.

How did she get here? Was this her old home, outside the dungeon? There was so much wood. And *leather couches*. She had to be. Where else would she be? She couldn't see to confirm the sunlight, but there were *windows*.

Was Katherine even real? Her dreams always *felt* real. Would she collapse into a pile of rats, squeaking and screeching as they rushed out of her limp clothes on the ground again?

She steeled herself, wrenched her arm to the side, and punched herself in the mouth.

It . . . hurt.

"Emhreeil—did you just— Okay, *please* calm down. Please. Do you . . . recognize my voice? It's me, Katherine," the woman rushed out, her tone just shy of pleading.

Emhreeil didn't have the space in her head to process words, focusing on the throbbing sensation in her cheek.

It hurt, but just barely. Just barely enough to not be sure if it was true pain or phantom pain, like her brain telling her she was in pain in her dreams without making her feel it.

Her breaths sped up, thoughts racing as she stumbled away from the bed, away from . . . from someone who *couldn't* be Katherine.

Her hand came up to fist into her hair, only to meet skin.

She was bald?

Was she a prisoner? She'd . . . she had killed two guards. They caught her, didn't they? Was this some weird form of interrogation? Illusions, psychics, she knew no punches were pulled in the pursuit of "justice." She might be talking to a particularly good actor. Shape-shifter?

It hurt too much to hope otherwise.

Needing something to ground her, something to make it *hurt*, she turned to her left and punched the wall, with far more speed than her body could handle, the [Haste] too potent for her frail body, and the sharp crack of something breaking in her hand was what made all the haziness of sleep and ambiguousness of her conscious be washed away by pure, *real* pain.

"Oh," she breathed out, hollowly, [Pain Resistance] much too high leveled for her to feel anything more painful than a dull throb, and she spat out a hiss of a breath and tried to backpedal, her stump moving to cradle her broken hand with another that wasn't there anymore by sheer reflex.

Two steps back, she felt her knee buckle, collapsing backward onto something metal that slid away, a million metal little *things* clattering to the floor, around her, on her, and she kicked with her feet, backing up to the wooden wall.

She just— One *moment to think*. That's what she needed.

"Emhreeil, *please. Please*, calm down. You're safe. It's me. Katherine. You're in House Kervile's manor. We're on the top end of the third floor. The year is 6832 After Descent. The month is Hurile, day twenty-two." Katherine's voice was deep and as close as one could get to calmness, just like she remembered, getting closer one tiny step at a time, like she was approaching some rabid animal, and she sounded so *real*.

Who the *fuck* was Kervile? And she couldn't remember what year it was *before* she'd been dropped into a rat-infested pit. None of what she said held any meaning. Any proof.

Some part of her whispered to her that she was being needlessly paranoid. Another grumbled that she wasn't paranoid *enough*.

"B-bottom right, on your . . . on your back," she gasped out, scraping her heels against the ground to flatten herself against the wall even further, her muscles coiling. She considered the window to her right, how likely she was to die if she jumped through.

How likely it was that she would jump through the window into another empty room, the skittering of a giant spider in an empty ruin being the only companion to her gasps.

Who she hoped was Katherine paused.

"Above the back of your hip. What is there?" she demanded, mana gathering into another [Sparkburst], more and more, every bit of the mana that had filled her to the brim of bursting, a little explosive held within her broken hand, ready to explode should she direct it.

She felt Katherine's features contort into pure confusion for a heartbreaking moment, feeling the fragile roots of hope wither inside her, dread pooling at her gut.

Then Kat's expression slackened with realization, her right arm dropping limp by her side.

"An L-shaped scar. Small one. I stumbled when tending to the rose garden, the thorns peeled my shirt up, and a particularly big one buried itself in there to the hilt. You stitched it together three days later, cussing me out for pretending to be tougher than I am and hiding it," Katherine said, a healthy dose of fondness in her voice as she resumed her steps, passing the couch and carpet, the metal table that smelled far too much like disinfectant, a mere dozen feet away now.

Something tight and warm roiled in her chest, pushing against the back of where her eyes used to be, anger, adrenaline, and desperation washing away like water through a sieve.

It hurt to *hope*. To hope that this wasn't another feverish lucid dream, to hope this wasn't some elaborate interrogation ploy.

But the proof was there. The throbbing pain in her hand, the memory nobody but the two of them had, and one of the two faces she feared she'd never "see" again, the voice she'd started to forget the pitch of, after two impossibly long years of separation.

"K-Kat?" she croaked out, her voice warbly, her energy leaving her, and she felt her pants turn into shuddering gasps, tears soaking into the fabric wrapped around her eyes, her body going limp.

"Yeah, it's me, Em. A little . . . hard of sight because of that spell you threw, but it's me. Can I come closer?" she asked tentatively, her features lightly pinching in concern as her steps slowed and stopped, lifting the hand rubbing at her eyes to give her an earnest look she couldn't possibly know that Emhreeil could see.

She felt something in her chest crack open like an egg, something warm like joy and liquid honey enveloping her clenching heart.

Instead of answering her, she pushed off the wall with her forearm, forcing her legs to curl beneath her torso and push her off the ground, forward for just two rushed footsteps before her legs gave out and sent her tumbling.

Katherine darted closer with speed she didn't expect from her, and she crashed into Katherine's chest, her left arm loosely throwing itself over her right shoulder, her nonresponsive weak fingers tugging at her smoking coat, unable to form the fist she wished to make.

"K-Kat—" she started, wanting to speak, to say something that was intelligible, an apology, but all that came out was a choked sob.

An arm snapped shut around her waist, the other coming up to the back of her head and pressing her head into her shoulder, and she flinched violently, something instinctual she couldn't quite withhold.

Katherine tried to pull away but aborted the effort when Emhreeil let out a garbled "*No!*" and tried to tighten her half hug.

She tried to speak again, a stuttered, shuddering sequence of letters coming out of her mouth before she choked on air, grinding her head into Katherine's coat, trembling from head to toe, sniffling and sobbing uncontrollably because *she was here*, she was *alive* and *real*.

She'd almost fried her friend's eyes out by sheer reflex. She couldn't ask for forgiveness enough. She couldn't explain how much she missed her.

"*Gods*, you're so *skinny*," Katherine whispered, sounding horrified at the way she could fit three people of Emhreeil's size into her arms, and she choked out a broken imitation of a laugh at the fact that *that* was what she'd first noticed was wrong with her, feeling Katherine's hold tighten a little in response, the only thing keeping her upright.

"Hey, you're okay. I've got you. You're fine. You're safe. Nobody's coming for you," Katherine whispered, barely audible over her own sniffling and choking, something oddly hard in her tone, nuzzling her head, a familiar motion that lacked the blood-soaked fur she was used to, a familiar notion that felt wrong *without it* but felt much too comforting to care.

Emotion crushed her heart, seared thoughts to nothing, demanded release lest it crush her sanity to bits. Warm joy, crushing guilt, cold despair, hopeful relief, empty *loss*.

Emotion left her a wordless wailing mess, fingers scraping at a scorched coat as she babbled half words mixed with choking sobs, apologies without structure, limp, drowning in the scent of smoke and Katherine, letting the comforting words that passed through one ear and went out the other lull her to unconsciousness before she'd even noticed it.

A sharp twist within that phantom sensation of *presence* in her mind made her gasp awake again, hearing a familiar voice call to her, the thudding rhythm of boots hitting stone.

She ignored it, frozen, feeling a distant *pull*, a direction, a faint brush against her mind.

That direction was *up*.

The mote of sensation moved, a tiny space with steady strides, just far enough to where she didn't know *what* it was doing but was close enough to *feel* it. Faintly.

It . . . *wasn't* a dream.

"He's alive," she croaked out with a breathless sigh of relief, feeling like a two-ton block of steel was lifted off her chest.

Then she laughed, a weak, bright thing, and blasted mana into the room, feeling Katherine's wide eyes settle on her.

"Katherine?" she asked, smiling, mildly delirious, ready to announce to her that her friend was alive and she had to go find him, ask her to come with her, but hesitated for a precious moment.

A smile across a face tight with worry. A nod.

This was real. Katherine was real. Her murderous canine friend was *real* and *alive* and fighting something *right now.*

There were a lot of words, speeches, possible conversations she'd play out within her mind when the wolf would drag her through the pipes, about what she would say, and how, to her best and longest friend.

Her mouth opened as she struggled to push herself higher up on the bed, then dropped open, slack, feeling like someone had just pulled the rug out from under her, her body freezing.

She couldn't feel him anymore.

Just like in that sump, there one moment, and like a lightbulb flicking off, gone the next.

But that didn't mean death the first time, apparently, and likely didn't mean death *now.* That didn't even mean he was injured, as far as she knew. It could be a skill it was toggling on and off, or something erratic by nature.

Besides, he was a *wolf.* He was a tough bastard. He was still alive, likely strolling along some alley after whatever fight he'd just had, munching on someone's hand.

She knew he was somewhere above too. And she still had Katherine, staring at her with a concerned pinch in her features, extending a hand to her shoulder and squeezing wordlessly.

Her breath stuttered, and she quickly swallowed.

"I . . . hi. I really missed you," she eked out, unsure of how to begin or what to say, mind mildly overwhelmed by the suddenness of everything. Should she tell her? Was it safe? Did it *matter?*

Katherine's smile widened.

"Hey, Em. I know you did. You told me plenty last night," she said in a tone laced with mild teasing.

Before she could respond to that embarrassing tidbit, Katherine forged onward. "It's a little early, but do you want to eat something? You *really* need it. We can talk later."

The casual tone *really* helped with calming her down. If she just stopped thinking so hard, she could almost forget she'd not seen Katherine in two-something years, and her other friend was, against all odds, alive.

She tried to wet her lips, but her tongue was as dry as sandpaper. All too aware of the black hole eating through her insides where her stomach was supposed to be, she sighed.

"I . . . do you have blood? And water?" she murmured, and felt herself shrink even further into her warm, soft blankets at the blank stare she perceived on Katherine's face.

"Em. Why are you drinking blood?" Katherine bluntly asked her, her voice hard, and her head snapped to her, despite the lack of eyes to convey her surprise at the sudden change in her voice.

"I-it's . . . it's a trait. Vampiric. Blood heals me and feeds me. So . . ." She trailed off, and Katherine opened her mouth, then her jaw clenched, and she clicked it shut.

"Later. Later," Katherine repeated quietly, seemingly to herself, and nodded with an audible sigh. "Okay. Give me a second. Do you need it straight from the source, or would a syringe work?"

"I don't know," she breathed out, and Katherine nodded before turning away and walking to a metal table on the other side of the room, covered in little pots full of medical tools, and began the process of drawing her own blood.

She took the time of silence to try and process everything.

It felt wrong to sit here, comfortable and warm, when she had so much to do. She had to go find the wolf again, she had to finish that creepy guy's chore from the sewers, sell the—

Where was that golem core?

Judging from the plain, light clothes she was wearing, someone stole it, or if she was willing to be *very* optimistic, it was being kept in a safe place somewhere around here.

"Don't touch that," Katherine's voice snapped, and she turned in her direction, brows furrowed.

"What?" she croaked, confused.

"Not you, the goblin," Katherine clarified, voice soft, and another pulse of mana revealed what she meant, a childlike figure skulking back into its corner to curl into a ball, its oversized shirt mostly being used as a rucksack, its large pointy ears curled back like a scared puppy as it wrapped its hands around whatever was in its shirt.

She couldn't really feel what was in there, nor did she care enough to try.

Her mind drifted back to the man in the sewers and the job he'd given her.

"Third floor, fourth quadrant, walk down street ninety-three, just past the open square. Ask for the bishop. Tell him the password, sell the golem core to him, and give him the compass. The password is the phrase . . ." She trailed off in her mutterings, her brows furrowing as she struggled to remember. "I saw a . . . ghoul on a conveyor belt, and it turned around to smile at me."

Right.

That didn't mean anything as long as she had neither core nor compass, but having that hanging over her head was disconcerting at best. Would he get mad at her for not doing her "job"? He could probably easily kill her.

Nobody weak delved that deep into the sewers, and nobody sane stayed there for long. That freaky mutant hanging from the pipes down there was *proof* of what happened to those who did stay there too long.

Right, so, she had to find out where the wolf was. Fast. Then finish that man's orders and . . .

Use whatever favor she gained from the priest of that church to beg them to find a vampire to turn her. Something which might not even work. But even if it didn't work, she could "see." She wasn't weak and helpless anymore, despite her emotions being an erratic mess.

Katherine strode back toward her bed, one hand clamped around a cupful of blood and the other applying pressure to a small needle puncture above her elbow.

"Stay in bed, please. You *need* rest," Katherine chided as she continued walking, and she stilled in confusion before realizing she'd been coiling up to throw herself out of the bed, her waist bent, legs half hanging off the bed, her teeth gnashing together in excitement.

She nodded and consciously settled back into the bed, struggling to tamp down the urge to throw herself out of bed and just *run* up, trying to catch the wolf and drag Kat with her.

And the urge to rip the cup out of Kat's hands.

Katherine placed a hand beneath her neck, the other bringing the cup down, and she tensed in discomfort and embarrassment before quickly relaxing, warm tears pooling at her eyes again as a surge of nostalgia flooded her chest.

Even if this situation was far more morbid than simply being sick on a warm silk-covered bed with Katherine trying to keep her fever from being too frustrating, their positions were too similar to not let her mind drift to simpler, easier times.

Then the cup tilted, and her next inhale brought forth the scent of iron and something deeper, gamey and *sweet, so sweet*—

Her hand moved up to clutch Katherine's fingers tight around the cup, and she brought her head forward, wide, draining the cup in three hurried, open-mouthed gulps, rubbing her tongue over the top of her mouth, noting the subtle tastes hidden under layers of iron and copper, unidentifiable.

She sagged back into the bed with a satisfied groan and a deep breath, letting go of Katherine's hand and the cup held within.

"Sorry. It's hard to control myself. Are you okay? A cup's worth of blood isn't . . . a little," she awkwardly said, trying to not be too obvious in the way she was licking every crevice in her mouth to chase the taste.

Before Katherine could reply, she felt her lips move, words without forethought leaving her mouth.

"You taste good."

Whatever Katherine was about to say devolved into a choked sound like an aborted word, before devolving into an undignified fit of coughing, halting laughter, her hand moving up to cover her mouth as her shoulders shook, her eyes scrunching up with amusement.

She winced.

"Sorry, sorry. I— That was a weird thing to— *Can you stop laughing?*" she grumbled, and felt a smile tug at her lips as her friend's laughter redoubled, her own chest and stomach starting to convulse with quiet amusement.

It genuinely did feel like they'd only parted yesterday.

After a minute or so, the amusement faded, and silence came over them, an easy, albeit fragile, one.

Katherine broke it first.

"Emhreeil . . . what happened?" Katherine asked, voice soft as she came up to the elevated bed, turned around, and leaned against the very edge, staring at her face over her right shoulder.

She swallowed, heaving a sigh, feeling like her mind was swimming in an ocean of remembered events.

"I . . . it's a lot. And I don't know how much I can tell you," she murmured, and felt Katherine's right hand extend over her body to grasp her left wrist, a gentle pressure that just stayed there as a sign of support.

"Tell me everything you can," Katherine said, earnest and soft, so she swallowed past the lump that was settling in her throat, and nodded.

"After we parted, I . . . spent a lot of days floundering around, trying to figure out how everything worked down here. Then I went to the Adventurers Guild to register and bought a [Haste] spellbook." She stopped once she felt the muscles in Katherine's neck and jaw stir and flex, followed by her face.

Katherine's face tightened in a way she couldn't decipher.

"*Why* did you want to be an adventurer?"

"I was stupid. And naive, and just . . . so *fucking stupid*," she muttered, her voice hardening in self-loathing, her chest tightening as her mind wandered to days spent in dirt-cheap inn rooms, waking up covered in sweat and sticky fluids with bile tickling the back of her throat and rope burns searing her skin, cigarette smoke mixing in with the scent of sweat and sex to make a miasma that seared her nostrils.

Her stomach momentarily clenched, but having nothing but a bit of blood in it, it didn't even try to heave its contents back up through her throat.

"I just . . . I thought adventurers were synonymous with free individuals, you know? People who did as they wished, moved where they wished, lived as they liked. I never wanted to go into the Factory. Just . . . find a team, maybe skirt around the sewers taking extermination quests, level up, eventually leave Carmera and go to someplace nicer. The Kotetha Empire was . . . probably still *is* taking back the desert after the whole Ascendancy fiasco, and they always needed more adventurers to help. I'd wanted to go there afterward, maybe with a couple adventurer friends if they too got sick of the dungeon. Or . . . maybe you, if you didn't . . . hate me." Her voice grew weaker and heavier.

She cleared her throat a bit and grimaced.

"Could you get me a bit of water?" she asked, and after a moment of silence, Katherine nodded and hurried to a sink at the other end of the room.

As she did that, she simply relaxed back into the bed, anger sparking in her mind the more she began to remember how she'd acted, what she'd done without a shred of forethought. God, she wanted to just . . . find her old self and bash her skull in with a rock. How the fuck was she so *stupid*? Well, no, she knew the answer to that. It just didn't quite make accepting her past absurd naivety any easier.

Katherine came back, and she quickly drank the small cup of water before gesturing to hand the cup back to her, feeling immediate guilt for treating her like a servant.

"I—I can . . . take it back," she offered, drawing the cup away from Katherine's reaching hand.

A slow, confused blink, a tilt of her head.

"You're exhausted and recovering. And I want to hear your story. Let me."

With a slow nod, she gave the cup back and felt the blanket until Katherine had taken her post beside her once more.

Before she could resume, Katherine sighed.

"Em. You're my best friend. I don't hate you. At all."

"You should," she replied quietly, and instantly regretted it, feeling the flash of pain that crossed Katherine's face. Fearing a little, that Katherine might follow logic and agree with her regardless.

"Em, the only thing you've ever done that has wronged me is dropping freedom into my lap and walking away without giving me the chance to enjoy it by your side," Katherine said softly, and grabbed her wrist again.

Warmth and confusion warred for dominance in her head.

That— How could she even *think* that?

Her jaw trembled as warm tears dribbled out of her tear ducts, guilt stabbing icicles into her chest, and her throat tightened like someone had put their boot on it.

"I . . . y-your ba— Your b-back." She sniffled, gritting her teeth because *why couldn't she stop crying—*

"Is *not*. Your. *Fault*," Katherine ground out. "I don't *care* about my back, Emhreeil. I'm not crippled, and looks hardly matter to me. It's just a bunch of scar tissue. Stop beating yourself up over that. It's been *years*."

"B-but, all th-that pain. They would *whip you* . . ." she hissed out, before pulling her head back and digging it into the pillow under her. "*Okay*. If you say so, okay."

"Okay, as in, you'll stop beating yourself up over an old and forgotten bunch of injuries, or . . . ?" Katherine asked leadingly, softly, and she gulped.

"I'll try."

Katherine nodded, smiling a little, rubbing her thumb into her left wrist at the pulse.

It was immeasurably comforting.

"Good. That's all I can ask. But we got off track. What happened?" her friend asked, and she took a moment to think, to digest.

"It . . . long story short, I found a team. Th-they looked decent, weren't complete newbies, but were looking for someone who could buff their party. Everything looked perfect. I bought a spellbook for [Haste], I had some minor telemancy and another spell that made sparks, but they told me they really wanted me to get another one. A light spell, because without light, fighting even a rat is near impossible in the sewers, and you never know when a lamp or a flashlight will break. I didn't have money to buy that one, so they offered t-to . . ."

She trailed off, swallowing once, twice, trying to clear her throat as if it could clear the phantom rock that had nestled into its base.

"You used to like hugs. Do you want one?" Katherine offered softly, and her clattering teeth tried in vain to grit against each other.

"Y-yeah," she warbled out, and then a moment later, she felt two hands settle around her shoulder and hip, dragging her to the edge of the bed, before warmth and softness enveloped her, Katherine's hair tickling her nose as an arm wound around her back and waist to lift her up just a little.

Her left arm curled around Katherine's shoulder, and she let out a shuddered exhale of relief as she placed her own head on Kat's left shoulder.

"Thanks," she mumbled, muffled even further by Katherine's coat pressing into her face.

"Go on," Katherine prompted, and she nodded faintly.

Her coat still smelled like smoke.

"They offered to lend me the money to buy an [Illumina] spellbook. Gave me a long slip of paper, just a simple loan contract with a blood-drop signature. Then, as soon as I'd signed, they . . . I—I don't want to talk about it. Long story short, I became their slave." She *felt* every single muscle in Katherine's body tense and flex, her grip becoming almost tight enough to hurt.

"Was it as bad as Irythiel?" Katherine whispered, steel in her voice, and she tightened her hug, trying to burrow into her friend to drive away the shame and disgust crawling under her skin like a thousand writhing worms, her stomach clenching painfully.

"Worse. My mom n-never . . . They w-were w-worse," she spat out, her shoulders quivering, her nails digging into Katherine's coat.

"I fucking *hate* crying. Why can't I stop?" she warbled out, and couldn't contain the little sob that followed.

"It's okay to cry. I'd be a lot more concerned for your mental health if you *weren't* crying, Em," Katherine murmured, poorly concealed rage in her voice as she forced her muscles to relax a little. "The things you've gone through are harrowing to *listen to*. So just cry. It's okay. I do it myself sometimes. You walked into hell, and I'm sure you'll walk out of it stronger than ever with a bit of time."

She spat out a sound, a choked, mangled thing between a sob and a bark of laughter.

"I've killed people. I killed people, Kat. I'll n-never . . . I'll never be the same. I'll never be the person y-you rem-remember again."

"That's all right, Em. People change all the time. Besides, I don't think you had a choice," Katherine softly soothed. "What happened after?" she questioned, preventing her from replying to the first part of her comment, likely on purpose.

"W-we, we went to do a r-regular rat ex-extermination request. In one of the waste pits. Th-they hadn't real—" She cut herself off to choke down another odd sound that tried to come out of her throat, allowing her friend's warmth to drive away the bone-rending cold in her insides.

"They hadn't realized h-how many rats there were down there. And then they asked me for light, s-so I gave it to them, and . . . there were so many rats. Not fifty or a hundred like we'd thought, it was *hundreds*, just, just a wave of screeching fur almost as tall as we were. We tried to retreat but couldn't do so fast enough. We got overrun. *I* got overrun. Th-they . . . ate my eyes, my skin, my f-f—" She gagged on nothing, a dry heave, her body coiling, legs instinctively curling up to her stomach and hitting Katherine's ribs in her panicked rush to curl into a ball.

She could never forget the feeling of rotten teeth digging into her body. The grimy, sandy, branch-like texture cutting through into places that had never been exposed or touched before, the unimaginable discomfort and revulsion, the searing agony of her flesh snapping apart like a network of strings and goo.

The feeling of her eyes being pulled out, trying to tug her brain out of her skull with thin strands of agony that snapped and tore.

Instead of letting go, Katherine gently shushed her, rubbing soothing circles in her back, barely reacting to the strike.

After a few seconds of harsh breathing, she growled through shuddering breaths, wiping the wet blindfold on Katherine's shoulder as more tears just *kept coming*.

"I hate feeling s-so fragile. How did I kill two people without blinking a-and now I can't even t-t-talk because o-of some f-fucking *rats*. I'm s-sorry," she ground out, feeling her nails protest against the leather they were stabbing into.

"Don't apologize. You're . . . not just human, but the expression remains. I won't judge. Just take your time. When you're ready, tell me what happened after that."

"No, I . . . " she weakly protested, then immediately hesitated as she thought of what happened after . . . the rats.

Her unnamed furry companion was a *wolf*. If *anyone* knew there was a wolf alive, there would be a hunt. And if that information somehow reached the kingdom . . .

There would be an army.

She hadn't read up on why wolves were so zealously hunted. It was just a reality she needn't look into, she thought, because nobody had even heard whispers of a wolf in centuries, beyond baseless rumors or botched attempts from mad biomancers trying to bring them back for whatever reason.

But complete control over biology . . .

What if her friend decided it should procreate? How long would it take before he would have birthed a dozen other wolves, and a dozen more? It's not like he couldn't just change his gender on the fly.

What if he could concoct plagues to wipe out human life in the dungeon? What if he didn't *need to*?

The more possibilities arose, the more the vague threat of a lone, intelligent wolf loomed in her mind, and there was no doubt left in her that if the kingdom heard of this, the dungeon would *burn* to get to her . . . inhuman friend.

She really needed a name for him, at least in her head. Later.

The simple, current fact was that she wasn't sure she could share the truth. Not the *whole* truth. At least not yet. She didn't know when, but *not now*.

"We, uh . . . w-wouldn't make it to the latch anyway, we were getting overrun. And then . . . something broke the staircase. I didn't get a good look. We fell down, crashed around the trash pit. My 'teammates' all died. I didn't. There was this . . . creature. Beast, maybe monster," she said awkwardly, and felt Katherine's encouraging nod against her shoulder, her hold tightening a little.

She wasn't about to say anything that pained her like Katherine was probably expecting her to, but she still appreciated the gesture.

"It was . . . smart. And for some reason, it helped me. It brought me a healing potion, nudged it into my hands, and after I drank it, helped me by dragging me out from underneath the debris. We sort of just . . . hung around after that. For what felt like weeks. Nobody came for us. Kat, it-it fed me. Kept me alive," she whispered, and felt Katherine's brow furrow within her mana field.

"Kat, it-it fed me. Kept me alive."

She frowned in confusion.

Why was it so easy to form expressions around Emhreeil? She usually couldn't even figure out what her facial muscles did, but now everything just . . . clicked in her head. To frown, do this. To smile, pull the cheek muscles back.

Idly, as she considered Emhreeil's words with suspicion and disbelief, she wondered if this was how normal people felt.

"The creature fed you?"

Em nodded.

"Y-yeah . . . My legs were broken, s-so I couldn't even stand up. I-it would just hold dead rodents over my head and let the blood drip into my mouth," Em breathed out, voice full of warmth.

What?

What?

Why did Em sound so *fond* of the memory?

She was *so confused.*

At least that part of the story explained how and why she had a vampiric trait. And the couple dozen parasites and diseases Lady Anna had to cleanse out of her system before they started showing serious, debilitating symptoms.

"Hold on. Are you sure it was an animal?" she asked, giving Emhreeil a comforting squeeze, rationalizing that maybe the elf was a little bit delirious or hallucinating at the time. Or maybe just met some kind of shapeshifter type with a mysterious streak.

"Yeah, Kat," Em mumbled. "It would growl and snarl, and it dragged me out from under t-the debris by biting into my clothes and dragging me out. It— I even cuddled with it at some point. I can't tell you . . . *what* it is, but it wasn't a humanoid of any kind. Four legs, fur. Kind of felt like a dog, but . . . very mutated."

She felt amusement trying to tug her lips into a smile of disbelief.

"You *cuddled* with some . . . unidentified creature? In a trash pit?"

"Well, no, in the pipes *below it,*" Em said.

Trying to imagine Em even *touching* a stray kodzer or dog of her own free will was hard, but the mental image of her cuddling with some unidentified furry creature in some sewer pipe was just . . .

She felt like her brain was shutting down.

Change wasn't supposed to just . . . smash her in the face like this, but here it was. Some part of her was proud and intrigued at how different her friend had become, while another whispered to her that change wasn't always good, especially if it came from such suffering.

"But, yeah, we sort of . . . huddled together down there. It was . . . nice to me, beyond some hiccups at the start where we were both tense and unsure. I would have died a thousand times over if it wasn't there. It even used its own *blood* to feed me later," Emhreeil whispered, her tone blatantly nostalgic and warm, and she couldn't quite find the words to express the strange mix of emotions she felt.

The only one she could identify was a sense of disgusted, disbelieving wonder and intense confusion. She hadn't even known that emotional cocktail was possible.

And . . .

Its own *blood?*

"I . . . okay. What happened next?" she asked.

"They f-filled the pit with poison gas to get rid of the rats that were coming back up. The-the mutant, or whatever it was, dragged me into the trash pit as it activated, and we fought between the gears against . . . a *lot* of rats. It protected me. I still don't know why, but it did. After we fought off the rats, we just found some pipe and crawled into it. Then we just crawled and climbed around the sewers and some abandoned factories until we found an open tunnel that led us to a toxic sump. That's where some . . . giant aquatic monster found us, and fought my . . . uh, buddy. I ended up getting flushed into some . . . facility with those two guards, and after realizing they wouldn't help me, I killed them to . . . drink their blood. And live."

Emhreeil's voice quieted toward the end, but before she could figure out a way to soothe guilt that was entirely unnecessary, Emhreeil continued.

"I . . . I thought it died, but . . . just a few minutes ago, I felt it, fighting somewhere. Way up above," Emhreeil finished, voice tight with worry and anxiety, her tone almost like she was asking her for something that she couldn't quite piece together the contents of.

A few minutes ago. So that was what had woken her up.

She blinked rapidly at the wall, confusion making her mind stutter as it tried to parse through what she'd heard, backtracking in the conversation for a moment. The questions mounting with every second were swamping her head.

Way up above?

How did the damn thing get up to the *second floor* from the bottom of the third, in just two days? Was it using lifts?

"I— How did you know you were going through abandoned factories?"

"Oh, I have . . . a skill called [Mana Touch]. I can feel things if I throw mana at them."

That . . . she'd never even heard of such a skill, likely because it sounded way too specialized and way too out of her league to even grasp the coattails of.

So she just nodded, grateful that Em had a way to navigate.

"Okay. And *how* did you 'feel' it fighting?"

"I . . . I think it might have a skill. I don't know. We could feel each other whenever either of us was fighting something. Position, where we were directing our attention, stuff like that." Emhreeil pursed her lips, thinking.

Then her eyes widened.

"[Pack Hunter]. That's the skill it has. So it is definitely an animal of some sort. At least by origin," she asserted, and a short silence stretched after Em nodded again.

"How did you lose your arm?" she blurted out, then immediately winced, not wanting to put Emhreeil through the pain and trauma of remembering that when it wasn't even something that mattered anymore.

Contrary to her expectations, Emhreeil giggled, a small, teary, but blithe sound.

"It got infected. I asked the, uh, beast, to bite the limb off. Then I cauterized it with [Sparkburst]. Hurt like hell. A-and th-then, the smug little fucker started *eating it* like I'd given him a snack." Emhreeil snickered a little, her shoulders jumping, relaxing her body, her legs sliding back down to lay flat against the bed rather than pressing into Katherine's side.

She just goggled down at the teary, laughing mess in her arms, wondering *what the hell could possibly be funny about that*, and breathed out, low and deep, letting the information sink in.

All that suffering, the betrayals, the apparently *thousands* of times she'd have been dead if not for some unidentified furry thing with [Pack Hunter].

Mutant dog, maybe? A Tillenhall experiment that they'd discarded again without thought nor interest in the harm it would cause?

She was getting sidetracked.

What she could focus on was how *easily* this meeting could have never happened if just one thing had gone wrong. How unbelievably lucky she was that Emhreeil could even be there to laugh and cry and dirty her coat with fire and tears.

"You said you felt the, uh, creature, right? Somewhere up above?" she asked, and the remnants of laughter quickly subsided from Emhreeil's skeletal frame, a sight which had her skin crawling with unease and a motherly desire to stuff her full of food until she looked like a balloon.

"Y-yeah. I . . . I *need* to find it again. I . . . I wish I could stay with you, I—I *want to*, but I can't just let it roam around, I *can't*. It's going to get itself killed. It probably doesn't understand how much danger it is in. And . . . I can't just forget about its existence. I don't want to . . . abandon my friend." Emhreeil gulped.

Katherine's jaw clenched.

Try as she might to tamp down on such feelings, she couldn't help it.

"So it's okay to abandon your *human* friend, again?" she whispered hollowly, her hug tightening, struggling to tell the chill of betrayal in her chest that Emhreeil was just a little dense and likely had no idea what was going through Katherine's head.

Rationality unfortunately rarely worked on emotions. Curse them.

"What? *No*," Emhreeil hissed in reprimand. "I— Wait . . . you want to come with me?" Emhreeil breathed out, all her fire gone, replaced by surprised, hopeful awe.

Gods, this girl . . .

She was going to smack her one day.

"Why would I *not*? Em, of course I want to come with you, are you *kidding me*? I'm not letting you out of my sight again until I'm old and gray and stuck in a wheelchair," she said, voice firm. "Beyond protecting *you*, I also just . . . can't keep going like this."

"I— *Keep going like this* . . . ?" Em whispered, voice distant, utterly still. "Are these . . . Are your new employers like my mother?" Em asked quietly, her voice tight.

Then Katherine shook her head, and Emhreeil seemed to mentally stumble, expression shifting against her shoulder.

"No. I just . . . I feel purposeless. I want to be by your side again. If not as a maid, then as a bodyguard. Nothing else feels right. So yes, I want to come with you. Both for you and myself. And I can *fight* now. I'm not just a meat shield. We can find your mutant dog together, if it means so much to you, and I can protect you while you do that."

And with those words, Emhreeil fell silent.

For ten seconds, it was awkward.

After thirty, it became a little concerning.

She pulled back a little, and felt Em's arm tighten around her.

"Just . . . just give me a moment to think. You said . . . What did you mean 'abandon me *again*?'" Em asked, sounding completely, genuinely clueless.

She sighed.

"Em, do you remember what you said when we . . . parted ways? You basically said I deserved to be free and live a nice life, that I 'deserved better.' Because you have a very guilty conscience about things you *shouldn't*. But you never asked me if I *wanted* to go and be free alone. It's not worth it, from what I've experienced. I'd rather be your maid again."

Emhreeil shifted in her arms, growing lax. "I—"

"No, Em. You pushed me away because you were feeling guilty, and you were beating yourself up over things I didn't care about anymore. You gave me freedom then just . . . left me behind. And I understand why. I don't blame you. I *know* why you did it. But please don't do it again. I don't want you to leave me behind again as you go off chasing whatever it is you need in your life. Let me come with you," she finished, softly and earnestly, and felt a full-body shudder course through Emhreeil.

"I—I hate crying," Emhreeil ground out through a small series of shuddering gasps, and Katherine rubbed her back, nudging her head with her own.

Then Emhreeil took a deep, stuttering breath and pressed her forehead into her collarbone as she began to speak.

"Okay. Okay, I—I'd love it if you came. I m-missed you. Not as m-my slave or bodyguard, though. Just my friend. B-but just *promise me*. When, w-when a sudden realization comes, *promise me*, you will not s-share anything to anyone about me or the . . . creature. T-to *anyone. Ever.* Please. I can't tell you, not yet, but . . . *please*, d-d-don't . . . don't hate me," Emhreeil rushed out, her voice wavering and warbly, gradually going smaller and meeker.

She squeezed her tighter, tight enough to feel the pressure in her arms, crushing her friend's tiny form into her chest.

"I can't hate you. Ever. No matter what, Em. I promise, whatever you can't tell me, if and when I know, I'll keep it to myself. I'd swear it on a blood oath," she said, and barely heard the jumbled sound that Em sniffled into her coat, which vaguely sounded like "Thank you."

"Let's stay like this for a bit. We'll grab your stuff and go to my apartment tonight. We can't stay here," she breathed into the light fuzz growing on Em's head, and felt her nod.

"Then, we'll go find your friend."

CHAPTER 8

Finding an empty nook it could stuff its body into was surprisingly easy. These underground nest tunnels were full of them.

It took a bit longer to find a *good one*, but it managed.

It had to kill a few stray rodents to get to it, but even in its half-dead state, that wasn't very difficult, and so it had found itself a clogged little tunnel with a metal grate in the middle, which it shuffled into, pointed its snout at the entrance, and *finally* fell into [Devourer], with both the time and peace available to see what it could improve on.

And the list was *long*.

After healing itself to functionality again, just in case, the first thing it did was add more strips of the wood-like underskin armor. It had saved its life when the human stabbed it in the neck, stopping his blade before it could go any deeper and pierce something like an artery, so it simply considered where these strips would be needed, where its weak points were, and wrapped the thin mesh around them.

Four wide strips across its abdomen, with a bit of overlap, one *very long* strip running across the back of its neck down its spine, almost to its tailbone, and two vaguely cylindrical tubes around its legs, to protect tendons and arteries once more.

It would take a couple days for those to grow in, and the cost was *enormous*, but that was all right. It had more essence than it could even try to use in one session.

Next were the things it had gained from that spearhead shark.

They were all incredible. But almost none of them fit well with its biology.

The shark's skin was almost like the wolf's in its layered and protective form. Its topmost layer was like a sponge that sucked nutrients and food from its environment, a *very efficient* process, then underneath that was leatherlike skin, stretchy and bouncy but tough to cut or pierce.

Under those layers was a tightly packed thicket of tiny bones within a thick pocket of fat. So even if one got through the skin, they'd then have to cut through what must feel like flexible bone, so tightly packed within the fat as it was.

It was fascinating, but the skin and its layers were far too heavy and thick for the wolf's biology. And making them thinner would very negatively impact how protective they were, how mobile. It was just not something designed for the wolf's size. The spongelike layer that passively fed the shark was useless, as its fur was incompatible with that, and the wolf wasn't *swimming through its food* most of the time, so that was another great thing that simply didn't fit with its body.

The next thing it gained was the thing's cell structure.

In short terms, it had just gained agelessness and natural, infinite growth. Which would be great if it didn't have those already.

In longer terms, the thing just *didn't age*. Its cells did not age, it never stopped growing. A spearhead shark that was five years old would be just as spry as one that was five hundred years old, even if significantly smaller.

On any other animal, it would have been a great power-up. For the wolf . . . it was already functionally immune to aging, and it could force its body to grow to whatever lengths it wished, so long as it was careful about strain on its heart and such details that might harm it.

The next few things were most definitely usable, however.

First, braided muscles.

They were functionally *twice* as powerful as its current muscles, without adding any bulk to its form or weight.

Which explained how that colossal thing could whip and twist around in the water like it was a snake floating on empty air.

The problem was its bones—and energy consumption.

Bending bones was one of the best upgrades it had done so far, and they were the anchor to which muscles were connected.

So if it used muscles that were too powerful, every pull would force its bones to bend and fray in strange, uncomfortable ways that would contort its body in the middle of a fight.

It also reasoned and *saw* that twice the power didn't mean it used the same energy. Fully contracting a braided muscle took twice as much energy as a normal muscle. Which meant it would tire out *twice* as quickly if it began using its muscles to their full potential.

Which meant that it would have to be very careful with how much force it used. Unnecessary force was energy being wasted.

So it had options now.

It could either strengthen its bones and give up on a lot of their flexibility, but not all, to replace all its muscles with braided ones.

Or it could only use braided muscles in places where it really needed them, like its "fingers" or its jaw muscles. Bones with surface areas too small to bend, in places where it could definitely use more power.

It opted for the first option, at least for now. Making sure not to work its muscles too hard would take some practice, but it would be worth it.

It slowly replaced all of its musculature with braided muscles and tightly packed its bones with hardened connective tissue, without adding any micro-tendons through it to balance out the hardness.

The result was a slight increase in weight, a big increase in durability, and the added option of having its bones actually crack and snap with enough force. They still bent more than any bone should, but they *could* snap in two now.

Hopefully it wouldn't come to that, but it knew better than to get its hopes up.

With that change finalized, it focused on the shark's tail.

It was an almost vertically flat piece of biology, with flesh and bone and tendons in the middle but a specialized rubberlike mass of . . . scar tissue covering the top and bottom of it.

Its purpose was simple. Absurd shock absorption on the upper and lower portions of the tail. The shark could make three-foot-wide pillars of stone crack with a single blow, and it wasn't merely its toughness that let it do that without its tail snapping in two. It was in fact that the scar tissue shielding its tail was seemingly *designed* to minimize or neutralize impact for the shark to the point where it was ridiculous.

It was even disconnected from the flesh itself, *just* enough to not slide around when it moved its tail, but just disconnected enough to where the impact physically couldn't really travel through its tail.

The wolf was sure this had some great applications.

It just couldn't figure them out.

It could cover itself in this and be invulnerable to blunt force. But it was the same issue as the shark's skin. Too heavy, too thick, too awkward.

It could put this scar tissue on its *own* tail easily, but it would only hinder the prehensile nature of it. Rubbery scar tissue or not, it was *thick*, and it wasn't *liquid*. It would get in the way.

With a mental sigh, it discarded that idea, and instead got to work on figuring out how to add a second tail to its body. Its tail had saved its life many, many times, so more of something good couldn't hurt.

At the start, it considered just making its bottom spine branch off into two separate tail bones, but it would have to mess with its walking that way, its hip bones would have to be redesigned, and it would feel and work very awkwardly. Instead, it picked the vertebrae where its tail connected to its spine and significantly thickened them, gradually, before taking the first base vertebrae of its tail and making it even wider, having to redesign a bit of its muscles and tendons to do so.

The end result was that where its tail began, the first vertebrae was enormous enough to fit a whole other tail, which the wolf quickly added.

It had the feeling it could add a hundred limbs and control them all without much issue.

Which gave it . . . *ideas*. A lot of them. And while some of them might stretch its own self-definition of its body, many of them *didn't*. They weren't big or drastic enough to where it would feel like a brain connected to a mass of flesh that wasn't really its own, no longer a wolf.

Putting them in the backburner for a second, it copied its original tail, a comfortable length twice as long as its body was, and simply told [Devourer] to make another one on the free space its tail bone had to offer.

That change, surprisingly, [Devourer] said would only take a couple hours.

It tried to find out why, but at this point, it had learned not to question everything about its skill or how it worked. It wouldn't get answers, and any answers it would get wouldn't really help it, as far as it knew.

That done, it went back to what it had gained from the spearhead shark. The most important and the most troubling aspects it had saved for last.

That thing had multiple brains and hearts.

It had one . . . biggish brain in the middle of its triangular head, and then, like the branches of a wire system being undone, stems of tissue extended to the edges of its massive skull, peppered with tiny versions of its own brain, the bare, most basic parts. Then, through its gargantuan neck, two tubelike tunnels full of nerves and brain tissue extended down into its body.

Unfortunately, it hadn't eaten the thing's torso, so it had no real idea what those were doing. It could assume that they would add more tiny brains into its body, presumably connected to other sensory organs, which would transfer the information back to the main brain, already processed and translated.

These brains were all . . . thoughtless. Nothing but a mass of neurons and fats and proteins and cells that were all completely and utterly dedicated to processing information, offloading the strain its main brain would be under from having to use slightly higher thought as well as parse through its regular senses.

It had eaten . . . a lot of human heads. It knew what parts of the brain did what, what glands did, which neurons did what. The structure, the stem, the base, the odd division most brains had.

So it could say with relative confidence that it *could* add these brains to its own biology. They had no memory, no thoughts. No emotions, no ingrained reflexes to stimuli. There were no chemicals in there to do that, no glands, no neural connections. Just mindless brainpower.

Which sounded odd, but was true.

And on top of that, they worked *amazingly* with its own skills and biology.

One of the only limitations it had run into with its vibration antennae, for example, was informational overload. But if it could add these tiny little auxiliary brains along the inside of its torso, it could probably add *hundreds* of antennae to its body, make every footstep give it a detailed feeling of everything within hundreds of feet, without even really trying or focusing.

It could make its nose as sensitive as it wanted. It could add more ears, more—

More *eyes*.

It wouldn't have to fight annoying flying things by having to turn its whole body and head toward them. It wouldn't force itself to face its attackers due to that tiny insecurity that between one footstep and the next, in that tiny instance a dashing human might be off the ground entirely, they'd do something strange and manage to hurt it. It wouldn't have to *guess* where projectiles were going.

And nothing would really be different for its *main* brain. It would think at the same speed, do everything the same. Maybe it would even be *better*.

But those were still . . . brains. Parts of one, at least.

So it hesitated.

It thought long and hard, ran through possible problems. Did it again. Dismissed them one by one.

And in the end, it didn't really have any reasons left *not* to add them, and a mountain of reasons to do it.

With its heart beating fast enough to make its sleep uncomfortable, it made a little pocket in its abdomen, which was a mass of bunched muscle and a few glands, and put *one* auxiliary brain in. Ran nerves up its spine to connect it to its main brain, and then extended two thin tubes to the side of its waist, like the shark had done, and at their ends, it modeled crude sockets, eyelids, and eyes, jutting just a little bit out of its waist. It took the normal protective film around its main eyes, made it several times thicker, several times denser, strong enough to where one could reasonably bounce a pebble off its "testing eyes" without even making them flinch. Then it ran thin networks of nerves back to the auxiliary brain.

It confirmed its changes with a mental affirmation and dove out of [Devourer], pushed away the updates of the symbols, and anxiously slept for a few hours before noting the eyes and auxiliary brain had finalized, and shocking itself awake with adrenaline.

It didn't really feel very different. Oh, sure, it could feel its own flesh cannibalizing itself only to be replaced by a braided superior one, it could feel plantlike strings wriggle under its skin as they grew from its own flesh, it could feel how its body was a little heavier, a little more *stable* and *firm* on the ground, but mentally?

Nothing had really changed. Its memories were still there, there were no . . . strange, murky visions of places it had never seen before, no strange instincts to go dive into a puddle of water somewhere. None of the things it was worrying about.

The first thing it noticed was its new tail.

It felt like it had been there all its life. Swirling it around the confined insides between its hind legs, and the grate of the tunnel wasn't even weird or difficult. And it certainly felt as strong as its first one.

Then it turned to the new eyes, positioned on either side of its waist.

Getting its body to realize those were there was a bit more difficult and time consuming, but after ten or so minutes of fiddling around, it managed to force the eyelids open.

And resisted the urge to howl and yip with joy, its body vibrating in excitement. It scraped its claws at the stone as its tails slammed into the stone, wagging, keeping a messy bunch of happy sounds contained in its chest.

After so much pain and misery and constant fighting, this little bit of joy felt a thousand times sweeter.

* * *

The sight wasn't the same as its normal eyes. The protective film over its auxiliary eyes was so thick and dense that everything was fuzzier, less colorful, and shorter-sighted. Even while staring at stone that was a mere six inches away, it could tell.

But it had *eyes* in its *waist*. It had gone from one point of view to three.

And it wasn't . . . terribly disorienting, somehow. It felt like . . . as if someone had taken the area at the side of its main sockets that prevented its eyes from turning, and replaced that empty void with sight. Like its world had expanded.

Moving them around wasn't quite as easy, as they were rather weak, but it had put the muscles in there in the sockets, so it *could* make the eyes swivel and look around independently. It was wonderful.

It really wanted to go back into [Devourer] and add more of them, and after an hour or so of vibrating with excitement it had no outlet for, it managed to knock itself out with a healthy dose of melatonin and do exactly that.

The brains themselves weren't big. They were thin and long, merely the root of a brain, really, just enough for reflex and momentary, relatively weak processing, and thus no more than half an inch wide and three or four inches long. So it could put in a lot of them. Especially with how much bigger it was now. It was entering the "huge canine" territory, or so it felt. It had only seen something as big itself maybe once when it was a pup.

So it put in a lot of these brains.

Two at the bottom of its gut, where its intestines used to be, for the pair of eyes it had built, which it moved down to its hips. Putting them there was a pain, as so many moving parts meant that it had to be careful of the nerves extending too much or pinching and breaking from its wild chaotic movements in fights, but it thought it managed it.

Six more brains in the middle of its gut around the glands, which it connected to the antennae in its legs, before adding even *more* antennae, making a loose network that peppered its forearms.

Two at the top of its guts, which it connected to another pair of eyes it placed at its waist, just under its rib cage.

Then it connected all its auxiliary brains to each other, and then to its spine, leading them up to its real brain, finalizing the connection. A network of information.

The auxiliary brains would take in stimuli, take the burden of processing that stimuli into things that made sense, translating reflected retina light into vision, translating vibrations to position and feeling, and then move the processed information into its main brain. It was a little slower than the tiny amount of time it took for its main brain to process vision from its main eyes, mainly due to the smaller distance the information had to travel through its nerves, but it would *work*.

It would work perfectly.

It woke itself up again as soon as its eyes were finished, which it assumed was more than a few hours, just to see if having six eyes instead of four would be any more disorienting.

It wasn't. Anything around itself in a circle, it could see now. Sure, not as clearly, not as quickly as its frontal eyes, but no more guessing, no more spinning for a flying enemy it couldn't track. It was satisfied.

It even noticed how much *lighter* and *faster* its thoughts were without a thousand stimuli distractions demanding its mind to process them simultaneously. The auxiliary brains were so incredibly useful it wanted to howl in joy.

But that incident next to the burning rivers had taught it its lesson. It was being hunted, for reasons it didn't know anything about. Best to keep quiet.

It pushed that out of its mind for the moment, then it tried to go back to sleep, with the vague desire to open its skills and change itself further.

Then [Devourer] opened the moment that thought and desire finalized and processed in its mind.

While it was awake.

It stood there for a moment, all of its eyes glazed over, confused and bewildered.

It tried to check its body, to dive into its biology, and the rush of information was a sensation of panicked confusion rapidly building as images and sensations and understandings flooded its eyes and ears and mouth, and it could taste blood for some reason—

Then something snapped and made its brains all shut down.

It came back to the real world almost ten confused, dizzy seconds later, fully aware it had just spent a dozen seconds staring thoughtlessly into empty space, wondering what the hell was happening.

At first, it experimented.

It tried to delve into its own body on a surface level, as detached as possible, and found it nigh impossible. Then it closed its eyes and ears to focus, tried harder, and it . . . sort of worked. It could feel itself on a surface level. Tendons, flesh, skeleton, the easy parts.

Trying to delve into something too much, too deep, like individual cells and such, it just made the wolf black out again, finding itself completely thoughtless for another few seconds until its brains all . . . restarted, for a lack of a better word.

It was fairly certain that if brains didn't have that self-defense mechanism, it would have just given itself either some kind of aneurysm and killed itself, or at least massive brain damage. Just from using its skill.

Now it could understand why [Devourer] had so far insisted it should be sleeping to use it.

Maybe the paradoxical inactivity of its own mind sleeping had allowed [Devourer] to sneak into the picture and deal with the massive amounts of information without burdening the wolf. Maybe there was something more mystical going on, but it didn't know what, and it doubted it would ever really know.

But it still wanted to try, so it experimented again.

It could still "see" its body, as long as it focused and reduced outside stimuli. Anything up to seeing individual muscle fibers was . . . doable. Organs were generally fine. Anything more in-depth made its head swim and stumble, but if it pushed for things too overwhelmingly complex, like trying to read into the nerves of its eyes or something even more complicated, everything shut down.

After half an hour or so of finding out its limits, it delved into a different part of [Devourer].

Saved patterns.

What felt like a lifetime ago, it could idly remember making . . . experimental templates of sorts. A version of itself with a pair of ears on its neck, for example, just as a test. One it had never applied, of course.

If it wanted, instead of thinking and directing [Devourer] into doing something, which took time and effort in the moment, it could have just spent some time a couple days ago, for example, to make a template of the changes it wanted, and tell the skill to apply it to its body whenever it decided it wished to add it.

It still had to make the changes itself. The only difference was that they just didn't apply until it told the skill to. Saved but unused.

It was an interesting part of its skill, but it had just never found a use for it. It had always been rather redundant. It felt more tedious and worrisome than just putting a bit more mental effort into making sure things in its body were topped up with more direct attention.

But maybe . . . it had finally found a use for it. Because templates were *easy*, even on its exhausted mind.

It barely had to think of that old neck-ear design, and mentally prodded [Devourer] into applying it, before it felt the tingles begin, felt a small fistful of its fur start getting sucked back into its skin.

Hurriedly, it pounded its main brain with melatonin, forcing itself to sleep, and took manual charge of [Devourer], canceling that change and pushing its fur back into place.

And that's when it noticed something it hadn't been paying too much attention to.

Two of its auxiliary brains were inactive in its abdomen. They had only just finished forming, and the nerves were still creeping through its flesh to connect with each other, and so, without any stimuli, these brains were effectively inactive for . . . now . . .

Inactive.

As in . . .

Asleep.

It paused for a moment, thoughts racing, threatening to pull itself out of sleep again with its frenzied, racing speculations.

[Devourer] was a skill. It came from the symbols.

And as far as it knew, the symbols were just . . . something made from the world, weren't they? Another unthinking phenomenon of the world, like gravity. They were just there. Strange and difficult to predict, but they didn't seem to be alive.

They were like a universal law or maybe a fixture, or so it thought of them by now.

So, if the symbols, or whatever rules guided them, weren't intelligent . . .

How would they differentiate between "main brain" and "auxiliary brain"? Would they even care or bother to make a distinction?

[Devourer] might have activated simply because *one* of its brains was asleep, and the wolf had thought of how it wanted to use the skill then, making it open automatically.

Maybe the skill and the symbols that made it thought that one completely mindless brain being asleep was enough to keep the wolf from harming itself. An artificial safety block or something, which it had just bypassed by complete accident.

It thought back to the *other* thing it couldn't use without being asleep. The symbols themselves.

Not wanting to interrupt the process of the two brains making a connection, it made another even smaller one, designed to be inactive and forever without stimuli, and placed it right outside the small loose cluster it had safely packed within its abdomen with shock-absorbing fluid. Isolated from the network.

Then it waited for a bit, enough for the melatonin to flush out of its system, and forced itself awake for what felt like the hundredth time, the moment all of its brains and eyes were finished.

It called the symbols, and they answered. They didn't rush in, white squiggly shapes across a swimming black background with aftershocks of light in the background, not like before. They just sort of . . . filled its sight. *All* of its sight, all of its eyes. It was strange.

-Species: Wolf
-Race: None
-Name: None
-Path: [Hound of The Keeper] Level 29

Base Attributes:
Strength (+1)
Speed (+1)
Dexterity (+0)
Endurance (+10)
Perception (+1)
Resolve (+1)
Intelligence (+6)
Soul (+1)
Available: 8

-Racial Skills: [Pack Hunter], [Quick Learner], [Devourer]
-Acquired Skills:
[Pain Resistance - Level 28]
[Infection Resistance - Level 9]
[Poison Resistance - Level 29]
[Corrosion Resistance - Level 8]
[Disease Resistance - Level 4]
[Magic Resistance - Level 6]
[Mental Resistance - Level 29]
[Electricity Resistance - Level 4]
[Restful Awareness - Level 26]
[Tough Skin - Level 18]
[Iron Stomach - Level 7]
[Mana Perception - Level 15]

[Mana Manipulation - Level 17]
[Soul Perception - Level 4]
[Echoes of Oblivion - Level 8]
[Bloodrush - Level 8]
[Logotexnia - Level 6]
[Sonic Blast - Level 8]
[Tremor Sense - Level 7]
[Maddened Frenzy - Level 6]
[Mana Conversion - Level 4]
[Danger Sense - Level 4]

-Acquired Titles:
Witness of Divinity: You have seen a being of divine nature in their own realm. Your illuminated gaze shatters all illusions and pierces through any and all falsehoods.

Glutton Beyond Compare: You have eaten multiple times your body weight over a single uninterrupted period of consumption. You gain +1 in Strength and Speed while your stomach is adequately filled.

-Acquired Traits:
Survivor (3 / 5): You have felt the chill of death many times, and survived. You have fought against impossible odds and won. You are significantly tougher than your frame might suggest.

Hunter (1 / 2): You hunt living creatures, whether it is for survival, sport, or personal gain in one manner or another. You are slightly harder to notice when intending to hunt.

There was no headache, nor stab of pain or confusion.

The only difference was that no matter how much it focused on the symbols, that flash of knowledge and understanding of what it was looking at was immensely muted. It could still remember the rough numbers and understand that it had gained an absurd amount of levels in almost every skill, and that its "Struggler" trait had progressed to . . . *something* better, it assumed, but beyond the barest hint of a concept, the symbols gave it nothing.

Experimentally, it tried to put an attribute point into Speed.

Speed (+2)

It didn't feel any huge difference beyond feeling like a few pounds of weight were just removed from its body. Not from its mass, but from the force that gravity exerted on its body, without drawing back on the force its body exerted on the ground beneath its feet.

Simply put, it didn't make any sense.

It felt similar to putting a point in Strength, but less . . . present. It was like its body was just a little bit more detached from the laws of the world than before, and it couldn't quite understand how no matter how much it waved its arm around in a circle and wriggled in the tunnel to figure out what was different.

Still, it could use the symbols while awake now.

So it could . . . theoretically, give itself attribute points in the middle of a fight? It didn't know if that was a good idea, to throw points into whatever might save its hide in that present moment rather than something that would save its hide in a future fight, but it was something to consider.

Considering that it gained levels from using its skills and killing things, it could gain a level in the middle of a fight and then put that attribute point into something immediately.

That was incredibly, immensely helpful.

It had to take a small break, just to let its mind process everything. It felt . . . oddly dazed, in a good way.

It still had a couple of changes to shift through. The flying lizard it had eaten and the furry orange thing, it hadn't even checked on yet. It still had to figure out the possibilities of how it could put this accidental boon to use.

It certainly would not be able to delve into its body and patch itself up in the middle of a fight. It had difficulty doing so while completely safe, in nigh-perfect darkness and relative silence. It would be completely impossible while dodging and getting battered around or running.

And then it remembered the templates, the . . . copies. It wasn't sure what to call them in its head. It just knew that they were easy to use.

So if it simply made a copy of its body every time it rested, and told its skill to revert to that state . . . the skill *should* theoretically heal it. It wouldn't be fast, not when thinking in the terms of a chaotic fight, where a minute was a lifetime and a half, but it would be fast enough where the wolf would never have to worry about its condition getting worse in the middle of a fight. Bleeding, open wounds, as long as it stalled, it would inevitably end up better and better until it was healthy again. It would only lose a few hours' worth of progress to its ongoing upgrades.

In fact . . .

Energy was . . . technically, for the most part, just how much oxygen was in its blood, as far as it understood. Lactic acid was just what caused muscle weakness after exertion when oxygen supply was not enough.

It was a fledgling idea, but it just realized it might have just found a way to make itself completely inexhaustible.

If it made a template that simply told [Devourer] to pump its bloodstream's cells full of oxygen . . . and briefly jumped into [Devourer] in the middle of a fight to activate it, it should, theoretically, just . . . not get tired. Or at least make getting tired to be a very, very, very long process.

Of course, it was more complex than that. Nutrients and proteins and enzymes played a big part in the whole mechanism too. Its muscles would still fray and get worn down over time, needing rest to repair, and its mind would still need rest as well, so it wasn't like it could just devote such a process to stay on permanently and never bother with sleeping. It would just be a waste of essence.

Plus, sleeping and napping was fun and nice.

But if it turned on that template in a fight, coupled with its points in Endurance, it might as well be a biological machine. Utterly inexhaustible, slowly healing. Every missed swing of its enemies would be energy they'd expended, energy the wolf didn't have to worry about, and after the fight, it would just eat them to replenish any lost essence.

Then it could just turn the process off the next time it went to sleep.

It was . . . honestly a bit in disbelief of how quickly it was getting stronger. It wasn't *strong*. It still had to run *all the time*, and it grated on its newfound pride like a knife scraping at its vocal cords, urging it to growl and snarl. It made its fur bristle and its teeth gnash, but it was *true*. It wasn't strong *yet*. But it was getting stronger so fast it felt a little overwhelming.

Its sense of time was shot and useless, but it couldn't have been that long ago that it was a tiny bag of failing organs and melting skin draped atop a brittle skeleton. It felt like years, but it could just as well have been a month alone. It just didn't know.

Its mind was getting a bit lost, in both emotion and memory, as well as speculation, so it took a brief moment to parse through information and sort of . . . recap. Calm down and reassess things that were actually important.

After all, it wasn't completely free and safe yet. It could feel the humans. The suspicious ones, and the scared ones too. Prowling about the winding, mazelike tunnels, in and out, all around for hundreds of feet, looking for it.

They hadn't gotten close yet, but it didn't have the delusion necessary to think that it was completely free and completely safe. So it had to be productive, and *not* linger on feelings and memories.

Despite how difficult it was not to, when this tunnel reminded it oh so much of a rusty pipe and affectionate fingers playing with its ears.

It shook its head and body a bit, both to get rid of the flies that were slowly gathering to lap at the drying blood in its fur, and to shake its thoughts away, physically.

It sort of worked.

Reassessment. *Now.*

It had . . .

Eyelids slid open on every side of its body.

Six eyes. Two at the hips, two right below the ribs, two in its head. Full view of its surroundings from all sides except above. Well, the fur got in the way a little bit, but it couldn't do anything about that without making *far* too obvious weak points in its defenses.

And then it realized something.

There was a little too much light in the tunnel the moment it opened all its eyes. Very yellow light.

It turned around, bent its waist a little, and looked into the glowing eye sitting at its left hip, half obscured by crusty, blood-matted fur. Then it moved that eye to the side to look at its own head.

Looking itself in the eye from two directions. It was . . . unsettling.

This would take some getting used to.

The problem was that *all* of its extra eyes were glowing like its normal ones. So much for stealthy sensory organs. It would have to come up with a solution to that sooner or later—

Then it remembered it had [Echoes of Oblivion] and exhaled in annoyance. It could just cover itself in darkness and hide such weak points without even noticing the mana drain. Its mind was going too fast, racing too fast. It was like . . . emotionlessly panicking. It was annoying.

It tried to focus.

So, a full view of its surroundings, except above. It had to add one more eye, at around . . . the crux where neck met torso should be fine. Wouldn't compromise any weak points either, like its spine, since there was a *lot* of material in the way, more than the middle or top of its neck had.

What else?

It had a faint smattering of antennae going up almost to its biceps, connected to its new auxiliary brains.

It had a new tail.

It was fun twisting the tails around each other like a braid of sorts. Made it look and feel like it only had one *massive* extremely fluffy tail. Also helped conceal the second one. Would be good for surprise attacks.

Its bones were more solid now. Its muscles were slowly being replaced with braided ones.

And for now, those were all the changes.

It quickly dove back into [Devourer], squeezing its abused melatonin sac dry, and immediately began working. It adjusted the slime sheath a little, moving the seam down along its back, and quickly put an eye where its neck met its torso between its shoulders, connected it to the brain network.

Then it got to making a template for [Devourer] that would oxygenate its blood when applied, regardless of its body composition, and immediately after, it started looking at what it had gained from the small furry thing it had eaten.

The biology was blessedly simple. After everything it had gotten from the shark, it was a relief, almost.

It noted the way the cat's claws could be extended from within their sheaths using little tendons, and wondered if it could do something with that.

For a mild experiment, it focused on its claws, trying to see if it could add something like that to its own hands, and once again paused, confused and overjoyed.

It could change its claws now.

It had only noticed because it was focusing on them, but that stone-solid knowledge that told it '*you cannot change this*' was no longer there.

With trepidation and excitement both, it focused on the flawless pieces of what . . . *should* have been bone or keratin but was something else entirely, something it couldn't even try to identify.

Experimentally, it grabbed one with its mind and told [Devourer] to change it, make it thinner and longer.

And the skill didn't protest.

It tested the limit of how much it could change one, and found none besides time and . . . whatever accounted for mass with such a strange material. Asking the skill to make them bigger simply didn't work. Asking the skill to warp them, shift them, did.

A single claw could be thinned and extended down to the cellular level almost, a thousand times thinner than a piece of paper, into a flat circle almost three hundred feet wide, a size that was mind-boggling to the wolf.

The only problem was that such a change would take literal *decades*. Asking the skill only brought forth a sense of flashing sunsets and dawns, of trees being stripped and filled in the blinks of an eye, in the very mountains and landscapes shifting slowly, a time it couldn't comprehend.

Decades. Tens of *years*.

It dialed back and wondered how much time it would take to move some of the mass from inside the claws, hollow it, and move it to the outside. Making them both longer and wider.

The answer was still far too long for its liking, but a bit more reasonable. Stretching the length of its teeth and claws by about an inch would take about two weeks.

Possibilities came to mind, each crazier and more appealing than the last.

It took one of its crusher teeth, a rather redundant inhabitant of its mouth, and tried to move it up around the inside of its skull, stretching it to form an impossible-to-penetrate bubble around its brain.

And it worked. It would take something like three *months*, but it *could* do it.

It tried to add another tooth to the new protective mass to speed things up, but the skill refused to do it, acting like each tooth was individual and impossible to merge or combine.

Still, three months, for making sure its brain couldn't be scooped out of its skull, no matter what hit it? It was a cheap price.

Of course, there were weak points. Where its eye sockets were, the hole at the back of its skull, its ears, if one were dexterous enough. It had to have access to those senses, and a fully impenetrable brain wouldn't be able to do that.

So in truth, it wasn't an impenetrable defense against a skilled enemy. But against anything else? It wouldn't have to worry.

It had precisely forty-two teeth. Twenty of them were crushers.

First, it moved all of the crushers out of its mouth and into a padded pouch of nerveless flesh on the top of its gut, and told [Devourer] to fill the gap that would form in its mouth with regular, albeit significantly hardened, teeth. A process which would only take a dozen hours or so.

From there, it could hold these [Devourer] teeth inside its body and mold their shape to something more protective over the course of a few months. Four of them would be stretched into jagged hollow rectangular bars that would replace the normal crusher teeth later on, and the other sixteen would be turned into armor plates.

It would have to make sure they weren't dug out or somehow removed from its body, because then it would have to restart the process all over again for each one it lost, as [Devourer] only seemed to wish to regenerate them as teeth. Or claws.

But in a month or two, with semi-regular thought and molding, it would have sixteen little armor plates it could use to protect its most important and most vulnerable parts. It wasn't sure yet of how or where it would put them, but that was a problem for its future self.

It had thought of making them into bones, but flesh refused to attach to them for some reason. The muscles just sort of . . . slid off.

Then, it turned to its sharper teeth. Canines and cutters.

It didn't mess with them too much. It took the small tendons that the cat used to pull its claws in and out, and weaved a small system like that through its snout bone, then told Devourer to lengthen its cutting teeth and canines by a solid inch.

Two weeks for those to lengthen too. It told [Devourer] to roughly sync those systems together, so it wouldn't have semi-retractable teeth without needing to, and turned to the last useful thing that cat had given it.

A ridiculously flexible spine.

Seriously, the thing could twist itself into a spiral if it wanted, and not get injured. It was absurd.

A cat's spine could rotate more due to simple structure, and their vertebrae had a special, flexible, elastic cushioning on the discs, which gave them even more flexibility.

The wolf, of course, had no real reason not to put this into its own spine, and even its tails. It could curl them into tight spirals with this, which meant it could exert more grabbing force since it wasn't fighting its own tail structure to curl.

Besides, the flexible spine allowed it to absorb impact better than its own super-rigid one, though it was a *little* weaker in how much added force it could give to its movements.

The cat also had a sort of . . . built-in reflex system in its mind, something to do with balance, but the wolf didn't know enough about how it worked to add it. It wasn't sure it even needed it, really.

Then, it moved to the annoying flying thing.

[Devourer] said it was a thrakling. Something like a small drake, whatever that was. Its biology, generally speaking, wasn't anything all that incredible. It was incredibly average. The wolf couldn't even use its wings, because it was far, far, far too heavy to fly. Not without wings the size of a small human nest.

But the liquid fire the thing spewed was thankfully a biological process, not a mana-related thing, as it had assumed.

The explanations it got from [Devourer] about it were, frankly, extremely complicated and almost as difficult to follow as going through the structure of a human brain.

But it did roughly understand how it worked.

It was essentially an incredibly thin, unnamed chemical mix that was kept in a gland sac like any other.

This sac, however, connected to a muscle and tissue system that was expressly designed to launch it with high pressure.

It was essentially a gland that would make the chemical, the chemical would be moved into a holding sac, then there was a launching sac, a valve which kept the launching sac from leaking back or forward, and a bunch of muscles that would utterly *crush* the launching sac when the wolf clenched.

Then the valve would unlock with a small muscular contraction, and the launching sac would spew this chemical out into the open air.

The chemical, upon coming into contact with oxygen and carbon, or at least sufficient amounts of it, would ignite. The heat would make the chemical and cell connections change, making the liquid that was thinner than water somehow thicken into a thin, clinging slime.

It was beautiful, and its purpose was entirely savage.

The wolf wanted this so bad it felt like it was salivating with its mind.

It was so wonderfully designed. The liquid was safe within the inside of its body, and when exposed to air, would ignite, before thickening into something its prey would be entirely unable to just brush off or gather. Sure, it hurt the spread of the fire a little in exchange for making sure the fire *stuck*, but this whole system was designed around *precision*.

The little thrakling was designed to be a sniper, firing liquid flame onto its enemies and watching them scream and writhe in agony from afar until they collapsed and died. After which, it would swoop in for its free, wonderfully charred meal.

The wolf didn't even have to think about it. It added the fire-spewing organs as high up in its gut as it could fit it into, and weaved the pressure system through the organs in its chest, using its esophagus as a guide, and formed the exit points, two tube endings that ended at the entrance of its mouth to either side of its tongue.

It was entirely aware of the fact that if any flaming liquid dripped onto its tongue or mouth, it would immediately burn its mouth, at least until the wolf shut it and ruined the chemical solution with its own spit.

It just didn't care.

A bit of pain in exchange for something this powerful, something this versatile and brutal and scary? It was nothing.

What more? It felt like it was forgetting something, but then again, it had learned so much that that feeling was almost permanent by now.

. . .

. . .

. . .

The shark hearts! It had been planning to give itself a second heart now that it was growing large enough to justify it, and the shark had a great valve system in place. It wasn't even all that different from the wolf's, besides shape.

So it began working on changing that shape into something it could fit into its own chest. It was rather easy. Giving itself a second heart was only tedious due to having to shift all its other organs around a little, shrinking or enlarging some others. Within an hour, it was done, and confirmed its change, feeling [Devourer] start to work on it.

With two hearts, its blood flow would go even faster, smoother, and it added the safety blanket of knowing that even if one heart got ruined or somehow failed, it would have another to keep it alive until it could fix the problem.

And then . . .

It stood there for a bit, feeling oddly lost.

It . . . didn't really have anything else to change. It knew how human brains worked decently enough, and their intelligence didn't seem to be born of anything more than size and the frequency of the wrinkles in the tissue. The wolf couldn't make its brain larger without making its whole head awkwardly larger, and "decently enough" was not a level of skill it was comfortable with to start adding wrinkles to its brain or making such drastic changes to the absolute most important part of itself.

Besides, the more wrinkles it added, the slower its brain would process. Smarter did not mean *faster*. It was slowly beginning to wonder if it even wanted to make its intellect match a human's. It didn't feel too motivated to do it at the moment.

The symbols were a bit more of an immediate interest.

The points might be . . . No, it knew what it wanted. It knew *exactly* what it needed.

It flicked the symbols open, finished with [Devourer] for the moment.

Speed (+5)
Perception (+5)

It felt hasty, to dump all its points into two attributes like this, even if Perception was necessary for Speed to even be useful.

But suddenly feeling like weight, momentum, torque and strength were no longer significant factors into how fast it could go, into how its body felt even while *asleep*, it couldn't much care. It knew it had made the right choice.

So now . . . now it would just . . . wait for all its changes to finish, make a template copy of its body once they were done, and go on its way.

Half of the changes were already done in the day and a half or so it had been blinking in and out of sleep.

It could wait for another day or two without much issue. Naps were nice.

It would have to keep an eye out for patrolling and searching humans, but it wasn't terribly concerned. It hadn't picked the first little nook it could find. It had felt as much as it could with its vibrations and picked the most remote, convoluted, nonsensical path it could find that led to one. It was also pretty far from the entrance to the tunnel networks it had taken.

It went to sleep peacefully with a deep exhale of both immense joy and sadness, and idly wished it had the luxury to turn off [Restful Awareness] and dream of the last time it was in such a pipe, with its human packmate by its side.

CHAPTER 9

Sleeping while having multiple skills active or activating was an odd sensation. It had discovered a while ago that it could do so, but it just hadn't crossed its mind whatsoever to actually *use* this strange skill interaction.

Back when it was climbing up the shaft, it just wanted to sleep, and it wasn't in the best mental state, nearly delirious. It hadn't even been using [Restful Awareness] for many of its naps, feeling like its head was stuffed full of acrid dust.

Then, after another couple close brushes with death, it ended up in a cage surrounded by humans, and it was in no mood to reveal or draw attention to itself more than it already had.

In short, it was *trying to get out of the tunnels then getting captured and nearly dying like seven times in a row,* while juggling the far too numerous possibilities of its own flexible biology, so it had its own excuses as to why it hadn't dedicated much thought to how the symbols functioned.

It once again felt stupid, however, which was a mild prickle to its pride.

Maybe it should be focusing even more on Intelligence.

Regardless, it had a . . . not a theory, but an untested realization.

As it sank into the warm embrace of sleep, it used and kept activating as many skills as it could. No, actually, it didn't *just* use them, it pushed them to their limit.

It kept [Mana Conversion] at maximum power, sucking mana out of its environment and funneling it into [Echoes of Oblivion], pushing way more mana than was needed into the skill. It activated [Bloodrush] the moment it came off cooldown, it tugged its own limbs around to further level up [Restful Awareness], it clumsily made . . . *noise*, meaningless sounds with [Logotexnia], confident [Echoes of Oblivion] would eat the sounds up before they traveled the tunnels.

Judging by the pings on the back of its mind as it slept for nearly two days straight, its theory was correct.

And it was on the verge of slamming its head into a wall for not doing this sooner. The amount of levels it got during a two-day period of basically doing nothing was *ridiculous.*

[Echoes of Oblivion] has Leveled Up. Level 8 → Level 15
[Bloodrush] has Leveled Up. Level 8 → Level 14
[Logotexnia] has Leveled Up. Level 6 → Level 14
[Restful Awareness] has Leveled Up. Level 26 → Level 32
[Mana Conversion] has Leveled Up. Level 4 → Level 13

Seeing the levels go up, but without knowing what those numbers represented, was rather moot. That visual improvement didn't mean anything. So it began to prod and push, trying to figure out *how* they improved. Not only its recent level-ups, but those it had gained from the fight as well.

Most of them were rather self-explanatory, like [Tough Skin] making its skin act more like thick, treated leather when struck rather than thin skin, at least with its current level. Some of the more opaque ones took a bit of mental trickery to figure out.

[Echoes of Oblivion] had gotten a little easier to use, but considering how used to it the wolf was, that was not particularly noticeable. It felt like flicking a switch by now. What would have been noticeable, had it bothered attempting it, was that its range had increased significantly. The range at which it could push out this . . . puffy, all-consuming darkness was not mere inches, but *feet.*

The skill refused to tell it a number, or even a vague impression. It was more like it just helped the wolf control the darkness outward.

It would take a bit of practice, but it could quite literally cover itself in a cloud of darkness if it wanted. Any kind of melee combat would be impossible for whoever was trying it. They would just lose their senses and get shredded to ribbons without even knowing where their opponent was.

If it practiced control, it could pretend its form was multiple times larger than it really was. Which would have been very useful back when it was leaving the lift.

Moving on, [Bloodrush] leveling up just made the boost it got from the skill more potent with every level, without impacting anything else. The same went for [Maddened Frenzy].

The level-ups in [Sonic Blast] were a bit more impactful. Control, speed, and efficiency. The distinction between power and efficiency was very important.

How quickly it could gather a blast, how well it could control it, and the efficiency of its mana when gathering up air and propelling it. It didn't make its blasts stronger or louder directly, but indirectly, through helping the wolf be more *efficient*. It would likely reach a level where the efficiency was near perfect, and then that progress would plateau completely, but it had no idea at what level that would happen.

The concept was a bit complicated, but it . . . *somewhat* understood it.

[Tremor Sense] had a sort of . . . dual purpose and improvement. It seemed to be adding exactly ten feet of vibrational sense to its natural senses per level. Which was negligible with what the wolf was currently operating with, but the real benefit came from the detail the skill added to its vibrational senses.

Whereas normally, it should have been feeling rough, hazy guesses, like knowing there was a gap in the stone sixty feet to its left, some kind of pipe twenty feet below, the skill instead intercepted that vague information and sharpened it, added detail, before feeding it to the wolf.

The vague gap in the stone turned into a room, the muffled idea of something in the corner turning into a pulley box it could almost feel the inner mechanisms of. Because this applied to the nearly four hundred feet of distance it could feel while barely paying attention, the value of such a low-level skill was immediately apparent.

Looking back on all this, it made sense. Before it got the skill, everything was hazy and vague with the vibrational senses, which was normal, because that's how antennae worked. It was an organ that was never meant to be long range or accurate. It came from a *cockroach*.

The wolf just hadn't noticed that incongruence until now. It had just assumed it was some kind of natural progression, just it getting used to its own new senses.

With that simple realization, [Tremor Sense] became one of its most treasured skills.

It moved on to the next one, its least-liked skill thus far.

After a few minutes, it realized that it was also the one skill that had improved most drastically compared to its first level.

[Danger Sense].

All the levels truly did was increase its detection range. But when its starting range seemed to have been barely two feet, it had been more of a nuisance than an assistance back when it was getting chased, constantly pinging in its head of danger that it could already see and was already in the process of dodging. Now, its range was about eight feet.

It wasn't great at math, but at level four, it could assume that each level-up added two feet to the range. If an attack was coming, and it hadn't *seen*, heard, or felt it coming, this could be the final line of defense to prevent it from getting stabbed by another pointy flying stick or needle.

And . . . that was about it.

It didn't really have anything else to do. It figured its skills out; its changes were just about finished.

The urge to go back to resting mindlessly was tempting, but it went into [Devourer] instead.

It wasn't really sure what it was here for. Usually it identified problems and found solutions to them.

Now, it just wanted to . . . do more. Not just better, *more*.

Earlier, it was just relieved to be alive and free. Now that it had had plenty of time to relax and calm down, it was more *upset* at the fact that it was happy about being able to run away. It had resolved to stop running, hadn't it? Yet it was still all it could really do.

It had to do more.

It didn't know exactly what the feeling was. There was something of an uneasy, emotionless sort of panic in the back of its mind. That wasn't . . . *entirely* new. It was always there, begging the wolf to think and think and think and overthink until it passed out.

What was new was that there was a vague idea of *change, change, something has to change*, an insistent scrape at the back of its mind. It felt something similar many, many times, but never so strong or insistent. It could usually ignore it. But two days of suddenly doing nothing but sleeping had brought the notion to the utter forefront of its mind.

Coupled with the umpteenth time it had almost died . . .

It knew, in the back of its mind, it was still restricting itself. There were still some loose threads holding on to something it thought it had discarded, some background thought in its mind that made it push less than it might have to.

It had just changed itself a lot, that cautionary remnant would say. It could take a bit of time to familiarize itself with its new changes, the cautionary remnant would say, of a time before it was fighting for its life constantly, a sentimental piece that didn't even want to change its own paws because it would be changing its form *too much*.

There was no time, no essence, the remnant could use as an excuse, and for once, the wolf grabbed on to that subconscious thought and crushed it.

There was no time?

There was nothing *but* time. What could come here? What could find it here before the wolf did first? Nothing could ambush it. Nothing could kill it, not in these decrepit little sewer tunnels. It could feel a half dozen exits the humans didn't even know about at the edge of its perception, all leading back to the outside world a couple hundred feet below. It could escape any time it wished. It would just take a bit of time.

There was no essence?

Its attention turned to the *dozens* of humans it could feel, patrolling, searching, chalking up the walls with little sticks so they wouldn't get lost. Its lazy mental glare focused on the few hundred rodents the humans left behind as they searched, the other few hundred that hadn't noticed them to rush to their death yet.

There was essence *everywhere*.

It turned to the pouch of slime in its back, putting into perspective the amount of space and weight that added to its body. The things it prevented the wolf from putting there. Out of some sort of sentimentality.

The human was *dead*. Burned, boiled, melted, eaten, and vaporized. She was *gone*.

It didn't matter if even the logical part of itself told it that there was still a decent chance she was alive. It knew that. This wasn't about what was *true*, because truth didn't matter. This was about the wolf getting over its *feelings*, and focusing on being alive to feel the damn things in the first place.

No, not just alive. That was complacent. It wanted to *thrive*. It wanted to be the hunter, rather than the prey. It was sick of running.

So it repeated the mantra to itself, over and over, until it began to convince itself.

The human was dead. Gone.

And the pouch of slime on its back would never be needed again. What would it use it for? Holding heads? Judging by the lift incident, it could get more whenever it felt like it.

Pragmatism. It needed *pragmatism*, not sentimentality.

It turned toward [Devourer] with a determination that it hadn't felt yet. Ideas did not waft and waver, they stuck to its mind and *sank their hooks in*.

It got rid of the slime glands in its back, removed the slime veins entirely. It added a branching vertebrae to its upper back, and added another t—

No, it was no *tail*.

Just a tentacle that came out of its upper back, almost vertically, a couple inches below its neck eye. It was made of equal parts bone, muscle, and thick, ropelike tendons. There was no fur. The last vertebrae was extended into a ten-inch-long hardened blade that moved past the flesh and skin to stand proud in the air.

It used the cat's spinal structure to make the thing as flexible as it could. It added a network of intertwining flesh that snaked around the base and through its back muscles to latch on to ribs and spine, adding strength and structure to its motions.

It nestled the tail into the back pouch, which it severely reduced the width of, and increased the length, just to hide the extra appendage better. This look also made its back look wider vertically, paradoxically making it look *more* like a canine, while also shielding its spine.

Any whisper of doubt that crept in, the wolf crushed it.

It had gained a pressure system, hadn't it? It had been *trying* and *failing* to find ways to use its paralyzing poison, hadn't it?

There was nothing bad about just blindly adding more firepower, literal and not, to its body.

The remnant of its cautious self hesitated, and the wolf pushed it away, crumpled it into a ball, and stomped it into the back of its mind.

It took the pressure system that it had used for its liquid fire and reduced its size to what the small thrakling had been using.

It copied this system nine times, and for six of these copies, it changed the inner chemical to something thinner than water, but equally harmless. It planted those six copies at the base of its new tentacle, surrounding it, half burrowed into the significantly smaller pouch, and ran the tubes up the sides of the tentacle.

It replaced the normal launching sac muscles with several layers of thick braided ones, just for added force, after doing the same to the launch sacs responsible for its mouth fire.

It borrowed the structure of the two fangs it had hidden in the tip of its two tails, enlarged them several times over.

It straightened them, melted the joints, turning them to thin, straight hollow spikes made of brown-black chitin, with catch grooves on the bottom, extending outward. It even added some small hooked barbs, so they couldn't easily be removed.

It used the nerve structure of the slime veins to make a thin film of nerves and fat that lined the inside of the spikes, one that would automatically contract without the presence of the nerves in its tail to keep the films dilated, causing them to push whatever liquid it placed inside them out of the thin hole at the tips the moment they were disconnected.

With the spike structure done, it placed them around the top of its tail in two layers, three four-inch-long spikes that began four inches below the bone blade and crested upward to end where the skin ended and the blade began, then added the other three in between the gaps of the first, just a couple inches below.

In the tentacle, it built small glands that would pump the hollow insides of the spikes with its paralytic poison from the side, enough in each of them to kill a human several times over, and built a small, separate network of muscles that would be able to tug the spikes around in whatever direction it wished, for aiming purposes, creating odd bumps in its tentacle.

It hooked the spikes up to a valve system like the one it had in its lower chest for the liquid fire, but made of cartilage and muscle for the most part, allowing the wolf to launch the spikes, or thorns, with a small effortless contraction and a spew of harmless liquid.

It had not changed the other three launching systems, which still spit flame, nestled at the bottom of its rib cage where intestines used to take up space a long time ago, and ran the exit tubes around the rib cage and out of its back, through the base of the tentacle and all the way up to just under the spikes, ending them in three equally spaced reddish holes which it could clench open or shut.

The result was a tentacle whose tip was covered in six venomous spikes, and three exit points for liquid fire.

Now that it had this system, why stop there?

It added more glands in its stomach, more pressure systems. Ten of them, nestled amongst the auxiliary brains and other various glands, snug but not tight.

It was amazing how much it could fit into its abdomen and still have it just over half full and almost skinny compared to the rest of its frame.

It ran the flamethrower systems up to its arms, two ending at its shoulders, two ending at its forearms, and six going backward to its actual tails, three for each. It copied the spines and muscle structures and overlaid them atop what was already there, adding three maneuverable spikes to each forearm, shoulder, and tail.

It wouldn't be able to launch the ones on its upper body individually, as each triplet of spikes was connected to the same system, but it didn't matter. It wanted firepower. Something to *kill* with, not something it could use to *run*.

Out of the corner of its proverbial "eye," it saw a small pouch of its teeth nestled into the top of its gut, in the process of turning into armor plates.

Without allowing itself to form doubtful thoughts, it took four of the sixteen future plates and told them to shift into twelve-inch-long spikes, thin, sharp, long, and covered in triangular jagged protrusions that would shred and widen any wound it made with them.

It quickly double-checked to make sure all its inner teeth were set to be blunt, and resolved to watch carefully for the spiked ones, to make sure they wouldn't put pressure on things they shouldn't.

Four months, the skill said. It didn't care, it accepted, regardless of the ridiculous timeframe.

Then again, it used to take the skill ten days to give it *human eyes*. Now, such a change would barely take a day. Fixing its whole body was the work of a dozen hours, even if it was on the brink of death.

In two months, [Devourer] might say it would only take a week to shift its teeth.

Prodding the skill provided no rebuttal. Good.

More. It wanted more. More change.

It took the shock-absorbing scar tissue of the spearhead shark, scrutinized it.

Why had it thought there was no use for this?

It built a wide abdomen-shaped strip of it and shoved it under its skin, snug against its abdominals.

It wasn't like it used its abdomen to curl all that much. Its structure wasn't like a human's. And its abdomen was *full* of useful things now.

What else? Where else?

Skull. Blunt impact. *Obvious.*

Why hadn't it thought of that?

That emotionless panic, that scraping whisper of *change, change you have to change, change now*, it gradually receded, turned into ideas and open concepts.

It took a thin film of the scar-absorbing tissue and removed any and all fat that was around its skull, replacing it with a little less than half an inch of the bouncy tissue instead, making sure to keep the tissue disconnected from both the muscles below and the skin above, but held firmly in place by surrounding pressure.

What else? It wanted more.

It thought of other "crazy" ideas, ideas it had discarded, old ideas.

Once, what felt like months ago, it wished it still had human arms, just to be able to fiddle with their annoying devices and ladders and the like.

Why not? It had room. It could *make* room.

It took the structure of a human shoulder, severely lengthened the arms. It removed all fat and a lot of muscle, replacing bulk with tight, wiry networks of interlacing flesh, replacing normal muscle with braided ones, and put these shoulders right under its pectoral muscles, to the side and a little farther down to not interfere with its main arms.

The shoulder structure was surprisingly easy to graft in, just weaving the muscles between its obliques and attaching them to its ribs, the scapula being draped over the side of its rib cage like a thin piece of armor, the shoulder joint simply shoved against one of the ribs and stuck onto its surface, a mass of cartilage. It added another two more curving bones at the bottom of its rib cage and extended lateral muscles down to attach to them, around its sides, just to add pulling power to the arms, to be able to use them to lunge forward even farther and faster if it had to.

The finished look was like it had swallowed an elongated human, and it was trying to burrow out of its torso.

Just to not have the arms stick out from the rest of its body, it covered them in a rough, thin layer of fur and made the skin dark gray, the nails black and humanoid, but *very* thick and slightly sharp. Just in case.

Now, it looked like it had just added some parts of shoulders and back muscles under its existing ones. They didn't even take up much room. It should still be able to use its main arms in all the usual ways.

The new arms were . . . perfect. They had multi-jointed *fingers*, not like its own, which were short and stumpy, barely usable for anything other than running, scratching, and climbing.

Dexterous, light but powerful, not like its main arms, but good enough.

Then it paused.

There was no such thing as "good enough."

It had room. It *still* had room.

Two more flamethrower systems, nestled under its new, rather thin and short ribs, which ran through the underside of the secondary arms. The launch tubes curled around the wrist to the back of the hands and split into four exit points placed at each knuckle.

It didn't want precision, it wanted brute force and destruction. It had more than enough precision.

Its abdomen and gut in general were about three-fourths filled up by now, and it resisted the urge to fill up the last quarter of space with more liquid fire.

For the last touch, it made sure the tendons of the arms were as thick as it could reasonably make them, and went to remove the by-now-useless fangs under its bottom jaw.

Had it even gotten to use them once? It didn't think it had, and they made resting its head on its paws awkward, so it removed them without much thought, the venom glands connected to them as well.

It added two more flamethrower systems in its tails, the exit points nestled right next to the venom fangs. It might burn the fang and fur a little when it shot, but so what? It was just fire. It had felt worse. It had felt its insides melting as a pup barely able to reach a human's shins. A little fire was nothing, despite its stupid instincts insisting it's dangerous.

More. A little more change.

It vaguely remembered how annoying it was to constantly have to chew and cut and bite to eat. How time consuming it was.

So it took its esophagus, and just . . . *widened* it. Significantly, all the way down to its stomach.

If that meant its vocals would get deeper too because of the windpipe and vocal cords being shifted around, it wouldn't complain either.

After confirming that change too . . .

It felt . . .

Calm.

No, *satisfied*. It had reached a point where no matter how much it pushed itself, it just couldn't find more ideas it could feasibly add to its body without bloating itself and making certain ways of fighting inefficient. That mild sort of frenzy that kept whining and pleading for change was no longer there, sated.

Without a hint of second thoughts or regret, it briefly checked over its work, did some small corrections and minor structural improvements in the way the muscles were woven, and sank back into thoughtless rest, idly activating skills as they came and went.

It knew it *barely* had any essence left. It knew its passive essence consumption had almost tripled with the amount of glands and organs it had added, its increased size. It knew the nutrients its body needed to not only maintain itself, but *grow*, were in the realm of at least three-fourths of an entire human body per day.

It just didn't care.

Essence was everywhere.

And it had nothing but time right now.

* * *

Another day and a half was spent with it going from hiding spot to hiding spot and napping the hours away, not even bothering to test anything before *everything* was done. It was barely making any progress through the tunnels, but doing very much the opposite with its body, so it was satisfied.

Besides, the humans were seemingly starting to give up, the search parties lessening more and more, so it was in absolutely no hurry.

It woke up for the umpteenth time with a lazy yawn.

Four days of strolling around sewage tunnels and finding little hidey holes to sleep in was surprisingly fun and relaxing.

It asked the symbols for updates.

[Echoes of Oblivion] has Leveled Up. Level 15 → Level 20
[Bloodrush] has Leveled Up. Level 14 → Level 17
[Logotexnia] has Leveled Up. Level 14 → Level 16
[Restful Awareness] has Leveled Up. Level 32 → Level 36
[Mana Conversion] has Leveled Up. Level 13 → Level 16

Why hadn't it been doing this before? It felt like strangling its old self with its tails. Both of them. Just . . . *free levels!*

With a grumble of annoyance, it shuffled out of the tight vent pipe it had burrowed into and quickly confirmed there was nothing nearby but rushing wastewater. With a small puff of darkness on its legs and paws, it landed soundlessly on the mossy cobbles underfoot and straightened, stretching.

Not that it even got stiff anymore, not really, but it still felt nice after being confined in a tight tube of iron.

All of its changes were done, and its essence storage was nearly empty, the drain only off-put by the wolf idly snacking on whatever rodent it could find. It had to get food *soon.*

First, testing its new tools.

It turned to the left and opened its mouth wide, clenching a pair of muscles in its gut. The pressure built and built, and then it tugged another muscle, the one for the inner valve, and pried it open.

Two twin streams of liquid fire traveled a clean *thirty* feet in a completely straight line before even beginning to curve down to the stone below, and it was around forty feet away that the liquid finally met mossy brick, pooling and thickening in a rapidly expanding, slimy puddle that dripped into the trash waters below.

That felt easy to use.

And it was *very* beautiful, it noted. It really liked flames.

Its mouth *should* be getting burned from how the liquid instantly lit on fire while still contained within its jaws, but the most it felt was a building, irritating heat.

It loved Endurance . . .

It kept the stream going until it began to run out of liquid, after three seconds or so.

As the liquid ran out and the pressure lessened, it felt the stream lax before abruptly cutting off, and its tongue burned from a stray drop or two that hadn't joined the pressurized stream. It grimaced as it clicked its mouth shut, suffocating the fire before rubbing the thick liquid into the roof of its mouth and mixing it with spit, sloshing its tongue around, feeling it dissolve.

It tasted really bad.

It opened its jaws again and let out a relieved exhale when its mouth didn't light on fire.

Next thing to make sure worked right . . .

Well, the secondary arms worked exactly like they should be, and it had gotten to know that very well when they'd grown long enough to drag on the ground as it walked, which was really annoying.

Finding a comfortable way to rest or suspend its secondary arms took a while, until it had managed to sort of fold them over each other and across the bottom of its chest, and tuck the hands into the armpits, its forearms snug against its ribs.

That, combined with their light weight and rough fur, provided enough friction to let the wolf let them rest without having them dangle and drag down on the floor.

It had tested them a *bit*, and discovered them to be . . . about a third as strong as its main arms. Which made sense. They were missing a lot of supportive structure and muscle mass.

But the fingers were perfectly dexterous. Only thing it hadn't checked was their reach.

It unfolded them, feeling its wrists and knuckles hit the ground as it brought them out from under its main arms and between them. Then it extended them as far as it could. They were about four feet long, far longer than actual human arms, but it hadn't extended them so far.

Two and a half or so feet away from its snout, they stopped. That didn't sound like a lot, but it was farther than its main arms could reach by quite a lot.

It was still rather odd to have four arms.

It turned them over, palms up, and brought them close, tilting its head as it examined the skeletal-seeming limbs. Fingers wriggled, wiggled, closed and opened.

So odd.

It folded them back around the bottom of its chest, out of sight, and moved on to the next thing.

It burrowed the tentacle out of the back pouch, extending it toward the ceiling, and stared at it with the eye it had on the base of its neck, wriggling it back and forth, admiring the black-brown spikes that almost gleamed in the firelight, the black skin making the appendage look oddly stout and hard, the pure white straight bone blade jutting out of the tip, adding even more contrast.

In short, it looked *brutal*. Five feet of wriggly murder.

It looked like something the wolf itself would see on another creature, and immediately decided to keep its distance.

It twitched the muscles around each spike and found the process to be a lot harder than it had thought. Some spikes turned to the side, some up, some down, and it took a solid five minutes for the wolf to feel confident in what it was doing.

It did note that the display was immensely disturbing and intimidating, and for once, it found an odd sort of sadistic joy in the thought of making humans stare at it with enough fear to soil themselves, running away before they'd even fired a bolt.

It was still preening over how it had handled the lift, yes.

It brought the tentacle low and turned to the opposite wall of the tunnel, lifting a spike to jut perpendicularly out from the limb. It aimed that singular spike with as much care as it could manage, slowly, and began squeezing.

It kept the pressure up, until it felt those muscles begin to cramp, and then finally used a different group of them to peel back the hardened cartilage over the grooves keeping the spikes embedded in its tail.

The *millisecond* the cartilage had slipped off the grooves, with a strange sound like a sharp, short whistle combined with grinding sandpaper and a violent burst of fluid, the spike . . .

Disappeared. At the same time, the sharp crack of stone echoed down the tunnel, its tentacle rocking back a couple inches from the unexpected recoil.

It blinked, turning its head to stare at its tentacle with at least four incredulous eyes, spread over its side.

The eyes on its right side focused on the wall and stared uncomprehendingly at the dripping black thorn embedded an entire inch into solid stone, the stone cracked around it with a little spiderweb pattern that extended about three inches from the center.

Its tentacle fell limp, tip on the ground as the wolf turned its full attention on the thorn, squinting at it, tilting its head left to right.

That . . .

That didn't make sense. That shouldn't even *happen*, even if the wolf had the force necessary to do it. Which it thought it did, because a multilayered sac of braided flesh squeezing something smaller than a human's fist until the muscles began to cramp was a *lot* of pressure.

But even *if* it could throw them with such force, its spikes were made of *chitin*. No matter how incredibly hard it squeezed the launch sac, it should have just bounced off. *Maybe* dug into the stone enough to stay in place by the tip, or just outright shattered, considering the speeds involved.

It shouldn't have *cracked stone*.

They weren't light, but they weren't *that* heavy. They weren't *soft*, but chitin could *bend*, it was *not* harder than . . . rock . . .

It remembered its Survivor trait for a moment.

Every time that trait upgraded, it had felt a very noticeable improvement on how tough it was. And considering the number had risen to three out of five, maybe the improvement got even steeper as it leveled up?

That speculation was centered on the ridiculous idea that *maybe* Endurance applied to its projectiles.

It dove into the rushing waters below, and with energetic paddling, made its way to the other side of the tunnel in four short seconds, clambering up with scraping claws, taking a brief second to shake the water out of its fur.

It went up to the thorn, tilted its head, and gripped it between its crusher teeth, yanking it out of the wall.

Then, it tried to crush it with as much force as it could muster.

It squished, a *little*. It barely noticed it. And that was it.

It *knew* that it was more than strong enough to crush a thin hollow spike into nothing but chitin chunks. Stone, too, if it tried a bit harder.

It extended the right secondary arm around and up, and the wolf grabbed the spike out of its mouth with its fingers, holding it up for inspection, twisting it around contemplatively as it tilted its head, feeling the spike's texture on the naked black skin that covered the underside of its fingers.

The symbols made no sense. That was *not* a part of its body. Maybe the hardness would fade? If it didn't, would the humans be able to grab its spikes and use them like weapons? That wasn't an actual concern, but more of just . . . where did the symbols draw the line between what was and wasn't its body? It didn't make sense.

As with most things that didn't make sense, the wolf decided to leave it for later, or never.

With a flick of its wrist to toss the spike into the waters, it folded the human arm back out of sight.

It turned its head down to stare at the three spikes lying flat and a little diagonally on its right forearm, tips aimed at the ground. They were something it could use as armor, weapon, *and* projectile. It flexed the extra muscles it had put around its arm.

The spikes came to life, wriggling, four-something sharp inches of slowly wavering chitin.

Just for show, it wriggled the antennae it had spread throughout its forearm too.

The sight was uniquely disquieting, even to itself.

It took aim at the opposite wall again by putting its forearm parallel to its chest, took a short second to amp up the pressure, and shot.

Same result as the first. Three spikes embedded into the stone, a solid inch each.

Disbelief and joy were an odd mixture, but the wolf found itself liking it. How could it complain about something like the symbols helping it too much?

It extended its secondary arms out from the side, under its main ones, took aim at the wall with its knuckles.

The liquid fire that spewed out was not so much of an accurate stream as much as it was a wild, vaguely rectangular spray, droplets and mist breaking off from each other and almost *detonating*. Rapid ignition was surprisingly loud, a short bassy *fwoom* sort of sound echoing down the tunnel.

With four shared exit points, the spray also only lasted a little more than a second, and the range was barely ten feet. Trade-offs.

It wasn't disappointed at all as it stared at the giant stretch of brick merrily being charred just five feet away.

For when it couldn't afford precision and needed to just make whatever was in front of it cook, this was perfect. It could increase the capacity later when its essence storage wasn't practically empty.

Folding its secondary arms out of sight again, it took aim with the tentacle, down the left side of the walkway it was on, and found the range to be the same as the flamethrowers in its mouth, albeit less of a twin stream and more of a triangle-shaped spew, the streams hitting each other and spraying wildly after the thirty-foot mark. Two seconds before emptying. The exits to the tubes were a little wider than it thought.

The entire tunnel smelled of smoke by now, and was extremely well-lit by the giant stretches of burning liquid squirted about, and so, it kept itself vigilant for wandering humans. None within two hundred feet. None approaching.

Its tails were next.

They had by far the most accurate, tight stream of fire, the longest range at fifty feet, and the longest fire time, at six seconds. It had taken care to make the exit point as small as possible, so that made sense.

The spike shots were the same as all its other shots, without any delineation. It was much harder to aim the ones on its shoulders, but it could manage, somewhat. They did work great for intimidation as well.

It did realize that aiming these spikes would take a bit of practice in general, but it would have time for that. The extra eyes certainly helped it aim, what with the added perspective they gave it.

The last test it wished to try . . .

It activated [Echoes of Oblivion], like it had been doing for hours and hours of sleep, and just like before, it didn't let the skill be; it pushed mana into it, as much as it could drain from its own cells.

For a moment, a familiar fog embraced it, like a comforting blanket. Then the next moment, the blanket expanded, turning into a genuine roiling cloud, a little over three feet in each direction, shaped almost like a squashed sphere around its body.

Of course, with the wall and ground and its legs touching it, that just meant it was sitting in a roughly seven-something-foot-wide and tall sphere of void-black fog. Enough to conceal its movements, make the enemy guess what they were even fighting.

It extended its secondary arms forward, and the fog roiled forward to match them. It swished its tails, each almost as thick as a human's arm, and the fog did the same. Using the skill this way did consume a surprisingly large amount of mana, though.

It tried to push even more mana into the skill, but the skill sort of . . . rejected it? It was like it refused to let the wolf extend the cloud a farther distance than its level allowed the wolf to.

That was odd, but it couldn't complain about the ability to completely conceal its form, even when in plain sight.

It wouldn't be able to cover a room or anything like that, not anytime soon. But it didn't need to.

It felt its tails begin to furiously wag, joyful and hopeful, and it quickly located the most jittery, isolated search group within its range.

With a black hole in its stomach, an empty pit in its soul, and self-satisfaction wriggling in its chest, it howled.

[Echoes of Oblivion] devoured its declaration of a hunt.

With a long exhale of impatience, it focused on the search group under the pipe it was resting within, waiting for them to walk out of the tight corridor they were shuffling through and out into the brick lip that surrounded the bizarre cycling room.

As it did so, it thought about how being able to feel almost four hundred feet in all directions without even paying much attention or putting any effort in, from a mixture of its vibrational senses and [Tremor Sense], it was . . .

It was an awareness so immeasurably comforting that it filled the wolf with this sense of bone-deep *safety*. It would always know if someone was coming, where they were coming from, how heavy and tall they were, read their stance to know if they were coming after it or just wandering. It felt like an omniscient creature, almost.

The three humans, clad in coverings and basically vibrating with nervousness, jabbered and hiss-barked at each other as they tensely walked in a line on the thin, crumbling brickwork, eyes twitching amongst the ominous ruins to their right.

The wolf didn't pay much attention to them, despite the strangeness of seeing something like a mangled temple made of bricks sitting in the middle of a sump, its crumbling remnants half filled and being worn away by chemicals and waste.

Three hundred feet to its left, in parallel pipes and through at least three walls, it felt two groups talking to each other through their mechanical talk-pads.

Below, three confident and well-armored humans walked with practiced, meaningless stealth through the crumbling innards of a control room, likely trying to find ways to cut off its escape paths into as few places as possible, funnel it into a predictable path.

They couldn't set traps down here, but they could try to corral it into predictable spots when it inevitably went through the sewers and came out on the other side, and *that* would be where it assumed they'd set the actual traps, or so it assumed. Because the best moment to strike was always when one's guard was down.

They wouldn't succeed.

It waited until the three humans were almost right below it, and activated [Echoes of Oblivion], feeling the skill's soft, coiled fingers wrap around it in a comforting, eddying motion. It grabbed onto the lip of the pipe and carved out a large triangular piece of heavy iron.

Then it handed it to one of its tails and whipped it away with all its strength at the stone ruins, the massive metal fan whirring away at the center under the waters.

It crouched, head tilted down to stare at the humans, reveling in the idle waft of fear it could pick out from underneath the cloying scent of aging trash water, while the eye in the base of its neck stared at the flying piece of iron. A moment later, it slammed into stone with enough force to echo in the room ten times over, and one of the humans, the middle one, *squeaked*, pulling a sharp blade—

A sword, it suddenly knew.

Pulling a sword out, and blindly aimed it toward the hazy outlines of the forgotten building, arm shaking.

With their backs to the wolf, right below it, sitting on a three-foot-wide piece of crumbling brick walkway while just three feet below them wastewater trickled away, they had no chance.

It could just tilt its forearm down, and, assuming they didn't have a lot of points in Endurance, put a spike through the top of their heads. It might take less than a second to kill them all.

They smelled and felt like . . .

The humans in the lift.

Their morale was horrid too. Two were frozen, the third in the middle looked and smelled ready to faint.

It could probably kill them all instantly. But it didn't want to do that. It wanted something more than just essence out of this encounter.

Besides, the humans hunting it seemed to put more worth into quantity rather than quality, and that was just fine by the wolf. More essence for itself. [Devourer] never stopped being hungry, and by extension, neither did the wolf, no matter how good it usually was at suppressing it. Now? Without even essence in storage? It felt *hollow*. Cold and empty, unsure. It hated the feeling.

Still, it kept its patience. Somewhat.

It hooked its nails into the iron pipe, swung its body down, and stared at them through the gap between its legs as it hung in place.

Then it dropped, legs curled to its stomach and arms wide.

It waited until it was only a foot or two above the quivering human in the middle before it whipped its tails to coil around the necks of the two men on either side of him. Before any of them could react, its legs unwound like a spring and slammed into the scared man's skull with a gut-wrenching crack that caved in his skull, instantly knocking him out.

His forward-leaning posture made him jerk and crumple down like a folding piece of paper, right where the wolf was trying to land, and the wolf had to hurriedly jerk its feet up again, mid-fall, to land on his back, surprised by how easily its weight and strength did such damage.

Damn it. It hadn't even meant to do that. It shouldn't have aimed for the soft spot of the skull.

It didn't waste time with the other two. The moment its legs landed on the middle man's body and its hands hit the floor, it tightened its tails, one far more than the other. The left one's windpipe was crushed instantly with a fleshy crunch and a gurgling sound, his hands fisting in its fur and trying to peel its tail off with surprising strength and ferocity, his lantern hitting the ground and starting to flicker, damaged.

Which was not the plan, because that was the tail it *hadn't* been tightening at full strength.

The one to its right, a stockier, bigger human, let out a choked gag, jerked and swung his sword at the wolf's tail with as much speed as he could muster, and the wolf mourned the loss of a couple dozen hairs as it watched the sword bounce off and leave the human's grip from resistance he was likely not expecting, tumbling into the waters.

That swing was either really weak or its fur was made of iron by now, because it barely felt anything. It sincerely hoped for the latter.

It was also rather surprised that this human hadn't met the same fate as his kin, especially with how much effort the wolf had put into snapping his neck. It felt like it was trying to crack a support beam in twain.

It didn't *mean* to crush the fragile one's windpipe; it had just underestimated its own strength, but the one on its right at least had some decent points into Endurance, it seemed. Which was good, because it needed at least one of them alive, and the unconscious one . . .

The dent in his head was a little too deep for the wolf to have much hope of coherence from him, even if he did wake up.

It jerked the fragile one back, ignoring his frantic, surprisingly painful struggles, and dragged him off the brick lip that lined this bizarre chamber before dunking him into the water. It stepped off the unconscious human, kicking his body to the side, flush against the wall.

Then it turned off [Echoes of Oblivion] as it calmly trotted up to the edge of the brickwork and curled up, hands stacked atop each other under its snout as it stared at the fragile human's struggling form beneath the water, felt the gentle thumps of his fists beating at its tail as it held him down. Judging by the speed of said thumps, that was where he'd put most of his attribute points, assuming he had access to them, which it still wasn't sure about.

The tough one continued to struggle, and the wolf let him exhaust himself, tugging him closer or away from itself whenever he tried to advance or do anything but pluck hair out of its tail, tightening it whenever he tried to scream or call for help.

That tough one, he had common sense. What good would Speed or Strength do if he'd gotten his neck snapped before he could even react?

If he had common sense, maybe he would be easier to communicate with too. It felt quite lucky.

It opened the eye on its left hip, staring blankly at the tough human, and it smelled his fear spike suddenly. It filled the air, the scent faint but bittersweet.

The eye roved over him to land on a familiar metallic device, and the tentacle in its back dug itself out of its pouch before whipping forward. The human jerked and stiffened even further as the speaking tablet clattered to the floor, his hip coverings cut and frayed along the string that held the blocky thing up.

It curled its tentacle into a spiral, bone blade pointing straight at the device, before spearing forward and through it, bone tip embedded into stone. With a violent flick, the wolf threw it into the waters, just for good measure.

Its attention returned to its temporary toy, still struggling under the murk.

The fragile human was already dead, really, what with his crushed windpipe, and his struggle was only making him exhaust himself quicker.

But the wolf was not in a merciful mood.

So just to mess with him further, it began jerking him around randomly, pushing down then pulling up and randomly going left or right, preventing him from mustering his wits or any sense of balance as he flailed about desperately.

The human lasted about twenty seconds before he went limp, and the wolf twisted its tail until it felt a satisfying pop-crack reverberate through its flesh as his neck snapped. Just in case. That done, it dragged his corpse out of the water, dumping it by its side before vigorously shaking the appendage to get rid of the water soaking the fur in a sort of twitchy wagging motion.

That was . . . cathartic. It felt *good*. It felt fun.

It knew that playing with its food was fun. It had learned it a long time ago, from the rodents back in the pit when it had gotten bored of killing them or eating the dead ones.

It just hadn't quite realized *how* incredibly fun it was when it genuinely hated its prey too.

Because yes, it had gone past just being *upset* at the humans trying to capture it when certain realizations came to it as it prowled through the tunnels and thought of recent events.

Not only had they almost gotten it killed or captured a dozen times by now in just the past week, refusing to just *leave it alone*, the reasoning it suspected for their actions was *infuriating*.

It had debated lighting one of them on fire as it choked them to muffle or choke out their screams, but it didn't feel like burning its tail fur by trying that, and it liked its food uncooked and fresh, preferably.

More painful for the human trash that thought they could control it, but too much of an annoyance for the wolf to bother.

If this whole hunt was about the humans eating it, it wouldn't even think twice about it. That was the way things worked. It was natural, normal. Why would it hate something just trying to eat and survive? That was literally the wolf itself, until recently.

No, it hated them because they didn't have *any* interest in that. Much like the rats, psychotic little things they were. The rats were frenzied mindless nuisances. The humans . . . or rather, *these* humans . . .

It had reviewed that chaotic mess of a fight it had gone through almost a week ago, and it slowly became apparent that very few of the attacks launched at it were lethal in any way. Ropes, nets, paralytic poison, which its immune system had grown a little better at combating, as a side note, then light-nets connected to arrows . . .

They were trying to capture it alive.

Which ruled out the possibility of them wanting revenge, or trying to extinguish a threat as a result of it killing their kin, like that female down by the burning rivers. They either somehow didn't know or didn't care.

From what little it knew, and ruling that possibility out, it had to assume they wanted it leashed and commanded like those of its kin it had seen, dragged by a leash. It, and only it. It couldn't fathom any of them going to such lengths for a regular canine. And the only thing unique about the wolf was that it was *not* a regular canine. It all clicked.

Which meant they knew it was a wolf, or at least knew of how potentially powerful it could be, and thus wanted it as a . . . a tool, weapon, or something . . . *subservient*.

A pet.

The word came to mind suddenly, and it felt its lips curl into a soundless snarl as its fur bristled across its back.

And that *reason*, the reason the humans were hunting it with such fervor and numbers, that pissed it off a lot more than if they'd just been trying to fill their stomachs.

As if he had some kind of second wind, the human planted his feet to the ground and abruptly yanked back with all his strength and body weight, actually moving the wolf a little.

It tilted its tail, a light twist and jerk, and in the blink of an eye, three thin barbed spikes were pressing into the human's neck, just shy of breaking skin. Its low warning growl mixed with the human's heaving breaths as he froze, slowly lifting his hands off the tail, holding them up by his side, palms open and empty, his fear churning into that bitter scent of terror.

Its chest still burned with low, seething contempt as it dragged the tougher human's body to its knees behind it, letting its tail slacken enough for the red-faced man to gasp in heaving breaths without worrying about self-impalement, his wide, terrified eyes nailed to its waving tentacle.

It opened the eye on its left hip to stare at him, and the human's skin turned almost bone white as his eyes jerked to it, tentacle momentarily forgotten.

His hands began to shake.

It felt a surge of satisfaction at this situation. It felt so *nice* to be feared for once.

Just to add to it, it slowly undulated the tentacle's spikes in the air as it got up and turned to face him. It flattened the tentacle against its back again, wiggling it back into its sheath, out of sight.

Its second tail wrapped around the neck of the human it had killed, dragging his dripping corpse to sit next to itself, half of it on top of his unconscious kin's body. Its secondary arms unwound and extended to the sides, and the human let out an inarticulate whimper-sob kind of sound at the sight, leaning back as much as the spikes on his neck would allow.

With a twist, it folded the spikes flat against its tail again, not wanting its captive to accidentally or purposefully kill himself, then tightened the tail again and sat down on its haunches, face-to-face.

The size difference was significantly smaller than it was used to. It was nice to be getting bigger. The human *was* on its knees, but still.

It formed a fist with its left secondary hand before extending the pointer finger to point at the dead human's head.

"Hheeeeaaaad," it growl-whine-snarled with minimal assistance from [Logotexnia], and the human's eyes widened significantly, looking like they were about to pop out of their sockets. It looked almost painful.

Then it twined its fingers around the corpse's head fur, pulling its slack face off the floor.

It pointed at the hair itself with its right-hand pointer finger and used [Logotexnia] to imbue a vaguely inquisitive feeling into its following chuff. It was obvious. It sounded *questioning*. So the human should know it was asking a question. It was *easy*.

"W-w-w-w-what?" the human squeaked out.

Or not, because that was *not* what the *what* sound meant. It wasn't sure what it meant beyond being used for questions, but it didn't mean that. Emree-eel would say *what* all the time, but never to bring attention to her head fur.

It growled, making him flinch and grimace. It shook the head for emphasis, dragging the corpse forward then raising it a little more, and used its right-hand finger to poke at the hair directly.

It chuffed again, questioning.

The human swallowed audibly, once, twice.

"H-h-head?" he eked out.

It used to have a lot more patience than this.

As it was, it simply let out a short snarl of frustration, letting its teeth show, ignoring the human's sob-whimper, and slammed the head down into the bricks below with a muted crunch as its face flattened.

It caught itself and took a deep breath to calm down, then leaned back a little, waiting for the human's eyes to open again.

After four seconds of silence, they did, the human timidly staring at its main hands that still sat on the floor, and so it pointed at the corpse's back with its humanoid arm again.

"Chuheesssst," it chuff-hiss-whined.

It pointed at the human's legs.

"Lheeehg," it growl-whined.

It pointed back to the head.

The human was still just staring at its main arms like he was about to pass out, uncomprehending, not lifting his eyes beyond glancing at whatever the wolf was pointing at.

No eye contact. A show of submission. Which was good, but *not* what the wolf was looking for.

"Hheeaaad," it snarled.

Then it grabbed the corpse by its head fur again and used its other hand's pointer finger to very specifically tap at the strands it was holding the body up by.

It let out the same questioning chuff.

"I— H-hair?" the man warbled out through the tears in his eyes, his rough voice not well suited to the tones, and the wolf tilted its head at the new sound, dissecting it.

"Hhh . . . aaaairrr," it growl-wheeze-snarled.

The human jerked his head up and down frantically, some weird gesture it couldn't parse the meaning of.

The eyes on its right side opened and stared at the ruins.

There were plenty of things here to point to and learn the name of. And this human had eyes, unlike Emree-eel.

Time to see how much knowledge it could wring out of him before turning him into essence.

Three hours and a lot of frustration later, it couldn't say it was . . . *entirely* disappointed.

It knew from the [Devourer] skill that there were differences in what humans called a "forearm" and a "wrist," so it knew what to look for. It just didn't know the sounds the humans used for specific body places yet.

That was mostly where they stumbled upon frustration. The human was stupid, and it took another half hour to even get him to understand what it was trying to learn.

It could say with relative confidence that it could make any sound that referred to most of the human parts by now, with quite a bit of specificity.

It learned how humans called those glass lamps they held, "lanterns," which was oddly pleasing to say. Their coverings had multiple names to refer to them, again, for no reason. Upper thing was a "shirt," lower was "pants."

It learned that the human didn't know what to call it, making pleading gibberish and making sad yipping noises whenever it would point at itself questioningly. It wasn't sure if that meant they didn't know it was a wolf or if they didn't know what a wolf *was*, and thus had no sound for it.

That's when it began running into difficulties, because human body parts were easy and specific. Environment, apparently, was not.

Pointing at the floor made the human give it a dozen different sounds for it, like "floor, rock, stone, bricks, ground, pleaseletmegoplease" and a bunch of other annoying sounds, all depending on how displeased the wolf looked, as if he was just trying to appease it but didn't know what exactly it wanted.

Even though what it wanted was rather clear and simple.

That was roughly when it gave up and decapitated him. It made sure to eat every tiny piece of the group and kick their clothes and equipment off to be carried by the sump waters, then went on the hunt for another team.

Still, it learned plenty. Maybe the next group would be less annoyingly stupid.

It couldn't be *that* hard to just give the same damn answer twice in a row when it pointed at something.

It was wrong.

The next group was not much better. It learned how they called their blades, their belts and buckles, their foot coverings. Their metal speaking device. The "comms tablet."

Ugh, its thoughts were getting all muddied by it using the human sounds in its head when thinking of stuff now. It was endlessly annoying, to have its thoughts start shifting from . . . thinking in images and concepts and objects to *sounds*. Why did the humans do this to themselves? It was so much harder to think this way, so much noisier, in a weird way.

So bizarre.

Still, it wished to understand human speech. If not to use it to communicate with them, then at least so it could extract information from them and figure out why they were such complete, nonsensical, suicidal creatures. Maybe ask them questions about the symbols. What this stupid mana thing was, how it could better control it so it would be able to do the amazing things its Path vision showed it, like devouring spears with blankets of void.

The more it thought, the more questions popped up, and much to its displeasure, it knew that the humans were its best chance of getting answers. Meaning that the wolf would have to know how to ask *and* understand the given answers if it wanted to satisfy its curiosity.

By the third group, it realized that no such thing was likely to happen anytime soon. The damn sounds they used were all so . . . varied. It started to cross-reference what the humans agreed on, just to understand if the ground below its feet was "rock" or "stone," if it was "ground" or "floor."

It was leaning toward stone. Two out of three score on that one.

The lessened gnaw of hunger in its stomach and soul was a light balm upon its frustration, but it was enough to make the wolf realize that it had stocked up on enough maintenance for about a week.

Thus, it decided to hurry out of this metal plate's innards, focusing on vibrations, periodically activating [Bloodrush] to extend its range.

As easy as prowling these rather desolate tunnels was, despite the slowly increasing number of rodents, it could actually *feel* itself getting more impatient and irritable, hour by hour, as it descended.

There was no reason for it. It really could not understand why it felt this way. No amount of silent introspection helped.

Maybe that odd sense of inner panic, of needing to change, was not something derived from its subconscious dissatisfaction, but its frustration at something it couldn't locate? It really didn't know.

As it descended deeper, the humans lessened more and more, until it could only feel two groups of six moving through the tunnels with a purpose and determination that let it know it should probably avoid them. They were not patrolling, however, just following a predetermined path through the tunnels. Very quickly, it might add. Very violently too, because the inhabitants of this place did not enjoy their trampling steps.

It also began running into more and more bizarre things as it got closer to the middle of the plate's innards, and deeper down, near the underside of the metal plate, it felt said bizarre things lessen, as if all the strangeness was contained within the middle of the tunnel network.

Why? How?

It was dying to know. One thing it seldom managed to refrain itself from following was its own curiosity.

The bizarre *things* it saw were . . . both locations and creatures.

The first thing it had felt was the faint sensation of an elongated humanoid creature with its legs fused together, made of sludgy flesh and fat, briefly scraping at a wall before vanishing back into the waters, where the wolf lost it.

It didn't even *want* to investigate that one, despite how morbidly fascinated it was by the creature.

The second one was some kind of . . . mass of dozens of chitinous legs and spikes and hooks the size of four humans, making some kind of . . . nest, or something, covered in squishy bits. The wolf actively avoided that one.

Locations were . . . dizzying, and there were far too many. Control rooms that were, for some reason, upside down. A small room filled with coffins and rotted skeletons. It even saw something like some . . . crypt, covered in twisted metal statues.

It didn't explore those either. Not much point in it.

The only odd location it decided to visit was an inert pump room, which was basically already in its general path. Judging from the vibrations, it had been turned into a human's living space. This far down, that was a bit bizarre.

When it finally got to it, the door was made of something strange like . . . paper, painted and covered to camouflage into the surrounding metal wall, and it would have worked if the wolf didn't have vibrations to see through it.

Witness of Divinity also just *told it* the wall was fake, but still.

The door didn't really open so much as it just crumbled into a wet, rotten heap at its feet with the lightest shove, the wires holding it in place just snapping from the shift in weight, rusted through completely.

It walked in and swerved its head around. The room was a perfect cube, about thirty feet big, and still felt cramped.

There was a point where there was so little light that even night vision was meaningless, and this room definitely reached that point.

It spewed a small line of flame onto the floor, next to its foot, and wandered forward.

The smell was . . . horrid, even for the sewers. It was rotten flesh and decay mixing with a miasma that it could actually *taste*, like rotten flesh and ancient dried paint that never aired out of the room until now.

In the left corner, some mass of rotten pillows and feathers and fabrics, almost like a bird's nest. Crates flanked the odd nest's right side, some wooden and crumbling, some metal and dented inward.

Still, enough survived to give the room a very strange feeling. An odd sense of importance and untouchableness, as if it was in a place it shouldn't, an invader of a sanctum with no guardian.

It ignored it, because it was curious.

In the right corner, it saw and felt the corpse of a human, half machine and half a rotten skeleton, curled up into a ball in the corner as it lay amongst the broken fragments of a mirror, one large, dirty piece clutched in its right hand in a reverse grip, limp on the floor, the other still clutching where its hair might once have been.

Rotten pieces of paper lay on the nest and around the body, haphazardly discarded, thin and withered, but it could glean some kind of mess of human squiggly lines in their yellow-brown bodies if it squinted.

To its left, there was just a gigantic pile of . . . fabric and wood and paint, crushed and melted together as if by acid all the way up to the ceiling. There was even dried paint on the floor, covering almost half of it in a chaotic blotch of colors.

To its right, two giant pumps rusted away, taking up about a fifth of the room in total, their pipes burrowing into the middle of the wall.

And leaned against them was a bizarre assortment of . . . metal cans filled with brushes, glass canisters on rotten wooden benches, strange three-legged stands that supported a long line of rotting . . . fabric, it looked like, stretched over rectangular wooden frames, so decayed that the wolf feared the entire line would slump down into wet chunks should it breathe too hard in their direction.

It breathed another small jet of fire to its right, and the extra light made its eyes widen as they fixed upon the fabric again.

Canvas, the ether whispered, and the wolf didn't need to be told what it was used for, staring curiously at the faces painted onto the fabric, each the same but progressively changing with each new picture, seven of them in total.

It trotted up to the first one in line, the left one, recognizable by the simple fact it seemed to be the oldest one.

It was an extremely detailed painting of a single man with a receding hairline and tired eyes, his face lit by what seemed to be candlelight. Behind him, the wolf could idly recognize the door it had just pushed through, a lumpy mess of painted cardboard-like material. It assumed that this painting was the human drawing himself. What for, it didn't know, nor try to understand.

It was . . . oddly pleasing to the eye, even if with age, the paint had cracked and splintered and lost most of its color, giving an oddly eerie feel to the picture.

The second picture was like the first, except . . . sloppier. The shadows were lengthier, the human's features a little lopsided. His smile looked worried. The improved condition told the wolf there was likely something like months or *years* between each piece, which didn't make much sense either, but it ignored it for the moment.

The third was . . . not the same person. The colors were difficult to parse under firelight, but they were a little off. The human's jaw and features were more like a lumpy mask clipped onto a human's deformed head, rather than the carefully rendered strokes of paint it saw in the first one.

His smile was too wide, one eye too bright while the other was just splashed over with black paint, like a hole in his face.

It was like the human's skill was actively regressing. If it wasn't for the visible improvement on the paint's condition as it moved along, it would have assumed it began its observation on the wrong side, going backward.

The fourth painting looked angry and sort of desperate. It was all reds and straight lines, spikes and angles and no curves, forming a jagged oval shape with the barest suggestion of human features. The mouth was an open pit in this one, the color of his mouth pure black. The picture looked as if a human was being flayed alive and screaming.

It was both . . . confused and mildly intrigued.

The easiest and most logical explanation it could come up with was that some strange human went in here, decided to use it as his new home, and slowly started losing his mind.

But why would a human even do that? This place was neither safe nor comfortable to live in. The humidity was grating, even by the human nest's standards.

The fifth painting had some faint return to detail, in that half the face was some malformed, vaguely spiral-textured mess with an eye and a cheek, while the other half-and-something of the face was a bunch of parallel lines like pipes and squiggly . . . circles.

Were those supposed to be gears?

Well, the human was half machine from what it could feel, so maybe it was a metaphor for how he . . . replaced his legs with metal ones?

The sixth drawing was . . .

Just a black-and-gray mass of vague shapes, a few hard lines indicating the malformed lumps, which it assumed were the edge of a jaw and a shoulder. In the middle of all this, a sloppy white circle remained, with a textured black dot in the middle, a tiny one in comparison to the wide sphere. It assumed that it was supposed to be an eye. If it was, the eye looked quite terrified.

The seventh drawing was a shredded mess, torn apart.

It tilted its head, going from the first to the last painting again. Then to the human form curled up in the corner to its right.

It walked to the human corpse in the corner and extended a human-oid arm out to the side, grabbing onto one of his metal legs and dragging the half-mummified corpse out of the corner, straightening the body in the process.

The metal was . . . odd.

It flared all of its antennae and tapped the lumpy, dented mess of half circles with its main arm's knuckles.

Its ears straightened in surprise.

There was still bone in the metal.

It was crushed and seemed to be almost . . . assimilated into the iron, with the odd way they were melting into each other, but it was still in there, trapped and preserved.

If that was a gradual process, it looked *really* painful.

It thought back to the human who had fought it with a metal arm, and winced as it thought of how much time and pain he must have gone through just to turn his whole arm into metal. It felt a sense of respect for him, actually.

The iron was not exactly uniform on this human, however. It was like . . . a shell, almost, still clinging onto bits of decayed brown flesh, almost mummified, or melted *into* the flesh.

Actually, not quite. It looked more like the metal was eating the human alive from the outside, or like the human was growing a shell of metal, except it went from the outside, then inward. The metal snaked around his hips in a wide, segmented cast, leaving him fully mobile as far as the wolf could tell, but likely in a lot of pain.

Was it all on purpose? Did the humans do this to be stronger?

They *were* pretty weak without their mana things.

It couldn't figure anything out about this strange scene, not beyond speculation.

It just looked like a human decided to live in the tunnels, progressively lost his mind, and killed himself with a piece of a broken mirror in the middle of his changes, for no reason.

Curiosity sated, it turned and walked out of the room, continuing on its way down.

Over time, the deeper it went, it noticed the rats slowly getting bigger and more *twisted*. It got a firsthand look at this, as the rats that it ran across steadily became more misshapen and simultaneously more annoying to dispatch without wasting fire or spikes on them.

At first, the teeth were more crooked than it thought possible, much too large, occasionally jutting out of their gums like gnarled branches of spiky bone, almost. Not an issue, but bizarre.

Then, their bodies just started getting *weird*. Their legs bent wrong, some of them had skulls shaped more like someone made a rat's skull out of clay before bashing it with a hammer a few times and letting it dry.

It vividly remembered one rat that had one eye in its neck and the other almost on its nose, and the thing couldn't even move its head right to keep the wolf in its line of sight.

It still ate them after messing with them for a bit, snipping off limbs or seeing how long it could hold them down until their bodies just became too exhausted to even move.

The answer was that they didn't actually do that. They just struggled until their heart gave out and they died. The sheer tenacity was almost admirable, if the wolf didn't suspect that they had no real choice in how they reacted to living things.

Then the tunnels started getting weird. Not quickly, but as the dozens of feet turned to hundreds and the wolf came closer to the center, it was like someone had taken a normal grid of tunnels and bashed them together, mixed them up with surrounding rooms that didn't belong, sumps covered in wires and control rooms mixed with winding, shredded vents.

Instead of there being twenty conventional, natural exits it could feel that led to the outside, there was just this crushed, winding strip of labyrinthian tunnels that led to each other in vast loops, with only six big ones that all funneled toward the nest's wall and some kind of facility that awaited their cargo there.

Six exits sounded like a lot, but when they all led to two near-identical human facilities, they really weren't.

It could feel the dozens of humans prowling about inside both, sitting on rafters and checking every nook and cranny, setting traps.

Unfortunately for them, it could feel a fair few more exits they had no idea about, should it decide to leave. But it didn't want to.

It had to get to the heart of the tunnel system, where it belonged. Back to where it should be.

Not yet, though. It was just . . . too curious to rush.

By the time it was getting close to the middle of the tunnel network, the rats started being larger than the canines it saw in the human nest, easily reaching up to a human's knees. Considering the wolf could reach a human's upper thighs, the size difference was slowly shrinking, and the rodents were getting increasingly more . . .

Some part of itself wanted to say "absurd, inefficient, disgusting," while another felt an odd sense of burning envy.

It wanted to be more too. To change more, to be more. Flesh to flesh, flesh to steel, steel to flesh.

Some had legs almost as long as their bodies, making them stumble and shuffle like crippled heaps of flesh trying to sprint while on mangled stilts. It was ridiculous—

And awesome in a morbid way.

Some, like the one currently trying to kill it, were so malformed that they were just clumps of fur and flesh that had absolutely no resemblance to an actual rodent anymore, and were just . . . useless. It had no idea how they survived. Maybe they just ate the moss that clung to the walls.

It stared down with a sense of annoyed envy and mildly confused amusement at the enraged ball of awkwardly flailing limbs grinding against its right arm, bashing against it, gurgled whistles coming out of . . . somewhere.

How did this thing even eat . . . ?

It wanted this. It wanted to change, to change, until it shed its form like a cocoon, unrecognizable . . .

That . . . wait, no.

It tilted its head.

It still wanted to be and look *somewhat* like a wolf, didn't it? Yeah, it did. Impulsive thoughts.

It didn't really matter.

The wolf brought out its humanoid right hand to grab onto what looked like . . . the flailing, furred hand of a human toddler with the elbow joint backward, if instead of ending at five fingers it just ended in two pincerlike nubs.

It lifted the creature by said hand and satisfied its morbid curiosity by just . . . holding it up and admiring the thing, almost as big as itself but entirely useless.

It could *almost* puzzle out where the gurgling sound was coming from, but not quite.

How did this . . . *thing* even happen? Why did they only get like this deep in the sewers? They'd been normal, if increasingly big, until the past day or so when it decided to just speed down the tunnels as fast as possible.

It debated how it would even begin to eat this thing, how it could even play with something that was already so deeply tortured by its own form—

A stray drop of liquid went into its eye from the thing's useless jerking, and it felt a surge of boiling fury spear through its nerves like an electric shock, instant and thoughtless.

It threw the thing into the wall to its right with a crunchy squelch, making it bounce off and leave a smear of fur and goopy flesh behind, then took half a step forward in preparation, ready to crush it to pulp, to beat it into a formless chunk of meat patty, its lips curling back over its teeth with a low snarl.

The faint tug of a skill leveling up in the corner of its mind briefly distracted it, and for a moment, it felt something like the most tiny, imperceptible caress of a string against its mind, shifting just enough for the wolf to feel it, like a weight that it had grown used to and forgotten was even there.

It hesitated, feeling its anger waver, something in the back of its head reeling in confusion.

Why was it so angry?

Why was it even *here*? It could leave without going anywhere near the center of the sewer system. There were unmapped shafts everywhere. There was absolutely no need for it to be getting so close to someplace so obviously dangerous, even if the prey got bigger and bigger. Why was it only questioning what it was doing *now*, after several hours or days trying to get to the center of the tunnels?

A vague sense of disconnection filled its mind and body, and it stumbled in place, taking a step back. It stared at a pair of furry arms, both humanoid, both right.

It felt like it was observing something through a pane of glass, like it was using puppet strings to make the limbs move, like they weren't even its own.

Why had it been wanting to change itself so much? It made sense, of course. It knew that it had that subconscious block, it knew it needed fire-power. It wouldn't revert the changes; they were amazing.

But that itching sensation, that frenzied feeling that just told it to *change, right now, as much as possible, more*, that was not something it had felt before. On one hand, it made sense. It had almost just died multiple times in a single day, just a bit ago. It made sense to want to change, hard and fast.

On the other hand—

That weird mana symbol it had felt etched into its skull, ages ago, briefly flared, and it felt its thoughts scatter for a moment, [Mental Resistance] straining, allowing it to realize what was going on. It felt the body's head shake with a growl, and felt that confusion evaporate.

It opened the symbols, that tug of a level-up still insistent.

[Mental Resistance] has Leveled Up. Level 29 → Level 30

It stared for a few moments, brows furrowing, the gaping chasm between mind and body groaning wider.

It tugged the puppet strings. The arms moved, back and forth. Sluggish. The puppet was weak.

The misshapen ball of flesh rolled and scrambled toward it again, and the wolf used the puppet's right arms to drag it to the side, into the waters. It let the thing drown in the current, standing in place.

It thought back to how it kept getting increasingly impatient, angry. The first stages of it were normal; they felt fine. It was *right* to be angry at the humans, it felt nice to toy with them a bit before eating them.

But as it thought back, it began to wonder if its normal, usual self would toy as much as it did with the rats it found deeper down.

It thought back to one of the larger ones it had caught, one that it had grabbed onto with its human hands and held down while it ate it alive, reveling in its enraged, agonized screeching, and started second-guessing whether that was its own mind or something else influencing it.

Of course, it didn't feel bad for the thing. It didn't even feel remorse.

But usually, it wouldn't come up with something that bothersome just to satisfy some newly grown sense of . . . sadism, or whatever it was that had guided it to do that.

It thought back to what it had felt when it saw the rodent it had just swept off into the waters: a sense of vague, reverent awe and respect, before the thing attacked and more normal feelings slid into place.

It focused further.

Why had it wanted to get to the center of the sewers so much? Why had it felt a sense that it *belonged* there, that it should be there?

Back to where it should be, it remembered thinking, and it wondered what that even *meant*. It didn't belong anywhere.

Something was wrong.

[Mental Resistance] was always on. It was always at full power. It had learned its lesson a long time ago when some human had muttered "control beast" and forced it to obey, that it shouldn't put the skill down.

So it focused on the skill, sightless eyes staring into brick, the puppet's body still.

A minute passed, five.

Occasionally, it could feel *something* brushing against its mind and inflaming certain things, finding its feelings and subconscious desires and just . . . gently brushing against them, tugging them forth. Digging them out, selectively. Twisting them to some unseen purpose.

Something was trying to influence it. Control it. And it was somehow getting through its skill.

This was not the same thing as what it had felt from the pitch-black titan that gave it its path. That was like two clawed gauntlets, forcing their tips through the seams at the gates of its mind and forcing them wide open so it could walk in, unashamed and uncaring of its notice.

This felt more like imperceptibly thin spiderwebs, weaving themselves through the gates' seams, something so subtle and rampant that by the time something else might have realized what was happening, it would be too late.

Was that what had happened to the human before? That half-metal corpse? Is that why he'd lost his mind?

[Mental Resistance] has Leveled Up. Level 30 → Level 31

It had to get out of here. *Now.*

It tugged the body's strings, and the puppet sluggishly turned. A whisper of doubt crept into its mind as the mana construct in its skull briefly came into awareness again.

Cold, calculating fury coiled around its lungs, and it turned [Pain Resistance] all the way down before extending its right secondary arm in front of it, palm open.

Then it spewed a short burst of fire onto its furless paw, and the gaping crack, that widening chasm between its body and its mind, thinned.

Not enough. Even on bare skin, it was too tough to feel *real* pain from fire, not quickly.

It brought the hand up to its mouth, and with the puppet's teeth slightly blunted, it raked them through its paw, stopping just before the bones, blood hissing and boiling as it began to mix with the burning slime.

The pain of its flesh splitting, without even a single level of [Pain Resistance] to assist, was enough for the chasm to snap shut.

The feeling of looking through its own eyes like a telescope, the feeling of moving its body like tugging at a puppet's strings, they just puffed into smoke, the pieces of itself clicking back together in an instant.

It shook its head again with a snarl, its fur bristling across its back as it regarded its surroundings with eyes that had life renewed in them, suspicious of everything and anything as it clenched its fist shut, smothering the fire, reveling in the pain to keep itself *present.*

It could feel exits. Small shafts, tubes melted through iron and stone.

They were too distant, too difficult to access.

It could make its own entrance to them.

It didn't trot or lightly prance forward, it *ran.*

Away from the center of the sewers, up.

[Bloodrush] activated, once, twice, three times.

It rushed to an endless shaft made of stone to its right, nestled behind a tunnel wall. It was a familiar sight and feeling, but one without pipes going through it like the last one it had been in, instead just metal frames that would occasionally brush against endless metal cables.

Digging through six feet of stone sounded difficult, and it would have been, had it not had the human arms to shovel the debris out of the makeshift tunnel between its legs as its main arms focused on raking through stone and breaking off chunks of it at a time.

It was three long, mildly paranoid hours before it judged the stone to be thin enough.

It punched through clumsily, not having all that much space to move its arms in the jagged tube it had clawed, and used its human arms to assist, punching through the stone a second and a third time.

Then it squeezed through, growling and snarling in effort as it contorted itself to fit its upper body through, right shoulders and head first, legs scraping at dusty rock to push itself forward. It could still faintly hear the trickle of rushing water from behind it as it breathed in fresh air for the first time in about a week.

It took a short moment to breathe it all in, turning its head to look down, its two right arms bracing against the stone.

The shaft looked like it was more than a thousand feet tall, which was a rather strange thing, because it felt like the stone and metal plates holding the smaller human nests up were not nearly that thick. And this entire sewer system was held within one such plate.

Still, it couldn't exactly complain, as it could see the end of the shaft, a tiny block through which light came in from below.

It would take a *long time* to get down . . .

Or it could just . . .

It eyed the thick steel cable a foot or two to its right with three critical eyes, squinting in thought.

Its fur was starting to get really, really, really warm from all the friction.

Still, it was having a lot of fun right now.

Sliding down the metal cable was just . . . *fun.*

A little terrifying too, because it was going down head first when the nearest flat surface was likely more than a thousand or more feet below, but it had two tails, two legs, four arms, and a tentacle, all tightly wrapped around a six-inch-thick cable made of steel.

Short of a fireball exploding in its face, nothing could make the wolf detach.

It tried not to ruminate too much on what it had learned in the tunnel system, but it was difficult not to, when the ride was *this* long.

First things first, it *had* to get rid of that mana symbol in its skull. It hadn't *done* anything before now, as far as it knew, and [Devourer] was definitely not connected to it, so it felt more than safe enough in removing it.

No, it felt safer *to* remove it, actually. It had no idea why the thing started acting up in the tunnels, nor why its first action was to try and make the wolf go deeper, try to control it. It didn't make sense. It made the wolf not just *uneasy*, but downright scared.

It felt like if it wasn't for a very set amount of coincidences and events, it would have never been able to feel the construct, nor resist it. And where would it be now? *What* would it be now?

It didn't know. It just knew it would have to dig out a large portion of its upper skull completely, and shift it out of its body before replacing it.

It was going to be *such* a chore, and likely dangerous too, so the wolf began mentally preparing itself for another half a day or so of sitting around in some nook and cranny somewhere with half its skull missing until it grew back.

How joyous . . .

But the alternative was far, far worse.

As its mind wandered, it started developing some kind of abstract theory that maybe the tunnels were just *evil*. Maybe it was making odd connections and nonsensical theories, but something about it just clicked. It explained a lot.

Why were the rats completely insane and psychotic?

Well, they lived in the tunnels, didn't they? The wolf had no doubts that if it lived its entire life with those strings winding around its thoughts, it could end up like them itself. Though not the same, but similar. It still had no explanation for most of their behaviors, like rushing at anything alive except each other. But maybe the tunnels treated certain things differently?

Another question: Why had that human gone insane and killed himself?

He stayed too long in the tunnels, most likely.

Why were those experienced, dangerous humans almost running through the tunnels in their search for the wolf?

They likely felt the strings too, or at least knew about them. They were rushing to stay down there for as little time as possible.

The more it thought, the more little strings and theories kept popping up. It remembered the human that had killed itself, covered in metal that, in hindsight, looked more like it was *consuming* him. It remembered the deformed human that it had seen clinging to ceiling pipes shortly before it lost its own human.

It remembered that envy it felt toward the malformed abominations, how it, too, wished to change, that odd . . . *panic*, almost, when it decided to add all these spikes and flamethrowers on its body.

What about that golem made of steel it had fought, back when its human was still on its back? Was that really one of those constructs the humans created down by the burning rivers, but instead of being stone it was iron that they used, or was that just a human who had been consumed by the metal?

It started to feel like the tunnels were some kind of . . . alive, sentient thing, a corruptive presence, the more it thought about it.

It was all centered around change. Forming and deforming, without much cause or reason. One human turned fleshy and elongated and strange, another was eaten by metal. How and why?

It would also explain why the rodents' biology was so much better suited to something smaller. Why they kept getting more twisted and bizarre and bigger the deeper the wolf moved. Logically, their biology shouldn't even work. Many of them shouldn't even be alive. That clump of flesh and limbs could *definitely* not hunt or feed itself.

Did the tunnels sustain them? How? Mana?

Why did the tunnels under the human dwellings want to twist and change things? Even the tunnels themselves at some point looked like they were being affected the closer it got to the center. It remembered looping spirals and crushed hallways and vents merging into each other, how it had wondered, briefly, if its antennae were acting up, or if what it was feeling was actually real.

And why did the symbol in its skull seem to be connected to the tunnels? It had never activated or done anything before then. The wolf had almost forgotten it even existed.

It was like it was solely placed there to make it easier for the strings to infiltrate.

Why hadn't it activated the last time it was in the tunnels, then, with the human? Was it too far from the source of this . . . presence, or corruption? Or had it activated and the wolf just hadn't noticed?

It did vaguely remember getting delirious and angrier over time back then, but it was so much milder and slower. Considering its circumstances back then, it was just natural. Additionally, most of the time it had spent in those tunnels after killing the roof tumor, it was going upward.

And who or *what* put that damn symbol there? The wolf knew it hadn't, and it knew [Devourer] definitely hadn't. Why had they put it there? Was it born in the tunnels and released outside? That didn't make sense. There was nothing like itself down there, not even close. Canines didn't exist in the sewer tunnels.

Did the tunnels put the mana symbol there in its skull, to lure it deeper in the future somehow?

But that also didn't make sense. It vividly remembered its first memory being one of itself waking up as a pup in a giant broken box made of wood, somewhere around the burning rivers.

It had dreams of sleeping in a pile of kin under yellow light, but those were dreams. It couldn't trust dreams to be memories rather than wistful constructs of its own mind, born out of desire for a pack, not really.

So it considered its first memory to be that box.

In hindsight, *why* did it wake up in a broken box in the middle of nowhere, all alone?

It had *so many questions about **everything***.

It was frustrating. So, so, so frustrating, and its head felt like it was slowly being filled with dry cotton, one wad of it being added every time it spiraled back to the same question or formed a new one.

After such a tiring day, such an overwhelming week, it just wanted to relax.

So it just let its head hang limp and stared at the slowly approaching lights below, feeling oddly content and lazy, consciously emptying its mind for now.

It could, and *would* deal with all this later. It would find a little hole to do skull surgery on itself soon.

It would ask the humans about the tunnels when it knew how to speak. When it had room and had well and fully escaped the reach of whatever group it was that seemed dead-set on hunting it.

Now, it just watched the pretty lights, letting the ropelike texture of the metal wire caress the underside of its chin like a mild massage.

CHAPTER 10

Gathering their belongings was, predictably, a short affair.

Katherine had all her things in some dingy apartment somewhere, and Emhreeil herself, well . . .

She only had that guard's outfit that she had grown . . . oddly attached to, and the little goblin she'd apparently, unknowingly, acquired.

The panic about that particular bit could come later, when she would be forced to make a decision on what to do with the little thing.

She felt along the cleaned jacket, made for a man three times her size, and felt a strange sense of importance hidden within a simple weave.

This wasn't just a jacket to her, not really. This was the blanket she'd been swaddled in after her baptism of acid and blood. The sole comfort she had as she stumbled through empty hallways and felt her body slowly fail. A thick, oversized, padded jacket that was still warm, that made her feel like she was being hugged, back when she thought her friend was dead.

It was also a reminder.

Both of what she'd done and the version of herself she'd had to leave behind.

She grabbed it by its nape and lifted it, before shuffling her left arm into the jacket's, then lifting the arm and sort of . . . awkwardly shuffling her shoulders into the jacket by shrugging and wriggling around.

She examined herself with a small flare of mana.

One sleeve hung down, empty. The other was oversized, but not too long. The jacket didn't even need the buttons to close, it was so big compared to her frame that it simply draped over her front like a blanket or a robe.

It was a bit difficult to visualize how she might seem to another, but in her opinion . . . she looked oddly good in it.

It gave off this sense of . . . lazy, uncaring authority, almost. An imposing jacket that obviously belonged to a guard that wasn't being worn properly or did it fit on her.

That thought, of how she looked, brought a bit of insecurity to the surface.

Kat was sitting silently on the couch, lost in thought.

Emhreeil felt a pang of embarrassment in her gut for what she was about to ask, a reminder that maybe she hadn't left as much of her old self behind as she would have liked.

"You really, really shouldn't wear that," Katherine said before she could even open her mouth, and she turned slightly to face her.

"Why? This is the third floor, right? Guards don't wander around here . . . usually . . ." She trailed off, her brows furrowing as she tilted her head. Why had there been guards in that waste disposal facility?

Katherine opened her mouth, then closed it. Squinted at empty air a bit.

"How long did you say you were in the sewers for?" Kat asked, and she felt an odd sense of foreboding.

What had she missed?

"I can't say with any accuracy, but it felt like months. Realistically, at *least* one? Maybe a bit less?" She started, turning to face her friend fully, and felt her knees wobble from the motion, one of her knees suddenly just giving out without any warning, nor sign of actual strain.

Katherine was out of her seat before her yelp had even finished, before her outstretched hand could even reach the couch, hands fisted onto the jacket, pulling her up and closer, straight.

Goddamn it. She had to eat again. And not just . . . these little snacks.

She straightened with a sigh and could feel the worried twist to Katherine's features as she used the jacket to hold her up, pull her straight.

"I'm fine."

"Are you sure—"

"Kat, you're not princess-carrying me through the streets."

Katherine's mouth clicked shut with a nod, and after making sure she was stable, stepped back.

"Anyways, why did you ask? What did I miss?"

The deep, deep breath that Katherine took before exhaling it all out in an equally massive sigh, was all the warning she got before those three words left her mouth, and she froze in the middle of trying to straighten the jacket one-armed.

"A civil war."

Her sightless glare crawled to meet Katherine's as her slack jaw jerkily closed.

"I . . . explain?"

"It's . . . a lot of things. I don't know the whole of it, but Lady Anna does, and she likes to rant when she's upset. Long story short, there was an attack on a teleporting station near the Golden Road, by some adventurer's group based on the third floor. Second strongest, right after the Scions, and according to the newspapers, it was a very small gap. I think their team name was Seven-Six-Two. The station . . . well, it burned down. The highborn didn't take kindly to all this, flooded the dungeon with the Guard to bring the place to heel, but it's only escalating. I expect a full war to begin soon."

She remembered that station.

Thus, that statement didn't make any sense.

"What do you mean the station burned down? There's nothing flammable there," she uttered quietly.

The jacket was starting to weigh on her weak frame.

"I mean that it turned into a giant lake of molten metal and glass, Em," Kat said, with an odd tone of having given up on thinking about how insane that was.

Emhreeil tried to picture it. That building, so impossibly gargantuan, two floors of epic proportions that made any human that walked within them feel like an ant in a human's palace, enchanted from top to bottom almost, all turned to molten slag.

It was genuinely too hard to even imagine that. The scope was too wide, the feat too ridiculous.

"There's literally nothing left of it. There were some vivid descriptions in the papers about it. There was this . . . vortex of almost-white fire that could literally be seen from the royal palace across half the country in broad daylight, and by the time the Crimson Guard managed to smother it, the station was melted and vaporized along with a hundred feet of the surrounding area being torched black. The latest death report was almost two and a half thousand dead, and counting. A lot of tradesmen, some minor nobles, adventurers too. Not just civilians. People call the station's remains 'The Brand' now, because from above, that's what it looks like." When Katherine finished, her tone had a tiny inflection that suggested she was explaining as much as she was reciting to her what she'd read.

Wordlessly, she walked up to the couch Kat was leaning against and did the same, arms limp by her side on its leathery back.

The Crimson Guard. She remembered reading about them as a teenager, not by her own choice, but intently all the same.

They were essentially demigods, by most people's standards. The best of the best that Carmera's royal family could afford, the ones who delved two, three levels down into the Factory just to keep leveling. The ones who would get sent overseas in place of an actual army, to deal with whatever uppity kingdom decided to send ships over the Black Ocean to reach Carmera.

They were never enough to *hold* the territory, but that wasn't their role. They were a walking team of weapons. Declare war on Carmera, the country with the most profitable, largest, and most brutal dungeon in the entire world, and you could expect these six to drop out of the sky, raze a couple of your port cities to the ground, annihilate your navy, then disappear again.

Carmera hadn't been at war in over ninety years, and part of it was attributable to the Crimson Guard. Of course, the giant, dark ocean covered in unspeakable horrors and leviathans also contributed heavily to making Carmera unable to expand or be invaded by sea. The lightning cannons covering the mountains and walls made aerial assault impossible as well, at least by any large force.

But the Crimson Guard were a big part of this . . . untouchable nature of Carmera. At least from the outside.

All of a sudden, she was rather glad she'd read up on the basics of military history. The added context was immensely helpful to help her frame these events in her head.

To hear that even with the Crimson Guard at the scene, two thousand people ended up dead, was difficult to even comprehend. They were a team built for war, but still, they had to have barriers, some kind of damage-control capabilities, right?

And what Kat had mentioned about a full-blown civil war erupting . . .

Carmera had a standing army, yes.

But it was *tiny* in comparison to the actual population. How would this even work? Would they just conscript literal *tides* of mercenaries from overseas with the next metal shipment?

Or would they just conscript from the various factions that inevitably would form from the kingdom trying to expand into the dungeon *properly?* Then, it might not be "the kingdom versus the uppity undersiders," it would just be common man versus common man, fighting for who would hold their leash.

Like slaves.

Like *dogs*.

The whole situation was only just unraveling itself to her, and she already hated everything about it. She wanted nothing to do with this.

So with a heavy heart, she sighed and shrugged off the red jacket, which Katherine quickly noticed her struggling with and helped by tugging the sleeve off her hand.

"Thanks," she muttered, and flexed her shoulder blades a little, leaning back. Katherine nodded, gathering the jacket and folding it on her lap, likely out of habit.

A minute passed in silence, both of them lost in their thoughts. She was just trying not to think too much about the civil war.

Eventually, Katherine tapped her forearm, and she focused back on the present.

"Did you run into a golem, by any chance?" Katherine asked, and nodded her head toward the goblin girl, who was sitting cross-legged, holding the bundle made of her own shirt tight against her stomach.

Emhreeil startled as she realized how Katherine knew that.

"I— Yeah. Wait, is *that* what she's been holding on to this entire time?" she asked, voice rising in hope.

Katherine nodded.

She groaned in pure, unadulterated relief, slumping slightly.

Feeling oddly reinvigorated, she pushed off the couch and quickly walked to the goblin, who watched her like a wary owl chick, eyes wide and body curling down like a wary animal trying to mold its body to the wall.

She tried to crouch down, but with how weak her legs felt, she only just managed not to fall on her ass, fumbling down to sit cross-legged next to the goblin with jerky, clumsy movements.

For a moment, they just "stared" at each other.

Emhreeil found that the goblin was . . .

It was *adorable*. And something about that was so . . . disconcerting on an emotional level.

Her entire life, she'd been told goblins were these horrid, malformed creatures with gigantic triangles for noses, beady red eyes, mismatched teeth, and a permanent sneer of hatred. Subhuman wretches that were too lowly to ever enter their walls, not as servants or slaves or pets.

In the dungeon, she'd seen a decent amount of them, which clued her in to the descriptions being rather exaggerated.

But seeing something in crappy lighting through a crowd, usually from a fair distance away, was not nearly enough to realize *how* exaggerated.

Her eyes were *huge*. Her hair was short and scruffy, not reaching past her shoulders, and her nose was like a little button. She almost wanted to press it.

She couldn't see her eyes beyond feeling the surrounding eyelids and tension in her features, but she assumed they were not beady red holes of hatred.

And her ears were not these . . . leathery, scrunched flaps of skin she'd been expecting. They felt more like *Emhreeil's* ears before she lost most of them, just upsized by twenty times, being longer than the goblin's head from chin to hair, and subtly moving with muscles hidden behind the ear's base. It was cute.

She wanted to touch them.

The goblin uncurled the shirt-dress hesitantly, and fished out the objects Emhreeil had been inwardly stressing about and suppressing. A compass and a golem core. She sort of held them in her open palms together, making an odd, questioning croak.

Emhreeil couldn't help but feel her lips twitch into a small smile. She sounded like a squeaky little frog.

For a thoughtless moment, she moved her arms to take them, before remembering her right arm was no longer there and awkwardly abandoning the motion. She licked her lips.

"Kat? Could you grab and hold on to these?" she asked, and gestured to her stump as if to answer a question not yet spoken.

Katherine simply nodded and marched over like a soldier, making the goblin tense a little bit, before extending her hands to Katherine.

Her friend shoved the things into her coat pockets with genuine care, as deep as they could go, and the goblin shifted, pulling up the stretched shirt until it was on her knees.

Which had the very unfortunate side effect of making Emhreeil momentarily feel her . . . private bits with mana, and she froze, immediately halting the small pulses she'd been sending in her direction.

God*damn it*, it was already awkward enough trying to regulate the mana pulses enough to not go through Katherine's clothes and accidentally "feel her up." Now she felt like some disgusting creep.

She dropped her face into her open palm and groaned.

"Why is she *not* wearing any clothes besides the shirt?" she miserably whined, and after a moment of silence, Katherine inhaled sharply before clearing her throat awkwardly.

"Oh. *Oh*, uh, um, we didn't . . . I mean, she didn't really grab enough attention for someone to notice. I—I didn't think about your . . . skill. I'll go ask Lady Anna for some garments in her size. The things I requested from her should be ready as well. I— Sorry? I'll be back." Katherine fled, and Emhreeil couldn't help but snicker a little at how easily flustered her friend got by the insinuation.

Then she remembered her previous request she hadn't gotten to ask, and jerked her head up.

"Wait! Could you grab some bandages and a veil too? It's just . . ." She waited until Katherine turned around and vaguely gestured at the disfigured mess that was her head.

Katherine nodded, expression not shifting in the slightest from the mildly embarrassed purse of her lips, then turned away again and fled.

With nothing else to do, she sent another pulse of mana, a small one, roughly where the goblin's head was, taking great care to direct and weaken it.

It was staring at her, its head tilted, blinking lazily.

She wanted to pet it.

Wait, no.

Her.

The girl wasn't an animal. She was told they were like one, and it certainly didn't seem much more intelligent than a human child, but it felt *wrong* to call her an "it."

Thoughts freshly organized, she doubled back on the initial impulse.

She wanted to pet her.

She shuffled forward a little bit, before slowly extending her hand toward her.

The goblin sort of . . . scrunched her shoulders up, eyes widening as she tried to curl her neck down to hide her head between her tiny shoulders, likely staring at Emhreeil's hand, judging by the angle of her head.

The same hand that had turned a man's head into charred paste a mere foot or two away from her, back in the factory.

With that thought in mind, Emhreeil was fully expecting the goblin to flee or just lean away in fear at least, but proving her previous bravery in both helping her initially and not fleeing when Emhreeil walked away, she just progressively tensed, but stayed put.

Her fingers brushed against scruffy hair, and it was exactly what she was expecting.

Greasy, dirty, and likely stiff with errant chemicals that had glued onto the strands and made them feel more like coarse hay. It oddly reminded her of the wolf's fur.

She didn't feel much revulsion, truth be told. She'd licked blood and spider slime off her buddy. She was beyond such things by now. She didn't feel much beyond an odd sense of gratitude.

Had this little thing not given her that health potion, "wasted it" according to the guard, could she have even been coherent enough to realize what she had to do? Would she have been able to even coordinate her body and mind enough to kill the guards?

Was this yet another person or something *close* to one, that she owed her life to?

She didn't know how she could fit the goblin into her little makeshift team, nor what she would do when she'd find her friend again. Hell, she didn't even know *how* she would go with him, if she could even keep up with him and help him or just be a burden. She wasn't even sure if he'd want her to come with him.

And if she did go, what about Katherine? What about this nameless goblin that she was now apparently in charge of?

Part of her, a guilty, whispering, feral part of her, wished to leave all this behind, completely and utterly, and stalk back into the bowels of this hell pit, as long as her friend was by her side. To leave civilization and connections behind, to kill her old self completely and utterly disconnect.

But she couldn't do that to Katherine. She couldn't do that to herself after all that struggle to find her again.

When the time came, maybe she could work out some sort of compromise. A halfway, some way she could keep her pie and eat it too.

Her fingers inched forward into the strands, an inch, two, and tension melted off the goblin's shoulders, lowering.

Her palm came to cover her head, and she awkwardly brushed her fingers through the dirty locks, back, in a way she was unfamiliar with, a way she barely remembered Katherine doing to her, ages ago when she'd been at her lowest and needed someone to care.

A sniffle made her pause, her brows rising in surprise, and she drew her hand back as she felt with phantom fingers, the shy crawl of tears moving down the goblin's cheeks.

Before her fingertips could extract themselves fully, an odd garbled whimper left the goblin's lips, and small fingers clasped around her wrist for the second time since they first met, tugging her hand back.

Confused, she just let the goblin drag her hand back onto its—*her* head, and then let it sit there for a moment as she wondered what she was doing. The goblin poked her fingers, nuzzled her head into her hand, pushed against it, and Emhreeil experimentally moved her fingers, brushing through her hair.

The goblin's hands retreated to sit on her lap, and she leaned her head up into Emhreeil's touch like some kind of needy puppy, sniffling again.

Her expression slackened in understanding, and without needing more prompting, she continued her ministrations, pressing firmly down and through her hair.

She could easily picture herself in the goblin's position, years ago, when her father had pet her head as a child. If she just removed some inhibition, if she added a dash of naivety, and removed the first few years of her life spent in happiness, she could very easily put her old self right where the goblin was, needy for a caring touch.

Goddamn it. For *fuck's sake*.

She didn't need more emotional connections. She *really, really, really* didn't want more. It was both a weakness waiting to be taken away, and a rope around her waist that held her back from letting go completely, going with her wolfen friend the moment she could.

But the girl was just too adorable. She'd saved her life, and even held on to her belongings for what, according to Katherine, must have been close to a *week*. Never letting go of the rumpled shirt, stalking around corners, holding on to her things for her until she asked to have them.

She let out a sob-sigh of frustrated resignation, giving herself over to the mercurial things known as "feelings," and hung her head as she used her thumb to rub around the goblin's temple, before thumbing at the base of her ear when she moved her hand forward.

The soft little sounds of contentment were not enough to mute the sound of rapidly approaching footsteps, and the moment the door opened, the goblin turned her face away, using one hand to rub at her eyes with a sniffle, but did not lean away from her touch.

Katherine paused at the door, staring, the bags in her hand swaying from her abandoned momentum.

Emhreeil wet her lips before looking in her direction and shrugging helplessly.

Katherine let out a soft, bemused *huh* sound.

She took a moment to feel the odd contraption in her hands. Just big enough to fill up one of her hands, a sphere made up of a thousand tiny metal segments. It was embedded into a big, heavy necklace that needed a thin steel chain to even stay on her neck, the frame rectangular enough to prevent it from rolling across her collarbones with every movement.

It looked heavy and was even heavier than it looked.

"Okay, so . . . just put mana into it," Katherine provided, rather unhelpfully, and after a moment of struggling to push energy through the circuit in her throat, she just decided to touch the frame with her hand and push mana into it.

The necklace-eye activated.

A world of black and white, crisp and sharp and moving, burst into existence within her mind, and she gasped, loud and sharp.

It was odd. The point of view was centered on just under the base of her neck, and she couldn't exactly turn her head to shift her view, just the eye itself within its giant, *heavy* metal frame.

Her hand slowly waved in front of the necklace, and she felt the shifting, moving parts of the necklace twist to move the lens's focus point to her fingers.

Her throat constricted, something like a wide grin of joy forming on her face, a pressure building up in the base of her throat.

She stumbled back and collapsed into the couch, letting the eye observe the glittering light crystals of the chandelier above, colorless but wondrous.

"I assume it works?" a soft voice asked from above and behind her, and a shuddering breath preceded by a nod was her reply. The eye flitted upward, and tears prickled at her eye sockets.

Katherine looked almost exactly like she remembered.

She felt a little hand poke her own, and she sniffled, feeling her cheeks start to cramp and strain from the unfamiliar tension of a grin.

She lifted her hand and ran it through the goblin's soft silky hair as Katherine lips curled into a barely there smile before turning away to continue packing.

Whatever Katherine had done to the goblin's hair when she'd dragged her away for a bath, it felt like a soft cloud of silk now. Brushing it was extremely calming. Her pleased grumbles as she laid her upper body on the cushion, her knees on the floor, were also soothing.

She felt energized. She felt *ready*, even if she wasn't sure what exactly it was that she was ready for, a mixture of having her sight back and being well-fed doing wonders for her spirits.

Katherine knew of a place where she could get a decent food supply without draining her, and their first sample had made her satisfied. Comparing it to the wolf's blood was like trying to compare the taste of cardboard to a chocolate cherry strawberry cake, so there was no point. There wouldn't ever be anything superior.

As if a signal born from fate, summoned by her thoughts, she felt it again.

That tug, that directional pull.

Her friend was fighting something again. *Already?*

A mere ten seconds later, the sensation vanished again.

She hoped that meant he'd just gotten into a fight with a . . . rat, or something equally nonthreatening.

With any notion of calming down gone, she hissed out a sigh through her teeth and turned to the goblin.

She took her hand off and poked her in the side of the head.

A confused gibber came out of the goblin as it turned its face to look at her, and she pointed at its nose.

"Your name is Scruffy now. Is that okay?"

A moment of either confusion or contemplation, and the goblin nodded.

She nodded back and got up to walk to where Katherine was organizing the giant bundle of clothes and . . . *stuff* into something that could fit into a single large backpack.

A single outfit was laid on the table to her left, separate from the rest, and she walked up to it, blasting the outfit with mana.

It looked . . .

Honestly, it looked like Katherine just decided to take her own pitch-black wardrobe and replace the leather trench coat with a black cloak and hoodie. Long shirt, long pants, boots. Next to it was a wide, long, thin black scarf they'd use to cover her face until they could get their hands on a pair of masks of some sort.

The next hour was a blur of silent preparations and packing and changing, during which the only notable thing that happened was Scruffy dragging a chair to the desk that Katherine was organizing on and learning how to fold clothes that were about as big as herself.

She even looked like she was having fun. That was something nice the goblin could do. Be their . . . sort-of servant?

It was slow and hard, but it was a cute sight, and Katherine was more patient with Scruffy than before, so Emhreeil simply watched in silence, appreciating the fact that she *could see*. Black and white, but still.

The grin seemed to be permanently etched onto her face.

She couldn't wait to find him again. She couldn't wait to *see* him. She wondered if he'd be as horrific as his voice and species. Hopefully not.

Meanwhile, Katherine gave Scruffy some of Lady Anna's old childhood clothes, which were . . . high quality and criminally adorable and *very* unfitting with their own color scheme, but that was all they dared ask for. Kat quickly shooed her away to dress up.

A green-skinned goblin in a white silky skirt and kid's shoes with a vaguely brown button shirt was such an absurd sight that Katherine started snickering to herself when Scruffy trotted back to them, pulling and glaring at the clothes that were likely so comfortable they were *un*comfortable to her.

Soon, they had nothing else left to do, and so, unescorted and without much ritual, they walked out of the side gate they'd been directed to, waved through by heavily armored guards, and walked out into the dungeon.

Since when were the streets so damn *loud?*

It wasn't even the sounds she'd been expecting, like . . . actual violence, fighting, a *civil war*, or explosions or *something* like that.

She'd never heard anything like this when walking through the third floor's streets. People were too downtrodden and depressed to do things like what she was hearing. At least not on such a scale.

Even as she walked beside Katherine, the goblin pulling and tugging at her new clothes like they were something magical and strange as she jogged behind them, she could identify at least three different, very distant chants from different directions, echoing and melding together into this hum-buzz of noise. There were posters on every main street wall, bright paint was used to write slogans on a genuinely mind-boggling amount of walls and alleys, lifts and chem-tanks, walkway supports and storefronts.

They couldn't go more than five minutes without seeing some catchy or cheesy phrase like the higher they're born, the harder they'll fall scrawled across any vaguely flat surface. Including the floor.

After an hour, which left Emhreeil mentally and physically exhausted from the sudden overstimulation of both senses and thoughts, they took another lift down.

To be able to see that sprawling vista of ominous wires and lights and fading bridges and walkways intersecting and haphazardly going through each other was so comforting. She could almost add color with her imagination.

The commotion and general buzz of activity somehow kept getting more intense when they arrived at their destination.

The station had so many people out and about that for a moment, she froze, feeling oddly disconnected, like a wrench within a pile of nails, just something that didn't fit. It felt so odd to be around people again, and so many of them.

It felt odd to see even a passing glance directed her way. She felt strange. It felt *wrong* to be amongst a crowd.

She adjusted the black bandage-like fabric that Kat had wrapped around her head, just to be sure nobody could see her face or, really, anything at all under her hood. Another note of insecurity rang as she realized her mangled fingers were on full display despite the long-sleeved shirt, and she stomped down the desire to grab a glove from somewhere just to hide them too, instead shoving the hand under the cloak.

As they went down, farther and farther away from her furry friend, even if temporarily, she couldn't help but wince and grimace every time his existence would flare out into the back of her mind, a subtle thing that rarely lasted more than ten to thirty seconds, repeating every ten to thirty minutes.

The surroundings got a lot more intense as they continued. Not hostile, but just . . . riled up. Ready and energetic.

Shouldn't it be the other way around? The higher up, the more intense it would be? Why was it like this?

She tried to focus on shifting the eye necklace around, staring at the odd sight of metal barricades suspended sideways several feet off the floor in every major street by amateur pulley systems and chains welded onto random buildings everywhere, all facing outward. The fact that there were no irate shopkeepers or enforcers tearing the things down for defacing their businesses or cluttering the air and forcing the passing wires aside was even more odd.

Someone was playing . . . very energetic jazz music through a loudspeaker, somewhere below, echoing up the vast edifices of weaving metal and glass. The distorted sound was oddly disturbing from up here, like someone scraping at a machine's coiling innards.

The people were the biggest difference. They were *loud*. Some smiled, some just talked, all things that people didn't really tend to do from her experience, not down here.

Another couple lifts down, with her energy flagging and her body feeling like a sack of rocks, not at all helped by Scruffy holding on to her trench coat, more rough, vaguely melodic sounds gripped her attention.

She turned the eye necklace to the side as they walked through a crowd in a vast overhang, seeing a big group of seeming strangers all huddled around the statue of some dungeon baron or another, while on a metal table right next to it, some guy with a guitar was giving the performance of a lifetime, nodding his head and swaying to his own beat. Even with the way the fighting lyrics were barely audible and the way the sound carried terribly through the commotion, she felt like his song and raspy smoker's voice was revitalizing her, filling her blood with adrenaline, scratching at her eardrums in a way that made her want to move.

It had been so long since she'd last seen any kind of bard or music-related Pather just . . . giving a performance outside. No shop, no bar, no special occasion at a guild, no kind of payment she could see, just . . . a guy with a guitar singing fight songs while the crowd cheered or tried to sing along. Almost like some bizarre impromptu concert.

"Is there really a civil war going on . . . ?" she muttered in disbelief as they turned a corner, flitting into one of a dozen alleys on the outskirts of the marketplace.

"It's certainly a strange thing," Katherine said. "I guess having something to unite over, a common purpose, or at least common *disdain* toward some-thing, is making people a lot more energetic and communicative. At least, that's Lady Anna's theory. I will *never understand* how a civil war made the third floor *better*."

Emhreeil couldn't help but find that comment ceaselessly hilarious because it was *true*. "How are people this . . . changed, I suppose? I haven't even seen someone shake a guy down for his money yet. Where are the gangs, what are they doing?" she asked, and Katherine sighed.

"I don't think it really matters, Em. They're pretending to be turning a new leaf, 'one with the people' or some such drivel, but in truth they're just letting up on their usual activities a bit to raise morale further and steer people toward fighting the kingdom instead of inviting it in. As far as Lady Anna knows, it's not working the way they wanted it to. It's like people are seeing that life can be more than what it was, better without gangs *or* the kingdom involved, and the tension's gone three ways now." Someone came near them, and Katherine briefly paused as the man walked past them.

"The gangs are trying to play nice while keeping a hold of their authority and are barely managing to do either, the people seem to be forming up with the Crow's Church and the Struggler's Mantle as their chosen representa-tives, and it's gone from a possible two-way civil war to a four-way civil war, with a dozen small factions forming each side. In short, I don't really think it matters. It's an absurd, gigantic mess with millions involved. Lady Anna is following the developments closely, and even she can barely make sense of it. Best to stay out of it as much as possible, I think." Katherine finished as they turned another corner, and a simple question ate away at her.

"But what if the kingdom wins?" she asked quietly, and Katherine's shoul-ders drooped.

"I don't know. Whatever happens, I'm with you. Worst-case scenario, we leave. There are worse places than this, but also much better ones. We could figure something out."

Could they?

Her mood dropped, but she said nothing more as they shouldered past a crowd cheering and hollering at a pair of men fist-fighting in a makeshift ring of palettes and wire fencing, smacked down into the middle of a wide commercial road under an arched bridge of steel, surrounded by shops like bakeries and tailors and blade sellers, lit by crystal lights.

The shops were sending people out to try and sell stuff to the people making a mess outside, instead of trying to tell them to pack up and leave. The gang enforcers were nowhere to be seen.

The scent of cigarette smoke, booze, fresh bread, and sweets and oil was a strangely addicting mix of smells, she noted, as the crowd thinned around them before cutting off, leaving them with a long road covered in people that *weren't* glaring at everyone in sight suspiciously or trying to disappear into the walls around them.

She felt like she went into one dungeon and came out into another, a copy, one too improved over the original to make sense.

She idly remembered reading about how in the days before magic became so widespread, before the system even existed, tens of thousands of years ago, a kingdom would cheer when a war began, and celebrations would commence. It was the most absurd, nonsensical thing she'd ever heard in her life.

Maybe back then, wars did not mean that two groups of a couple high-level people would raze half the respective cities of each other until both sides gave up. Maybe back then, wars were not held back due to the mutually assured destruction of having high-level Pathers in their employ that could level a city within an hour, but some other factors like genuine diplomacy.

It was still *absurd* to think about people cheering for a war, even back then.

Now, she felt much the same, but she could at least see some kind of thought pattern that made things turn out like this. That sense of a common enemy, as Katherine, or Lady Anna, rather, had put it.

Her roaming eye landed on a newspaper held up by what looked like a teenager, halfheartedly moving it around for people to see, while a stack of them rested on his other hand. Behind him, a Bazi shop gave out hot beverages from an open counter.

She would have glanced away had the first words she'd seen not been "Awakened hound slaughters dozens—demon or highborn puppet??" printed out in gigantic black letters on the front, taking up almost half the page.

She paused, causing a confused croak from Scruffy as she almost ran into her legs.

"Wait," she said, and felt Katherine slow, turn around, and stop, before wordlessly following the eye necklace's gaze.

She should go up to the kid and buy it herself.

But it felt like her body had turned into half-set cement.

"Kat. Could you . . . buy that? A copy?" She whispered, feeling some hissing, squirming, vile little thing in the back of her mind scratch at her pulse, taunting her with a far-stretched possibility.

It was a coincidence, surely.

Katherine quickly did as she asked, turning the newspaper around in her hands with a blank look, reading as she came back toward them.

Emhreeil stood in place, silent and unmoving as a statue.

Katherine glanced up at her face before flicking down to the metallic eye on her sternum, and that was when she knew Kat had already connected the dots of *why* she was so interested in this paper in particular, that concerned, knowing glint in her eyes as apparent as ever despite the lack of color.

She took the newspaper with stiff fingers, and began to read.

Last night, on the upper ends of the second floor, commotion broke out. It was an ordinary, standard day for the passengers of Station 2-3-36. That was, until, according to people who have come to us with more information as well as folks interviewed on scene shortly after the incident, a giant black dog with glowing golden eyes crashed through an apartment building's window near the station, landed in a worksite, then charged straight through the metal gate and onto the outer edge of the platform. It immediately began running. Some reported it weaved between them, some said they only caught a glimpse of it before being bowled over and thrown onto the floor. But almost all of them reported that a mysterious group of men were very vigorously hunting the creature.

She felt her meager confidence crumbling already, caution and a fearful sense of determination settling in.

Glowing golden eyes.

She'd only caught a glimpse of them back at the staircase before the world collapsed out from under her, but that bit of description ruined any chance of this being a coincidence.

It hadn't even been outside for more than *two weeks* before something went horrendously wrong. Any plan she had of concealing its existence evaporated. At least to those who mattered. If it was already being hunted by professionals, the barons likely knew what was up. Or maybe if she'd be lucky and it would only be some independent group trying to catch a dog with glowing eyes for a quick buck, which would end up in deeper shit than they thought.

Optimism was nice, but it often led to disappointment. She'd bet on the former. Someone *knew*.

For a few hundred feet, this group hunted the creature, and it evaded them. That is, until a gigantic explosion of unknown origin bent the outer walkway, and unfortunately, that is as far as anyone we'd approached had seen. Most fled, the rest were herded away by men dressed in black.

Normally, this would be the end of our story. A monster appears in the dungeon, it is caught, and its fate is then decided by its captors. As you can guess by the headline adorning this very paper, such a happy conclusion did not come to pass. As the fight with the creature moved toward the center of the station, it would appear some lifts had stalled or been attempted to be halted, pointing to the suspicion that this was all either premeditated or very, very well organized.

Another massive explosion rocked the dungeon soon after, a fireball seen from all the way down Brightman's Alley. We do not know precisely what happened after, only the tragic ending. One of the lifts leaving the station seemed to have been burdened by the creature's presence, likely using the lift as an escape from its pursuers. All thirty-one passengers and a man presumed to be one of the hunters arrived mutilated and torn to shreds beyond any hope of recognition.

Her metallic eye moved up to the start of the paragraph. Down again.

She read it three, four times, before taking a deep, deep breath. Her throat felt dry.

One of the people we've reached through much risk and expense, who was at the scene and wishes to remain anonymous, has described the monster. They have said its color was darker than the most absolute, deepest black, a featureless, roiling void into reality, hazy as if covered by writhing fog, and mounted atop its back, three mangled heads dangled down from writhing tentacles that held on to them with black veins of nothingness.

The darkness of its form dripped blood endlessly, but neither its steps nor its breaths made any sound whatsoever. And so, armed with all this loose, vaguely connected info, we are left to make our own conclusions, our own speculations. Was this another case of a madman losing his experiment and trying to reclaim it? Was this a real, genuine demon, as it appears, and does that mean the Church of the Six-Winged Dove will descend into the dungeon for its head? Or perhaps the highborn decided to let their monsters out to play within our home, hoping to kill our morale—

She stopped reading, lowering the newspaper. The eye on her neck ran out of mana, and she didn't bother turning it back on, finding the darkness helpful in just . . . processing all that.

Thirty-two.

It was hard to visualize, to digest. Past a dozen faces, it started shifting, turning into a number rather than a group of people.

She turned, feeling like a blocky machine glued onto stilts, wavering in place a little as the newspaper fell from limp fingers. She lifted her hand to touch the necklace, charging it.

The fighting ring, the people within, without. She began to count them.

By the time she'd reached thirty, almost two-thirds of the people around her were a victim in her eyes.

It was a lot easier to drink in and understand the impact of her friend's actions when she could see the people around her and imagine them turning into shredded piles of meat.

"Em? Is it . . . you know . . . ?" Katherine asked from behind, a steady, firm hand landing on her shoulder, keeping her stable in more ways than one.

Emhreeil took a deep, deep breath that made her lungs burn, and nodded.

She felt . . . stiff. From the fact that despite the guilt churning in her gut, despite the resigned sadness for the lives lost and the acceptance of what exactly her friend seemed to be fighting every time his presence would flare out into the back of her head, she still could not bring herself to even consider changing her answer.

The line she'd drawn in her mind was carved into unyielding stone, and she could only wish her emotions would reflect that, in time.

"What do we do?" Katherine asked, tightening the hand on her shoulder.

Scruffy bent down to pick up the newspaper and then hesitantly planted her knuckles on Emhreeil's leg in some strange gesture of solidarity.

She felt unstable. And for once, it felt so nice to have people there to keep her upright.

She took a deep breath.

"Nothing different, Kat. I knew it was going to kill people. I'm not sure I'll be able to even stop it. And I'm not sure I'd turn away, even if I couldn't. It's . . . you don't have to be here, you know? You can still back out of this," she said, her voice oddly firm and quiet even to her own ears, despite feeling like a stone had settled into the base of her throat.

Kat had *said* she couldn't and *wouldn't* ever hate her, but this was the first time that promise was brought to bear between them since it was made.

The hand on her shoulder squeezed with a deep, tired inhale, laced with uncertainty.

"It's . . . Em, I'm . . . disappointed, even if I'm not sure about what. And I can't say I understand whatever bond you have with it," Kat continued, and like a sentenced man accepting the strikes of the whip, she stood there, stiff, tanking the blows in silence, waiting for the final strike of the guillotine.

"But I already said I'm not leaving you. I've told you three times already. If you're sure we don't do anything different, then let's just go to the apartment and regroup, plan. You still have a lot to tell me. And we could use a day to process, think. So let's just keep going. Okay?" Katherine squeezed her shoulder, and she nodded, the lens of the eye unfocusing, relief releasing her tongue, snipping away the invisible ropes keeping her glued in place.

But it quickly faded, even as her legs stiffly turned and began walking.

"Thank you," she mumbled, and Katherine's steps slowed until she was walking by her right side, their pace matching.

An arm tossed itself over her shoulders, rather awkwardly, as Katherine was half a head shorter than her.

"No need. Come on."

Scruffy swapped her grip to hold on to Katherine's trench coat.

The apartment, if it could even be called that, was in one of the most unwelcoming spots she'd ever seen, at least from first impressions.

The visual of this large squat metal dome being entombed by the dreary towering skeletons of buildings once full of life was very striking. Surrounded on all four sides, and with multiple fenced paths that led to it, she theorized that this could have been something like a central command point of sorts, long ago.

The uncomfortably tall factory complex around the structure smothered all light from outside, hiding it through monstrous containers, machines, and pipeworks, all half nestled within its concrete floors. Only bare hints of bleed-over light peeked through the blurry expanse above, most of it serving to make the fog along the top floors seem like it was softly glowing.

Opposite the entrance to the dome was a thin alley they were currently walking through that led into the large complex, and behind them, across the street from the alley's entrance, an open tavern restaurant stood, well-lit with warm light, the lower floor an open sprawl of activity, and the upper one a cozy, curving vista of glass and likely much higher prices. Baron Simian's enforcers prowled about to make sure nobody started any trouble.

The sheer contrast between these two environments, despite being mere feet apart, was a strange feeling.

It was like she'd just walked into an alleyway and entered a different world, the clamor and chatting from behind them turning muted unnaturally quick, as if they were transitioning through limbo as the alley's walls retreated behind them.

She took the opportunity to just gaze upon this bizarre, haunting scenery. The grandiosity of it, mixed with the cloying darkness not allowing her to see much more than vague shapes and impressions, the eerie silence broken only by distorted whispers of activity from someplace that sounded incredibly distant but was a mere hundred feet away, the fog accenting corners and pillars and gears and dizzying stretches of exposed machinery grafted into stone and steel buildings, blurring and fading.

It didn't even look *real*. It felt like she was gazing at the frozen memory of a dream.

Nothing moved. Nothing talked.

Just the gray impressions of dusty, hollow windows surrounding them like a cage of glass, stretching toward the white fog above, hinting at light they wouldn't be seeing anytime soon.

Something moved out of the corner of her gaze, and the golem's eye whirred to the side so suddenly she worried she might accidentally break its inner mechanisms.

A fleeting shadow, maybe? A trick of the eye? Whatever it was, she couldn't find it again.

Even stiffer than before, she did naught but keep walking.

She was sure someone lived in those ruins around them. She couldn't find a reason for them *not* to. Buying or renting a place was a luxury for many down here, no matter how small or pathetic. Finding an abandoned little spot to live in was a good idea, if one was willing to deal with the very real possibility of being suddenly murdered or worse, away from people and any notion of safety.

The fact that behind each and every window, a desperate soul might be staring down at them, only made the place more uncomfortable to her.

How the hell did Kat *live* in this place?

The metal floor abruptly turned to a mix of cobble and concrete, uneven, seemingly ancient, slick with chemicals and half-melted moss.

To her right, the faint roar of rushing liquid drew her attention, and she turned the eye to catch a peek of a geyser of superheated water spraying out of a gigantic pipe toward the sky, turning into warm fog before it could even properly pressurize back into water.

That revealed where the absurd humidity was coming from. With the scarf in the way too, it felt like she was trying to inhale slime.

Before she could consider whether or not she should adjust or remove the scarf, she felt the arm around her tighten, Katherine's steps slowing.

A surge of mana revealed why, crawling all over a massive pair of curved metal doors as the eye on her sternum kept roaming the haunting, towering emptiness above.

Katherine's arm swung off, and without much preamble, she stepped forward, opened an inconspicuous metal plate to the side, just six inches long, revealing a pad of buttons, unmarked.

Practiced and likely by rote, Katherine tapped at the buttons in a pattern, and the doors hissed open.

She stood there, staring at the pitch-black hallway of metal that apparently led to Kat's apartment.

Katherine gently placed the metal plate over the button pad, hiding it once more, then stepped into the hallway, absent-mindedly stretching her hand to press another button without looking, with a familiarity that was oddly effective in settling Emhreeil's unease.

Kat knew this place well. Undue surprises were unlikely.

Weak sputtering light bulbs lit up the hallway, hanging from the ceiling on exposed wires, and she mutely followed, Scruffy nervously sticking to her side.

She curiously split her attention between sight and feel as they moved through the hallway, which was surprisingly cramped and short considering the dome's size.

It was full of locked metal doors of surprising variety, some double doors with faded glass windows, some single, some made of heavy, enchanted metal, and the weirdest one being a door that had a massive glass wall to its left. She couldn't see what was behind it, as the entire glass was covered up from the inside with glued paper and random trash, smeared paint and dried sludge. She could only assume someone lived in there and didn't want people peeking at him.

Up a flight of stairs that rattled in place, cutting the dome in half, and they were on the upper floor, in the middle of a cross-shaped hallway that cut the upper floor in four equal parts.

Katherine turned to a door on the left, walked up to it, and repeated the same process of digging out a number pad and inputting a password to open the door before putting the plate back and reaching in to open the light.

Then Kat turned toward her and awkwardly extended a hand into the room in invitation.

She hesitantly walked in, pulsing mana and letting the golem eye, or perhaps *her* eye now, roam.

It was rather nice, surprisingly, and much smaller than she'd expected.

It was shaped like the top-left quadrant of a circle cut in four equal parts, the left wall flush with the door once opened. In the middle of the large curving wall opposite the entrance was a small skylight of curved glass, though the view was rather dreadful.

It hung over a giant metal storage cabinet with a mattress thrown atop it, and on the right wall was a single heating cell with a metal heating plate on top, a couple cooking implements hung across the wall on hooks and the like around it, while above and below it rested more metal cabinets.

In the left corner was a small open shower with a small depression in the floor and a series of small grates for the water, with a single curving curtain to hide the outside world, and just next to it was a single . . . nightstand, of sorts.

It was obviously some kind of storage closet, before whoever owned this building turned it into a small but functional room.

Her eyes landed on a pristine-looking necklace sitting on the metal nightstand, and she paused as she observed it, surprised to see something like that amongst Katherine's near-nonexistent belongings.

It was a rather intricate little piece of silver, not much bigger than a coin, and from its surface jutted out the portrait of a youthful smiling woman with pointed ears.

Was that . . . her?

Katherine's and Scruffy's steps followed her in, and before she could think of a way to ask, the door had closed.

Katherine took three steps before noticing her gaze, and paused mid-stride.

"I got that from an old man in the corner of a square. Did portraits on silver pieces with some tiny tools. A silver for two, he said. I . . . didn't know if I'd ever see you again, so I asked him to sculpt you. Just as . . . a sentimental reminder, I suppose. Haven't gotten to wear it much. People will do a lot of stupid, rash things if you look like you can afford to be carrying jewelry around."

Her lips curled into an exhausted smile.

"That's . . . really sweet," she mumbled, and felt Katherine relax a little behind her, before snapping her gaze to Scruffy, who was poking around the heating box.

After working in a processing facility, the goblin probably knew a couple things about machinery. Still, Katherine didn't seem to appreciate its clumsy poking, and quickly dragged her away by the scruff of her shirt to deposit her at the foot of the makeshift bed.

With three people in a vaguely triangular room that couldn't have been bigger than twelve feet across in any direction, with a low ceiling and cluttered with sparse furnishings, they barely had room to walk around each other.

Katherine seemed to realize this too, when she turned around and almost stumbled into her shoulder before peering around her feet to see where she could move without stomping on anyone's toes.

Em just kept looking at the necklace. It was nice to think that someone had been thinking about her back then, even if only occasionally.

Katherine cleared her throat as Scruffy stuffed herself into the corner next to the heating box, trying to find a comfortable way to sit in a skirt.

"You get the bed, Scruffy gets a large pillow I have, and I'll sleep on the floor if you want."

She snorted, amused and nostalgic both, her shoulders shaking a little as tension fled from her frame.

"No, we'll sleep in the same bed. We can fit. But . . . remember when we did that back at the manor, back when that royal event was happening and my parents were gone? And we overslept, so—"

"So Amelia came in because she thought you were out of bed, and then spent the next day panicking 'cause she thought I'd bedded you. By the time I'd caught her and asked her to keep quiet, she thought we were having some affair of sorts, and was wondering how to cover for us. She was a good girl," Katherine announced, a wide, amused smile on her face, a reminiscing look in her eyes.

"I didn't know her name was Amelia," she simply replied, and went to sit on the bed, letting her thoughts focus on something nicer and less complicated than her current predicament.

"I think you just forgot. Anyways, let's go to bed. We plan tomorrow."

She hesitated for a moment before nodding, and began to shrug off the jacket. The scarf around her head remained.

The hands of a nonexistent clock spun until the metal wore away, hours spent thinking, jumping from one spiraling pit to another, until she had some vague notion of cohesion left in the tangled yarn that was her mind.

And finally, sleep came, hours later.

She dreamt of herself, wearing blood-slick fur, surrounded by the horror-filled screams of dying men and women.

The next day began with an odd experience.

Waking up in a bed, relatively comfortable and warm, to the scent of food.

It was nice. Domestic. Unusual.

They all sat on the bed side by side with mushroom-paste bread slices Katherine had bought for them, a taste like bread mixed with mushroom sauce, strong and savory. She liked it. Even if she could only lick the small slice she had for the flavor, unable to actually eat it, it was still nice.

Her actual meal came in the form of a thick paper bag, tightly sealed and full of blood, sitting on the heating unit with a small preservation charm on it. Katherine didn't tell her how much it cost, but she could guess it cost far more than anything her companions needed combined. The guilt of that was another drop added to the lake.

After opening the bag and carefully gulping down the whole thing to not spill any on the floor, she felt ready to face the world.

Or its diseased underbelly, at the very least.

"So. What do we do? If you have a plan, I'd like to know," Katherine asked, a vital question, and Emhreeil set the paper bag, now empty, down by her feet.

She cleared her throat, feeling well for the first time in a while.

"I've been thinking about this for a . . . while. It's why I slept so late last night. First, we do that errand I mentioned. It's on our way up anyways. It'll put some padding to our pockets too, if that man is to be believed."

"If. From what you told me, he did not sound reliable or trustworthy."

She nodded.

"Still, nothing to lose from doing that. We do that, then we find *it*. That's where things get a little messy. For starters, he's already being hunted. He's already *somewhat* known. That newspaper was a local one, and it releases daily drivel. I recognize it. That means it was only a front-page story for a day or two, with some luck. Thirty people dying can't be that big of a story with a literal war slowly breaking out, not for long. Also, this is the third floor. Not that many people can read down here. Maybe something like one in three? So . . . people might have heard or read about him, but I doubt it's made him infamous. He's not like what is described at all either, so it's not like anyone will recognize him on sight. Regardless . . . the general plan of action is to go do that errand, find him, figure out some way to properly communicate. Likely while tagging along with him. Then I could explain things to him. Teach him *who* to hurt, to not have the entire dungeon screaming for his head. There's a difference between killing thirty innocents in a lift and killing thirty gangster scumbags spread out over half a floor. Another thing I want to do is finish this . . . vampiric trait. I want to turn." She briefly paused to check Katherine's reaction.

She looked a little cautious, in a way, but interested. Not disapproving, so far. Good.

"I'm not sure turning into a vampire is a good idea, or even possible, but if you're sure . . ." Katherine mumbled, almost to herself, thousand-yard stare focused on the closed door.

Then Katherine's expression shifted into incredulity, and she turned to her with wide eyes.

"Wait, teach it—*him* how to speak? How?" Katherine asked, obviously disbelieving.

She grimaced. She hadn't had time to mention that in much detail.

"He can do it already. I told you it's a smart beast. I wasn't kidding. It kept trying to get me to talk so it could mimic me. I think it was trying to learn how to speak," she said, idly flicking the eye on and off, trying to get used to the sudden snap of stimuli that happened each time she did so.

"You do realize how that sounds incredibly disturbing, right?" Katherine asked.

"Just wait until you hear its voice . . ." she mumbled back with a shudder, before deciding to get back on topic.

"Okay. After I teach him who to hunt without getting half the country on his tail . . . well, I don't know. That's quite far in the future already. A more immediate problem will be money. You need actual gear, I need spells. The reason is rather obvious. If you had any notion of having a peaceful life, I'd suggest you either throw it away, or leave before you're too deep and have that choice made for you." She felt Katherine's features twist into an annoyed frown.

Yes, she'd said it like three times. She knew that. But she wanted to make sure Katherine knew what she was getting into.

Emhreeil had accepted that she'd leave any notion of a normal life behind by doing this. Maybe Katherine hadn't quite realized that yet.

"I'm not leaving," Katherine coldly said, and she nodded.

"Okay. Thank you," she mumbled, and extended her hand to the left to give Katherine's hand a brief, grateful squeeze.

"So . . . money. I'm not sure how we're going to get a whole lot of that. We might need to buy certain things for him too," she vaguely said, wondering if it would be better to raid auction and trade houses for exotic, dangerous animals or just outright buy them.

After all, there were only so many things in the dungeon it could steal body parts and organs from. It would hit a wall eventually. A wall she could help him overcome.

Conversely, that same ability of his might be able to make them all the money they could possibly need.

She could convince him to grow a bunch of rare, excessively overpriced organs that belonged to exotic animals and make a gigantic fortune from slicing them off him and selling them.

But she couldn't exactly *say* that to Kat. That'd give away the . . . big secret. She would, eventually, have to tell her.

But just . . . not yet. Not before Katherine had seen him, seen that he wasn't what his species or the stupid newspaper said he was. Or maybe that he was, but that wasn't *all* he was.

"That plan seems deceptively simple," Katherine said, and she could only shrug in reply, because it was.

"If we get too caught up in the details, we'll never get anything done. So, yeah. We need money and connections. I have some ideas for the first bit, some good, some not that great. The latter is unlikely," she admitted.

Money and connections formed the best and biggest shield one could have. She knew that, she'd seen that, she'd *been* behind that shield. And while the second part was highly unlikely, the first was not as unobtainable.

"Do you have any ideas for making a few crowns?" she asked, going through possibilities in her head.

Katherine hummed.

"Some, but I doubt they'd make nearly enough, nor be the kind of work you're thinking of. I worked in a club for a bit, for example. The pay was . . . enough for me to eat. So that's likely not going to cut it. What did you have in mind?"

She sighed, putting her elbow on her knee and supporting her head with her palm.

"The first idea I had was one you're not going to like. I could make a new adventurer team. The guild doesn't share information, and furthermore, any beastly 'pets' or companions do not have to be registered. Meaning that if I could convince him, and with some luck, we could almost have a legitimate career as an adventurer team. You, me, him, and Scruffy. Just taking up some jobs while we do whatever we decide to do on the side. Nothing too attention grabbing or dangerous, and we'll keep a low profile. Alternatively, we could make a team in the Mercenary Guild, but it's all rather . . . risky? I don't know if we want to get involved in that crowd. The Mercenary Guild was essentially a third arm of the dungeon barons, as far as I know. I doubt that's changed. We could also just loot whoever he decides to eat, which would be decent . . . pocket money." She mumbled the last part, feeling a vague sense of moral alarm at how her words sounded.

She cleared her throat and turned to Katherine, who looked contemplative for a few silent moments, the hum of the vent fan and Scruffy's shuffling being the only sounds in the room.

Katherine nodded.

"That sounds acceptable. Makes sense. We do have *some* money, though. I kept the vast majority of the crowns you gave me back then. It's in the central bank on the second floor. So we could buy another spell with that, and buy some half-decent armor for us both."

She thought about it and bit what remained of her lip.

Are you sure you don't want to keep it? was what she *wanted* to ask, but she already knew what Katherine would say.

"Okay. Let's go," she said instead, and reached for the hooded cloak on the nightstand, her eyes briefly lingering on the necklace.

Katherine nodded and grabbed the backpack she had prepared, stuffed full of medical supplies, some money, and clothes. Mostly clothes.

CHAPTER 11

The Great Tower was the central mode of transportation for the entire dungeon.

If one unfocused their eyes, it was a gigantic cylinder with a clock as its crown at the first floor, a megastructure a thousand feet across and several dozen times as tall, farther than anyone could see up or down.

If one focused, they'd see a dizzying network of moving parts within and without, framed by a great shell of stations and pulley systems.

The outer rim was covered in square metal cages, thousands of them, arrayed in tight formations, stopping wherever the platforms around it allowed, to pick up individuals and small cargo like simple luggage. The inner ring was a latticework of countless metal beams framing moving platforms, for larger cargo like supplies, or simply large crowds. The center ring of platforms was the biggest and hardest to get access to, used for moving gigantic shipments of steel, stone, and machinery, right in the center of the tower.

Even now, all around them, she could see small bridges of metal extend from the metal plates around the Great Tower, inching toward it, locking onto platforms, lifts, and cages before retracting with well-oiled mechanisms once they were clear.

It was just as jaw-dropping and terrifying to behold now as it was the first time.

A touch on her elbow startled her, and she spewed mana around herself by reflex with an involuntary jerk, only to relax when she realized it was just Kat holding their tickets, gesturing toward their lift.

As they moved forward, she lingered on the ticket that Kat shoved into her hand, crumpling it a little as she reached up to tug her hood down.

It was so *fucking loud*.

There were so many people here.

It made her intensely uncomfortable.

She shoved the ticket into her pants pocket. Twenty coppers per person, ten for pets and animals smaller than a person. One silver for them in total, because Scruffy was considered more of a pet than a person, at least generally.

A week's worth of labor for a factory worker, if she remembered right. A long trip with the lifts was expensive, but it was worth it.

Hopefully.

She couldn't help but feel some frustration at paying for what was once built to be a public commodity. The kingdom had built the tower without expectation of pay.

But of course, gangs existed, so like the leeches they were, they grabbed on and refused to let go.

The cage, or lift, stayed open for another ten minutes after they had settled into their corner. Some people came in after them, a small group. They gazed at her in particular with an air of caution that made her stiffen, tensing.

At not even one-fifth full, the lights above the lift's doors began flashing in warning.

A minute later, they closed, and she let the eye on her neck gaze out into the passing world from beneath the murk of her cloak, drawing comfort from Katherine's hand by occasionally grasping her wrist, as if she could *feel* her tense discomfort but couldn't quite help her with it beyond a bit of token affection.

She still appreciated it.

She whispered the instructions to herself occasionally, mildly paranoid she would forget them, and before long, they were in front of the church in question, legs aching and chest tight.

She had been expecting a little chapel, maybe a place of prayer.

This was more of a cathedral.

A gothic structure made of metal, painted pitch black in anti-corrosive paint, nary a single nail or welding mark upon its complex surface, towering within its shadowed crypt of buildings, its aggressive black spires mere feet below walkways and weaves of wire.

For such a majestic building to be nestled within such tight confines was a strange thing to see. This looked like something that should be towering over a square, a marketplace flanking it on either side.

Despite the tight alleys around it, however, there were still people here.

Outside the gates were two men wearing feathered cloaks, standing at ease on their posts beside the massive double doors, the crow-shaped masks upon their faces leering eerily at passersby, the giant round goggles glinting in the sparse light.

Or maybe it was her imagination.

As they walked forward, she caught glimpses of more feather-headed men patrolling around the building and alleys, likely to ease the worries of the worshippers or simply to declare their presence.

As they neared, she noted what kind of people would attend a gathering of the Six-Eyed Crow's Church.

It was rather surprising to see that it was mostly groups. Few people walked alone in the dungeon if they could afford not to, of course, but it was such an . . . ordinary sight to see a family going to a church, no matter how weary their eyes as they passed them.

Or a young girl flanked by two tall hard-eyed men that resembled her, likely her brothers. Something normal outside, but scarce below.

This was a place where a sense of community existed, at least enough for people to trust bringing their relatives.

She could have sworn she heard cawing as they neared, and her brows furrowed a little.

They walked up the steps, and just as they were about to pass, a guard extended a gloved, armored hand to indicate they should stop, his beady-eyed mask trained right on her.

Of course, the doors were far too wide to be blocked by one man's arm, but it was the spirit of the gesture.

They both paused, but she stayed calm. The man didn't seem aggressive; even his gesture was rather slow, almost reluctant.

"Greetings, brother forgotten. I'm afraid that golem parts are rather frowned upon within these halls. The taint of the dungeon has no place within a holy place. Can you remove it?"

She opened her mouth, closed it, licked her lips.

Should she be offended he thought she was a man?

"She is blind. It is the only way she has to see," Katherine said for her, and both guards peered at her own eye with a sense of hesitant . . . stiffness. Disgust or wariness, she couldn't tell from under their layers.

"All right. But do use it as little as possible. Have your friend assist you if you must. We have no reason to give its eyes more than they already see," the guard finished, his voice thrice-muffled by his mask, giving it a rather intimidating, distorted trill, and with that cryptic wording, he lowered his hand and nodded to them.

She shut off the eye for a bit as they climbed up the stairs just to appease them, sending out small pulses of mana, just enough for her to feel vague shapes within a six-foot radius. It was enough to not embarrass herself.

Then they were inside, and Katherine gasped, her steps pausing beside her.

She flicked the eye open, and her brows rose high, her jaw slackening.

"Whoa . . ."

They sat in the middle of a long, twenty-foot-wide walkway that separated the pews on either side. The floor looked oddly twisted, glittering like an expanse of glass shards melted back together.

Maybe it was, she couldn't tell.

Above them, a solid hundred feet tall, stood the half-cylindrical ceiling, supported by spiraling metal pillars twisting like metallic ropes, four feet wide each, pierced through by jagged metal spears, dozens of them for each pillar, uneven and seemingly randomly placed. Their spear tips were capped with powerful light crystals, lighting up the whole church.

And upon every spear sat a murder of crows, cawing and croaking and preening, swooping down to observe the worshippers, some of them even landing on people's heads and shoulders, pecking at their hair or hats.

The half-cylindrical ceiling ended at a dome, highlighting the altar at the forefront of the church and the massive church organ that loomed over it. She could see various spots where the ceiling just opened up to the dungeon above whenever a crow would get near it, an automatic enchantment that baffled her.

From the center of the dome extended a massive chain that held a chandelier, except instead of crystals, from its chains hung two semicircles of gleaming silver bowls, where hundreds and hundreds of crows sat and ate, two diligent servants scooping up any falling feed or feathers that drifted down to the altar.

Her gaze wandered back up to the pillars.

From some spears hung strange dream catchers, woven spiderwebs of rope and glittering glass, while from some others hung nets full of gleaming silver coins, shiny bottle caps, burnished bronze, small skulls, fragments of broken mirrors. On either side of the altar, just before the pews, were two long tables, where she could see people go up to and offer whatever they wished to part with.

There were not many people in the church right now, little less than a dozen, spread out healthily over the massive cathedral. But she could see some of them up front.

She saw a man go to said tables and give the broken bottom of a bottle, a girl a few copper coins, another giving a furry coat.

The only thing that was rejected by one of the altar servants was from a man who tried to give a bag of *something* to the table and was turned away, still holding it in his hands.

The lights from the spears and the chandelier covered in feeding bowls glittered off the floor, the metal surfaces, the black-painted pews, the dream catchers, giving off a bizarre effect like the fragmented insides of a colorless kaleidoscope, or light reflecting into a flat surface through shifting water.

It was nowhere near strong enough to be blinding, but the inside was *bright*, brighter than she was used to or was expecting from the half-lit windows of the cathedral.

"What on Ergos . . . ?" Katherine mumbled, taking a hesitant step forward, and Emhreeil let out a breath she hadn't realized she'd been holding.

"This is incredible," she murmured, and then startled when a black form rushed down from above to noisily flap above her head and land on Katherine's, who jerked and hunched her shoulders in surprise, a half-aborted motion leaving her hands half raised as she tried to look up at the . . .

No, that wasn't a crow, that was a raven. It was *way* too big to be a crow.

It croaked oddly as it shifted on Katherine's head, trying to find its balance, wings spread out in case it fell.

She just turned her torso toward the spectacle to stare.

Katherine's hands lowered, giving her a wide-eyed look that screamed *help me*, which she ignored because what was she supposed to do? Shoo away the holy bird that had chosen Katherine as its perch? That would likely get them kicked out.

"Uh. Just leave it?" she suggested with a small shrug.

Then the bird cawed a very, very strange caw mixed with a trill.

Katherine didn't seem to notice anything wrong with it, but she did.

She was the one who had to mentally translate unintelligible animal *noises* into words enough times to be able to connect the caw-trill sound into something that sounded like "Hello."

Still, she wasn't sure if she'd heard right. It felt like she was just hearing something and giving it meaning in translation.

"What?" she asked, somewhat dumbly, and the raven turned to her.

It let out the same noise, slightly altered, a croaking trill this time, and it was unmistakable.

It was literally saying "hello." Quite cheerily as well, if she could ascribe human aspects to its behavior.

Katherine's brows furrowed as her eyes moved up to the raven, then down to her and back, mouth open in confusion.

"Are you intelligent?" she asked bluntly, and she got her answer when the bird's eyes seemed to sharpen even further, its gaze shifting down to stare very pointedly at her . . . hips?

No, her *pockets*, where the golem core and compass were.

She sucked a breath through her teeth, suddenly nervous.

What the fuck *was* this place?

The raven jerked its head toward the altar, and she turned to see a man emerge from behind the metal statue of shifting fabric and feathers, the only one she'd seen with their face uncovered.

Then he began walking toward them.

Thankfully, the walkway was *long*, so she had time to glance back at the bird, curious and disturbed.

Unfortunately, whatever hint of higher intelligence she'd seen in its eyes seemed to have left. It just kept repeating "hello" over and over again, pecking at Katherine's hair occasionally as her friend stiffly stood there, unsure of what to do or if she was even supposed to move.

It took two minutes for the old man to reach them, a kind-faced, gray-haired individual with a mild smile on his face, feathered cloak swaying with his steps.

"Greetings, sisters forgotten. I saw you sitting here, lost. Is there something that troubles you? Any troubling dreams, any odd objects you'd like to part with?" he asked, and she realized what he was doing.

Still, shouldn't they at least get some privacy? This felt a bit strange to just . . . do in the open.

She nodded.

"Yes. Are you the bishop of this church?" she asked with confidence she wasn't quite feeling, and the man's smile widened as he nodded.

She squared her shoulders.

"There are some things that trouble me . . . Father," she started haltingly, unsure of church-speak. She had seen the Dove Church's naming conventions. Did the Crow's Church use the same? "And some things I'd like off my hands."

Judging by his demeanor, she hadn't offended him.

"I saw a . . . dream. I saw a ghoul on a conveyor belt, and it turned around to smile at me," she said, and the man's brows straightened, his smile shifting a little.

"I see. What would you like to be rid of?" he asked, quietly, and she briefly glanced around them.

Strangely, nobody seemed to be paying attention to them. But she couldn't feel any magic around. Coincidence, hopefully?

"I'd like to part with these. If you understand," she added, and with stretching fingers, managed to squeeze both the golem core and the compass into her hand without dropping either as she presented them, blindly hoping that she wasn't about to give away something as precious as an untouched golem core.

That thing was usually worth at least fifty silvers, half of a gold coin. Enough to buy a half-decent detachable prosthetic.

The bishop's eyes glanced around, the motion so quick and violent that it was disturbing considering how still the rest of him looked, smile included.

His hands came up from beneath his cloak and gingerly took the "offerings," a crystal-looking ball covered in runic scratches, and the plain-looking compass. With a sleight of hand she wasn't expecting, a single ring was dumped onto her palm, more felt than seen, as if just materializing above her palm.

"Compensation," he clearly whispered, his lips not moving whatsoever, and she could only wonder how he did that.

Her attention turned to the jewel for a moment, a rather plain thing with a simple crystal at its top and a silver body. A faint sensation registered a moment later, the prickly feel of mana compressed into the silver touching her hand.

She stiffened in surprise, her fingers slamming shut around it.

An enchanted ring for a golem's core? That was . . . a good deal. An amazing deal, even, depending on *what* exactly the ring did.

As inconspicuously as she could, she snuck the ring into her left pocket.

"Hm. Is there perhaps some wish you might make of the Crow, in light of your generous donation?" he asked as he openly cradled her "donation," and it took her a moment to realize what he was asking.

The man in the sewer mentioned a minor favor. And she was going to cash in.

"I'd wish . . . very fervently, that the Crow might let me meet a vampire who could turn me. I'm already . . . set on the path, so to speak," she breathed out, just loud enough for him to hear.

He simply nodded, not a twitch of surprise on his face.

"We shall ask," he whispered again through closed lips, and they all stood there awkwardly for a moment, unsure of if there was more to say.

The man extended his arm to the raven on Katherine's head, and the bird took the offer, hopping off to perch on his wrist.

"Farewell, sisters forgotten. Come back anytime, should you wish to know more about the Crow. Or perhaps simply to bring the little one to play with the other little troublemakers. And remember . . . should you find an unwanted soul, a scavenger, or something cursed and spurned by fate, do direct them to us. The Crow protects the unwanted." He glanced at Scruffy with a slight smile, whose eyes widened, half hidden behind Kat's leg.

She was surprised by his demeanor toward Scruffy. Most public establishments, and even some places of worship as far as she knew, didn't even allow goblins in them. Or maybe that was just the Dove?

The odd duo simply walked away, the raven mindlessly cawing its greetings to the bishop as he laughed heartily and stroked its head.

She turned her torso to face Katherine and noticed her blank, empty stare, tainted with a hint of confusion.

She swallowed.

"Well, that was . . . a lot faster and less troublesome than I thought it would be," she said, and her words seemed to shake Kat back into awareness. They didn't really have anything to say, so they just turned and walked away, out of the cathedral, back out into the open square.

"That whole place was really creepy. It screamed 'witchcraft' enough to make my skin crawl . . . What did he give you?" Katherine whispered as they wove through the thinning crowds.

"I'm not sure. It's an enchanted ring, but I can't really test what it does out in public. I'll wait until we find someplace to sleep."

Katherine nodded, straightening the pack on her back.

The inn they found after several *hours* of walking was about as low in quality as it was in its pricing, but it wasn't like they needed luxury. Just one night to sleep and keep going.

Still, if Kat's apartment was the size of a storage room, this room was the size of a bathroom. They barely fit.

She didn't quite sit on the bed as much as she fell on it, her weak knees crumpling the second a hint of tension bled out of her.

She groaned in pleasure as her protesting muscles finally got to rest, feeling Katherine lethargically shrug the backpack off and flex her shoulders and back with a worryingly loud series of cracks.

As her body rested, her mind began to pick up the slack.

Most importantly, whatever the hell did "we shall ask" mean? She hadn't thought to ask at the time, but what the fuck was that? Was she supposed to come back every once in a while and ask how the search was going? Or would they find her first?

Both options weren't great, but the latter was both disquieting and downright creepy.

She'd go back there in a week or two and ask. It seemed reasonable, even if it made her oddly embarrassed.

"Sorry for using you as a pack mule, by the way. Once I turn, I'm carrying everything for a month," she said, rubbing her burning thigh with her hand in the hopes it would relieve the incoming soreness.

"It's a good workout," Katherine replied, lightly shrugging, then fell onto the bed beside her, half twisting so that she'd land with her head on the pillow diagonally, legs hanging off the side.

As the mattress's springs creaked and groaned from their combined weight, she fished the ring out of her pocket and paused.

"Hey, could, you uh . . ." She trailed off, holding the ring up, and Kat raised her head to look at it for a moment before nodding, groaning as she raised her torso.

After grabbing the ring and slipping it onto her middle finger, Kat collapsed back into the bed.

She sent a slight prod of mana into her finger and felt a small bundle of objects form in her mind.

She gasped so sharp and fast that she almost choked, jerking upright to gape at the ring.

"Em? Em, what's wrong?" Katherine spoke hurriedly, and her jaw clicked shut.

"Dimensional ring," she breathed in complete disbelief.

Katherine went silent for a moment, before hissing "*What?*" and scooting closer.

"It's-it's a dimensional storage ring." She looked dazed.

This . . . this was worth, what, *ten* gold coins? This wasn't a *fair deal*. They'd basically *robbed* that man.

"Did he give us the wrong ring?" Katherine asked, brows high, and she briefly considered that possibility.

She focused on the items inside and paused.

A bloodied knife, an . . . eye in a tiny jar?

And a folded piece of paper.

She focused on the paper alone, and it came to the forefront of her mind, a three-dimensional object she could move around and position. She turned it, mentally placed it so it would drop onto her open palm, and yanked it out.

With a tiny puff of displaced air, a blood-speckled paper dropped into her hand.

She shook it open, and just like she thought, it was a letter. A dreadfully short and concise one.

I caught a mouse sniffing around. It didn't say much, but the clean air in its lungs and the state of its fur said enough. A nest grown fat is looking for the fledgling leech. It wants its blood back.

"What is this gibberish?" Katherine scoffed.

"It's not gibberish. Give me a second," she snapped, scowling at the letter.

She ran the words over and over again in her head for a solid minute, until she realized what it meant.

A deep breath rushed into her lungs before leaving them, her shoulders drooping.

"*Fuck,*" she hissed, dropping the letter to bury her face in her hand. "I think Irythiel is looking for me."

"Your mother . . . ? Why now? How did you reach that conclusion?" Katherine carefully asked, picking the letter up off the floor and reading it with a confused frown.

"It's not exactly complicated. Mice sniffing around. Like an assassin or a kidnapper, trying to find something. Someone caught him, likely tortured him. It says the clean air in its lungs and the state of its fur said enough. That means this was someone from outside the dungeon, well clothed, or at least well equipped. A nest grown fat could also mean a *rich* nest, or rather, a wealthy family, if you think in terms of rodents who don't have coin or land. 'Grown fat' also implies inaction, until now. Looking for the fledgling leech—"

"Means they're looking for *you*. And 'it wants its blood back' could be taken several ways with the other things said in the letter, but with context . . ." Katherine trailed off, realization settling on her face.

"Great. Another thing to be paranoid about," she growled, feeling a low, boiling fury coil in the bottom of her gut like a snake getting ready to strike.

If her family wanted her back all of a sudden, she wouldn't be terribly surprised. Elves bred incredibly slowly. With the sudden unrest and uncertainty happening, it was obvious that her family would want her back to wipe her mind and start anew.

They'd tie her to a chair, empty her head of everything, pay some psychic a fortune to scrape out every inkling of personality or meaningful memory, and raise her up again, like a mentally disabled adult who just had to be "reset."

It wasn't *unlikely* that they'd force her father on her as well.

Combine the elven kind's low birth rates with their incredibly stupid "pureblood" mentality they adopted from the old human ruling class, and the lack of defects due to incest, and there was a recipe for some very disturbing scenarios. She wouldn't put it past Irythiel to stoop that low.

Maybe a long time ago they hadn't thought any such actions necessary. Maybe until now they hadn't been able to find her, or maybe they just thought they'd make another child, only for this civil-war business to make them realize they did not have such time on their hands.

This time, she doubted they'd take the risk, not after her defection and the general chaos around.

The mere thought of what would happen should she be caught made her sick.

Her breaths deepened, her nails digging into her palms.

"Okay. Adding to the list of potential future actions, *killing my parents* goes to the top of the list. We're also going to have to be even more paranoid and quiet, it seems."

"Agreed. Do you think the man from the sewer wrote this?" Katherine asked, and Em nodded.

Who *else* would do this?

She focused on the knife and let it out, dropping it onto her palm with another puff of displaced air. It was rather strange, with a thin handle, a very small guard, and a vaguely triangular, four-inch-long blade. It also exhumed mana, just a little bit of it.

She couldn't figure out what that enchantment did, but as she brought it right next to the golem's eye at her neck, she could take a guess. Its blade was speckled with still-present blood and *still* looked sharp enough to cut glass.

Trying to shove mana into the blade did nothing, unfortunately, so it seemed to be a passive enchantment.

Then she paused and brought the knife to her face, tugging the scarf up to run her tongue along its bloodied blade.

She sighed in satisfaction at the taste and snack, before realizing that Katherine looked vaguely disturbed, and stopped.

Right, what was she doing . . . ?

Knife, ring, testing.

She focused on the knife as she pulled it away from her face and mentally tried to . . . sort of *shove* it back into the ring, more of a test than anything.

It obeyed effortlessly, popping back in instantaneously.

She turned to the letter still loosely held in Kat's hand and tried to do the same.

Nothing happened.

She reached for it, brushing her fingers on its surface, and mentally shoved.

It went into the ring as well, half-folded and still lightly crumpled from where Kat's thumb was pressing into its side, seemingly frozen in time. Trying to manipulate the paper and fold it with her mind did nothing.

Finally, she popped out the tiny jar with the eye still in it and brought it closer to her sternum.

Eye to eye, so to speak . . .

She was still too upset and worried to snicker, but her lips did twitch up in amusement for a sparse moment.

It was quite grotesque, its pupils shrunk to a pinprick of terror, little veins crawling over the few white parts that were still visible. Some of the nerves were still attached. It even looked *wet*, the blood at the bottom still fresh.

As she was struck with the sudden urge to take the eye out and lick it like a lollipop, she decided instead to just shove it back into the ring, mindful of Katherine's presence. She didn't want to gross her out even further.

Some background voice of alarm in the back of her head asked her why she herself wasn't grossed out by the thought, and she firmly ignored it.

As far as she could tell, this eye was just proof of his claims. Or maybe a warning too, of what he was capable of.

"We need to go buy you a dagger tomorrow too. And find another mortician to buy some blood from. A couple healing potions too," she mumbled, mind somewhat distracted with trying to figure out what this was all for.

This wasn't something someone gave to an errand runner, or a goon, or an employee. A warning, a *dimensional ring*, an enchanted knife, a severed eye.

She could recognize that something about all this was off, and it wasn't too difficult to guess what.

The man in the sewer was either trying to recruit her and her friends or was trying to build some kind of favor with her, for some reason or another. He was trying to use her for something; she just couldn't quite figure out what.

Was he hoping she had "tamed" the wolf and could order it around for him?

If so, he would be very disappointed. Her buddy was quite proud from what she remembered, as well as being a *fucking wolf*. She was sure that trying to control him in any way would only end up with her being ignored at best, torn to pieces at worst.

Men and women and legends, all far greater than her, have tried to tame wolves, and none succeeded.

"—istening?" Katherine asked, and she suddenly realized that the background noise she had been ignoring was her friend talking.

With a mild pang of guilt, she turned a little, slouching in shame.

"Sorry. Was just thinking about something. Could you repeat?"

Katherine put her hand on her shoulder and suddenly began pushing her back with strength she couldn't fight against.

As she flopped back onto the bed, Katherine began yanking her up so her head wouldn't be smushed against the wall, and with some squirming and help from her weak legs, mostly to not tear her new shirt, they were lying parallel to each other.

"Is there something else we need to think or talk about, or can we go to sleep?" Katherine asked, and her tone made it quite clear which option she preferred.

"Let's sleep," she murmured.

Then she felt something move under the mattress, and stiffened, then sighed in exasperation.

"Scruffy's under the bed."

"Ignore her."

"I—"

"Ignore her."

"Okay."

Katherine was saying something, and she knew she should be paying attention. If nothing else, simply to know exactly what their finances were like.

They were in a chop shop, as the common folk called it. It was a strange mishmash of standard medical equipment, alchemical potions, anything that could be used in necromancy or witchcraft, alchemical ingredients, basically just a shop geared toward the less violence-inclined Paths but also not the crafting-oriented ones.

But there was a box with two *rats* right *there*, and they were squeaking, and her blood was boiling because of them.

Their container was more like a small engine with half of it being observational one way glass and various little chutes meant for feeding and watering them built in.

It was only the small ventilation device glued onto the side of the box that kept them alive and breathing.

Her eyes itched and rolled, despite no longer being there, and her fingers twitched incessantly.

How could she break that? Was there a way to do it without the shop owner noticing?

The golem eye followed her commands, shifting to the side as much as it was able to on its holding device, just a couple inches, going from the top of the box to the bottom.

She couldn't find one.

"How much?" someone said, their voice colder than the barren north, and the conversation behind her abruptly paused.

It was only the click of her jaw closing that made her realize those were her own words, and a small pulse of mana revealed both the woman behind the counter and Katherine staring at her.

"How much for these?" she asked again.

"Well, if you buy *two* bags of blood, I'll toss that in for you for just three coppers." The crone behind the counter coolly said, fiddling with her rings.

At the edge of her mana pulse, she felt Scruffy gently poking at a broken clock, open wonder in her expression.

"Scruffy?" she asked, and after a moment of no reaction, as if unused to responding to that name, the goblin's head jerked toward her, hurriedly backing away from the clock, hiding her hands behind her back like a little kid caught with their fingers in the honey jar.

If she was slow to respond to Scruffy, what did her old owner call her? It certainly wasn't a name. Nobody named goblins, as far as she knew, and nobody understood their gibbering either, so she wasn't sure if they named themselves.

"Do you want the clock?" She asked, voice a little harder than she'd intended it to be, something she blamed on being amped up by the rodents' presence.

Instead of wincing at her tone, Scruffy's big eyes widened even further, confused. Then she nodded once, slowly, uncertainly, almost looking suspicious.

"Give us that clock too and it's a deal," she said, turning her head enough to make sure the shopkeeper knew that it was directed at her.

Scruffy's surprised, gleeful look made the cold fury in her heart a little less biting.

He was fighting something.

Again.

He just didn't *stop*. It had stopped being worrying by now, just making her wonder what the hell he was doing. If he fought *this* often, they were likely not large fights. Maybe he was just busy . . . stealing body parts from rats and insects or something. That was the optimistic perspective she'd decided to go with.

Besides the mild anxiety, it was also immeasurably reassuring to know and feel that they were getting closer to him.

"Are you sure we're heading the right way?" Katherine asked, and she paused, trying to reorient herself with the rough position she last felt him at. It took some mental remapping and a few seconds of silence before she continued walking.

"Yeah. I'm sure."

Katherine nodded.

"So, why did you buy rats?"

She didn't answer, walking on autopilot as she considered the question.

The main reason she bought them was to kill them. Some kind of . . . mindless catharsis, maybe. Revenge, as childish and meaningless as this particular flavor of it was. That wasn't the sole reason, though. She wanted to just . . . wash away that lingering fear.

She hated that even though they were encased in some glass-like material in an insulated box, six feet away in another person's grip, her gut was still a tightly clenched knot of unease and dread.

"It's . . . embarrassing," she mumbled, and kept walking.

Embarrassing wasn't quite the right word. She was just scared Katherine would think less of her for it.

She just needed someplace that was a little abandoned, some spot she could just—

To her left between two rumbling smoke chutes, she spied a small rectangular area nestled into the backside of some storage houses, little more than a back alley for the workers to get a smoke break or eat whatever lunch they could get. Sludgy gray mud covered the ground, a mixture of coal and dirt and overflowing sewage waters.

It smelled as horrid as she expected it to.

Perfect.

She turned on her heel, walking faster.

A barrel remained next to a pile of iron bars, fire still licking away at its insides, presumably from when the warehouse workers had cooked something up here. She sped up further, almost jogging, until she was standing right in front of it, Scruffy and Kat catching up as she stood there.

Her mind was blank for a moment, unsure of what she was intending to even do.

An idea quickly came.

"Could you . . . put them over the barrel?" she asked, throat dry.

She knew what she was doing was needlessly cruel and unethical. But as she turned to Katherine, her eyes flitted to their squirming forms, the disgusting vermin squeaking and sniffing in their tight enclosure, and venomous hatred boiled in her veins.

She wanted them to *boil*. To burn and *squeal*.

Katherine paused, giving her a searching look.

"Don't . . . don't ask, please? Could you just . . ." She vaguely gestured to the barrel, and Katherine sighed before walking past her and depositing the large rectangular box over the licking flames.

It couldn't fit in the barrel, but half of it almost did, while the other half jutted outward.

Which would leave the rats to scramble up a steep slope to escape the heated bottom, tiring them out. The fire would continue, their ventilation box sending in nothing but burning air, cooking them alive in their box.

A mixture between a sneer and a smile curled her lips beneath the scarf.

A cruel, vindictive pleasure bloomed inside her chest, feeling like a slight weight had been lifted, like an ever-present niggle had finally been soothed.

Katherine walked to stand by her side, and she basked in the moment.

She felt satisfied, vindicated, warm in a way.

Scruffy glanced at the barrel curiously before losing interest and going back to poking at the clock in her hands with a little needle.

Katherine mutely watched the rodents panic alongside her.

It wouldn't be a fast demise.

That was fine, they could use a moment to rest and . . . enjoy themselves.

As the minutes ticked by, the rodents began to try and bite and scratch through the glass and metal, the little cup of water in their enclosure having pooled at the bottom and steadily starting to boil, scalding their bleeding feet whenever they slid down.

Scruffy went to sit on the pile of metal bars to their right, tongue sticking out the side of her mouth in concentration as she wiggled the needle between the tiny gears.

Cute.

Her lips curled further, into something resembling a smile.

Another minute passed, and the rats were starting to hyperventilate, their whole bodies inflating and deflating rapidly from their deep breaths. They were too exhausted to keep trying to dig through the glass.

Good.

She imagined their panic, their hopeless despair, knowing she was the cause.

It felt like pure *victory*.

"Why?" Katherine eventually asked.

As the rodents finally began to die, one collapsed and occasionally convulsing, and the other weakly scraped at the metal wall, blood pouring out of its nose.

"Why what?" she asked, feeling pleasurable shivers race up and down her chest up to her neck, to the back of her head. She struggled not to visibly shake from how good it felt.

Revenge was an ever-present allure, even before she'd come down into the dungeon. She hated her parents with enough vitriol to fantasize about various painful ways of killing them, even if she never thought herself capable of committing to a single one of them.

But never had she thought revenge would feel so good, so easily. It was the most twisted kind of happiness she had ever felt.

She cussed and hissed and snarled and giggled at them with a voice that sounded like her own, all in the safety of her head, where nobody but her could see or hear. She pretended they could hear or understand her and her taunting, and it only got sweeter, the fantasy all too perfect.

Something touched her left shoulder, and she jerked away so quickly she felt a nerve pinch in her back. The eye whirred to see a surprised Katherine, arm half raised, and they both stood there, half turned, staring at each other.

"Sorry. I—"

"Sorry I just—"

They spoke at the same time and stopped.

She spoke first this time.

"Sorry. Just very . . . jittery right now," she explained, and allowed a shiver to pass through her, the eye on her sternum twisting to the side a little to stare at the rats.

One down, one to go. Good, *good, fucking **die**.*

Katherine pursed her lips, eyes flicking to the box.

"Can I hug you?"

The eye didn't move from where its attention was focused, but she didn't need it to feel the uncertainty in Katherine's stance as she asked.

Instead of replying, she lifted her hand to shift the eye to the side as much as she could, and took two steps forward, throwing an arm around her friend's shoulder, tugging her forward.

Two steely arms locked around her, and she rested her cheek on Katherine's shoulder.

"What I was going to ask is why are we doing this with the rats? Why do you want to turn into a vampire? I won't dissuade you, I'm just . . . curious. A trait can be undone. This one seems a little more frustrating than most to get rid of, but I'm sure you could do it." Katherine spoke softly, and she thought about it for a minute, a long, comfortable minute, with the wonderful view of the last rodent starting to convulse on top of its brother.

As its dying throes played for an audience of one, she began to speak, deciding to ignore the first question.

"I don't want to get rid of the trait. I like it. I *really* like it. Every meal is like a . . . a potion that strengthens everything. And turning . . . turning would give me power. Personal power, not financial or social power, just . . . *me*. Which I will need, all I can possibly get."

It sounded too simple. Too easy, too empty without context.

"Before I came into the dungeon, you know, I had this . . . strange worldview," she murmured. "I thought the powerful were evil, and the weak were virtuous. A result of faulty pattern recognition caused by Irythiel, I'd say. I thought if one was poor or weak, they were nothing but a victim, and that if someone was powerful or wealthy, they were the abuser. Of course, I learned quickly that that was not how things worked at all."

Katherine made a noise of encouragement, nodding slightly into her neck.

"Power is . . . a tool. I thought it corrupted people back then, but I realize now that it simply brings out what is already there. Can someone who is weak really be a virtuous man because he hasn't hurt someone, when the only reason he hasn't done so is his inherent weakness? Power just . . . brings out the real person under all the inhibitions and restraints inherent to being weak. And I want that power. To be . . . unrestrained. To find out who I really am under all these . . . layers. To be able to run with the monster I call a friend, to be able to protect you and myself, if the need arises. The price of my humanity . . . well, I'm not human, so elven . . . ity? Elvenhood?" she fumbled, struggling to find a way to say what she meant in Carmeran.

There were some things she could only say in Elvish without having them sound like funny gibberish, and this was one of them.

Katherine chuckled.

She huffed, amused by both the convulsing rodent and the turn the conversation had taken.

"Yeah, the price of my 'elvenhood' seems like an all right price to pay for that," she said.

After a moment of silence, Katherine nodded. "All right. Thank you for telling me."

If Kat noticed how she dodged the question about the rats, she didn't say anything about it.

The second rodent died eventually.

A few more minutes passed, calm and comfortable as they stood, not bothering to dissolve the embrace, the fading crackle of flame mixing with the clicking of clockwork and hum of smog chutes into a pleasant background tune.

"We should go," she eventually said, feeling like their break had gone on long enough.

"You're okay, right?" Katherine asked as they separated.

The eye turned to the side a little, glancing at the silent box.

"Yeah."

Their funds were running out.

She had put the coin bag they had into the ring, and though that lightened the load on Katherine's back somewhat, it was soon to be the end of the second day of constantly walking and taking lift after lift.

[Pack Hunter]'s utterly ludicrous range was starting to sink in.

Having to walk and pass through most of the third floor, it was a little easier to put the sheer *distance* into perspective. Two days of taking lifts, free and not, of walking several hours a day until she couldn't even feel her legs, and they were only just now getting to the top parts of the third floor.

It was somehow much worse than down below.

Their path used to be relatively straight until now.

Walk to a station, ask people for landmarks and directions or consult some shoddy maps, go there, take a lift or walk up the winding, endless staircases around the spires, come out onto another plate, and repeat.

Now, to make their way to a station or a landmark, they had to dodge roving bands of gangsters, citizen and adventurer militia prowling the streets and looking for a fight with the uppersiders, or genuine conflict.

Judging by the incessant clanging of steel on steel, the shouting, the sounds of explosions and roaring fire, getting anywhere *close* to the *actual* fights was a bad, bad idea. So they had very meticulously avoided them.

The path there was . . . rough.

The dungeon was full of deteriorating buildings, some crumbling, some rusting, some were just improvised boxes of sheet metal stuck onto I-beams, forming strange makeshift neighborhoods in the lowest ends of the third floor. So she was used to seeing abandoned, shoddy, and crumbling buildings.

She wasn't used to smelling smoke in the air as they walked through the remnants of what once might have been a two-story storage building, half collapsed onto its side, its brick walls scorched black and crumpled into piles around them as glass crunched under their feet, the wood little more than charcoal now, anything not nailed down already looted.

She certainly wasn't used to seeing guards' corpses swinging from light posts, their entrails hanging down like ribbons, the miasma of rot and death so present in such blatant open space.

In the distance, she could see a makeshift clinic operating in the middle of the street, three people with white shirts darting between people laid out on the floor. She saw a stocky man bring another, put them on the floor, then run back out of sight. Another guarded them and the medical supplies, occasionally helping where needed.

There was a battle somewhere to their left.

It looked like the third floor was slowly being reclaimed.

They stalked through the tight underpass of a metal bridge, overlooking a cracked concrete slope that led into a gutter, and her eye lingered on the crumpled corpse half slumped over the side of their path, just about ready to slide off.

Katherine stepped around it.

She would have too, had she not noticed the gang tattoo on his exposed forearm.

Instead, she hooked the tip of her boot under his ribs and kicked him off the path, letting his decomposing body melt into the river or be feed for the rats below.

There was noise ahead, but then again, she'd gotten used to it by now. Shouting was nothing all that alarming, not anymore.

But maybe that corpse should have warned her that there were gang members around, even if their presence was less tolerated than ever.

It didn't quite cross her mind, it seemed, because as they turned the corner, they saw a group of four men lounging around the street smoking and laughing, while a fifth pounded on a metal door.

Their steps paused simultaneously, Scruffy peeking between them to watch what stopped them.

Four men, one woman. They all wore the same clothes, some mixture between dark-gray cloth coats and brown pants, and if that wasn't enough to surmise some kind of uniform, she could see their gang symbol boldly and shoddily embroidered on the breast of their coat. A twin-headed green snake forming a heart with its heads.

She had seen it before, but she couldn't quite remember which gang they were.

She just knew it wasn't a small one.

Weapons both concealed and obvious swayed from sheaths and bulged their clothes from within, yet they didn't seem terribly concerned with harassing passersby. Maybe they could walk past . . .

"Open the fuck up, old man, before we bust the door down and fuck up everything you have! You didn't pay up!" the man pounding on the door boomed, and her eye flicked to the side, watching for the people's reactions.

There was a bakery across the street, where a stocky young man snuck glances at the gangsters with open hatred and contempt in his eyes. Two customers who were awkwardly sitting inside, unsure if it would be safer to stay or leave.

And there was a single unconcerned old man just casually walking down the street, a cigarette in his mouth. He stumbled into an alley and disappeared.

They could just turn around and try to find another way to the station. But it would take ages, it would slow them down even further. Assuming they didn't get lost.

And a smaller, less rational part of her simply decided it did not want to continue dodging conflict. She'd been doing that her whole life, and it never worked. They'd run into another gang, or another blockade, and lose even more time, more energy, more money. They were bleeding resources they couldn't afford.

Better to slam her horns forward than try to keep her head away and simply reveal her neck for the knife.

"Act confident. Walk behind me," she ordered quietly. "If they talk to us, treat me as a bodyguard, act diplomatic. Scruffy, just hide behind Katherine. We're not fighting if we don't have to." She fished the ring out of her pocket before popping it into her mouth.

Katherine did nothing but nod with a displeased, worried expression, despite being behind her, correctly guessing she would be flaring mana the entire walk through.

Which would drain on her mana a bit more than she'd like, but she couldn't take chances.

As she began walking forward, she maneuvered the ring around using her tongue, until the thinner part was clenched between her teeth and the small gemstone was pressed into the inside of her cheek.

She had tested the summoning range.

Not one single part of what she was trying to take out of the ring could be farther than about seventeen inches, not even the tip, or else it wouldn't come out.

More than enough range.

Muffled shouting and voices came from within the house, one rough and one high pitched. The guy at the door sighed, straightening his coat, glancing at his fellows. The group's leader seemed to be a particularly large man with a scimitar at his waist, and he just scoffed, picking at his ear.

As they got closer, the voices became more intense, legible.

"No, no! Mother, please— Stop! No!" a girl shrieked through the door, the metal distorting the sound into a wail, and her steps stuttered for a moment. Something in her mind slid apart, a platform without supports, tilting. Metal and glass walls turned to marble, pipes melting into trimmed bushes, the ground turning to chalk-white brick, color and light bleeding into the scene. The hanging wires above them turned into whips, dripping red. Katherine's vague figure crumpled onto the ground, bleeding, teased at the edge of her mind, somewhere to the left.

She turned the eye off, frozen, the sight crumbling into the void.

Someone moved through her mana behind her, and she snapped back to the real world, resuming her steps just as Katherine's brow began to furrow in confusion. It smoothed over quickly.

She kept walking, not turning her head or eye toward the approaching gangsters.

"Please—"

The door slammed open, and a small figure was *thrown* outside with a girlish shriek. Her eye snapped to the left, her steps stuttering once more. She recovered faster this time, barely noticeable. The gangsters certainly didn't notice, all turning toward the girl and her mother.

A furious-looking woman, barely dressed, with a blotchy, twisted nose, stains covering her nightgown, staggered in place in the doorframe, a sneer on her face.

"She enough?" the woman rasped, her patchy, greasy hair and wrinkled skin making her look ghoulish in the dim light.

"Nononono, please— Mom, I'll be good, *please*—" the girl screamed as she scrambled up off the floor, terrified, lunging with open arms toward the woman, who reared her leg back as if to kick her.

A gangster's hand darted out to grab the girl by the arm, yanking her back with enough force to nearly dislocate her shoulder. She struggled for a moment, yelling, before he punched her in the stomach and she collapsed like a broken doll with a strangled gag, her knee-length skirt tangling her legs.

Emhreeil's teeth gritted, pain shooting through her gums as her movements grew stiffer, anger and the creeping tingles of something horribly unpleasant pooling low in her gut. The bastards weren't paying any attention to them, however. They would pass through without even being looked at.

The leader yanked the girl up by the arm with one hand, the other grabbing the girl by the chin and tilting her head back as she heaved, swaying and trembling as he appraised her.

They were just across the street now, a mere fifteen feet away. The distance made it so hard to detach, to mentally back away from the interaction.

One of the gangsters was staring at them quite blatantly, leaning on the wall, unconcerned but not stupid enough to ignore them either.

"Eh, she ain't a beauty but she ain't bad. She'll do. You know where to go if you want your next dust hit, hag. Pleasure doin' business with ya," the leader said, and the girl let out a strangled, heartbreaking sound, trying to twist out of the man's grip.

"Sto-*ngblgh!*"

His knee slammed into the girl's stomach, and with a guttural sound, her legs went limp as she vomited, the gangster sneering in disgust as he let go, letting her convulse on the floor.

"*Eugh.* Bitch. Aitel, grab her, I ain't dirtying my new coat."

Barbed wire scraped against her spine, her teeth grinding and gnashing and shivering, her fingers twitching. Her body rebelled against her mind. She ordered it forward, to keep walking.

They had enough fucking problems. They couldn't act like they had any measure of power when they didn't. They couldn't afford to care for others as well as themselves.

What was special about this girl? Her wolf friend could have killed thirty of her and even if her heart would clench and her stomach would heave, she wouldn't do anything to stop it.

They couldn't afford to draw attention. Irythiel was prodding around for them. According to Katherine, she was already known to a small neighborhood for being the first to kill a guard down there.

There was a trail one could follow, and adding another footprint on that track would only bite her in the ass later.

But no matter how many sound, perfectly valid arguments she made, no matter how much she pointed out the moral dissonance of objecting to this girl's fate because it wasn't her friend's fangs around her neck but a gangster's fingers, her body kept getting stiffer, slower, tenser.

Her walk was now a struggling shuffle. She was barely moving.

The gangster woman was staring, eyes narrowing, her long curly hair shifting on her shoulders as she tilted her head in open curiosity.

Emhreeil wasn't looking at them, so maybe the bitch just thought she was weird. She could still walk away just fine.

Weren't these the thoughts of everyone else who passively watched her suffer in Ghar's clutches for almost two years? Wasn't *she* the naive girl on the floor a while ago, wishing someone would spare her more than a glance, offer a helping hand?

A choked sob came from her left.

"Shut up and stop squirming or I'll make you shit blood and cum, you worthless cunt. Got it?!"

Her jaw cramped, and the pain anchored her to the real world.

The eye flicked to the side briefly, staring at the crumpled lump on the ground.

"Kat," she breathed out, the sound a little awkward with the slowly deforming piece of silver in her mouth.

She wasn't walking anymore.

Katherine's expression was tight and twitching in suppressed discomfort, but at the tone of her voice, it all washed away, something like fearful determination replacing it.

Maybe they could negotiate. Maybe the bastards would trade the girl for her knife, even if its enchantment was minor.

Or maybe she'd reveal they had such things on them and the heartless scumbags would immediately try to kill them so they could take it all for themselves.

She knew better than to expect the best. Especially out of people.

"We're killing all of them," she breathed out. "Tell Scruffy to hide."

Katherine turned and dropped to her knees, appearing like she was talking to a child from the gangster's view as she quickly whispered instructions to Scruffy.

The gangster woman raised a hand to tap at one of the men's shoulders with the back of her knuckles, and when he turned, she muttered something and jerked her chin toward them.

Scruffy walked to the bakery, opening the metal door and scurrying to the side to hide.

Two people were looking at them now, the other three bickering and trying to haul the girl up without getting any vomit on their hands or cloaks.

"What are you lookin' at? Move along," a man gruffed, despite neither of them staring at them, squaring his shoulders and puffing his chest out as he walked toward them, arms tense, his coat tight on the muscles below. Combined with the scar on his chin that raced up his cheek, he would be quite intimidating, if she hadn't cuddled with things far worse than him.

Through the bile in her throat, she spoke.

"Why, a potential customer," she said loudly as she turned, her voice rough and sharp without meaning to, mixing with the involuntary snarl in her throat. Those who hadn't been looking glanced over, three considering, the seeming leader unimpressed, and the woman suspicious. The girl's mother slammed the door shut and retreated into her derelict home.

She knew the ways of the court, how a noble spoke and emoted, how a merchant did. The mask slid into place easily, hiding the serpent coiling beneath.

"If you wish for some good meat, I've got my own toy with me. She's much better than chattel trash like her," she fake-sneered, the golem's eye being exceedingly obvious in where its gaze was directed: straight at the girl.

Katherine froze beside her, unable to hide the widening of her eyes, confused as to her angle here. Just speaking like this made her want to bash someone's brains out. She hated it. She hated it *so much*.

"She's a beauty, she's capable, and I've already trained her well enough," she explained. "She's eager to please, if you catch my meaning. Been looking to get rid of her for a while now, and this is as good an opportunity as any. You fine gentlemen seem to be looking for meat, I have meat." She spread her hand in a magnanimous manner from underneath her cloak as she squared her shoulders, the odd lisp from her trying to keep the ring in place and only being able to use half of her jaw only furthering what she was going for.

A mysterious, strange man who drew attention, and most importantly, directed it.

She moved her shoulder subtly to draw their eye to the motion, then swept her arm behind her at chest height and tucked it into the small of her back, the motion and the accompanying swish of her cloak flaring in front of Katherine before falling, not unlike the drama of pulling the cover off an item at an auction.

A sense of flair that people fell oh so easily for. She lowered her shoulders, shrinking, and opened her cloak to the nearest light source, turning the golem eye off. Darkness drew the eye, but so did the contrast of light against it. By revealing what was beneath her cloak, she made herself lighter, and without the glowing yellow eye of the golem, she faded into the background even better.

She moved a foot backwards just to add to it, making sure her footing was like her dance lessons. A sliding foot, minimal movement, a graceful backwards slide. She tilted her shoulders so that she was facing Katherine, because people paid more attention to someone who was turned straight toward them.

And her little performance worked perfectly, all five eyes landing on Katherine who looked stiffer than she'd ever seen her.

Gods, she would lick her boots clean for this later as an apology, and she'd still feel like she owed her.

The man who seemed to be their leader walked forward, his leering eyes roving up and down Katherine like she was a drug he was appraising the quality of. At his hip was a sword, and at his wrist she could see a folded dart launcher. Two darts.

The gangsters spread out, leaning to the side to catch a glimpse of Katherine, curious, all but one who was halfheartedly holding the gasping girl's arm. It was like they'd forgotten she was there completely, despite being only a foot away.

She reached behind her head, cracking her neck as she massaged her nape. The woman's eyes moved back to her. Four people not paying attention was still more than enough.

Her muscles felt like steel threads, stretched to their utter limit. One twitch, just a little closer. The man reached his hand forward, grasping Katherine by her chin roughly, tilting her head up. She felt spikes and needles dig into her synapses, a pure, boiling hatred finally finding an outlet.

She let her hand begin to drop. Mana gathered, her attention split into four equal parts, her mind straining and slipping. One made shapes of force, brute and not, one focused on an object, another on a spell, another on her targets and the space between them.

This close to her mouth, the ring could reach. With a tiny pop, the dagger flashed under her lowering hand in a reverse grip, and her fingers slammed shut around the hilt. [Haste] activated, taking a healthy fistful of her mana with it.

Half of the mana stored in her body over several days went into [Telemantic Construct], coiled around the neck and chin of the woman watching her like a hawk, snapping into existence for a mere millisecond with the faint crack-whistle of air.

Her neck didn't quite snap so much as her head twisted backward a full 180 degrees in an instant with a sickening fleshy noise, the muscles and skin in her neck splitting apart and spraying blood in a wide ring as she was almost decapitated, her body trying to spin and failing as her shoulder slammed into the iron with a deafening bang and bounced off.

Her hand flashed forward as the leader tried to jerk back and away. The dagger slammed into the side of his neck, burying three inches deep before she could go no deeper, his ungodly Endurance making his flesh feel more like tightly wound layers of linen.

Kat jerked back and low, away from him, her hand flashing into her trench coat.

The leader tried to backhand her with his left hand as he launched himself away, his fist heading toward her armpit, and she managed to twist the knife a bit before pulling it out with a squirt of blood, managing to dodge by leaning her whole torso back and sideways, extending her arm up.

Her veins sang in ecstasy. Her skull filled with rabid butterflies, every flap of their wings oh so tingly, scattering her thoughts and leaving mindless adrenaline behind.

He was still in the middle of his strike. It felt like he was moving in slow motion, some separate time.

The moment his arm flew past her, she bent low and slammed the knife into the side of his knee, through the cartilage and into the joint, and didn't bother wasting time to dig it out, instead using the knife like a handle to launch herself forward to the next thug, who had only just begun moving his hands to his sword, and popping it into the ring right as it approached the edge of its range.

For him, this was likely all a slip's worth of time, no doubt a blur he could barely see or even process.

For her, it was more like five seconds.

His eyes lagged behind her, as if he couldn't keep up with her form, and he had only begun to abort grabbing his sword to try and raise his arms to shield his head. Her open hand slammed into his face, her palm over his left eye.

[Sparkburst] took a third of the mana remaining in her body.

The left half of his head exploded in a wild mixture of disintegrated blood and minuscule fragments of his head mixing into the flashing mass of sparks, and she felt his eye socket explode around her hand, allowing it to push through the missing chunk of his head.

Blood and viscera peppered her scarf, and for a moment, she lamented having it, wishing she could have felt that on her skin, on her face.

Then she realized her hasty error when she realized she couldn't change direction. She tried to bring her left foot forward and halt her momentum, or at least redirect it, and half managed it with a tiny step that had her knee crashing into the gangster's.

Momentum wasn't kind to her. Her left shoulder bashed into the corpse's chest, unable to fully stop or redirect herself, and felt her cloak's ties snap apart as she tried to move her arm to shield herself.

She spun 180 degrees from the impact, hastily throwing her left leg out behind her to grind her to a halt, and cursed her weakness when said leg buckled from the sudden strain, followed by her other leg.

Her back slammed into the iron wall at stomach height, followed by the back of her head, and her attention scattered with her cloak as she felt its hood detach, the sensation of things moving through her mana turning into a vague impression that slipped through her fingers.

Something was rushing at her, fast enough to almost feel like normal speed despite [Haste]'s boost.

She curled her stomach, threw her whole torso and head down. Something slammed into the wall above her with a slow, deep boom, and she bucked off to the side, scrambling up and away, the world swaying under her feet as she tried to swivel around and face her opponent. Mass whipped toward her head from the right, another from her left, going for her ribs.

No time or leverage to dash out of range.

She could only afford to take a strike in one of those spots, so she threw a hasty repulsion field toward what she could only think were fists, hoping to take some power out of the strikes, and moved her arm to the left, popping the dagger back into her hand mid-swing.

She did it too fast, too panicked, too disoriented.

The handle hit her thumb, and her fingers didn't quite manage to close around the guard, leaving it to uselessly tumble to the floor, out of range. She just barely managed to redirect the fist aimed at her head to the side with her palm, glancing off the side of her head as she leaned away, a bruising scrape.

The fist to her left slammed into her side, below her ribs, and pure agony burst out over her insides, the impact rushing through her organs as a shockwave that had her breath knocked out of her and her body locked up like a stone, her body going utterly limp in shock with a sharp wheeze, her left leg kicking like a reflex.

Someone was roaring, the sound as slow and distorted as every other. Something was screeching in her ear, a deafening, endless whine. A high-pitched voice screamed, sounding like the wail of a great bell being shredded. The scent of cooked meat and blood rushed up her nostrils straight to her brain as she inhaled the moment she was able to. She knew that the Speed attribute inherently broke reality, to a small extent. Everything from the System did.

Still, as she was left to fall without an anchor point to speed it up, to drag herself down, she felt like she was sinking through water more than falling. It was just slow enough to give her body and mind time to restart, to regain control of her limbs.

Too little too late. Her back met the cobblestones, and something in her neck strained as it went rigid, her head only narrowly avoiding another impact with the floor. A fist covered in spiked metal rushed toward her head, two hundred pounds of mass behind it as the gangster put all of his weight behind the strike.

She jerked her waist and head, managing to narrowly dodge a right-hand punch that was sure to have taken half her teeth with it, and her hand rushed toward his head from underneath his arm.

He folded his arm, his elbow stabbing at her wrist and throwing her aim off, her [Sparkburst] doing nothing but lighting his coat on fire. The same arm straightened right after, his fingers clamping down around her neck, his palm slamming into her windpipe, and something heavy and sharp slammed into her lower stomach, making her jerk and wheeze in agony as her legs kicked and scrabbled at the ground, her hips trying to buck his immense weight off her to no avail, only managing to tilt her hips into the gap between his legs, the knee on her navel sliding off to hit the cobbles.

She tried to grab his elbow, hoping to blow the joint apart, and despite the difference in speed, he managed to just barely twist himself upward and minimize the damage, making her dig a burning hole into the base of his forearm as a giant spew of sparks erupted between them, his scream feeding the hungry pit in her stomach.

His fingers went almost limp around her neck, and she gasped in a raspy breath that almost had her choke on the ring as he let go entirely, twisting his torso.

His left arm, previously busy trying to stabilize himself, curled in front of his chest as he dropped on her, trying to use his forearm to crush her windpipe, and she tucked her head and neck into her shoulders, moving the ring into the space between her left cheek and gums.

Something in her jaw popped and cracked as his forearm slammed into its side, and her hand rushed to his ribs at the same time his right hand moved to deflect it.

She couldn't get close enough in time; he wouldn't let her. She detonated early.

She felt his coat be blasted to shreds, his flesh be blown apart and scorched to the bones of his rib cage, but it didn't go deeper, and so she tried to detonate a second [Sparkburst], pushing forward recklessly to try and end this fight, despite his approaching hand.

His fingers clamped shut around her wrist and wrenched it away right as she felt his bones crack from the heat and the flesh be scraped off a mere moment before she could reach his lungs and blow him apart from the inside out.

The bastard pressed down, holding her wrist to the ground, his weakened grasp still just barely enough to make escape unfeasible, snarling in her face as they found themselves in a stalemate.

She snarled back, mana gathering in her throat as her brain grew fuzzy, and prepared herself for unfamiliar pain.

Her mouth opened, her jawbone grinding agonizingly from the motion as the thin, untrained exit point in her throat strained.

She twisted her head, allowing his forearm to finally press down on her throat, and just as triumph renewed his strength, familiar runes formed in her mind, her tongue flicking in patterns she'd trained a thousand times with fingers.

She didn't even know if this would work, but it should, in theory.

The spell's framework finished after a tense second and a half, which felt like a minute, and she opened her mouth, slamming mana into it.

Her tongue went bone dry in an instant, a searing numbness flashing through it as sparks spewed out of her mouth, the insides of her mouth burning and twisting like charred leather, her front teeth cracking from the sudden heat, a couple leaving entirely.

The moment he saw the light through the scarf, he tried to lean back, freeing up her throat, allowing her to blow air into the blast as well. The bassy, rumbling *fwoom* of rushing sparks combined with the sound of something like a million tiny crackles happening at once.

She couldn't feel what it did to him as it met his face, but she could feel the way he instantly jerked his head to the side and rolled off her with choking, hacking coughs.

He tried to get up, and she rolled up after him, fingers scrabbling at the floor.

For a moment, she felt the charred slate that was his head, nose gone, eyes smushed and leaking from beneath eyelids that were blasted apart, his hair still flaming atop his head.

With how much mana she'd put into that blast, she had been expecting his head to be missing, or at least the lower half of it.

Fucking *Endurance*.

She recognized that the fight was done as her legs curled and snapped straight, lunging at him like a rabid panther.

But she wasn't.

He swung blindly with his right arm, panicked, with a shout that had his voice crack like a scared little boy's, and it didn't even come close to hitting her as she rushed forward.

The scarf slid off, her inhibitions riding on its coattails, too damaged to cling on.

His left arm curled in front of his head, and her hand met his wrist on its way to his ear.

[Sparkburst], she snarled in her head, and found her voice rising to vocalize without her consent, the sound mangled through her half-cooked tongue.

The blast pushed him a foot backward, his posture going from leaning forward to being at a forty-five degree angle on the opposite scale, one foot flailing in the air and the other barely on the ground. She felt his joint torn to shreds as his hand hung on by what little remained of his inner wrist.

There was no mana left in her body, but her mana core still had plenty.

She drew a fourth of it into a vague repulsive construct that flared briefly against the gangster's chest, just enough to lighten the load.

Then she drew her arm back and tilted her right shoulder forward, slamming it into his sternum right after the construct pushed him, feeling something in her shoulder shift with a pop.

She was halted by the impact, but he wasn't. He flew back for a couple feet, upper back first, and with how close they were to the walls, he slammed into the bakery's door, his head crashing through the small window at its top as the door's body bent inward from his weight.

Her legs curled as she lowered once more, trembling and feeling far too weak for what she was trying, but she did it anyway, reckless.

His hands tried to reach for the doorframe, fingers limp and twitching, his torso heaving as he gasped in a single breath, bringing his head forward through the broken window to shield his neck with his chin.

He screamed something, his body shrinking, curling in on itself, and the distorted sound of him screaming "Stop, stop!" sounded so funny when it was all slow and stretchy and distorted by the flow of time in her ears, his intonations ruined, his rough tone turned to something that sounded so absurd, as if spoken by a chubby fairy tale merchant lamenting a stolen apple by the snappy hero in one of those stuffy plays she was taken to as a child.

It sounded almost mocking and sarcastic.

As it should be.

Why would she stop? Had *he*?

Her dry, burned lips stretched and broke as a grin split her face in half, full of broken teeth and bleeding gums.

His fingers tried to curl on the frame, to dig himself out as his legs crumpled, almost managing to bring himself to a half-standing crouch. Despite his strange stance, his presence became more solid all of a sudden, something about him shifting. Some skill, maybe.

It likely didn't matter.

She slammed into him, shoulder first again, ignoring the lance of dulled pain that arose from it, and felt the door give way underneath them as they went into the shop. Her hand hit the floor, and she moved her upper body away before he could attempt to grapple her with his fumbling arms.

"Stop," he pleaded, screamed "Please, I yield" as fast as he could speak.

Without [Haste], she could guess it would sound pleading, wheezy, desperate, a cry more than a shout, almost one single, continuous word.

With [Haste], it felt like he moved his jaw and what came out was a mangled sound between a deflating balloon and a yawn and a word spoken by a sloth. It sounded so stupid she almost wanted to laugh, had she the breath or levity to do so.

Her hand darted down, weaving between his blocking forearms, under them.

The center of her palm came flush with his chin, and he tried to twist and buck, almost managing to throw her off, if it wasn't for the fact one of her knees was on the floor.

A blast of sparks melted and tore through his jawbone, and he howled, swinging blindly.

The back of one of his hands, she didn't care which, rushed toward her head, and she ducked under it, feeling it just barely clip the back of her head.

Without his hands to protect his face, she simply slammed her palm down on his face, fingers digging into melted flesh, and activated [Sparkburst].

She felt his face melt under her palm, shredded and scattering with the sparks in a million little pieces. A limp wrist punched her in the rib as he spasmed, kicking at the trail of glass and broken hinges they left behind as she coughed out a snarl. She leaned forward even more, digging her weight into him.

She managed another [Sparkburst] before having to dodge his half-functioning arm, pushing her hand down into his crumbling skull for leverage to lean back and twist her collarbone out of a collision course.

[Haste] still had time before running out. She still had time.

The moment his hand passed in front of her chest, she reared her hand back and curled her torso down. Her palm met his face once more.

For a moment, she let herself feel it. Her fingers dug into cracking bone and charred flesh, flakes of skin and bleeding mincemeat finding refuge beneath her fingernails.

As he twisted his waist and began to shriek in agony, moving his arms for another worthless bout of flailing, she let herself feel the intoxicating sensation of victory and superiority, crawling up and down her spine.

Another blast of sparks, compressed into a mere fraction of a second.

She felt the sparks detonate against her palm and the flesh trapped under it, burning both but shredding only one, and the introduction of his shriek turned into a gargled sound like a choking frog as he jerked and convulsed.

Her hand sunk down, in, an inch further, and stopped once the last sparks petered out.

Still alive.

Another [Sparkburst], weaker. She had to save some mana. She could still feel forms shifting and twisting behind her in the street. Katherine needed help after she was done here.

"Die," she snarled, feeling her hand melt and become one with his skull, a mess of charred pulp, the ring finally slipping out from between her teeth to bounce off the gangster and mix with the glass shards below.

Another [Sparkburst], and he bucked to the side, his right leg kicking and jerking, arms going limp for a second before sluggishly trying to rise again.

"JUST FUCKING DIE!"

She threw whatever mana remained in her core into the next burst.

Her hand sunk through what remained of his face, into his brain, the back of his skull, and felt the squishy bits of his skull splatter and scatter on the floor like an overripe fruit that was scorched black and crushed beneath a hydraulic press.

He went limp, completely and utterly.

She panted for a few seconds, a wheeze grasping at the edges of each breath. Her head lowered to his chest as she felt her limbs begin to shake and quiver. She couldn't even see or feel anything, and likely wouldn't for a while longer. No mana left.

She'd won. Right?

The smell should be horrid. Blood and brains and scorched clothes and hair, a gut-wrenching stench. But it really wasn't. She took a deep, deep breath, stuttered. She felt her shoulders shake, her fingers twitch and spasm in the charred sludge filling the man's half-present skull.

She threw her right knee back over the corpse's hips, straddling it, before finally leaning back, feeling a layer of burnt skin in her hand stick to the gory mess it was embedded in as she curled it to her chest. Her fingers spasmed and shook incessantly.

They had a single healing potion with them. Somewhere in Katherine's pack. Katherine.

She froze, straining her ears. Harsh panting from behind her, far behind her. Twelve feet, maybe. Choked, panicking whimpers. Fifteen? And the breaths of at least four people all around her. The . . . bakery. She sent him into the bakery. Customers, owner, Scruffy.

It was just the person panting behind her that she had to make sure of.

"Kat?" she croaked out, barely audible even to herself. She grimaced. No way would Katherine hear that.

Her rising paranoia faded when a familiar voice rose.

"Fuck. Em?" Katherine asked, out of breath, and Emhreeil let out a breath she hadn't realized she'd been holding.

Pain was creeping in, the shivering aftershocks of an adrenaline overload rushing through her shivering frame.

"Yeh. H-h-hi," she stuttered on autopilot, a little dazed, and winced as those words sent a stab of pain through her jaw. "Pothion?" she gritted out as she stumbled upright, forcing her head to rise a little. Her tongue wasn't working right.

The System kept prodding her to check it, and it did nothing to help with the headache she felt rapidly forming.

It hurt. A lot.

A gasp came from one of the customers somewhere to the left, and she quickly recognized that [Haste] was just about to run out.

"Of course, of course, just—one second," Katherine said, her voice funny in that slow way, and her boots thudded on the cobbles as she rushed, presumably, to where she'd dropped their backpack.

The smell around her was making her drunk. Fresh breads and pastries, smoke and gamey iron, blood and death. She could taste it, all of it.

She was so hungry.

Plus, blood would help with . . . whatever injuries she got from that . . . the . . .

Fight. The fight.

She tried to raise her foot over the corpse so she could step to the side, and almost stumbled, stiffening. She felt like if she took another step she'd fall down.

"Schhruffy?" she mumbled, and a familiar questioning croak came from the girl, her shoes crunching on the glass as she approached, apparently not horrified by the show she accidentally put on.

"Wmring. Wriing. Ring," she fumbled, and pointed vaguely to where she thought it dropped. Trying to speak with a flash-charred tongue was hard.

And as the adrenaline continued fading, increasingly painful.

Scruffy moved around the corpse.

The gasp from earlier wandered into her mind, the tense silence registering.

She tilted her head vaguely to where she could hear the customers and the owner breathing, in the corner of the shop to her left.

"If you . . . speak. To anyone. This will . . . be you," she carefully enunciated, pointing down at the corpse between her feet, staring right at them with eyeless sockets.

The young man audibly gulped before speaking, his voice more akin to a whimper than genuine words.

"Yes, sir."

She didn't reply, and she did not have the presence of mind to feel bad about the threat, nor about being mistaken for a man for the fifth time.

A croak by her side, sounding vaguely cheery. Likely Scruffy finding the ring.

A rushed tempo of thudding boots behind her, and just as her knees began to feel like jelly, Katherine wrapped an arm around her shoulders, tilting her a little to the side.

"Dear gods, what did you even do?" Katherine gasped, and something prodded her lips. "C'mon, drink it all. I'm fine, just some scrapes and bruises."

After a moment of standing there, she got another idea.

"No, jutht . . . save it. I . . . drink from outthide. Thhe guys," she slurred out, and turned. "Give knife. Can't shee. See."

It felt like someone had stuffed her skull full of prickly hay. A burnt mouth didn't help with her speech either.

Fuck, she was concussed, wasn't she?

"No. Drink. At least enough so you won't deteriorate faster than you'll heal," Katherine ordered, and after thinking about it for a moment, she considered the slowly encroaching agony that followed every pump of her heart.

Her scorched fingers gently cradled the potion as she took a big gulp, less than a fourth of the vial most likely, and she almost moaned in relief as numbness crept over her weary frame. Her skin stretched and pulled oddly, likely growing new skin beneath the burnt remnants.

Whatever. Her fingers were already mangled sticks.

She gulped as she pulled back, some of the haze clearing.

Katherine briefly parted from her, leaving her to sway in place. Scruffy tried to help her by putting her hands on one of her legs, as if trying to stabilize a ladder, or a tilting support beam, and she couldn't help but let out a snorting chortle at her actions.

Kat came back, announcing herself with a whispered "hey." The handle of a knife was put in her hand, and no matter how much it hurt to do so, she tightened her grip on it.

Her tongue felt a little better. Her head didn't.

"Kat, take Scruffy and . . . loot the . . . fuckers. Take all, uh . . . useful stuff. I'll come help in a bit. I'll just . . . eat first. Take me to a corpse. Outside?" she mumbled, hoping her stop-start way of speaking was legible. She just felt so lightheaded.

"Okay," Katherine whispered, and gently tugged her outside, their boots crunching on glass.

After a few dozen steps, Katherine paused and grabbed her forearm, raising it a little.

"Person there. Uh, dead one. We'll loot the other ones," Katherine rushed out, likely just as high on adrenaline as she was. "One got away. I'm sorry. Their leader drank a healing potion before I could finish him off, and then he started fighting me with one of his lackeys, and when I finally knocked him out, the lackey ran."

She paused.

"Are you . . . okay?" she asked, remembering the giant scimitar hanging off the leader's hip.

"Yes. Just some mild cuts and a sprained wrist. I'll be fine. You, uhm, do your thing, we'll loot them. I'll hold on to the ring until your hand heals. And I'll direct the girl to the Crow's Church. She's obviously . . . unwanted. But we should get going, fast. The one who ran will likely tell people about us."

She stood in place for a moment, realizing the implications and the consequences of what they'd done here.

They'd likely made a mortal enemy of a large gang. Irythiel's mice might hear about this. But . . . she'd still do it again.

She nodded.

"Okay. I'll have . . . mana to see. In a minute. Go. And . . . sorry for how I . . . talked. Was just baiting them," she mumbled, and shakily tried to squat, only to fall sideways on her legs, one fist touching . . . some part of a corpse, she couldn't tell.

Katherine's retreating steps paused momentarily.

"I know. Don't worry. You just eat, I'll take care of everything else."

Her steps resumed.

She smiled as she began to prod the corpse with the knuckles, trying to figure out where its neck was.

A tug in her mind flared, lasting a mere couple seconds, pulling her above. She leaned back, head tilted toward the sky, considering.

He felt her too, just now, didn't he? She had been fighting.

"Hey, buddy . . ." she whispered with a growing grin. Soon.

Satisfaction and the honey-sweet taste of victory slowly bled into her exhausted frame.

How would her little wolf friend see this, were he here? Would he consider this her first successful hunt?

She liked the sound of that. She liked the sound of that a lot, even if it wasn't quite accurate.

She turned back to the corpse and paused once more when she heard a sound like a person taking a wheezing breath, somewhere to her left. Katherine was talking to the girl behind her in muted tones.

She felt for her mana.

Enough to charge the eye for a few seconds, at least.

She did so, and as the world blinked back into focus, she quickly looked around until she saw the leader. A beaten, bruised face, a dark purple neck, likely still internally bleeding to some extent, and an open, breathing mouth, drooling on the cobbles.

Didn't Kat . . .

No, she didn't. She didn't say the leader was dead, she said knocked out.

The eye turned off.

"Kat? Why is he . . . still alive?" she asked, and the conversation behind her abruptly stopped.

"Oh, that . . . I've never killed someone before, and I couldn't bring myself to do it. Do you—"

"Take me to . . . him real quick. I'll do it."

"Okay," Kat said with a sharp sigh of relief. "Just one second, the girl is still freaking out a little."

That was fine. She might have traumatized the girl, but it would be a million times better than whatever the gangsters wanted her for.

And killing someone who wasn't fighting back . . . She could do that much for her friend.

There was a hint of moral alarm somewhere in the back of her head as she considered what they'd done here, one that hadn't been there the first time she took a life. It was something that told her that her actions were wrong and she shouldn't be doing them.

But it felt . . . comparable to being a kid and trying to steal cookies from the cookie jar. She knew she shouldn't be doing it, but the guilt was so mild and the reward so sweet that it wasn't worth it not to do it, so long as she wasn't caught.

Katherine helped her up, arm around her waist, and she couldn't help but gasp and whimper, breaths going hard and fast from the sudden pain.

She couldn't even tell what she had hurt because her entire rib cage panged with every step, her mouth was still a ball of agony, and her right shoulder felt weird and twisty. After a few slow steps, taken with grunts and groans and hisses of pain, Katherine gently lowered her next to the leader, before immediately turning around to rush to the girl's side.

She let her breaths steady for a moment, reaching for the nameless gangster's body. Fresh blood just didn't compare to preserved, nor the one stilling in the veins of the dead.

For a moment, she considered the logistics of how she was going to kill him without wasting too much blood, then with some fair amount of pain and struggle, she managed to prop his head up on her thigh.

Her pointer and middle fingers hooked around the pommel of the dagger as she aimed down, her other fingers clenching shut around its shaft, using her elbow to stabilize him. She carefully felt along his head for the earhole before putting the tip in.

As she heaved and pushed down, she ignored the jerk of the corpse, thinking about how odd it was to feel cartilage and bone and brain tissue be torn apart through the handle of her dagger, how the resistance varied.

How it was a sensation that was both addicting and sickening.

She dug it in deeper, feeling uneasy, that sense of wrongness and distant guilt flaring. Her hand and fingers shook, and she couldn't tell if it was from some repressed emotion or the nerve damage she'd no doubt incurred from torching her own hand.

He convulsed one final time and went still.

She took a deep breath and quickly reached down and started feeling for a wrist. Once the heart completely stopped beating, sucking out his blood would be a pain. And she didn't want to waste anything.

She mentally paused for a moment.

Scruffy wouldn't mind eating human meat, right? It wasn't . . . technically cannibalism. Her kind did that in the wild all the time.

A question for later, she decided, as she peeled the sleeve back, sliced his wrist open, dropped the knife, and jammed the bleeding wound against her open mouth.

She moaned in pleasure as crimson nectar filled her mouth, those niggling bad thoughts and feelings washing away as warmth and numbness and strength entered her shaking limbs.

Scruffy, having nothing else to do for the moment, rushed to her side and held the hand in place for her, and after a moment of hesitation, she let go, allowing her hand to drop.

Then she reached up to pet her, despite how tender her skin was, and was rewarded with a pleased grumble. How the hell this little goblin wasn't terrified of her, she didn't know, but she didn't have the mental capacity to question it at the moment. As the blood flow slowly lessened, she idly wondered how the wolf would react to her having two companions with her. Would he consider them . . . How had Kat put it?

Pack members? Would they be included in that bizarre skill that let them find each other? Or would he consider them deadweight, a threat, too much hassle?

Would she be forced to pick one or the other?

The thought soured her mood, so she banished it.

She'd cross that bridge when she came to it.

CHAPTER 12

Removing the odd mana symbol in its skull made a lot of realizations occur.

And as it stared at the bowl-shaped cup of bone innocently sitting in front of its snout, the upper half of its skull just about done regenerating, it wondered if it was even *worth it*.

The first effect of removing it was immediate.

It felt dumber.

Not in the sense of when it made a very questionable decision, and wondered what its own thought process was when making said decision, but more in the sense that its thoughts felt sluggish. Complexity mentally exhausted the wolf faster than before, and everything about using [Devourer] became a little slower, a little more . . . foggy.

It wasn't a large effect, thankfully. It didn't feel like it had lost . . . five points in Intelligence, for example.

More like three or so. Which were . . . a lot, but it was a manageable loss.

Still, it was unpleasant.

The second realization it had came when it stared at a piece of glowing tube for more than ten minutes, focusing, and not a single word formed out of the aether to tell it what it was and roughly what it did.

Which answered the question of what it was exactly that kept feeding knowledge of various things to do with the world around it.

It also formed another thousand questions it doubted it would ever get answers for, so it didn't bother sticking to them too much.

Its eyes slid to the right, down, staring at a window that flashed a dozen colors a second with inner light.

This building was weird.

So much flashing light, so much *noise*. And the way the humans inside were acting was utterly ridiculous. Just a giant mass of . . . wriggling and jumping.

Was it some kind of mating dance?

Humans were strange.

Whatever this building was, it was a convenient spot to rest and do some minor surgery on itself as it slowly descended into the human nest.

Some parts of the nest had the unfortunate structure of *not* being able to be supported by those colossal metal-and-stone plates that usually held them up, and the end result was something like this. Something accessible, but isolated and most importantly, cornered against the walls of the nest.

It wasn't like any lucky humans could surround it when the building it was resting on was hanging over the edge of a gaping chasm. The cliff that led down the abyss was just sloped enough for the wolf to feel like it could just scrape its way down should anything unfortunate happen, and a cursory feel with its antennae confirmed that there was only one pipe going through the stone below, and it was clogged.

It stretched with a groan of satisfaction and lamented how big it had gotten.

The metal crawl space between two welded-together buildings wasn't designed for comfort, it knew that, but it was so very unused to having trouble shoving itself into every little crack it could see.

It had lost that sense of security that came from knowing it could hide behind every small box and fit into every little gap, in exchange for raw power.

It glanced down at its forearm, thick enough to be compared to a human's knee, wiggling the spikes a little bit for its own amusement.

Worth it.

It yawned and clicked its jaws shut.

After it had finished sliding down that metal cable and wiggling its body through a bunch of whirring mechanisms, the first thing it had done was simple.

Observe.

Observe *everything*.

And it learned a lot of things.

Firstly, [Echoes of Oblivion] was far more useful in making itself soundless than sightless. Turns out, being a black hole in space was a lot darker and easier to pick out than just another shadow clinging to the unlit underside of a walkway.

The skill's stealth capabilities had mostly been relegated to hiding the glow of its eyes and coating its hands and legs and claws whenever it scraped about or scaled a building. Considering its newfound ability to use [Echoes of Oblivion] to make itself a giant sphere of fog and obscure its movements, the skill was more combat-useful now.

Thankfully, sneaking came to the wolf naturally.

That didn't mean it was easy. There was so much light up here.

It was used to flickering lightbulbs, dark alleys, and broken networks of wires rendering entire stretches of the nest into complete darkness, vast expanses of foggy windows trapping the lights of the residents inside their little nests, smog and fog *everywhere*.

Up here, the air was . . . not *clean*, it still stank of chemicals a little bit, but it was far cleaner than below. There was no smog, no choking humidity making giant banks of fog it could stalk through. No humans came to tear down and pocket the light crystals either, so there were a *lot* of them.

And even when the humans were supposed to be sleeping, toward the end of the light cycle they followed, there were people patrolling.

It wasn't sure *what* they were patrolling for, but it could take a guess that they were looking for it.

The most useful bit of information it gathered was that humans had the odd tendency to *never* look up. Stalking prey became trivially easy when it noticed this.

The second-most useful thing it learned was that humans liked to walk into strange communal nests, then poison themselves until they were stumbling wrecks that could barely tell up from down, much like the building it was currently wedged into.

All it had to do was wait for the inevitable suicidal two-legger that would stumble outside and try to go home to his personal nest.

It was quite boring.

Its eyes flicked to the bony cap still sitting innocently on the dusty metal to its left. It was strange to think this was the top half of its skull just a few hours ago.

There was no mana in it anymore, nor anything useful.

Its human arm extended out of its side to grab it, and it blunted its remaining [Devourer]-enhanced teeth as it popped it into its mouth and began chewing on the bone.

It wasn't sure why, but it was so very satisfying to just be gnawing at something and meeting actual resistance.

* * *

It took another two hours, but *finally*, it found a good target, a lone self-poisoning human who had no companions with him nor stuck to the main big, well-lit paths.

Just when it was starting to feel that gnawing hunger again.

It could always dip into the underground tunnels for some rat snacks, but after that recent experience, it was very hesitant to do so.

It just made it feel uneasy, second-guessing every thought and action, whether they were its own or if the tunnels were doing it, or whether it was just being overly paranoid.

It was annoying. So it wouldn't go there if it could help it.

The human continued moving, and the wolf prowled above him, claws embedding lightly into a pipe that rimmed some building half-built out of glass.

Antennae and ears both twitched and spun, little balls of darkness obscuring all seven of its searching eyes, and impatience warred with caution as the human turned and stumbled down a long flight of stairs, clutching to the railing.

Thirty-two humans to the right building flanking the stairs, moving boxes.

Three on the left one.

Twenty-three above, walking on a metal bridge that connected two large gathering spots for humans, packing up their belongings and stalls.

It *could* pounce now, but . . .

It wasn't some preset condition or path that it was waiting for. Planning felt meaningless when its instincts had yet to fail it, not once.

Every time it thought about jumping down and just snapping his neck, there was a hint of reluctance in the background of its mind, a background pressure that told it that it was about to make a bad decision. So it waited.

The pipe went into the building, so it briefly jumped up to claw at the wall, then leapt up and grabbed one of the metal fixtures that held up the light crystals, its tails hooking into two others like them.

Another heave, and it was on the building's sloping roof, the thin lip around the smooth metal greatly assisting it in *not* slipping off as it slithered to the top.

It moved forward, waiting just a little more.

Then it paused, its head and attention swerving to the right.

Two people were running.

And as far as it could tell, the first was running away from the second.

It briefly wavered, looking down at the stumbling man.

Just from impact alone, it could tell the one pursuing was almost twice as large as its chosen quarry.

That, and it was curious.

It turned toward a stout bridge connecting two buildings, just fifteen feet away, and after briefly coiling and tensing its legs, it leapt. Two hands burrowed into the metal and two thinner ones grasped the lip as its lower body swung forward, and with a light snarl of effort, it swung itself up, grabbing the top of the metal bars and kicking to scramble onto the bridge.

It tried to map a route to intercept them, head tilting.

It was hard. Even harder now without the intelligence increase that weird mana symbol had given it.

Humans would one day pay for the ridiculously overcomplicated mess that was their nest, it vowed, as it grumbled and began to jog down the bridge that cut through swathes of buildings like a battering ram.

He breathed in harsh pants, feeling his legs nearly buckle with each step, but forcing himself to keep going, to keep running.

Stupid. Stupid, stupid, stupid!

Bossman had told him a thousand times to just poison their supplies and sneak away.

But he was hungry, like every other kid he knew, so he tried to leave a little bit unspoiled and carry it away under the Guard's noses.

He glanced behind him, seeing the giant guard still chasing him, looking much less tired than he was hoping for, and quickly turned back around, starting to feel a mind-hazing sense of desperation.

A sense of shame welled up as he wondered how stupid it would be that he might die because he dropped a damn food cube. Oh, that kid died 'cause he dropped a food cube? We'll mourn, but we're still gonna snicker at him inside our heads!

It was humiliating. He wanted to die fighting a dragon or something! Or not at all, preferably! He was barely twelve!

Drats, rats, rats rats rats and rackbats! Where the hell was he?!

He glanced to the left.

The head of a factory peeked out over a giant downward-sloping mess of thankfully well-lit metal stairs, running in a zigzag downward, tunnel entrances and pathways spewing out onto the path.

Could he try to change course? He had no idea what was in the countless holes in the wall and tiny alleys he ran past. What if it was a dead end?!

He glanced to the right.

A steep cliff-like expanse of metal, leading down to some kind of . . . open sump.

Too far, this stupid path was way too long—

A strange whistle-crunch preceded the sound of a large shuffling thud, and when the steady tempo of the guard's booming steps and heavy breaths stopped with it, he chanced a glance behind him to see what stopped the man, if his chances of living had increased.

Then he allowed himself to slow down, blinking in confusion as his dead sprint slowed to a jog, then stopped entirely, turning around, breathing in harsh pants.

The zigzagging path stretching down to the sump didn't leave much room for curves. He was on a giant stretch of cobbles, a straight line he could see from beginning to end.

And the guard had collapsed on the ground just past said stretch of cobbles, completely unmoving.

He caught his breath for a moment, wondering if this was some strange feint and if he should just keep running.

Then the light caught and reflected off the steady stream of blood slowly coating the guard's head from a wound he was too far to see, and his eyes widened.

Paranoia settled in.

He whipped his head up to the pipe-covered sky, to the left and right, before turning around, eyes wide and searching as his burning lungs protested.

Nothing.

What the fuck?

He turned back to the guard and felt his heart stop as his eyes rested on an empty path, nothing but a dragging smear of blood left behind to signify the man ever existed, leading into one of the countless pitch-black alleys weaving between the staircases.

He hadn't even heard a whisper, not even the drag of clothes.

He felt himself quiver before an involuntary whimper left him, and he stumbled back, turning around and sprinting harder than before, eyes wide in terror, every shadow another gateway for the unknown entity that did that to jump out from.

He didn't know if Bossman would even believe him when he told him how he got away, but that was a far distant worry as he wheezed and ran and ran and ran, too terrified to stop or even look behind him.

※ ※ ※

After two days of prowling about cables and slithering on the underside of bridges and walkways to dodge the lights and eyes that tried to follow it, getting a taste of proper meat was like . . .

Okay, it didn't have a comparison it could think of, but it was *good*. It felt great.

No mangy, sticky fur, no stupid crunchy bones with every bite, just red, squishy, *meat*. And thin rubbery skin. Human skin was so smooth and light on fur. It was great.

Humans were the best food *ever*.

Maybe it should have waited a little more before snatching the corpse off the street, but the human pup didn't see it.

Part of the reason it did that instead of just grabbing the pup too, was simply the thrill. Another part was how damn skinny the pup was. It could eat four or five rats and get the same amount of essence, it just wasn't worth the hassle.

Besides, seeing its bewilderment and fear was incredibly amusing.

It squinted as it dug its snout out of the human's chest, staring into the distance.

It could still see him, just *barely*. Stumbling and looking around as if expecting the wolf to jump at it from every shadow.

Its tail wagged in amusement as it snorted and dug back into the ribs.

One of its least favorite parts of a human.

On one side, the meat between the ribs was always nice and tender, and crunching and biting the bones was fun and felt nice in a . . . primal, instinctive kind of way.

On the other side, it was one of the most annoying parts of a human to eat. No endless meat or organs, just a bunch of awkward bites with four chunks of bone in it each.

The body began to slide off the pipe, and both its tails whipped down to nudge it back up, its human arms grabbing on to whatever they could reach to keep it steady.

Maybe it should have brought him to a flatter surface to eat, but it was just so hungry it didn't even consider it.

It's instincts weren't screaming at it, so it was probably fine.

It was gnawing on his upper spine when it felt it.

A sudden sensation that was familiar just a little bit of time ago made its whole body jump in surprise, partly because it was used to hearing, smelling, or feeling every surprise possible, at least during the past week and a bit.

Its head jerked up and to the side to try and stare incredulously through the floor twenty feet below, its hands all almost clasped together from the involuntary jump. For a moment, it was shocked into stiff silence, and by the time it realized that it wasn't its sight that was tilting but its entire body, it had already begun slipping off the pipe, its legs already off.

It yelped before trying to claw at the pipe, and only managed to bring the half-eaten corpse down with it as it dropped down.

Falling twenty feet flat on its back would have probably at least fractured a rib before.

Now, it felt like someone slapped its back a little harder than they should.

It snarled and threw the corpse off its body, scrambling to its feet and then just . . . staring at the floor, trying to stare *through* it in vain, seven eyes all wide and searching, as if any one of them could stare through solid iron somehow.

It closed its peripheral eyes, using only the front ones, and fractionally relaxed, blinking rapidly as it digested this . . . incredibly sudden revelation.

Its human was alive.

Its human was alive and fighting something.

Its weak, skinny, crippled nuisance of a human was *fighting something*.

And it couldn't tell what way she was positioned, if she was on top or bottom, if her moments indicated an offense or a beatdown, but it could guess from its memory that unless she was fighting a rodent or something, she was losing.

For a moment, it felt its fur turn to furious spikes, a shiver of fury raising them in a bristle that likely made it look half again as big as it truly was, its teeth curling into a soundless snarl.

It had already lost its pack once, and it did not want to do again, especially in a more permanent matter. Having its human by its side remained as the sole, genuinely pleasant bundle of memories it had of its life.

But no matter how much it wanted to sprint to the nearest ledge and jump off to reach her, it knew it couldn't possibly get to her in time.

It had no real way to measure, but she was just . . .

So incredibly far away.

How the hell did the humans bring it up here so fast?

Then it remembered.

A strange metal cage, attached to a gigantic, mind-bendingly large tower, crawling up its spine on giant cables.

It didn't have eyes to the outside world then, stuck in a little cage with a blanket on it, but it remembered feeling the scrape of metal going up and up and up near endlessly.

Its tails idly swished as it thought, slowly stalking forward, its meal forgotten.

If it could reach that giant tower . . .

No, if it could just use the humans' stupid platforms . . .

With a new goal and a clear destination in mind, it decided to wait until the sensation of presence faded.

The fight continued, and it stood there, anxious and angry, feeling *something* but knowing it was impossible to help.

Almost thirty seconds later, the feeling faded.

It didn't *snap away*, so it assumed that she won.

A squeaking rodent, attracted by the scent of fresh blood, wiggled out of a rusty pipe, and the wolf ignored its screeching as it approached, simply using the bone blade in its back to impale it through the back, before curling the tentacle to bring the weakening rodent in front of its snout.

She felt that, right? Did something as weak as a rat even register to [Pack Hunter] as a fight?

It had to get to her. It wasn't sure of the logistics of dragging her with it or how it was going to keep growing and running from its pursuers with her, but it didn't much care about such details either at the moment.

It calculated the distance to the sump a couple hundred feet below. With a flick, it tossed the rat away and crouched low, rushing forward, leaping over the railing, using it as a springboard to go even farther.

The sludgy, dirty waters were a perfect cushion for such a drop, thick and gooey and always frothing just enough to be soft on the impact as it crashed shoulder first into the concrete wastebox's insides.

The chemicals didn't even hurt anymore, a mixture of its own toughness and its mana cells working with its immune system to quickly identify harmful intruders and eviscerate them.

It still tasted *horrible*, though. It had to find some water to get that taste out of its mouth later.

As it clawed its way up the stone walls and out onto a small field of gravel and pipeworks, it broke into another sprint and wondered how exactly it was going to go about using the human lifts.

It loved its slime tentacles so much.

This was *so* much more fun when it was hanging *under* the moving lift rather than sitting on top of it.

And it didn't even have to put in any effort, beyond sneaking under the station's electrical wiring to grab onto a lift as it detached.

Getting to just limply hang from the underside and watch the pretty lights below was just so worth it.

It was magical.

And very time efficient.

It crossed about a day's worth of distance in about thirty minutes. It hadn't realized quite how slowly it was making progress when it constantly had to be paranoid and check every human's stride and posture, try to see where their gazes were directed so it could leap across a rooftop without someone seeing and notifying the people hunting it.

Because they *were* still hunting it.

Half-heartedly, like some pathetic predator that had lost its . . . "prey," and just couldn't give up without trying for a little more.

But it could still feel them.

It was mostly all the darts and vials they carried that betrayed them.

A lone human covered in pointy sticks, or arrows as the symbol in its head had called them, was a little suspicious. But a human covered in pointy sticks and twenty clinking needles presumably full of annoying poison? While another very similarly weighed one was always *somewhere* nearby?

That was just insultingly obvious.

It also made picking them off one by one all the more satisfying.

It let its head hang backward, tails lazily wagging as they hung down and opened all of its eyes.

It really liked the pretty lights.

Maybe it should start stealing those light crystals the humans used. Not only would more darkness be good for it down there, it could probably just . . . dig a hole somewhere and stash them in there.

Then it could nap on a giant pile of light crystals.

That sounded like a very nice goal to have.

It would unfortunately have to wait for the more pressing goal, which was to make sure its weird, fragile stick of a human didn't die again.

Well, not *again*, but . . . yeah.

The eye on the back of its neck turned to the left, staring at the approaching station.

With a sigh, it gathered all of its limbs and pressed close to the underside of the lift, trying to remember how the box fit into the platform and what parts had gaps so it wouldn't get crushed on docking.

The individual lifts were a lot more frequent, and significantly faster. So it decided to hitch a ride on one of them.

Additionally, they combined its two favorite things.

An isolated prey without escape.

And an equally desolate destination.

The boxes were pretty secure, at least without the wolf clinging to them. If the human noticed the added swaying, he didn't much show it.

When it reached down to swipe its claws through the lock mechanism, and a shadow covered the little window that was the only gateway of the man to see the outside world, his reaction was much more fun to feel.

Unfortunately, or maybe thankfully, nothing terribly exciting happened from there. The human tried to grab the door handle and keep it shut, the wolf yanked it open the moment his hand was on the knob, and as it yanked the door open, the human came with it, screaming.

A tail whipped around his neck before he could fall down into the abyss of lights and wires, and snapped it with a jerky twist.

Then it just slid into the metal box, dragging its food in with it.

Eating with an open, unobstructed view made it feel surprisingly . . .

Content.

They knew they were both alive. Or so it could guess.

Still, it made sure to try and pick off one of its pursuers every once in a while, just to let its human know where it was.

Its spikes proved immensely effective when aimed at the head. Only metal partially stopped it, and even then, the one human who had a head covering of metal got knocked out by the force of the thorn slamming into the side of his head and an inch or two into it.

So its fights were all very, very short.

Maybe if they were harder it would have leveled up more than just a single level in its Path, but it couldn't complain much about that when it was leveling up so fast in all other aspects.

It briefly flicked the symbols open.

-Species: Wolf
-Race: None
-Name: None
-Path: [Hound of The Keeper] Level 30

Base Attributes:
Strength (+1)
Speed (+6)
Dexterity (+0)
Endurance (+10)
Perception (+5)

Resolve (+1)
Intelligence (+6)
Soul (+1)
Available: 0

-Racial Skills: [Pack Hunter], [Quick Learner], [Devourer]
-Acquired Skills:
[Pain Resistance - Level 28]
[Infection Resistance - Level 9]
[Poison Resistance - Level 29]
[Corrosion Resistance - Level 8]
[Disease Resistance - Level 4]
[Magic Resistance - Level 6]
[Mental Resistance - Level 32]
[Electricity Resistance - Level 4]
[Restful Awareness - Level 34]
[Tough Skin - Level 18]
[Iron Stomach - Level 7]
[Mana Perception - Level 15]
[Mana Manipulation - Level 17]
[Soul Perception - Level 4]
[Echoes of Oblivion - Level 22]
[Bloodrush - Level 18]
[Logotexnia - Level 17]
[Sonic Blast - Level 8]
[Tremor Sense - Level 7]
[Maddened Frenzy - Level 6]
[Mana Conversion - Level 20]
[Danger Sense - Level 5]

-Acquired Titles:
Witness of Divinity: You have seen a being of divine nature in their own realm. Your illuminated gaze shatters all illusions and pierces through any and all falsehoods.

Glutton Beyond Compare: You have eaten multiple times your body weight over a single uninterrupted period of consumption. You gain +1 to Strength and Speed while your stomach is adequately filled.

-Acquired Traits:

Survivor (3 / 5): You have felt the chill of death many times and survived. You have fought against impossible odds and won. You are significantly tougher than your frame might suggest.

Hunter (1 / 2): You hunt living creatures, whether it is for survival, sport, or personal gain of one manner or another. You are slightly harder to notice when intending to hunt.

All that progress, and it hadn't even been trying too hard. [Restful Awareness] was an incredible skill.

Its human didn't return the favor of getting into frequent, if short fights, unfortunately, so it was all it could do to just keep heading down, very roughly in the direction it felt her.

Its sense of orientation was impeccable, thankfully. It wouldn't have survived long in the human nest without it. It had only lived as long as it had because it remembered spots and could just let instinct guide it to them again and again. It still remembered a leaking pipe that dripped water into a nice convenient puddle on the floor, the place it drank most of its water from before the symbols came.

And it still remembered some nest full of meat that had a nice human owner that would sometimes toss it some small snacks of intestine and the like.

It thought of briefly visiting him but wasn't sure for what purpose.

It wasn't like it could eat him. It felt weird and wrong to do that after he was one of the few that had helped it survive as a pup. Trying to thank him felt equally strange.

The point was, it was good at orientation.

So even if every lift added another tangled string to the yarn ball that was its path, it still felt pretty confident that it was going the right way.

And when it finally found that . . . utterly *absurd* tower that sat in the middle of almost every single miles-long plate in the human nest, it found its descent going from fast to *rapid*.

Climbing under a bridge and waiting for it to extend toward the colossal monstrosity of rumbling metal took a bit of effort, as did quickly scrambling across the underside and into the gigantic mess of interwoven, crisscrossing latticework of metal beams as thick as thirty humans sitting side by side.

Its claws were sore by the time it felt secure enough to take a breather.

Getting to the center so it could find a straight metal beam without much chance of interruption was *genuinely* difficult. Even with its vibration senses, it constantly had to dodge out of the way of a shifting compartment of steel or an outlining spine of rattling, blocky chains that were dragging some cage of humans up the outer rim, having to constantly be wary of something about to smush it to paste.

It was a shifting labyrinth of metal and gears and hissing pipes and iridescent steel and very strangely glowing liquids being sprayed into the moving mechanisms to vaporize the grease and oil buildup.

It avoided contact with those nozzles.

But when it got to the center and found a straight beam that wasn't ridiculously thick, all it had to do was wrap two tails around it, dig its nails in, and just begin to slide down.

Beside a few hiccups where seams and unexpected bolts and shudders almost made its claws slip out and forced it to tighten its tails and stop for a minute or two, it continued sliding down like a plummeting speck of shadow, catching faint glimpses of light and activity through the tiny gaps between the endless machinery spinning all around it.

As it stopped to try and find some still place to rest, it idly wondered . . .

If humans could build things like this, wouldn't . . . *everything* be a human nest of some sorts?

If it went up an unfathomable distance, for example, how clean and orderly would the human nest get? How many humans were there in this nest? Was there a limit?

Or was the entire world their nest?

The idea of angering the entire world felt like a very bad one.

But at the same time, running . . .

Running was starting to grate on its nerves.

Cradled in a hammock of wires as thick as its own legs each, between two rumbling blocks of gearwork, it went to sleep.

When it finally started getting somewhat close to where it had felt her, barring a couple thousand feet, it had to pause and go out for a quick snack, noticing its reserves going low again.

Unfortunately, it couldn't find any of its usual playmates. The humans hunting it must have lost whatever trail clued them in to its location when it went into the large tower. So it moved to grab someone random off the streets.

And it ran into a curious sight.

The humans were fighting.

Not its *own* human, unfortunately, or fortunately, actually. She was pretty weak.

Just . . . some giant crowd of humans.

One group was dug into some large factory complex, with trenches of gravel and makeshift barriers everywhere, peeking through the windows and walkways above to toss fire bottles and little rocks that exploded down at their assailants.

Glowing stone . . . insect-like things were moving with them, like the stone humanoids down by the burning rivers, except these had drills on their fronts and constantly moved back and forth in bizarre, start-stop manners, scaring away the red ones and then skulking back into the factory's makeshift defenses.

The second group was trying to get into the building complex and was vastly outnumbered. But they also knew how to fight and were far more organized, so they were somehow not quite being repelled yet. They threw mana stuff at the defenders, fire and glowing spears from a particularly large human that sat at the back of the attackers, while a large detachment of the attacking group was locked in a melee on the ground floor and around the wire fences.

It was interesting to see how humans fought. Not individually, but as a . . . a pack?

On the right corner, it could see another group carrying ladders, likely trying to sneak in through the upper windows.

It was such a strange thing to see. It knew humans fought, of course. Pack members did that all the time too, at least from what it had observed.

But never like this, never on such a large scale. Pack fights were scuffles, a lot of snarling, posturing, intimidation and domination, establishing a pecking order of sorts, the bigger dog asserting that it would be the one to get most of the meat.

So combined with previous things it noticed about them, it had to wonder if humans even worked in such a group. It had thought humans were like a . . . massive, cohesive, loosely connected pack. All of them, the nest itself.

That notion had been challenged when it realized that humans weren't exactly united in the task of hunting it, only a tiny group seeming to work toward that goal.

Now, such a notion was shattered.

Were humans split into many different packs? It certainly looked like that. Even their coverings—their "shirts" and "pants"—they had a kind of color pattern and similarity to distinguish group one to group two.

That was . . .

Convenient, actually.

It probably meant humans wouldn't get *too* upset when a couple of their kin vanished in the alleyways. It had been worrying that it was slowly drawing the ire of the nest in general with its actions.

Now it knew it wasn't. Or was . . . reasonably certain.

Humans were weird, there was always the possibility they considered this some kind of ritual. Or maybe they were just play-fighting but very roughly—

A man in red took one of the flaming bottles to his head, and his screams carried up to the wolf's perch.

Maybe not.

It had been idly glancing at another set of human packs fighting below as it jogged across a rooftop, trying to puzzle how to get closer to where it had previously felt its human.

And as if mere thought summoned her, it felt her, and its jog froze, almost stumbling over its feet from surprise.

She was so *close*.

She zipped around, fast enough to make it mentally blink in confusion, her attention jumping in a circle as she moved back and forth, but not away—

She was surrounded.

Its fur slowly began to bristle.

She turned, slowed, thrashed, fighting someone. Something impacted whoever she was grappling with, and then she began running out of the encirclement.

He wasn't sure how she healed so fast, or how she *ran* so damn fast, but it didn't matter. Someone was hunting her. More than one two-legger. Too far to feel them, but not for long.

Maybe complacency from the long stretch of silence had led it to unconsciously slow down again, to try and not attract attention. Now, it immediately gave up on any notion of stealth.

Its mind strained to not slip as it punched the metal with a deafening boom, denting it inward, focusing on the vibrations, mapping a path, some way to get to her, to find her quicker and kill whatever worthless meatbag was interfering.

Its lips curled into a soundless snarl as its tails hooked around smoking exhaust pipes, two human arms hooking their nails into the seams of the roof, its own fingers burrowing into steel.

It leapt off the roof, sailing in a near-straight line for a bit before slamming into the steel floor fifty feet below with a roll and a grunt of pain. It ignored the fighting humans who shouted and leapt away from it, breaking into a dead sprint toward a railing about two hundred feet ahead.

One of them moved as if to hit it with a lead pipe as it passed, fast and hard.

The tentacle in its back whipped out from its sheath to shoot a spike into his forehead and straight through it. It sped past them into the alley before his body hit the floor.

Wisps of smoke flickered and clung to its fur in random agitated bursts, a burning fury rising up in its chest, into the back of its throat, pressing for release, for a howl. A howl it kept down, clamping its jaws shut as its brows furrowed into a glare, venomous thorns rising across its shoulders and forearms.

Finally, action.

Finally, it was getting its pack back.

It leapt onto the railing and off of it, spreading all its arms wide open. A couple seconds of weightlessness and then its limbs clamped shut around the light-pole crystals that raced up and down for hundreds of feet, swinging once from momentum before sliding down.

It ignored the crack and sparkles of light crystals disconnecting and snapping as its weight barreled through the flimsily upheld lights, and a tide of darkness followed it as it descended.

CHAPTER 13

Katherine had led her and Scruffy somewhere, huffing and puffing from the messy load on her back, clanging and banging with every other step. She couldn't really focus.

Likely wouldn't be able to until the blood she'd gorged herself upon worked the stupid concussion away.

Katherine whispered things at her as she guided her to a corner, the air familiar in the way all places smelled when enclosed for a long time.

She wanted to sleep, she really did, but the System kept prodding at the back of her mind, and curiosity won over logic. Because it had been genuine *ages* since she'd last opened it.

So she slumped further into the corner and opened it.

You have progressed on your Path.
[Infuser] Level 17 → [Augmentor] Level 18

Already?

She knew Paths changed over time, whether because the person had changed enough or because they'd progressed enough in their Path to be considered something superior to before or some such drivel, but as far as she knew, Paths usually changed when someone had hit a milestone of some kind, an understanding, or just reached a very high level in whatever they were doing.

What prompted—

Fuck, thinking made her head hurt.

Still . . . she could not complain. [Infuser] was more of a "catch-all" path for people that imbued spells and properties into things and people. It caught craftsmen and rune makers and even most necromancers that were early on in their careers, just . . . all sorts of things.

[Augmentor] was very specifically oriented toward buffing or imbuing living things. Its bonuses to her [Haste] for example would be much better than [Infuser]'s, which was wider catching but weaker.

All this did was ensure that going into some kind of enchanting route would be much harder, and she was not interested in that whatsoever, in line with that supposed theory that the System could "tell one's fate."

Even if she wished to become some kind of enchanter, she was not stable enough, not secure enough, not connected enough to make something like that work.

Her more specific Path was much more combat oriented, and she had a feeling she'd be needing that more than trinkets.

Base Attributes:
Strength (+0)
Speed (+0)
Dexterity (+0)
Endurance (+3)
Perception (+2)
Resolve (+2)
Intelligence (+4)
Soul (+2)
Available: 5

The text stalled, and she pushed it to go on, having no clue what to put her attribute points into and only vaguely understanding the fact that allocating them while concussed and dizzy and sleepy and more than a little battle- and blood-drunk was likely a bad idea.

-[Pain Resistance] has Leveled Up. Level 24 → Level 26
-[Sparkburst] has Leveled Up. Level 19 → 21
-[Haste] has Leveled Up. Level 20 → Level 21
-[Mana Perception] has Leveled Up. Level 23 → Level 24
-[Mana Manipulation] has Leveled Up. Level 25 → 26
-[Mana Tank] has Leveled Up. Level 8 → Level 9
-[Mana Conduit] has Leveled Up. Level 8 → Level 13

-[Mana Touch] has Leveled Up. Level 10 → Level 14
-[Tough Skin] has Leveled Up. Level 7 → Level 9
-[Telemantic Construct] has Leveled Up. Level 15 → Level 18

She idly remembered [Tough Skin]'s existence and quickly realized that this skill had probably helped her hand stay usable almost as much as a mage's natural resistance to her own spells did.

Curiosity sated, she flicked it off, flipped it the finger mentally, and tried to go to sleep, feeling wired beyond belief. She felt exhausted but not sleepy. Like there was some scraping background thought that kept her nailed to the moment.

Scruffy eventually cuddled up to her, practically laying on her left leg, her back against the wall and her head on Emhreeil's lap.

She pet her hair as the goblin fell asleep.

It helped relax her a bit.

When Katherine joined the impromptu pile, leaning her head on her right shoulder and draping her trench coat over all three of them like a crappy blanket, she finally began to feel relaxed enough to slump into the corner rather than curl into it, and began to slowly drift off.

And even through the fuzzy space in her head, she understood why.

She simply wasn't used to sleeping alone anymore. It felt wrong. She wasn't sure if this sense of safety and comfort began after sleeping on top and cuddled up to the wolf for a couple weeks, or if it only really bloomed during the past few days of sleeping in cramped spaces in a tiny bed, waking up together with Kat and Scruffy, but it was there regardless.

She wished her skin could still feel temperature normally beyond the patchy mess of conflicting warmth and chill she felt. She assumed this was warm.

Fucking chemicals.

She fell asleep to the distant sensation of her friend fighting something above, briefly.

He was closer. Significantly closer.

He *had* felt her. And he was coming.

She fell asleep with a small smile.

After waking up and feeling like something a step or two above a walking zombie, Emhreeil had the chance to observe their surroundings.

As far as she could tell this was someone's abandoned basement. Cracked gray tiles over stiff stone.

Across the room from their cuddle pile of sorts, she could see a long stretch of organized objects.

Their . . . loot? Yeah, their loot.

It was a lot.

Half-processed memories from yesterday rose.

As hurried as they were to get away from the scene, preferably *far, far* away, they had to stop and hide somewhere, to not only arm themselves properly, but to rest and let all the blood do its work.

And it was doing it, she could feel it. Her hand almost had new skin. It felt smooth and waxlike, but it was there. Her fingers weren't twitching constantly.

So they'd found themselves here, wherever "here" was. It was dusty, it smelled like something died in the pipes above their heads weekly, but it was decent enough for them to sleep in.

It wasn't like they could just walk into an inn absolutely loaded with spare armor and weapons. They'd get found in a day and be gutted the next. Katherine had saved them a lot of time, if not their lives outright, by finding this place.

Eventually, she drifted off again, and woke up to the sight of Katherine poking and separating the loot.

After half an hour of waking up and stretching, she limped over to join her.

"Where's Scruffy?" she mumbled, bending down to access something that looked like a . . . curved cleaver.

"Outside. Sent her on lookout. She's smaller and sneakier," Katherine replied distractedly, and she nodded, going back to checking their haul.

"Em? I'm proud of you," Katherine blurted out before she could start, and she paused, confused.

"For helping that girl. You've . . . changed less than I thought," Katherine breathed out, genuine and oddly awed. "I would have walked away, personally. But you've always been the better person, so the entire time I was wishing you wouldn't, but I didn't know if you would stop them, because . . . well, like you said. You're different now. You're not quite the . . . bright-eyed sweetheart I remember. You're tougher now, harder. The same rose, but you've grown thorns, if that makes sense. So I thought you would walk past. I'm . . . really glad you didn't. I'm proud." Her fingers slowing on the sheath she was inspecting, lost in thought.

She took a deep, loaded breath, incredulous.

When was the last time she heard someone say they were proud of her? She must have been a toddler.

With a shuddering exhale, she stepped to the side and yanked Kat into a hug, ignoring her tiny yelp of surprise, her hand a tight fist in her friend's trench coat, forehead against her shoulder.

Arms wrapped around her, engulfing her.

"I'd have crumbled to pieces without you, you know that? If you weren't there when I woke up." she forced out from a chest tight with warmth, and Katherine didn't reply, simply hugging her tighter.

It took a few minutes of her breath breaking and stuttering, but eventually the lump in her throat vanished, and all emotions had been bled out of both of them. They separated, and with a final squeeze on her shoulder and a smile, Katherine stepped back to give her some momentary space, picking up the sheath she'd dropped before.

After another minute of thought and mental digestion, she joined her in picking through the loot.

She was lucky that the sheer surprise and speed of the fight didn't let any of the gangsters dig into their clothes and pull out some of the nastier stuff they had.

The inventory was ridiculous, and every passing item they laid out on the floor had her realize how absolutely *crucial* that element of surprise was.

Every other damn thing in this pile could have killed them.

They had an impact grenade full of acid the likes of which she could only guess would be found in the deepest ends of the fourth floor, for example. The thing frothed and *whined* when she brought it to her ear.

It felt and looked and *sounded* so toxic that she was pretty sure this thing would explode if it met air. Or water. Or anything that wasn't the enchanted insides of a complicated mess of plates and locks, which it was currently housed in, with a tiny slit of glass to look inside on the right side.

If it exploded, would it be in gas form or liquid? Gas bomb or liquid bomb?

She couldn't tell, unfortunately, but the idea of an acid gas grenade was horrifying.

She'd already felt herself melting alive once. She didn't care to repeat the experience. She missed not having numb skin, to some extent.

Then, irithite gauntlets. She wasn't sure how Katherine knew what that metal even was or what it did. Apparently it was some kind of alchemist metal. Self-repairing, to a decent extent. A bit less sturdy than steel.

How the gangsters had access to not *one* alchemist-sourced weapon but *two*, or how they could afford it, she wasn't sure. It was likely that the gang found some alchemist who hadn't gotten his guild's protection yet, and had enslaved him for dirt-cheap equipment.

The gauntlets were too big for her hand, of which she only had one, so Katherine got both of them and seemed oddly pleased as she curled and uncurled her fists in them.

She had to agree, Katherine and armor went together like milk and cookies. She was short, but that just made her look more . . . solid, in a sense. Like a small wrecking ball. Even if she wasn't sure what her friend's Path and skills were, if any.

They should discuss that soon.

Then, a small packet of rocks. Likely drugs. They threw it away, even if she had to admit to some curiosity.

Only two healing potions between the five of them, surprisingly.

Cocky pieces of shit.

Then . . . mostly a large assortment of light armor, under-armor, knives, more drugs, cigarettes, a couple coin pouches that Katherine was in the process of emptying into their own, a giant, gleaming scimitar that she had *no idea* how Katherine managed to beat with the crappy dagger they bought her, and the dart launcher. Along with a couple belts for all the stuff to clip onto.

Problem number one with arming herself was simple.

She was still incredibly weak.

She *felt* fine, true, but that was likely because she'd just gotten used to lifting ten pounds of weight like it was thirty.

So any of the heavier, more protective options immediately went out of the window.

Which left Katherine's loot pile absolutely *decked* compared to hers as she patiently reviewed the loot and kept tossing whatever she couldn't use onto hers.

Which was most stuff.

Iron treads?

It sounded good in theory, until she realized that walking with weights on her feet with her . . . "fighting style" and current strength was suicidal.

Gauntlets?

She only had one hand—better to sell them as a pair.

Besides, the dart launcher was a much better fit, even if Katherine had to spend an entire hour and a half readjusting everything around her twig-like arm and hand.

The whole thing was a single armor sleeve piece, unfortunately. It started with a thin sheet metal pauldron over a thick mold of leather, with straps that went around her chest and ribs. The pauldron connected down to a leather vambrace that hugged her forearm, a leather glove on her hand, and some leather protection around the arm. Simple but efficient and fairly light.

Only the lower half of her forearm had actual mechanisms, both over and under.

The dart launcher was snug with her wrist, and mercifully simple to load. It was just a little rectangular box with a button on the outer side, which she discovered she could bite to pop the box open, which split in half to reveal a groove for the darts and some kind of iridescent spring that would launch them when she performed two specific motions.

How Katherine knew all of this, she also didn't question.

After it swung open all she had to do was jam two pointy but factory-standard darts into the two slots and flick it back closed with her wrist. The little dart bandolier slung across her hips was also light and easy to clip on, with a metal clicking . . . thing. A buckle?

Then she got to testing it while Katherine replaced cloth with chainmail and holed leather, trying to avoid using mana bursts to give her friend some modicum of privacy as she changed.

Unfortunately the launcher was not mercifully simple to reload. That needed a second hand, or very fine telemancy to accomplish. Not rough fields like her constructs, actually grasping something with mana turned into force, which was more of a mana control exercise than a genuine use, broadly speaking.

Shooting the damn thing wasn't simple either.

It took Katherine around thirty solid minutes of explanations for her to learn what wrist and finger movements she had to perform simply to turn off the safety, turn the safety on, and how to shoot.

And after said half hour, she finally got to shoot the damn thing, loaded with one dart.

One barrel twanged violently, empty, while the other let out a much . . . meatier noise, sending the dart into the wall and bouncing off with a spray of stone chunks. The little cone of damage looked about an inch deep.

More than enough to pierce clothes and flesh, assuming no armor or ridiculous Endurance like with that fucker she fought.

When she asked how on Ergos she didn't get nailed by one of these darts, Katherine said he couldn't use the launcher because he was holding his sword with the same hand, and when he tried to twist his wrist to arm it, she just knocked the sword out of his hand.

Her evaluation of Katherine's combat capabilities rose even higher. She just sounded so . . . knowledgeable about it. Like she knew what a proper stance and parry and riposte was. Emhreeil sure didn't. She knew the definitions at best.

Before she could accidentally brain someone with a dart, she decided to turn the launcher off.

Bring hand straight up and yank to the right to disengage the mechanism, Kat had said.

With two short movements and twin clicks, the pull on her gloved fingers disappeared. Then she got back to trying to reload the darts on her own.

Fourth try, she *almost* got both darts in with the flashy motion, only for both to barely miss and hit the floor.

It was *possible*, but she needed some practice.

She liked this dart launcher. Even if she doubted it would do much for her, having options was wonderful.

The rest of her choices were similarly light. A thick shirt with a bunch of small bendy wooden plates sewn into the inside, presumably chemically treated, great for keeping her organs inside her. Then, a scarf woven around chainmail with two clips on each end to tie around her neck.

Well, that one was kind of heavy combined with the weight of the golem eye yanking at her neck with its chain, but she'd rather keep her arteries intact.

Then, simple shin guards made of some kind of dark blue wood, *extremely* light and oddly sturdy, a bandolier belt for her darts with a padded metal pouch for a single healing potion vial, and the enchanted ring around her finger.

Which was the biggest dilemma they faced as they slowly but steadily armed themselves, watching the loot pile on the floor steadily decrease in size.

On one hand, the amount of things they could buy with the seven or eight gold coins they might be able to sell this ring for was immense.

The most desirable of which was a golem arm prosthetic.

A *good* prosthetic. Four or five gold coins likely couldn't get her any of the enchanted or magitech stuff, not even close, but it would be enough to get something that was sturdy, reliable, and articulate. And *strong*.

Golems were strong already as far as she knew, but even compared to normal golems, that many gold coins got someone the good limbs, the ones that came from the really terrifying bastards down below.

And that was before anything from the System's attributes got factored in.

If she had one of those, she could have ended the fight yesterday by just reaching forward and crumpling the scumbag's windpipe into mush.

And it was tempting, it really was.

To have full functionality again. To feel a little more *whole* again, even if it would be patchwork and her flesh would never really return, not without a price she couldn't afford in her dreams.

But at the same time, the ability to just snap a dagger into her hand whenever she wished—

A dagger.

A stabby metal object.

Like her *darts*.

She let out an annoyed hiss, deflating like a balloon.

God, she was so fucking *stupid*.

She brought her hand down to her hip, and with a few quick taps had stored all the metal darts into the dimensional ring. They barely took up any space.

She bit onto the thin rectangular wrist launcher, managing to find the button with a fang, and swung it open.

The darts blinked into existence perfectly in the little grooves, and she swung her hand inward to the right to snap the box shut.

Just like that.

She took aim at the wall and fired off both darts.

Then she let the springs take a short second to reel back and teleported two more darts in without issue. With a flick and click, the dart launcher was disarmed, and she sighed as she bent down to port the darts back into the ring.

When combined with her current weakness, the weight of a *good* golem arm would really weigh her down. Pitted against the convenience and the sheer utility of being able to just throw anything she wanted into what was essentially a tiny pocket dimension, as long as it wasn't full, plus the quick reload, she was willing to settle significantly.

Maybe she'd buy a cheap little claw arm. Enough to grab stuff and hold on to them, nice and cheap and disposable.

With her track record, it probably wouldn't last long anyway.

Scruffy chose that moment to tumble down the stairs with a squawk, not even bothering to properly regain her feet before gesturing above with frantic gibbers, eyes wide.

"Shit," she hissed, feeling dread coil in her stomach.

This basement was a dead end. They had to push outside.

How the hell did they find them so fast? Blood magic? They'd certainly bled enough in that alley. But witches were *expensive* and fickle at best. How much did they piss them off?

Katherine wasn't one to be sloppy with things like this, there was no way this place wasn't remote and out of the way, wherever the hell they were.

Kat wasted no time in grabbing the long curving scimitar and clipping it onto her belt, then snatching up their backpack as Emhreeil stood there, trying to calm her heart down with deep breaths.

Her hand flitted down to the acid grenade dangling off her left hip, safe within a little pouch.

She wondered what it would look like, to see a crowd of human scum melting away into the gutter beneath their blood-soaked boots. What it would feel like to watch it.

Hear it.

"Kat. I know you haven't killed before. But please don't hesitate. It'll be either them or us," she whispered softly, hoping she wasn't inadvertently pushing her friend down some bad path.

Kat sighed, all bulky armor under a tight trench coat, her every step clinking softly as she walked to the stairs that led them down here.

"I won't, Em. Now let's . . . see how fast I can run like this," Katherine murmured, and glanced back at her.

They had to have a chat about their Paths soon. She had no idea how much Strength or Endurance Kat had. She had no idea if she could keep up with her, or the other way around.

Not that there was a chance in hell of her leaving Kat behind. Ride together, die together, or . . . something.

The golem eye flitted down to Scruffy, still panting. And very short of stride.

She ignored her startled squawk as she hauled her onto her shoulder, feeling her arm weakly shake from the strain.

"Grab on tight, Scruffy. Bumpy ride," she urged, and the goblin understood quickly as she followed behind Kat, her hands wrapping around her neck and feet digging into her waist.

She paused and bent down to grab a knife, handing it to Scruffy, who took it after a moment of hesitance.

Then she jogged forward, up the stairs.

She couldn't run well like this either, she had to admit. It felt heavy to climb up stairs with it, never mind sprinting.

The door to the basement creaked open, and Kat took a cautious peek.

"I see a couple of them. They're looking around the other doors and storage buildings. They don't know where we are right now," Katherine whispered.

She worked her jaw, trying to figure out a solution beyond just mindlessly legging it.

"I don't know where we are right now either," she simply said.

"Abandoned slave camp. These used to be storage rooms. There's a colossal factory to our distant right, and a smaller one to our left. Across from this door, a couple hundred feet down, are some of the higher sumps, and behind us, if we went around, is a giant stretch of open ground with spires and hanging tower buildings all over, leads down to a fighting pit a couple hundred feet off the end. Good for losing pursuers," Katherine rushed out in a breath.

Shit.

The sumps were a bad choice.

The factories were even worse. Far too large, far too complex. Workers got lost in factories, never mind random people running into one. Which might help them lose their pursuers, but then they'd be in a labyrinth of machinery and very likely surrounded on the outside.

"Fighting pit sounds good. Better, at least. How much speed do you have?" She offered, and Katherine hissed out a sigh, tense.

"I only have three points in it. And yes, it sounds good, but *open space*, at least until the paths narrow toward the fighting pit. We might get nailed and surrounded if they've got people that way."

"I think it's best if we just assume we're surrounded no matter which direction we go. Besides, I can speed us both up. How did you think I moved so fast yesterday?" she asked, leaning forward to peek through the door as well by sending a small surge of mana.

No footprints. They hadn't passed through this part yet, and Kat hadn't left any trail to the door.

"I really don't know here, Kat. All I have are your descriptions. I can make us both really fast for a while, and still have some decent mana left over. You know the terrain better, you brought us here. Which way?"

She knew Katherine wasn't used to taking initiative and was most definitely uncomfortable with doing so, but it wasn't like that was worth the danger her making a blind choice would put them in.

Katherine lowered herself closer to the floor, bracing against it, then glanced back at her head, before flicking down at the golem eye on her sternum, meeting her gaze.

"Honestly, I think you're right. Speed boost, then just . . . get into the tunnels and run toward the fighting pit. It's going to be crowded enough to let us slip away. Or start a massive brawl. Right. Okay," Katherine said, obviously psyching herself up, uncharacteristically jittery.

That contrast between them made her realize how much calmer she was in comparison.

She couldn't tell if that was a good thing.

"On the count of three . . . ?"

She nodded, crouching, her fingertips brushing against Katherine's back, two [Haste] spells at the ready.

A squeaky voice rose from the right of the door, getting closer, exchanging banter.

"One . . ."

Her mind checked the ring, the darts, the dagger.

"Two . . ."

The thrum of adrenaline, that sickly sweet thrill, coated her tongue, slathered her spine. Her aching, sore lips panged with tiny pricks of pain as they stretched into a small, tense smile.

"Three."

[Haste] left her body hollow, and Katherine gasped sharply at the boost she got, substantially more powerful than the one she gave herself.

The door exploded outward, and their boots kicked up a wave of gravel and dust as they both tilted left and pumped their legs.

A slow shout rose from behind them, a deafening whistle starting its trill by the time they'd almost turned the corner.

She was still weak and tired. Her head still felt fuzzy, and she still hurt all over. She was about half healed. Fighting was not the plan here, not even close. They just had to run.

The short, squat building they emerged from quickly retreated behind them, and she saw what Kat meant.

A wide expanse stretched forth like a field, peppered with giant piles of gravel and dirt and discarded scrap metal, flanked on either side by tall skeletal buildings. From above came light, spires and towers cut off a hundred or more feet before they met the ground, monstrosities of glass and lights and wire, the abandoned outlines of a giant greenhouse eerily dark and silent around them.

Someone shouted from the building up ahead to the left, and she gritted her teeth, pushing through the stiffness to pump her legs faster.

At the other edge of the vast mess of gravel and scrap metal hills peppering a long stretch of solid stone, she could see the buildings and fences slowly tightening to a small collection of alleys.

It was about four hundred feet away.

The way the golem eye bounced around was disorienting, so she turned it off, relying entirely on [Mana Touch], having seen what she needed.

She felt something rush through her mana field from where the shout came from, and she threw herself to the right, lowering her center and briefly slapping her palm on the ground to force herself upright again.

The air ruffled her cloak as the arrow narrowly missed her waist and Scruffy's leg. They only narrowly avoided tumbling into the ground, taken off balance by Scruffy's weight.

That wasn't a warning shot, not a net. It was a killing shot, center mass.

Her eyes widened as she felt another arrow, not even a full second later, whistling through the air, from the same direction.

Toward Katherine.

For a moment, she was about to slam into her side to get her out of the way, or try to push the projectile off course with a construct, something which took way too much time and mana to be without risk, not against something like an arrow.

Katherine drew the scimitar in one smooth motion, and she aborted that plan, trusting her friend, straightening back into a proper run.

Kat batted the projectile away without breaking stride, a motion that was impressive even with the slowed-time sort of feeling from the boost, and she again had to reevaluate her friend's combat prowess.

She mentally prepared another construct, just in time for another one to come, before the second arrow had even hit the ground.

In the brief moment it was blown off course, she realized that it was not an arrow, but a crossbow bolt.

A fucking repeater crossbow.

Fuck. Fuck fuck fuckfuckfuck—

Another deflection, hasty. She heard and felt the projectile bounce off Katherine's side, striking her on the flat end before spinning off behind them.

She heard something ahead, like the slide of a razor against brass, and briefly flicked on the eye. Katherine slid to a halt, head manically swerving around.

There was barely any time for her to register the sight of a half dozen floating motes of ghost light spreading just a dozen feet ahead before masked people replaced them with the sound of crunching glass, forearms clasped together in a wide semicircle.

Their masks were more like helmets, black steel and plain with a dozen little holes around the mouth as their only detailed work.

In the middle, a giant with a hammer on his back, bandages around his midriff, coat hanging open to reveal a chest and upper abdomen bursting with grotesque muscle. To his left, a wiry figure with gloves, wearing tight rags, covered in glowing runes. To the middle man's far left, a man with a mechanical spear. To his right, a man in a giant suit of chains, brown-black, dozens of bear traps hanging around his lower body thick enough to be forming an ankle-length skirt, his mask adorned with a childish chalk-lined toothy grin, the eye holes large enough to shove a fist through, yet still completely dark.

Behind them, some skinny short kid in a black mask and brown leather armor, holding on to their shoulders as they appeared, who quickly leapt away.

The man in the chains plucked at his suit and connected two chain ends to a pair of bear traps, quickly beginning to spin them like a flail, picking up speed as something on his back whirred, releasing and lengthening the chain links, his costume tightening up.

The man with the spear on his back *jerked* and twisted, as if his body was made of melting rubber, his right shoulder folding into his chest and hitting his left shoulder. A strange wavelike motion brought the spear into his hand and into forward motion over his shoulder, and he lunged for Katherine with a bizarre stance, shoulder almost to the floor, head turned completely away like a limp-necked doll.

An upward push from below, not much stronger than a shove, right as his foot was about to meet the floor to throw him forward, and he stumbled, tucking himself into a tight ball as he rolled even farther to the left, somehow managing to keep the spear vaguely pointed toward Katherine.

Katherine simply took the opportunity to back up and slap away another bolt, sending her a wide-eyed, desperate glance.

Neither of them had the reach to be fighting a twisting mannequin of a human with a spear that no doubt had a dozen tricks in it.

She kicked backward, mind reeling, the golem eye twisting and jerking around as she billowed mana like a smoke chute, looking for a way out that wasn't *through* them even as she drained herself utterly dry of mana to make a construct that would let them slip through, praying she wouldn't have to use it.

Because if she did, after casting *two* immensely charged [Haste] spells, she was essentially out of the fight from then on, excluding her dagger and darts.

A gigantic warhammer's head five times her own weight scraped chunks off the stone floor in an uppercut as the big man stepped forward in a sharp but ever-so-slow motion. The bear-trap man brought his left arm forward to whip a blacksteel trap straight at her head, equally glacial. The skinny man took a boxer's open stance, his gloves flaring as he stepped toward her, deceptively quick—

And the gap appeared as their movements made them lose their center of balance, tore their stability away.

"THROUGH!" she barked, fast enough that she doubted any of their adversaries would even understand the word beyond a strange shout, and the strongest mana construct she'd built yet by far, a flat plane of repulsion, slammed their line open, the big man getting thrown to the side into the bear-trap-wielding bastard, the boxer quickly shifting his feet as he was launched to the left, bringing himself to a stumbling pirouette to not fall on his ass, arms flailing.

She moved her upper body to the left, away from the flung bear trap, then dashed forward, momentarily digging her feet in to let another bolt fly past, tucking her stomach in, then resuming to move through the gap, past them. Katherine dashed forward at the same time, deflecting a jab of the spear, moving with her torso almost parallel to the ground.

She only had a moment to twist her torso around and meet the boxer's fist as he quick-stepped forward, crossing their distance in two short and measured pumps of his legs, despite Kat not only being closer to him but also directly trying to move toward her, almost sandwiching him between them.

Why were they all so focused on *her*?

Did the fuckers in the bakery talk?

Without any chance of dodging him, she caught his fist and tried to ease it toward her, doubting she could stop it in its tracks. The leather glove sizzled as his knuckles met her palm, but mercifully, it held.

She pushed back, barely slowing his fist down, simply wrenching herself away.

Scruffy's arm stabbed down with the knife from behind her back, aiming for the man's hand.

He twisted his footing and moved his body in a wave from his ankles, forcing himself forward in a quick jerk. His fist barreled into her collarbone, and she spun for a moment as Scruffy squeaked, the knife flying out of her hand, her hands scrambling for a grip on her.

She was dully aware that he'd broken her collarbone, her boots scraping at stone as she bent her legs to try and not end up on her back. She learned her lesson from last time, what happened when someone hit the floor.

She felt him step toward her as she keeled forward, throwing a hand out to catch herself and push off the floor before she could quite meet it, only to promptly lower himself and jump away from her as a scimitar slashed at where his fist was a moment ago.

Katherine's gauntlet yanked at her clothes as she passed her, and she gritted her teeth through the pain as she was essentially jerked up and forward by the motion, jostling the injury.

The mechanism on her wrist was quickly armed with a double twist of her wrist, and she blindly fired toward the bastard behind her as she unsteadily resumed running, hearing a grunt of pain but not having the time to feel what or where she hit.

Katherine placed herself between her and the sniper, swatting away bolts with gauntlet and sword, barely a second's delay between each shot. In the real world, it might as well have been a steady stream of endless bolts, a barrage.

She didn't have the mana to do anything other than see for about another two minutes, not after that giant push field, so she glued herself to Katherine's side, matching her pace for pace as they ran, covering hundreds of feet in mere seconds.

Then Katherine abruptly began to slow down, looking around frantically in between increasingly wild swats at the bolts.

She flicked the golem eye on and felt her heart drop to her feet as she watched detached groups of three sprint into sight from seemingly every single nook and cranny, filling the empty space before them, some of them being teleported in by the kid from before, a kid she just realized had seemingly *vanished* the moment the fighting began.

A mass teleporter?

Did they kill gangsters or a *dungeon baron*? Didn't they have better things to do with all this manpower? Why did they hate them *this* much?

She watched another four motes of light appear through a wall, quickly turning into four people, before the masked child just *disappeared* again into a ball of light and sank into the wall.

There were at least twenty people around them, forming a similar perimeter to before, wide and thin.

But they didn't have a chance to break through. She didn't have mana after having to toss a seven-foot giant and his hammer out of their way.

After everything she'd been through, she didn't want to die like this.

Another bear trap on a chain lunged for Scruffy on her back, as if in slow motion, and she easily twisted out of the way, turning around, struggling to figure out some path to escape.

The boxer took a wide path away from Katherine's side before seemingly sliding forward with a tiny hop that looked like it broke every law of physics possible, just barely slower than her, then lunging right at her.

She only just managed to throw her head out of the crackling fist's path, feeling her clothes spike with residual static, and her hand rose, a sharp metallic thud preceding the two darts that blurred forward.

They burrowed into something that wasn't flesh and were stopped. Armor.

Another fist, aimed just below her ribs.

A memory of what happened last time she took a hit there arose, and she spun with the hit as his fist met her padded shirt, feeling the strike take the wind out of her lungs as she spun, Scruffy losing her already-slipping grip and tumbling off of her—

Then the bear trap that had missed her caught on her single grounded leg as it returned to its owner, and swept it out from underneath her, the pressure plate mercifully too far to activate and sever her foot.

Someone was yelling something, but his voice was too slow to figure out what.

She landed chest down and bit down a shout of pain as her collarbone's pieces ground against each other inside her.

She felt the boxer zip forwards toward her, rearing his left leg up to stomp onto her waist, and tried to twist out of the way, only to see his right leg twist and kick him forward in a flying spinning kick that almost moved at normal pace.

His kick slammed into her face, and she only had the vague impression of noise and sound and *pain* as the eye flicked off, leaving her to swim in the air, to hang in limbo, not quite unconscious but just a hair off.

"EM!"

She couldn't afford to deflect the arrows anymore.

She let one slam into her shoulder and burrow half an inch into the chainmail, driving half a breath out of her, and in one motion, cut the strap of her backpack and dashed forward, letting it peel off her frame.

Then she realized that no matter *where* she stood around Em, she couldn't protect her. They were surrounded.

They were finished.

Just like that?

Why did they send so *many?*

She threw a leg over Em's semiconscious, groaning form, and slashed upward at another bear trap, knocking it aside with ease, before noticing the swirling chain leading up and up and up, out of her line of sight entirely, but perfectly aligned with her.

Her head jerked up just in time to see steel teeth descend toward her like a wide-mouthed shark, so much slower than it should be but a mere *inch* from her wrist, and she twisted her sword to align the base of its blade, unable to dodge and let it hit Em, un*willing*.

The sharp blade met the pressure plate in the center of the maw.

Then she watched the scimitar shatter like a mirror as metal teeth utterly pulverized the thin iron.

In one of the falling shards, she saw the reflection of her eye, wide and pinpricked.

She looked scared.

Something rammed into her knee from the side, only her loose stance preventing it from snapping but rather folding, accidentally kneeing Em in the back as she fell. The flat of a spear jammed into her right side, making her jerk with a short cry of pain and pushing her back in the middle of trying to get away from the boxer, off Em.

An arrow slammed into her thigh, going an inch through the thin leather armor under her coat, and she lashed out with a wordless cry like a cornered animal, throwing herself to the right.

Her hand *almost* brushed against the bottom of the spear before it was yanked out of reach.

The spear twisted, and *extended*, slamming into her solar plexus, and she let out a short wheeze as her momentum was cut short.

Someone slammed into her from behind immediately after, and the world spun.

An impact that numbed her face and made her vision swim, half the world covered by a stone wall, and she groaned in pain as a knee dug into her back, her arm wrenched behind her in a classic but efficient hold, before the second followed.

Her shoulders *burned*.

She panted in sharp gasps as she realized that she was on the floor.

Her eyes flit to Em, finding the spear wielder to be circling her, but not killing her.

They weren't going to kill them.

Not yet.

That was not comforting.

She could only watch in muted, mounting panic as the crowd around them thickened, watched between someone's legs as someone snatched up an unresisting Scruffy who was staring at them with wide, dread-filled eyes.

"Who do you work for? Beakers? Southpaws? Are you a merc?" the man above her said, barely sounding out of breath, and she gritted her teeth as his knee tried to fuse with her spine.

"No," she forced out.

"Which of you is the shot caller?"

She opened her mouth and hesitated.

Was she lying or telling the truth?

Which was more likely to get Em out of this alive? Would they kill the one who "knew less"? Or would they kill the leader first and investigate the others?

She had no naivety in her to assume they would both live. Neither probably would.

But she could at least try. Even if her self-preservation instincts were screaming at her.

The leader was always more valuable. The one who had more "info," if they were thinking this was some kind of organized attack on them.

She had no idea the Snake Eyes were this strong, this ready to spring into action. This well equipped. For a moment, she rescinded all previous thoughts, wishing they'd left that girl to her fate. It wasn't worth it. It simply *wasn't*.

"S-she is," she forced out, closing her eyes, gritting her teeth.

Its human had stopped.

It wasn't bothering with safety anymore, nor any kind of path.

It saw a gap, anywhere, that led down, and it jumped down with only the barest hints of caution and self-preservation.

It jumped off the building it had been sliding down, onto a moving platform, feeling wood and metal crunch beneath it as the crates tumbled off into the smog below, and it kicked off again, to an open horizontal conveyor belt, its claws barely keeping grip as they tore through the mechanisms and cylinders below, the belt fraying and spewing everywhere as it slowed to a crawl.

To its left, the factory twisted in a half circle, with a monstrous open gap that led downward, in the middle of which was a bundle of electric wiring that ran from the top of the building, out on a metal rail, all the way to the middle of the half circle, before it cut off and left the wires to fall down endlessly to whatever it was powering.

It twisted and kicked off, onto a ventilation shaft that lined the half cylinder of metal, one more solid than the rest.

The sheet metal crumpled like paper with a deafening bang, and it didn't waste time trying to stabilize on it, instead grabbing onto the metal wall beside it just long enough to swing its lower body forward and plant its feet on it.

Then it leapt again toward the wires, upside down, in a motion that was now as familiar as *breathing*, arms and tails and tentacles wide open.

It grabbed the mass of wire, thick and heavy enough to barely be able to grasp on or even move it with its weight, and laxed its grip enough to start free-falling face first.

It mercilessly crushed the small instinctive fear of seeing a bottomless abyss of smog below it into a pulp.

She was so *close*.

It felt her jerk and twist in the way someone could only do when being struck, and it choked down the sound in its throat, a pressure building but not releasing, a howl of bloodlust and fury.

It was barely putting any pressure on the wires by now, more or less hovering over them to not tumble off uncontrollably, each skim where its fur touched them almost like an impact.

Descending, the smog let it see vague outlines as it parted, the wolf's guts and blood pulling at its insides as it sped up more and more.

Giant pillars of wire and steel and glass extended from the bottom rim of this seemingly endless half tunnel, crawling downward from the mess of the factory's underside for hundreds of feet like unfinished pillars allergic to the floor.

Its human fell on the ground, jerked around, was *struck*.

A human on the ground was as good as dead.

From this far, it did the only thing it knew could reach her, could reach whatever bag of meat was trying to kill her and let it know that it was **dead**.

It took a gasping breath, opening its jaws to let the air rushing past it slam into its lungs instead, until they felt like they were about to pop.

[Mana Conversion] pulled mana from its body, from the air and space it was rushing through.

For a moment, a mere fraction of a second, it hesitated, remembering what happened the *last time* it decided to make such a racket without a care, telling itself that the humans hunting it would know where it was again.

It retracted its teeth into its jaws as much as the tendon system woven through the bones would allow, which was more than enough to not lose any of them, halving their length.

The next moment, it poured every hateful feeling and emotion into the sound it was about to make, every promise of a visceral, brutal death, every warning and tiny drop of hatred it could muster.

With shadows flickering and bursting violently around it as it descended, like a spike-covered black hole, it let go of the scream, the howl, let go of that ever-building roar in the back of its throat.

Its eardrums burst the moment it heard the first screech of sound coming out of its own throat.

Her mana weakly pulsed out as she focused back on sensation, on the real world, and her fingers slowly, sneakily opened the metal pouch and dug out the acid grenade, hearing Katherine's panting, pained confessions.

She pulled the pin, rolled it down to her knee with a flick of her fingers, and shifted her knee to cover the grenade.

One strong jerk.

One knee to its surface, and the impact plates would activate.

And she would take everyone here with her.

The shift drew attention, and in a flash, there was a razor-sharp blade pressing down on her nape in warning. The scarf would save her, but he didn't know that. She didn't need to alert him to that either.

She simply struggled through another couple pained breaths, going even more limp than before.

The boxer looked at her from where he was holding Katherine down. The spear wielder's head moved away from her, an opening.

"Kill the bitch. We don't need two," someone from behind said, their voice slow, and she barely had time to process what they meant before the giant man with the hammer stepped toward Kat. Something feral and senseless forced her to act, jerking her waist, her left knee rearing up, then down toward the grenade.

They'd all melt into sludge together then, a happily screaming puddle of flesh and leather and steel, in one final act of sheer spite.

Her world and thought process jumped as agony burst over the side of her head, and her knee met stone as she jerked, feeling her brain bounce around her skull like a pinball. She tried to move it up and to the side to try again.

The mannequin bastard leapt over her and snatched the little ball up in the middle of his leap, and in one twisting movement, like the unwinding of a demented spring, rolled to his feet, spun on every joint and axis, and pitched it away.

She flashed the dagger into her hand, the ring hidden beneath the glove, and tried to stab his ankle.

He flipped backward before landing on his toes and carrying his momentum into the longest winding spin-kick imaginable, and his foot slammed into her arm, into her side through it, sending her rolling in hitching, groaning gasps of agony, writhing on the floor, the dagger clattering to the ground.

The giant snorted, the goons around them laughed and jeered, setting her blood on fire, acid moving through veins throbbing in fury and fear.

The giant began to lift his hammer, still so slow, as if the very world was mocking her, like it knew she couldn't do anything and would stretch the moment out as much as possible just to watch despair crumple her heart into a ball.

Katherine bucked and twisted, her eyes wide, screaming as she failed to escape the boxer's hold, and frenzied desperation forced her to keep fighting, to keep fighting to the death because that was preferable to standing by while Kat was on the execution block.

She kicked toward them, a clumsy throw of her leg with a feral snarling sound, feeling her boot explode as her meager [Sparkburst] did nothing more than irritate their eyes, too far and too weak to do anything else.

The spear reared back, either to stab through her foot or cut it off, she wasn't sure. The start of an all-encompassing whine came from above.

Katherine watched the hammer rise, heart locked in terror, hyperventilating, bucking and twisting but achieving nothing—

For a moment, she caught the start of a faint whine, a foreign, distant sound.

Then the sound slammed into her like a physical force the next moment, exploding into an all-encompassing shriek mixed with a bestial roar, the scream of shredding metal mixed with the crunch of breaking bones, a rumble like a mountain breaking in two mixed with a million gnashing, grinding teeth, a whistle of screaming air mixing with a promise of a mangled carcass and the faint idea of a set of teeth wrapped around her throat.

She froze, completely and utterly, in sheer, heart-stopping terror, limbs locked in place, feeling the sound move through the floor, feeling the floor jump and shiver against her chest, feeling her bones crawl and writhe under her muscles, hearing the gravel piles around her click and crack in a million tumbling pebbles, hearing sheet metal rattle all around them like teeth in a shivering jaw, hearing glass crack and shatter above, showering them in fragments big and small as they all stood there, frozen solid, wide-eyed.

The sound continued, wavering and shifting, adding more and more, endless, louder and louder until she could feel its echoes moving through her bones, closer and closer, sharpening into a direction, building as she quivered in place, feeling a terrified, keening whimper press into the back of her throat as tears rushed to her eyes.

The sound finally ended, its writhing echoes twisting like a broken fractal into something otherworldly, leaving nothing behind but the frozen quiet of an equally terrified crowd.

Then Emhreeil burst out laughing, a light and genuine laugh, like it was the best thing she'd ever heard.

Some fought, some worked. Some spent their savings in the markets or at the bottom of a bottle. The dungeon was the same as ever, if one really thought about it.

Until that ungodly shriek squeezed a million hearts in an icy fist of mortal terror, and in its echoes, left behind a floor eerily silent, battles abandoned, citizens rushing to their homes, adventurers running for their gear, waiting for some unknown monstrous threat that they didn't know wouldn't come for them, not yet.

The large man unfroze first, his head jerking to her left, up and up as he stumbled back.

Katherine's teary gaze followed his own.

Among the falling spires of wire and glass, she caught a glimpse of a tiny dark shape, one with too many limbs, dropping out of the dark smog above. Golden laser-point eyes gleamed through the darkness, nonsensical and far too many, and she could have sworn one of them flicked to *her* before they all blinked out.

The air below it exploded, sending it into one of the pillars.

She heard the cocky hammer user snap himself out of it, scream at the goons, bellowing something she couldn't quite hear through the shrieking whine left in her ears, the *sound* still bouncing around and echoing in her mind.

She simply stared, terrified, as the dark shape bounced between pillars in its descent, launching itself down and to the side again and again, leaving behind a wake of sparks and falling glass, tumbling nonsensically, bouncing in ways that were disorienting to *look at*, much less imagine doing, with limbs fluid like spiked octopus legs and sometimes jointed like a man's, flashing in and out of the formless black hole that was its body.

It reached the end of a pillar and threw itself down a hundred feet.

A barely visible shudder of air, like a ball, rushed down and exploded before it could touch the stone, sending it flying down diagonally. It slammed into the floor, rolled as if it was a ball of limbs, sliding and hitting the ground like an urchin torn out of the void. Another explosion, and the gap of hundreds of feet was suddenly nothing but a mere second away.

She watched as, in the middle of flying forward, it shot another ball of air into the base of a pile of gravel to their left, the explosion of dust and pebbles

FLEABAG · BOOK 2

momentarily covering its advance with a wall of rocks that rained over them. The man above her scrambled off, but she couldn't find it in herself to even get up.

The spear wielder went to stab Em through the throat, likely thinking the scarf around it was an ordinary one, and before she could do so much as twitch and wonder if it could pierce through the chainmail, a black blur slammed into him, half the size of the man himself but with the speed of an arrow, sending him flying, spinning on one leg to stay upright.

Even with [Haste], she could barely keep up with what was going on, seeing little more than a whirr of black swing around the man's body, grappling with him, and then with a violent jerk, a round object whirled out of the mess.

A head, the flat metal mask now adorned with four gigantic claw marks where the eye holes were. It was followed by a spindly arm, spinning twice before hitting the floor.

Another limb burst out of the creature's back, and before the first body had even hit the floor, she watched liquid fire light up the dark underpass, pass over her, in tight streams and wild spews, coming from four different directions on its body, covering the pass in screaming, wailing bodies.

The hammer wielder went for a side swipe, covering his head with one arm and the other swinging his weapon.

The monster grabbed onto the hammerhead as it passed by and went with the swing, adding its own momentum to swing with it and then twist at the end to slam what she assumed were its feet into the man's head. Then, like an acrobat, it kicked off of him to spin and unveil another two limbs out of nowhere, fists pointed at the giant.

Fists which spewed fire.

The sound was not unlike an explosion, and with a blast of blinding light, the giant cried out in pain, his body engulfed from head to toe in clinging fire as he blindly swung a second time, backpedaling and writhing before dropping to roll on the floor, trying to put out the flames.

The monster whipped a tentacle at him, shooting some kind of projectile, before slapping away the pugilist's fist with three different limbs.

The giant slowed more and more, convulsing on the floor, until eventually, she couldn't see anything moving but the flames eating his carcass, and his panting chest, adorned by a gleaming spike.

The martial artist zipped forward again as the monster slapped aside a bear trap with a fuzzy tentacle.

Then the monster burst into a giant cloud of pitch-black smoke, and the martial artist froze, trying to backpedal.

It pounced on him in a zigzag motion, the cloud momentarily swallowing his form, and barely half a second later, she watched the cloud leap off of him, revealing a shredded torso, the man falling to the ground with his intestines spilling out of him, jerking and heaving in mindless shock.

The monster shot another ball of air that flattened everyone still up, sending pebbles everywhere once more, like a hail of buckshot, covering everything in fine gravel dust.

But she couldn't close her eyes, so she endured the burning sensation of dust pricking at her eyes as she mutely watched, frozen.

Through the cloud of dust that seemed to cover the entire underpass, she watched dozens of silhouettes writhe and run and fall screaming before the fire's light, hazy twisting figures locked in a twisted dance of death with a black shadow that darted in one direction and killed in another, something that moved like a rabid snake with nine limbs, that moved to one screaming shape and turned it into four twirling, bleeding pieces in the blink of an eye.

A cacophony of blasts of air and cracks of sound mixing with screams and battle cries was cut short, the sound of bodies hitting the floor mixing with Emhreeil's giggles.

She tried to get up, but it felt like her arms were made of paper, her legs shaking and numb.

Was she having a bad dream?

This couldn't possibly be real.

She watched silhouettes of chains flash through the air, cut through the dust, heard the thuds as they missed, until eventually, they didn't.

The black cloud suddenly jerked, dragged off a scrambling form by the shape of a chain, and her eyes dumbly followed it to the hulking figure of the gangster from before, clad in chains and traps, the mechanism behind his back reeling the chain back.

The monster was dragged out of the dust cloud, and she watched the pitch-black smoke cloud recede into its skin as it twisted and planted its limbs onto the floor like a spider, a scraping, alien *noise* that made her ears hurt answering the man's grunt of effort, sharp and fast.

She watched a black arm as thick as two men's be yanked forward as the gangster heaved and dragged the monster forward, watched another clawed arm snap to the trap.

Watched the sparks fly, the metal pieces clinking off the floor as it tore the trap off with contemptuous ease.

The gangster seemed to let his suit of chains snake around him to attach to each bear trap, after which he would just grasp a bundle of chains and spin them once or twice before flinging them forward with simplicity born of expertise.

The monster made a *sound*, some bizarre *noise* once more, nothing like the first, but enough to make her stomach cramp and ache in fear, kicking up dust, blowing the man's traps back like a strong wind.

It turned back into a smoke cloud and rushed at the man again, parting the tide of projectiles with unseen limbs as it slid forward like a jittery arrow.

Something popped into existence behind the man, and suddenly, with a small movement and a small mote of light that quickly disappeared, he was gone.

The monster paused for only a moment before retracting the cloud and, turning around to hunt the few survivors it had left, went back into the slowly settling cloud of dust.

She watched the outline of a man be speared through the chest, heard his gargling scream be cut off with a crunch as he was tossed away out of sight like a broken doll. She watched another swing a sword, only for his hand to continue without him as something black cut through it, his weapon and hand tumbling off as he screamed, before that sound, too, cut off as the shadow crashed into him, like someone hitting the stop button on a gramophone.

She watched, too terrified to even move, having to remind herself to breathe.

To remind herself that people don't feel pain in nightmares, and thus, this was reality.

She heard the screams get more and more distant, more and more out of sight as it hunted down every last person it could reach.

She . . . she had to get up. To get them out of here.

Her eyes moved to Emhreeil, still laughing and smiling as she shifted onto her stomach and began to struggle to her feet.

Emhreeil couldn't see him, but she didn't need to. The last man crumpled beneath him, and he immediately sprinted back toward her before the sensation faded.

She staggered upright.

Her fingers nearly slipped as she dug the glass vial out of its metal container, but she quickly bit off the cover and downed the whole healing potion in one go, panting in relief as injuries big and small began to heal. Some prissy corner of her mind lamented the loss of a few silvers, and she ignored it.

Then she let the vial drop to the ground, spreading her arm and stump wide as she laughed, a light laugh she hadn't felt come out of herself in what must have been ages.

His footsteps neared like a horse's gallop, and she delighted in this light feeling in her chest, of relief, of endless gratitude.

What's the score, buddy? How many lives do I owe you? she wondered once more, and beamed harder.

Then he crashed into her, tackling her to the floor, and she let out a grunt-puff of surprise and pain, her injuries protesting the rough treatment. And *holy fuck* he'd gotten so much larger—

"EM!" Katherine shrieked, and she felt him jerk against her, his head raising from where it was against her. His presence lit up in her mind again, another fight.

She snapped her arm around his neck before he could pounce on Kat, and felt herself be dragged two entire feet before he stopped, letting out a strange, questioning wheeze as he shifted to not step on her.

"No! No-no-no-no, she's a friend! Uh, shit, fuck, Kat, stand down, get on the ground, *ground, get on the ground now!*" she barked, and heard a hurried shuffle and thump as she assumed her friend did as she said.

She sent out a tiny pulse of mana to be sure, what little she had, and groaned in relief, slumping on the floor as the image that returned was her friend's furry, blood-slick head tilted in confusion, glancing between her and Kat, who was on her back, half raised, staring at them wide-eyed.

His presence retreated, no longer in fight mode.

"Meet my friend, Kat." She chuckled and tugged him down.

He obliged her with his previous enthusiasm, damn near tackling her to the floor again as limbs and twisty things all grabbed at her, and she laughed even more as she grinned and rubbed her forehead against his own frenzied nuzzling, the scent of wet dog and fresh blood not unlike mixing manure and roses, so bizarre was the smell.

She let out pained, hitching laughs as he smeared her red, tails around her legs and four arms trapping her to him as he damn near sent them rolling, twisting like a crocodile on her in mindless enthusiasm, his back to her chest, then back again, and then he was nosing at her bald head.

Then he licked her face and she sputtered, turning away, squirming as he continued his relentless onslaught.

"Bleugh! Ew, ew, ew, stop, ow— Holy shit you're fucking heavy—"

Then he got spit in her mouth and she gagged, turning aside to spit and choke on laughter, wiggling her arm between the half dozen limbs around her to wrap around his neck, dodging his overexcited wriggles by tucking her head under his chin and bucking around to dodge his bloodthirsty assault of spit and blood.

"Vile beast! I'll—" Then she grunted as a leg hit her in the stomach, and she let out a garbled sound that was supposed to mean *I'll have my revenge.*

Then he twisted, pulling her around, and halfheartedly nipped at her hairless scalp, and just like that, they were wrestling like rowdy pups, and she was wheezing with laughter, covered in blood and so happy she felt like a ball of honey and butterflies as she squirmed around on the floor with him, ignoring the pain.

It was so rare to feel so *happy* and excited to the point where it felt like its own limbs just weren't listening.

Its "template" quickly fixed its ears and vocal cords, and it somehow made the situation a little more *real.*

Despite having her here, doing her strange yipping and feebly struggling away from its efforts to clean her face and lick her wounds, it still took a little bit for it to sink in.

It had accepted so fully and completely that she'd died. Then when it learned she was alive, even then, it hadn't gotten its hopes up beyond trying its absolute best to keep her that way. It was like the idea of its human still being alive was in a strange sort of captivity until now, at least subconsciously, because it knew it might not get down here in time, it knew she might die regardless of its efforts.

It knew she was alive, but it hadn't accepted it yet, because until she was like this, next to it, doing her weird human yipping and nuzzling back and trying in vain to win their play fight, she might as well not be.

And now she was here, alive, and the odd sensation of not being alone was altogether far too pleasant to care about the other humans she'd decided to bring into their pack without its permission or consent.

It would toss her around a bit for that later, but now, it was too happy to care.

Somewhere along the ride, his voice returned, and his playful grumble-growling was so familiar it almost bowled her over with nostalgia, and then he was mockingly repeating her words back at her with grumbling little howls, and she was wheezing from laughing, from fighting, from the fact that he was suddenly one heavy bastard and he didn't seem to realize it yet.

But eventually, she stopped wrestling back, only squirming away from any licking, exhausted and breathing in harsh pants, so he stopped too, instead just flopping down on top of her with a sigh.

She sighed too, a sigh of contentment.

Finally.

It felt right again. *She* felt right again.

When lying down like this, he was larger than her, almost twice as wide on the shoulders. When walking he'd probably reach her damn thigh, maybe even her hip.

Wolves and their stupid cheaty, cheating bullcrap. It's been like two, maybe three weeks at most since they separated, and he was like twice the size and built like a rock.

"Where are you gonna squeeze into when you're the size of a dragon, huh?" she asked, flicking his ear, smiling when it flicked her hand back with a bratty grumble.

She sent a pulse of mana to Katherine, who still looked shell-shocked, staring at them from the same spot on the ground.

Then the wolf's head rose to the left, opposite Kat, and she felt him tense.

Another pulse of mana that left her dry, and she felt Scruffy very cautiously approaching from wherever she'd hid, in tiny steps.

She tapped him and pointed to the goblin.

"Friend."

Then she pointed back from herself to the goblin.

The wolf, bless his heart, wasn't stupid, so he quickly realized her meaning and flopped back down.

She wheezed, and after a small bout of squirming where she realized he didn't care too much to move off her, she snorted out a laugh and scratched between his ears, ignoring the sticky, congealing blood.

His absurdly bushy tails combined into one and wagged.

Then she turned toward Kat, still breathing deep and heavy as she tried to find words, now that the initial excitement had faded somewhat.

Katherine found them first, it seemed.

"So that's . . . your friend," Kat half stated, half asked, incredulousness and a heavy dose of fear in her voice, very cautiously and slowly starting to shift to get up.

Why was she . . . ?

She thought for a moment, then inwardly grimaced as she realized that having him slaughter something like thirty gangsters, after that *horrific* noise, however the hell he made it, was not exactly the best way to introduce him to Kat.

Embreeil almost pissed her pants from hearing it, and she'd *known* who made it. Katherine did not.

Kat was a tough cookie, mentally and physically, but from her own assumptions and snippets of conversations in lifts and inns, she could tell that Kat wasn't used to coming so close to death as to taste it, nor was she used to this much blood and carnage.

She'd spent the majority of those two years of separation doing training and going around as a bodyguard for Lady Anna. She didn't bathe in blood and guts, she didn't drink blood just to survive, she didn't have to kill to live.

She was shaken, in short.

She pushed at the wolf's shoulder insistently, and after a grumble, it got off her, quickly trotting off to snatch someone's head to chew on, with a parting lick that made her laugh.

A thought occurred to her as she noted that she was on the floor, the wolf chewing up meat a little farther away as the scent of blood and death licked and danced in the air.

Just like old times.

She damn near started laughing again from the ghostly sense of déjà vu, but she tamped it down for Kat's sake to a small quick of her lips.

She heard the crack of bone pause, then paws thud quickly toward her in a steady, quick beat, and ignored it, assuming he was just excited or something.

"Kat? You— Whoa!" she yelled, suddenly finding herself thrown up in an arc, a pair of muscled tentacles digging under her back and around her waist. She grasped at his tails for a moment for a sense of stability, legs kicking and accidentally booting him in the ass, and then she curled her knees in as she realized he was trying to carry her again, for some reason.

Barely a moment later, she was moving again toward Kat, and she stiffened, a pulse of mana showing a petrified Scruffy held in his arm, one of the lower pair.

He stopped just a few feet away from Kat, who looked stiff as a board, and tilted his back toward her, jerking his head to it with a short growl.

She didn't know why he was in such a hurry, but she didn't care. She trusted him far more than she trusted her own senses.

"Kat, just get on before he throws you on," she said, wriggling a little because there was something vaguely bony pressing into her rib.

"*Why?*" Katherine whimpered despairingly to herself, rubbing at her face, then turned around and began to sprint away. "Our supplies!" she yelled back, as if to explain herself, which was a nice gesture because for a moment she thought Kat had just decided to bail on them.

Her wolf friend snarled lowly, annoyed, and she quickly patted his tail, pointing insistently to the left, where two objects she very much desired were.

He turned to look, then glanced at her.

"Ssss . . . hwooooord?" he rasp-hissed, and she grimaced at the sound before nodding. Well, it was a dagger, but in his eyes, same thing.

Then she smiled because *where* had he learned that word?

He quickly bounded over, and with another small flash of mana, she found both the items she wanted. A bloodstained mask with four claw marks going through the eyes, head not included, and her dagger.

She just pointed at them and felt with fascination as a human arm uncurled from around his ribs to snatch them both up in a giant *paw* of a damn hand, and then just . . . stared at them, before he turned and chuffed a wordless question at her.

It took a moment for her to register it because the more she paid attention, the more changes she noticed and the more she inwardly goggled at how much of an amazing monster he was.

He even had an eye on his *neck*. That was just impressive and disturbing and perfectly suited to the absolute nightmare he was growing into. She smiled wider. She felt oddly proud of him.

Then finally his question registered, and she just made a universal "give that to me" gesture with her hand, and he twisted his waist a bit to present them to her.

Two taps, and they were thrown into her ring.

He stiffened before tilting his head further, then paused to shake and twist around, the blood matting into his fur most likely drying and making him feel stiff.

Katherine jogged back, something she didn't see but heard.

The wolf moved forward, and Kat immediately ground to a halt, stiff and uncomfortable as he came up close and began sniffing her, the low range allowing her a near-constant feel of the interaction.

Then he snorted, presented his back, and jerked his head there again.

Katherine stared at its back, looking equally disturbed by the intelligence on display and . . . *everything else*. She looked down at the wolf's impatient glare, then at her pleadingly, lost.

"Just, uh, lie kind of flat, and grab his shoulder—"

The tentacle in his back whipped out, wrapped around Katherine's waist, and yanked her forward and up, her stomach landing on his back and landing her face-to-face with Scruffy, who was dangling off his left side by the secondary arm.

She'd never thought she'd live to see the day where Kat would *squeal* like that.

She felt her jaw literally drop, and idly noted that she really had to make Kat less scared of him before it became a problem.

He only took a moment to maneuver Kat around and force her to grab his shoulders, wiggling the spikes on them and waiting for her to fist her fingers in his fur.

Then Emhreeil was the one who squealed in surprise, because she felt like she was suddenly dangling off the back of a fucking freight train as it bounded forward like an arrow, the bouncing irregularity included.

Little more than a dozen seconds later, a familiar sense of weightlessness came over her. A flash of mana revealed an edge behind them, retreating, and nothing around her.

Ah, he was jumping over something. Or a gap.

Something that was likely as dangerous as everything else he did.

Katherine let out a choked sound like a whimpering, high-pitched keen of terror.

They hit something, the impact jarring and painful on her myriad little injuries, but she didn't let that distract her besides a surprised grunt as she clutched at the bushy tails squeezing her like a paste tube.

She took a moment to examine the fear and exhilaration coursing through her heart.

She pushed the fear down and embraced the latter. She went to throw her hand up, stopped immediately when her collarbone stabbed a spike of pain into her chest, then whooped like a madwoman as she idly kicked her legs as if hanging from a swing, too happy to care, finally feeling like she was home, like she was whole again.

Maybe the repeated brain damage and the dizziness helped in her ecstatic joy, but that was something to worry about later, so she raised her hand to slap Katherine on the back from where she was glued to the wolf's back.

"Come on! They already heard us! Who gives a fuck for some more?!" she yelled through the shriek of tearing metal and rumbling machinery.

After a moment of hesitation, where they slowly slid down the side of a building, the wolf let out a howl imitating her whoop, a small hesitant one, and dropped.

And she screamed louder, exhilarated, and the wolf howled louder too on the next drop, Katherine letting out muffled screams as if to oblige her, but slowly getting swept into the atmosphere as they continued to tumble and scrape down pipe after pipe, building after building, down spires of wire and lift supports, even Scruffy doing her best to join in, though she was definitely more than a little terrified.

And like four nutjobs, they howled, whooped, screamed, and croaked their way down into the desolate walls of the dungeon, and she'd never felt happier.

CHAPTER 14

"Which of them survived?" he asked, his voice filled with pure ice.

Codek shifted in reply, his jaw clenched as he stared off to the side, a mixture of shame and anger in his eyes wreathed by the shadows of a candle. The manacles around his wrists clinked softly as he squirmed, brushing against the wooden back of his chair.

The man's spine was still solid, it seemed. He used to like that, a long time ago. Now, it just showed how much he struggled in reading people, his greatest shortcoming.

Ruling through fear was far, far, far more reliable.

If Codek were afraid of him *before* he fucked everything even further, he might not have pulled that stunt.

His metal fingers tapped at the armrest.

"Trapper, Mirdin, Swiftshot, and Gailo. Sermon got his head ripped off, Flasher got disemboweled. Mirdin got Trapper and Swiftshot out. Gailo played dead until we got to him. He needs a conjurative healer. He'll live, but he can't even fight a rat right now . . . Look, Ironheart—"

The chair's wood burst to splinters in his fingers with a sharp crack, making Codek flinch, dust and chunks dancing in the air between them like embers in a flame for a tense moment, before retreating to the darkness at their feet.

His gaze nailed the incompetent idiot on his chair. He did not blink, nor sneer, nor even make an expression, letting the contempt behind his eyes speak for him. Codek's eyes lowered.

With a slow, deliberate movement, he moved his hand to the side and unclenched it, allowing frayed wood chunks to drop to the stone floor of the cellar, moving his fingers down his palm as if sprinkling salt on food to clean the crap off his glove.

Then he shifted a little, lowering his brows.

"I don't care about your excuses, Codek. You sent the Butchers, our main strike force for Snake Eyes, as well as thirty greens, to hunt down two random bastards. Because they . . . what, hurt your feelings? Killed your old drinking buddy? Because we lost rep?" he asked rhetorically, lowering his voice to a metallic, mocking croon, allowing a sneer to curl his lip as he leaned forward.

Codek tried in vain to fuse with his chair, grimacing.

"The Syndicate had agreed with me that I'd station that team up to the top of the third floor to keep the red peacocks out, now that they've retreated. They were to be there, ready for when the kingdom sent the army, any day now. And not even a day after I make that agreement and tell you, you decide to cash in the favor we had with the witch without asking me, and send them in the complete opposite direction. Because you got arrogant. Because you thought *Oh, but it's just two people, I can deal with them before sending them up to do the real work.* Isn't that right? Did you stop to think of consequences? You made me look *incompetent.* Not in control of one of *my own gangs.* My position in the Syndicate was weakened, because of your *fucking stupidity,*" he snarled.

Of course, that wasn't the sole reason he was furious. But that could wait a little. Those thoughts had their time. Now was not it.

"I'm not here to hear excuses. I'm here to make an example of you. I'm tired of people just not quite listening right when I tell them things," he rumbled, and glanced to the side. Kolak's eyes met his, and he nodded, opening the door and stepping through it.

He didn't bother to close it. Codek would be hard-pressed to run without the tendons in his feet.

Besides, there was no point in doing this if nobody saw it.

He could see murmuring people outside, ranging from idle curiosity to grim-faced understanding.

Codek's eyes flit to the door as his breaths grew deeper.

"I swear—"

"Do you know . . . about Tillenhall? I assume you know something. Everyone does. They own the hospitals, they own the few healers that live in our little shithole. They own almost every alchemist, all the bio labs, and the sole high security prison the third floor has is theirs to do with as they please. The Cauldron. Nigh impenetrable, discounting Seven-Six-Two's team of freaks. But if you must know one more thing about Tillenhall that isn't as widely known . . ." he trailed off.

Kolak shoved through the crowd outside and walked in, a naked tattoo-covered woman under his arm, limp and moaning strangely, her hair dragging on the floor.

Faces on the outskirts twisted, naked horror for some, disgust for others, fear in most.

Good.

Codek's eyes jerked to his guard, then to the woman, and widened in horror, in despair.

Had he thought he'd forgotten her? What an unflattering assumption.

"M-Mia?" Codek croaked, going to rise from his chair as if in a daze.

In a flash, he was above him, and a fist made of steel slammed into his gut, slamming him back into the chair, through it, into the floor.

He took one languid step, then reached down, one hand crushing the man's shoulder, the other fisted in his hair as he hauled his heaving, gasping form off the broken wood, clean off the floor, then pushed him down to his knees. One quick movement had the manacles in his own hand behind the man's back, and he pulled them up, ignoring the strangled grunt the man let out.

He lowered himself until he was crouching behind him as Kolak made the woman assume a similar position across from them, kneeling, but too limp to show anything of her front, a mass of long hair like a curtain between them, patchy and dropping.

Codek's breaths deepened.

His lips were almost to the man's ear.

"Please, Manos, don't kill her, please. You know me. I know you, y-your story. We've saved each other in the Factory half a dozen times, one-one *fucking* mistake—"

"But if you must know one more thing about Tillenhall that isn't as widely known . . . it's that Tillenhall is more inventive with agony than I ever could be," he finished, ignoring the inane chatter.

He nodded to Kolak, and the man's meaty paw grabbed the woman's hair, pulled back, showing Codek what he'd done to his—unfortunately still-alive—wife.

Codek choked, his breaths growing hysterical at the horrific sight.

"Mia, Mia, no, no, no, no, no, NO—"

The man choked down a sob, thrashing uselessly with legs that didn't quite work, arms behind his back, before devolving into hysterical screaming about how he was going to kill them all.

Manos ignored it, feeling only a vague sense of vindictive satisfaction.

Shame about Mia. Decent woman, really. Bit of a whore, but a fun lass.

Unfortunate that she chose to love this *fucking* idiot.

Her face was gone, replaced by a deep furrow of melting flesh and chitin teeth, a long, thin V shape not unlike a wound that ran from her stomach to the back of her skull. Teeth and tongues and inhuman eyes wriggled and struggled to gargle and speak through the mess. Maggots crawled along the exposed flesh, curled around dead pupils blown wide in agony. Clicking centipede legs twitched and scraped at their own flesh, misfiring nerves and broken instincts.

A thousand mouths tore at their own flesh, fused into her undying body, each bleeding wound left behind replaced by another mouth to feast.

Maybe Mia was still in there somewhere.

He honestly hoped not.

But he'd been too soft for too long. He'd been cautious for too long.

With the wolf, the plan, and the gangs he controlled as well.

He would consider giving his men some *real* incentives not to displease him, only to reason that he might get deserters if he scared them too much.

He'd considered hiring some of those big-shot hunter specialists, only to say to himself how that might draw some eyes, make people question what on earth he needed so much muscle for.

He'd considered pushing harder to find the damn wolf, only to reason to himself that there were only *so many* things to eat in an oversized factory like this, only so strong the stupid mutt could get, that it wasn't worth the attention because it would inevitably run out of creatures to steal from.

Of course, it wasn't like he could have ever predicted how absurdly fast the damn thing would become such a menace, nor how on Ergos it learned fucking *magic*, but the point remained: He was done playing nice.

"Now, Codek!" he exclaimed, a savage growl in his voice, yanking at the man's hair, his hysterical thrashing all too satisfying.

"How about a kiss?!" he yelled, mostly to be heard over the commotion and the screaming, and dragged the man forward by the hair as he began to recoil and scream gibberish, spittle flying everywhere.

Blood dripped down Codek's scalp from the thrashing, the skin of his scalp splitting.

Mia's arms twitched, clicks and gurgles intensifying, things squelching and cracking as her torso split open even further, flesh parting, blood dripping from the wounds before turning to sludge and hardening to form brown chitin and clicking mandibles in its path, some eating their own flesh in the endless cycle of self-consumption.

One injection and an axe to the face to form *this*.

His admiration of Tillenhall and their insanity continued to rise.

He dragged the man forward as Kolak stepped back.

Mia jerked, legs twisting with horrific cracks as she launched forward, the flaps of her head snapping shut around Codek's.

He let go of Codek's hair to let the man drop to the floor with his wife, and jumped back in disgust, checking his coat briefly before stepping back to enjoy his handiwork, drinking in Codek's muffled, shrieking cries of agony as his former wife latched on with a hundred teeth and a thousand mandibles to slowly chew through him, jerking and twisting on top of his form.

Without much care, he stepped aside and walked away without looking back. He had so much work to do.

The snakes parted before him like a sea of frightened pups.

As they should.

"Ramina, you're the new boss now. Anyone trying to fuck with you gets the same treatment as dear old Codek. Got it?" he barked, his eyes roving the crowd to find nothing but nodding heads.

Bunch of fucking bobbleheads, the lot of them.

At least Ramina had a solid head on her shoulders, knew how to follow clear-cut orders and pass any ideas by him before going through with them. Codek had been loyal, but also opportunistic, backhanded, egotistical, and unimaginably fucking *stupid*.

Ramina shouldered through the crowd, looking genuinely surprised for a moment, her scarred brows rising, before she thumped her fist on her chest and nodded.

"Good. I'm off, got work to do. Get someone to heal Gailo and get the Butchers to the Grate. Take the funds out of Codek's stuff to do it. Burn the bodies once they're done wriggling back there."

Ramina looked puzzled, but nodded deferentially.

The Grate was where the second floor slowly melted into the third, into the true sewers of the dungeon. A fitting name, and a fitting new station for the strike team's disgraced idiots. If it weren't for their reduced number, they'd be holding the fucking frontline.

Maybe he should have made something more painfully creative for Codek.

Now to pay off every damn newspaper and person he could to try and brush away the scream incident.

He knew he couldn't quite do it, but he'd be damned if he didn't try.

The kingdom *could not* know about the wolf. Whether that was simply not knowing what it was or the more preferable option—not knowing of its existence at all—it didn't matter as much as the main point.

So even if his coffers ran dry, he'd try to make sure nobody would get curious enough to poke too much, to prod too deep, and find out the truth. It worked to some extent when it got on that lift. People took it at face value, because why wouldn't they? Wolves were basically a horror story for children at this point. *It was some kind of demon hound* was more plausible to think.

He could work with that or just spread as much bullshit as possible to make conclusions impossible.

Whatever other conclusion the public muppets reached, he had to try to keep interest about the damn thing low, keep people occupied with other things. Which, after its stunt, seemingly designed to fuck him over, would be very difficult. The window was closing, and he had to find it. He couldn't afford to drag his feet anymore in the hopes it would stop evolving at some point or make some stupid upgrade that would make it easy to catch. It was getting too loud, it was drawing too many eyes, and it somehow managed to figure out magic.

The last time that happened, people made a damn song about it. The Flaming Wolf, Devourer of Efleheim. The damn thing had too many avenues of improvement and progress available to it now.

He dug his communication crystal out of his pocket, pressing the sound bubble and tugging his scarf up his nose just in case someone was watching his lips from somewhere unseen.

Another few presses of buttons, and a prod of life force to swap it to the correct connection. It took nearly thirty seconds for the man to pick up.

"Stranger. How bad is it?" he asked simply.

"Depends on what front," the man's inhuman voice replied in a rasping series of hisses and clicks overlapping with each other, an ear-grating sound that he quite liked.

"What are the people saying on street level?"

"Most reached the same conclusion as last time. A demonic hound of some sort. It's got quite the reputation by now, you know? The Black Hound, they whisper. It's quite amusing what stories people will tell when times of strife and poverty pull them to the edge. Of course, information and narratives are as varied as people, so besides sightings of it running toward your men, and assuming it to be some kind of otherworldly presence, the narrative is fractured. Some cite the lift and curse it, some cite the scream and the Snake Eyes getting slaughtered and praise it as some kind of monster of cleansing flame or some such drivel. The charred corpses certainly make them think they're right. Many, thankfully, claim it is simply another of Tillenhall's wayward pets. With all the whispers of demons, though, the Dove might send warrior priests to deal with it if the narrative continues in that direction."

He worked his jaw, letting out a long, low sigh. The Stranger wasn't *wrong*. If the whispers kept moving in that direction, the Dove would inevitably try to come down and kill the damn thing.

"Won't the Crow object to that?" he asked, already suspecting the answer.

"Oh, they will. They'll either politely shove them out or finally decide to throw their spears into the theater of war. It all depends on how hard the Dove pushes. The Crow's been building strength for decades. The third floor is their domain. So I doubt your . . . wayward pet will be in trouble from the white cloaks. But if they can't push their way down here by force, the Dove will do it by stealth. Your pet will be in trouble from their more secretive squads, I believe. The Dove might not send any warrior priests, but a few spell blades? A team of assassins or some such to start poking their noses where nobody wants it? That, I imagine, is very likely. Do be careful on all fronts. I won't do your scheming for you." The Stranger clicked.

He made an affirmative yet thoughtful sound as he wracked his brain.

The way the Stranger said "wayward pet" might have held implications in it, if it weren't for his monotone clicks and hisses. As it was, he couldn't tell.

Regardless of that, he was, as usual, correct. The Dove was famously zealous for hunting down demons, and the Crow was infamous for being overly tolerant of them. He could drive some kind of spike there, some conflict, but he could also try to dodge it by misguiding the public in some other direction.

But the idea seemed to have picked up steam now. It would be very difficult to make them think there was something else going on, and it was too risky to make them move off a relatively safe train of assumptions into an unknown one. People said it was either some Tillenhall monster or a demon? That was not optimal, but he would take it over someone accidentally starting to spout something a little more dangerous.

Like pointing out how the claw marks were so clean it looked like someone *polished* the inside of each cut to a shining perfection, and drawing conclusions to the most definitive feature of wolves, which was their damn claws and teeth.

With the wrong tugs and pushes, they could be whispering something a little too close to the truth to be comfortable. Not worth it.

"No need to tell me things I already know. Any idea on what the connection between the two women and the dog are? Who they are? *Where* did they go?"

He wasn't going to rely on the Stranger, of course. Tracer was doing an admirable job of mapping out where the hell the trio were going, along what paths and where. It just hadn't been quite enough before, and he doubted it would be enough this time either.

After all, "somewhere around this six-mile-wide area" was not exactly fucking accurate. Figuring out that they were trying to get to the bottom of the third floor was much more helpful, but *still* too big and vague. Too many holes to patch, too many paths to make a trap. All he could do was cast an absurdly wide net and track anyone else the wolf picked off and killed to try and map its trajectory.

An expense he was willing to pay for.

The Stranger let out some kind of noise, perhaps his version of a sigh. It just sounded like a snake's crumpled hiss.

"None, I'm afraid. I may have a billion eyes and ears, but you reached for my assistance too late, with too wide a possible area. Haven't seen a glimpse of them, besides some rumors of laughing ghosts moving through the steel treatment factories, all along the Black Strip. Feel free to check there, but I haven't seen anything there either so far. And you know I cannot reach into the sewers, so if they've gone there, I am afraid you'll need another man entirely."

"I see. I'll deposit the usual check into your bank account. I'll ring you later if I have another task," he said quietly, the anger slowly having seeped out of him as he continued walking.

"And I'll be sure to name my price for that as well. Farewell, Ironheart."

A small flash of mana, and the call ended, the sound bubble dissipating. He pulled the scarf down and brought his left hand up, where an uncharacteristically bright and flashy ring rested on his pinkie.

He pressed a button on the outer side and cupped his hand around the ring as he brought it close. With a series of tiny clicks and the faint strain of tiny mechanical joints, the golden ring's flat top extended outward and unraveled like an umbrella, revealing a three-dimensional rendition of a spinning carousel, hidden from the world behind his scarred fingers.

Faded pink paper mixed with the yellow of age, drafted onto tiny metallic frills unfolding from its tiny cap. Unicorns and flowers filled the gaps, discolored, held together by nothing but enchantments. A distorted off-key jingle played as the tiny carousel spun, almost too low to hear, and for a moment, a mere few seconds, he let himself drift off to another time, a different place.

He let himself feel that familiar pain, to let her know he hadn't forgotten her. That he never would. That this was all for her.

Maybe he did so merely to brush away the guilt of what he'd done. Maybe this was his way of apologizing to her, for what he had become, a man he doubted she would ever be proud to call a father.

Even so, he allowed himself that small moment, knowing that in times to come, he could, and *would*, do so much worse.

With a deep breath, a weight on his chest, and a faint sting behind his eyes, he clicked the little button again and watched the carousel's aging corpse descend into its little crypt with a little click.

His hands dropped, and he pushed the emotions out of his mind, to be dug up on a late night with an escort in his bed and alcohol in his veins.

He still had work to do.

He always would, unless that mutt was in a cage.

ABOUT THE AUTHOR

SomeoneToForget is a LitRPG author whose debut series, Fleabag, was originally released on Royal Road. He writes to inspire in his readers the childish glee and wonder he has always felt upon discovering and immersing himself in new stories, and hopes his own stories will not soon be forgotten.

RESPAWN YOUR CURIOSITY

follow us on our socials

 podiumentertainment.com

 @podiumentertainment

 /podiumentertainment

 @podium_ent

 @podiumentertainment